Praise for *What We Find*

"Insightfully realized central figures, a strong supporting cast, family issues, and uncommon emotional complexity make this uplifting story a heart-grabber that won't let readers go until the very end.... A rewarding (happy) story that will appeal across the board and might require a hanky or two."
—*Library Journal*, starred review

"Robyn Carr has done it again.... *What We Find* is complex, inspirational, and well-written. A romance that truly inspires readers as life hits them the hardest."
—*San Francisco Review Journal*

"With this tale of the soothing splendor of the land and our vulnerability, Carr sets the bar for contemporary romance. The well-paced plot, engaging and well-defined characters, and an inviting setting make Carr's latest an enhancement not only to the romance shelves but to any fiction collection."

—*Booklist*, starred review

Praise for the novels of #1 *New York Times* bestselling author Robyn Carr

"A satisfying reinvention story that handles painful issues with a light and uplifting touch."
—*Kirkus Reviews* on *The Life She Wants*

"Carr's new novel demonstrates that classic women's fiction, illuminating the power of women's friendships, is still alive and well."
—*Booklist* on *Four Friends*

"A thought-provoking look at women...and the choices they make."

—*Kirkus Reviews* on *Four Friends*

"The Virgin River books are so compelling—I connected instantly with the characters and just wanted more and more and more."
—#1 *New York Times* bestselling author
Debbie Ma

P9-DDF-974

ROBYN CARR

What We Find

MIRA®

ISBN-13: 978-0-7783-1978-8

What We Find

Copyright © 2016 by Robyn Carr

Recycling programs for this product may not exist in your area.

For questions and comments about the quality of this book, please contact us at CustomerService@Harlequin.com.

www.MIRABooks.com

Printed in U.S.A.

This one is for Nicole Brebner,
my editor, my partner, my friend.
Thank you.

What We Find

Just living is not enough…

One must have sunshine, freedom,

and a little flower.

—HANS CHRISTIAN ANDERSEN

CHAPTER 1

Maggie Sullivan sought refuge in the stairwell between the sixth and seventh floors at the far west end of the hospital, the steps least traveled by interns and residents racing from floor to floor, from emergency to emergency. She sat on the landing between two flights, feet on the stairs, arms crossed on her knees, her face buried in her arms. She didn't understand how her heart could feel as if it was breaking every day. She thought of herself as much stronger.

"Well, now, some things never change," a familiar voice said.

She looked up at her closest friend, Jaycee Kent. They had gone to med school together, though residency had separated them. Jaycee was an OB and Maggie, a neurosurgeon. And...they had hidden in stairwells to cry all those years ago when med-school life was kicking their asses. Most of their fellow students and instructors were men. They refused to let the men see them cry.

Maggie gave a wet, burbly huff of laughter. "How'd you find me?" Maggie asked.

"How do you know you're not in my spot?"

"Because you're happily married and have a beautiful daughter?"

"And my hours suck, I'm sleep-deprived, have as many bad days as good and..." Jaycee sat down beside Maggie. "And at least my hormones are cooperating at the moment. Maggie, you're just taking call for someone, right? Just to stay ahead of the bills?"

"Since the practice shut down," Maggie said. "And since the lawsuit was filed."

"You need a break. You're recovering from a miscarriage and your hormones are wonky. You need to get away, especially away from the emergency room. Take some time off. Lick your wounds. Heal."

"He dumped me," Maggie said.

Jaycee was clearly shocked. *"What?"*

"He broke up with me. He said he couldn't take it anymore. My emotional behavior, my many troubles. He suggested professional help."

Jaycee was quiet. "I'm speechless," she finally said. "What a huge ass."

"Well, I was crying all the time," she said, sniffing some more. "If I wasn't with him, I cried when I talked to him on the phone. I thought I was okay with the idea of no children. I'm almost thirty-seven, I work long hours, I was with a good man who was just off a bad marriage and already had a child..."

"I'll give you everything but the good man," Jaycee said. "He's a doctor, for God's sake. Doesn't he know that all you've been through can take a toll? Remove all the stress and you still had the miscarriage! People tend to treat a miscarriage like a heavy period but it's a death. You lost your baby. You have to take time to grieve."

"Gospel," Maggie said, rummaging for a tissue and giving her nose a hearty blow. "I really felt it on that level. When I found out I was pregnant, it took me about fifteen minutes to start seeing the baby, loving her. Or him."

"Not to beat a dead horse, but you have some hormone issues playing havoc on your emotions. Listen, shoot out some emails tonight. Tell the ones on the need-to-know list you're taking a week or two off."

"No one knows about the pregnancy but you and Andrew."

"You don't have to explain—everyone knows about your practice, your ex-partners, the lawsuit. Frankly, your colleagues are amazed you're still standing. Get out of town or something. Get some rest."

"You might be right," Maggie said. "These cement stairwells are killing me."

Jaycee put an arm around her. "Just like old times, huh?"

The last seven or eight miles to Sullivan's Crossing was nothing but mud and Maggie's cream-colored Toyota SUV was coated up to the windows. This was not exactly a surprise. It had rained all week in Denver, now that she thought about it. March was typically the most unpredictable and sloppiest month of the year, especially in the mountains. If it wasn't rain it could be snow. But Maggie had had such a lousy year the weather barely crossed her mind.

Last year had produced so many medical, legal and personal complications that her practice had shut down a few months ago. She'd been picking up work from other practices, covering for doctors on call here and there and working ER Level 1 Trauma while she tried to figure out how to untangle the mess her life had become. This, on her best friend and doctor's advice, was a much needed break. After sending a few emails and making a few phone calls she was driving to her dad's house.

She knew she was probably suffering from depression. Exhaustion and general misery. It would stand to reason. Her schedule could be horrific and the tension had been terrible lately. It was about a year ago that two doctors in her practice had been accused of fraud and malpractice and suspended from seeing patients pending an investigation that would very likely lead to a trial. Even though she had no knowledge of the incidents, there was a scandal and it stank on her. There'd been wild media attention and she was left alone trying to hold a wilting practice together. Then the parents of a boy who died from injuries sustained in a terrible car accident while on her watch filed a wrongful death suit. Against her.

It seemed impossible fate could find one more thing to stack on her already teetering pile of troubles. *Hah. Never challenge fate.* She found out she was pregnant.

It was an accident, of course. She'd been seeing Andrew for a couple of years. She lived in Denver and he in Aurora, since they both had demanding careers, and they saw each other when they could—a night here, a night there. When they could manage a long weekend, it was heaven. She wanted more but Andrew was an ER doctor and also the divorced father of an eight-year-old daughter. But they had constant phone contact. Multiple texts and emails every day. She counted on him; he was her main support.

Maggie wasn't sure she'd ever marry and have a family but she was happy with her surprise. It was the one good thing in a bad year. Andrew, however, was *not* happy. He was still in divorce recovery, though it had been three years. He and his ex still fought about support and custody and visits. Maggie didn't understand why. Andrew didn't seem to know what to do with his daughter when he had her. He immediately suggested terminating the pregnancy. He said they could revisit the issue in a couple of years if it turned out to be that important to her and if their relationship was thriving.

She couldn't imagine terminating. Just because Andrew was hesitant? She was thirty-six! How much time did she have to *revisit the issue*?

Although she hadn't told Andrew, she decided she was going to keep the baby no matter what that meant for their relationship. Then she had a miscarriage.

Grief-stricken and brokenhearted, she sank lower. Exactly two people knew about the pregnancy and miscarriage—Andrew and Jaycee. Maggie cried gut-wrenching tears every night. Sometimes she couldn't even wait to get home from work and started crying the second she pulled the car door closed. And there were those stairwell visits. She cried on the phone to Andrew; cried in his arms as he tried to comfort her, all the while knowing he was *relieved*.

And then he'd said, "You know what, Maggie? I just can't do it anymore. We need a time-out. I can't prop you up, can't bolster you. You have to get some help, get your emotional life back on track or something. You're sucking the life out of me and I'm not equipped to help you."

"Are you kidding me?" she had demanded. "You're dropping me when I'm down? When I'm only three weeks beyond a miscarriage?"

And in typical Andrew fashion he had said, "That's all I got, baby."

It was really and truly the first moment she had realized it was all about him. And that was pretty much the last straw.

She packed a bunch of suitcases. Once she got packing, she couldn't seem to stop. She drove southwest from Denver to her father's house, south of Leadville and Fairplay, and she hadn't called ahead. She did call her mother, Phoebe, just to say she was going to Sully's and she wasn't sure how long she'd stay. At the moment she had no plan except to escape from that life of persistent strain, anxiety and heartache.

It was early afternoon when she drove up to the country store that had been her great-grandfather's, then her grandfather's, now her father's. Her father, Harry Sullivan, known by one and all as Sully, was a fit and hardy seventy and showed no sign of slowing down and no interest in retiring. She just sat in her car for a while, trying to figure out what she was going to say to him. How could she phrase it so it didn't sound like she'd just lost a baby and had her heart broken?

Beau, her father's four-year-old yellow Lab, came trotting around the store, saw her car, started running in circles barking, then put his front paws up on her door, looking at her imploringly. Frank Masterson, a local who'd been a fixture at the store for as long as Maggie could remember, was sitting on the porch, nursing a cup of coffee with a newspaper on his lap. One glance told her the campground was barely occupied—only a couple of pop-up trailers and tents on campsites down the road toward the lake. She saw a man sitting outside his tent in a canvas camp chair, reading. She had expected the sparse population—it was the middle of the week, middle of day and the beginning of March, the least busy month of the year.

Frank glanced at her twice but didn't even wave. Beau trotted off, disappointed, when Maggie didn't get out of the car. She still hadn't come up with a good entry line. Five minutes passed before her father walked out of the store, across the porch and down the steps, Beau following. She lowered the window.

"Hi, Maggie," he said, leaning on the car's roof. "Wasn't expecting you."

"It was spur-of-the-moment."

He glanced into her backseat at all the luggage. "How long you planning to stay?"

She shrugged. "Didn't you say I was always welcome? Anytime?"

He smiled at her. "Sometimes I run off at the mouth."

"I need a break from work. From all that crap. From everything."

"Understandable. What can I get you?"

"Is it too much trouble to get two beers and a bed?" she asked, maybe a little sarcastically.

"Coors okay by you?"

"Sure."

"Go on and park by the house. There's beer in the fridge and I haven't sold your bed yet."

"That's gracious of you," she said.

"You want some help to unload your entire wardrobe?" he asked.

"Nope. I don't need much for now. I'll take care of it."

"Then I'll get back to work and we'll meet up later."

"Sounds like a plan," she said.

Maggie dragged only one bag into the house, the one with her toothbrush, pajamas and clean jeans. When she was a little girl and both her parents and her grandfather lived on this property, she had been happy most of the time. The general store, the locals and campers, the mountains, lake and valley, wildlife and sunshine kept her constantly cheerful. But the part of her that had a miserable mother, a father who tended to drink a little too much and bickering parents had been forlorn. Then, when she was six, her mother had had enough of hardship, rural living, driving Maggie a long distance to a school that Phoebe found inadequate. Throw in an unsatisfactory husband and that was all she could take. Phoebe took Maggie away to Chicago. Maggie didn't see Sully for several years and her mother married Walter Lancaster, a prominent neurosurgeon with lots of money.

Maggie had hated it all. Chicago, Walter, the big house, the private school, the blistering cold and concrete landscape. She hated the sound of traffic and emergency vehicles. One thing she could recall in retrospect, it brought her mother to life. Phoebe was almost entirely happy, the only smudge on her brightness being her ornery daughter. They had switched roles.

By the time Maggie was eleven she was visiting her dad regularly—first a few weekends, then whole months and some holidays. She lived for it and Phoebe constantly held it over her. *Behave yourself and get good grades and you'll get to spend the summer at that god-awful camp, eating worms, getting filthy and risking your life among bears.*

"Why didn't you fight for me?" she had continually asked her father.

"Aw, honey, Phoebe was right, I wasn't worth a damn as a father and I just wanted what was best for you. It wasn't always easy, neither," he'd explained.

Sometime in junior high Maggie had made her peace with Walter, but she chose to go to college in Denver, near Sully. Phoebe's desire was that she go to a fancy Ivy League college. Med school and residency were a different story—it was tough getting accepted at all and you went to the best career school and residency program that would have you. She ended up in Los Angeles. Then she did a fellowship with Walter, even though she hated going back to Chicago. But Walter was simply one of the best. After that she joined a practice in Denver, close to her dad and the environment she loved. A year later, with Walter finally retired from his practice and enjoying more golf, Phoebe and Walter moved to Golden, Colorado, closer to Maggie. Walter was also seventy, like Sully. Phoebe was a vibrant, social fifty-nine.

Maggie thought she was possibly closer to Walter than to Phoebe, especially as they were both neurosurgeons. She was grateful. After all, he'd sent her to good private schools even when she did every terrible thing she could to show him how unappreciated his efforts were. She had been a completely ungrateful brat about it. But Walter turned out to be a kind, classy guy. He had helped a great many people who proved to be eternally grateful and Maggie had been impressed by his achievements. Plus, he mentored her in medicine. Loving medicine surprised her as much as anyone. Sully had said, "I think it's a great idea. If I was as smart as you and some old coot like Walter was willing to pick up the tab, I'd do it in a New York minute."

Maggie found she loved science but med school was the hardest thing she'd ever taken on, and most days she wasn't sure she could make it through another week. She could've just quit, done a course correction or flunked out, but no—she got perfect grades along with anxiety attacks. But the second they put a scalpel in her hand, she'd found her calling.

She sat on Sully's couch, drank two beers, then lay down and pulled the throw over her. Beau pushed in through his doggy door and lay down beside the couch. The window was open, letting in the crisp, clean March air, and she dropped off to sleep immediately to the rhythmic sound of Sully raking out a trench behind the house. She started fantasizing about summer at the lake but before she woke she was dreaming of trying to operate in a crowded emergency room where everyone was yelling, bloody rags littered the floor, people hated each other, threw instruments at one another and patients were dying one after another. She woke up panting, her heart hammering. The sun had set and a kitchen light had been turned on, which meant Sully had been to the house to check on her.

There was a sandwich covered in plastic wrap on a plate. A note sat beside it. It was written by Enid, Frank's wife. Enid worked mornings in the store, baking and preparing packaged meals from salads to sandwiches for campers and tourists. *Welcome Home*, the note said.

Maggie ate the sandwich, drank a third beer and went to bed in the room that was hers at her father's house.

She woke to the sound of Sully moving around and saw that it was not quite 5:00 a.m. so she decided to go back to sleep until she didn't have anxiety dreams anymore. She got up at noon, grazed through the refrigerator's bleak contents and went back to sleep. At about two in the afternoon the door to her room opened noisily and Sully said, "All right. Enough is enough."

Sully's store had been built in 1906 by Maggie's great-grandfather Nathaniel Greely Sullivan. Nathaniel had a son and a daughter, married off the daughter and gave the son, Horace, the store. Horace had one son, Harry, who really had better things to do than run a country store. He wanted to see the world and have adventures so he joined the Army and went to Vietnam, among other places, but by the age of thirty-three, he finally married and brought his pretty young wife, Phoebe, home to Sullivan's Crossing. They immediately had one child, Maggie, and settled in for the long haul. All of the store owners had been called Sully but Maggie was always called Maggie.

The store had once been the only place to get bread, milk, thread or nails within twenty miles, but things had changed mightily by the time Maggie's father had taken it on. It had become a recreational facility—four one-room cabins, dry campsites, a few RV hookups, a dock on the lake, a boat launch, public bathrooms with showers, coin-operated laundry facilities, picnic tables and grills. Sully had installed a few extra electrical outlets on the porch so people in tents could charge their electronics and now Sully himself had satellite TV and Wi-Fi. Sullivan's Crossing sat in a valley south of Leadville at the base of some stunning mountains and just off the Continental Divide Trail. The camping was cheap and well managed, the grounds were clean, the store large and well stocked. They had a post office; Sully was the postmaster. And now it was the closest place to get supplies, beer and ice for locals and tourists alike.

The people who ventured there ranged from hikers to bikers to cross-country skiers, boating enthusiasts, rock climbers, fishermen, nature lovers and weekend campers. Plenty of hikers went out on the trails for a day, a few days, a week or even longer. Hikers who were taking on the CDT or the Colorado Trail often planned on Sully's as a stopping point to resupply, rest and get cleaned up. Those hearties were called the thru-hikers, as the Continental Divide Trail was 3,100 miles long while the Colorado Trail was almost 500, but the two trails converged for about 200 miles just west of Sully's. Thus Sully's was often referred to as *the crossing*.

People who knew the place referred to it as Sully's. Some of their campers were one-timers, never seen again, many were regulars within an easy drive looking for a weekend or holiday escape. They were all interesting to Maggie—men, women, young, old, athletes, wannabe athletes, scout troops, nature clubs, weirdos, the occasional creep—but the ones who intrigued her the most were the long-distance hikers, the thru-hikers. She couldn't imagine the kind of commitment needed to take on the CDT, not to mention the courage and strength. She loved to hear their stories about everything from wildlife on the trail to how many toenails they'd lost on their journey.

There were tables and chairs on the store's wide front porch and people tended to hang out there whether the store was open or closed. When the weather was warm and fair there were spontaneous gatherings and campfires at the edge of the lake. Long-distance hikers often mailed themselves packages that held dry socks, extra food supplies, a little cash, maybe even a book, first-aid items, a new lighter for their campfires, a fresh shirt or two. Maggie loved to watch them retrieve and open boxes they'd packed themselves—it was like Christmas.

Sully had a great big map of the CDT, Colorado Trail and other trails on the bulletin board in the front of the store; it was surrounded by pictures either left or sent back to him. He'd put out a journal book where hikers could leave news or messages. The journals, when filled, were kept by Sully, and had become very well-known. People could spend hours reading through them.

Sully's was an escape, a refuge, a gathering place or recreational outpost. Maggie and Andrew liked to come for the occasional weekend to ski—the cross-country trails were safe and well marked. Occupancy was lower during the winter months so they'd take a cabin, and Sully would never comment on the fact that they were sharing not just a room but a bed.

Before the pregnancy and miscarriage, their routine had been rejuvenating—they'd knock themselves out for a week or even a few weeks in their separate cities, then get together for a weekend or few days, eat wonderful food, screw their brains out, get a little exercise in the outdoors, have long and deep conversations, meet up with friends, then go back to their separate worlds. Andrew was shy of marriage, having failed at one and being left a single father. Maggie, too, had had a brief, unsuccessful marriage, but she wasn't afraid of trying again and had always thought Andrew would eventually get over it. She accepted the fact that she might not have children, coupled with a man who, right up front, declared he didn't want more.

"But then there was one on the way and does he step up?" she muttered to herself as she walked into the store through the back door. "He complains that I'm too sad for him to deal with. The *bastard*."

"Who's the bastard, darling?" Enid asked from the kitchen. She stuck her head out just as Maggie was climbing onto a stool at the counter, and smiled. "It's so good to see you. It's been a while."

"I know, I'm sorry about that. It's been harrowing in Denver. I'm sure Dad told you about all that mess with my practice."

"He did. Those awful doctors, tricking people into thinking they needed surgery on their backs and everything! Is one of them the bastard?"

"Without a doubt," she answered, though they hadn't been on her mind at all.

"And that lawsuit against you," Enid reminded her, *tsking*.

"That'll probably go away," Maggie said hopefully, though there was absolutely no indication it would. At least it was civil. The DA had found no cause to indict her. *But really, how much is one girl supposed to take?* The event leading to the lawsuit was one of the most horrific nights she'd ever been through in the ER—five teenage boys in a catastrophic car wreck, all critical. She'd spent a lot of time in the stairwell after that one. "I'm not worried," she lied. Then she had to concentrate to keep from shuddering.

"Good for you. I have soup. I made some for your dad and Frank. Mushroom. With cheese toast. There's plenty if you're interested."

"Yes, please," she said.

"I'll get it." Enid went around the corner to dish it up.

The store didn't have a big kitchen, just a little turning around room. It was in the southwest corner of the store; there was a bar and four stools right beside the cash register. On the northwest corner there was a small bar where they served adult beverages, and again, a bar and four stools. No one had ever wanted to attempt a restaurant but it was a good idea to provide food and drink—campers and hikers tended to run out of supplies. Sully sold beer, wine, soft drinks and bottled water in the cooler section of the store, but he didn't sell bottled liquor. For that matter, he wasn't a grocery store but a general store. Along with foodstuffs there were T-shirts, socks and a few other recreational supplies—rope, clamps, batteries, hats, sunscreen, first-aid supplies. For the mother lode you had to go to Timberlake, Leadville or maybe Colorado Springs.

In addition to tables and chairs on the porch, there were a few comfortable chairs just inside the front door where the potbellied stove sat. Maggie remembered when she was a little girl, men sat on beer barrels around the stove. There was a giant ice machine on the back porch. The ice was free.

Enid stuck her head out of the little kitchen. She bleached her hair blond but had always, for as long as Maggie could remember, had black roots. She was plump and nurturing while her husband, Frank, was one of those grizzled, skinny old ranchers. "Is that nice Dr. Mathews coming down on the weekend?" Enid asked.

"I broke up with him. Don't ever call him nice again," Maggie said. "He's a turd."

"Oh, honey! You broke up?"

"He said I was depressing," she said with a pout. "He can kiss my ass."

"Well, I should say so! I never liked him very much, did I mention that?"

"No, you didn't. You said you loved him and thought we'd make handsome children together." She winced as she said it.

"Obviously I wasn't thinking," Enid said, withdrawing back into the kitchen. In a moment she brought out a bowl of soup and a thick slice of cheese toast. Her soup was cream of mushroom and it was made with real cream.

Maggie dipped her spoon into the soup, blew on it, tasted. It was heaven. "Why aren't you my mother?" she asked.

"I just didn't have the chance, that's all. But we'll pretend."

Maggie and Enid had that little exchange all the time, exactly like that. Maggie had always wanted one of those soft, nurturing, homespun types for a mother instead of Phoebe, who was thin, chic, active in society, snobby and prissy. Phoebe was cool while Enid was warm and cuddly. Phoebe could read the hell out of a menu while Enid could cure anything with her chicken soup, her grandmother's recipe. Phoebe rarely cooked and when she did it didn't go well. But lest Maggie completely throw her mother under the bus, she reminded herself that Phoebe had a quick wit, and though she was sarcastic and ironic, she could make Maggie laugh. She was devoted to Maggie and craved her loyalty, especially that Maggie liked her more than she liked Sully. She gave Maggie everything she had to give. It wasn't Phoebe's fault they were not the things Maggie wanted. For example, Phoebe sent Maggie to an extremely good college-prep boarding school that had worked out on many levels, except that Maggie would have traded it all to live with her father. Foolishly, perhaps, but still...

And while Phoebe would not visit Sully's campground under pain of death, she had thrown Maggie a fifty-thousand-dollar wedding that Maggie hadn't wanted. And Walter had given her and Sergei a trip to Europe for their honeymoon.

Maggie had appreciated the trip to Europe quite a lot. But she should never have married Sergei. She'd been very busy and distracted and he was handsome, sexy—especially that accent! They'd looked so good together. She took him at face value and failed to look deeper into the man. He was superficial and not trustworthy. Fortunately, or would that be unfortunately, it had been blessedly short. Nine months.

"This is so good," Maggie said. "Your soup always puts me right."

"How long are you staying, honey?"

"I'm not sure. Till I get a better idea. Couple of weeks, maybe?"

Enid shook her head. "You shouldn't come in March. You should know better than to come in March."

"He's going to work me like a pack of mules, isn't he?"

"No question about it. Only person who isn't afraid to come around in March is Frank. Sully won't put Frank to work."

Frank Masterson was one of Sully's cronies. He was about the same age while Enid was just fifty-five. Frank said he had had the foresight to marry a younger woman, thereby assuring himself a good caretaker for his old age. Frank owned a nearby cattle ranch that these days was just about taken over by his two sons, which freed up Frank to hang out around Sully's. Sometimes Sully would ask, "Why don't you just come to work with Enid in the morning and save the gas since all you do is drink my coffee for free and butt into everyone's business?"

When the weather was cold he'd sit inside, near the stove. When the weather was decent he favored the porch. He wandered around, chatted it up with campers or folks who stopped by, occasionally lifted a heavy box for Enid, read the paper a lot. He was a fixture.

Enid had a sweet, heart-shaped face to go with her plump body. It attested to her love of baking. Besides making and wrapping sandwiches to keep in the cooler along with a few other lunchable items, she baked every morning—sweet rolls, buns, cookies, brownies, that sort of thing. Frank ate a lot of that and apparently never gained an ounce.

Maggie could hear Sully scraping out the gutters around the store. Seventy and up on a ladder, still working like a farmhand, cleaning the winter detritus away. That was the problem with March—a lot to clean up for the spring and summer. She escaped out to the porch to visit with Frank before Sully saw her sitting around and put her to work.

"What are you doing here?" Frank asked.

"I'm on vacation," she said.

"Hmm. Damn fool time of year to take a vacation. Ain't nothing to do now. Dr. Mathews comin'?"

"No. We're not seeing each other anymore."

"Hmm. That why you're here during mud season? Lickin' your wounds?"

"Not at all. I'm happy about it."

"Yup. You look happy, all right."

I might be better off cleaning gutters, she thought. So she turned the conversation to politics because she knew Frank had some very strong opinions and she could listen rather than answer questions. She spotted that guy again, the camper, sitting in his canvas camp chair outside his pop-up tent/trailer under a pull-out awning. His legs were stretched out and he was reading again. She noticed he had long legs.

She was just about to ask Frank how long that guy had been camping there when she noticed someone heading up the trail toward the camp. He had a big backpack and walking stick and something strange on his head. Maggie squinted. A bombardier's leather helmet with earflaps? "Frank, look at that," she said, leaning forward to stare.

The man was old, but old wasn't exactly rare. There were a lot of senior citizens out on the trails, hiking, biking, skiing. In fact, if they were fit at retirement, they had the time and means. As the man got closer, age was only part of the issue.

"I best find Sully," Frank said, getting up and going into the store.

As the man drew near it was apparent he wore rolled-up dress slacks, black socks and black shoes that looked like they'd be shiny church or office wear once the mud was cleaned off. And on his head a weird WWII aviator's hat. He wore a ski jacket that looked to be drenched and he was flushed and limping.

Sully appeared on the porch, Beau wagging at his side, Frank following. "What the hell?"

"Yeah, that's just wrong," Maggie said.

"Ya think?" Sully asked. He went down the steps to approach the man, Maggie close on his heels, Frank bringing up the rear and Enid on the porch waiting to see what was up.

"Well, there, buddy," Sully said, his hands in his pockets. "Where you headed?"

"Is this Camp Lejeune?"

Everyone exchanged glances. "Uh, that would be in North Carolina, son," Sully said, though the man was clearly older than Sully. "You're a little off track. Come up on the porch and have a cup of coffee, take off that pack and wet jacket. And that silly hat, for God's sake. We need to make a phone call for you. What are you doing out here, soaking wet in your Sunday shoes?"

"Maybe I should wait a while, see if they come," the man said, though he let himself be escorted to the porch.

"Who?" Maggie asked.

"My parents and older brother," he said. "I'm to meet them here."

"Bet they have 'em some real funny hats, too," Frank muttered.

"Seems like you got a little confused," Sully said. "What's your name, young man?"

"That's a problem, isn't it? I'll have to think on that for a while."

Maggie noticed the camper had wandered over, curious. Up close he was distracting. He was tall and handsome, though there was a small bump on the bridge of his nose. But his hips were narrow, his shoulders wide and his jeans were torn and frayed exactly right. They met glances. She tore her eyes away.

"Do you know how you got all wet? Did you walk through last night's rain? Sleep in the rain?" Sully asked.

"I fell in a creek," he said. He smiled though he also shivered.

"On account a those shoes," Frank pointed out. "He slipped cause he ain't got no tread."

"Well, there you go," Maggie said. "Professor Frank has it all figured out. Let's get that wet jacket off and get a blanket. Sully, you better call Stan the Man."

"Will do."

"Anyone need a hand here?" Maggie heard the camper ask.

"Can you grab the phone, Cal?" Sully asked. Sully put the man in what had been Maggie's chair and started peeling off his jacket and outer clothes. He leaned the backpack against the porch rail and within just seconds Enid was there with a blanket, cup of coffee and one of her bran muffins. Cal brought the cordless phone to the porch. The gentleman immediately began to devour that muffin as Maggie looked him over.

"Least he'll be reg'lar," Frank said, reclaiming his chair.

Maggie crouched in front of the man and while speaking very softly, she asked if she could remove the hat. Before quite getting permission she pulled it gently off his head to reveal wispy white hair surrounding a bald dome. She gently ran her fingers around his scalp in search of a bump or contusion. Then she pulled him to his feet and ran her hands around his torso and waist. "You must've rolled around in the dirt, sir," she said. "I bet you're ready for a shower." He didn't respond. "Sir? Anything hurt?" she asked him. He just shook his head. "Can you smile for me? Big, wide, smile?" she asked, checking for the kind of paralysis caused by a stroke.

"Where'd you escape from, young man?" Sully asked him. "Where's your home?"

"Wakefield, Illinois," he said. "You know it?"

"Can't say I do," Sully said. "But I bet it's beautiful. More beautiful than Lejeune, for sure."

"Can I have cream?" he asked, holding out his cup.

Enid took it. "Of course you can, sweetheart," she said. "I'll bring it right back."

In a moment the gentleman sat with his coffee with cream, shivering under a blanket while Sully called Stan Bronoski. There were a number of people Sully could have reached out to—a local ranger, state police aka highway patrol, even fire and rescue. But Stan was the son of a local rancher and was the police chief in Timberlake, just twenty miles south and near the interchange. It was a small department with a clever deputy who worked the internet like a pro, Officer Paul Castor.

Beau gave the old man a good sniffing, then moved down the stairs to Cal who automatically began petting him.

Sully handed the phone to Maggie. "Stan wants to talk to you."

"He sounds like someone who wandered off," Stan said to Maggie. "But I don't have any missing persons from nearby. I'll get Castor looking into it. I'm on my way. Does he have any ID on him?"

"We haven't really checked yet," Maggie said into the phone. "Why don't I do that while you drive. Here's Sully."

Maggie handed the phone back to her dad and said, "Pass the time with Stan while I chat with this gentleman."

Maggie asked the man to stand again and deftly slid a thin wallet out of his back pocket. She urged him to sit, and opened it up. "Well, now," she said. "Mr. Gunderson? Roy Gunderson?"

"Hmm?" he said, his eyes lighting up a bit.

Sully repeated the name into the phone to Stan.

"And so, Roy, did you hurt anything when you fell?" Maggie asked.

He shook his head and sipped his coffee. "I fell?" he finally asked.

Maggie looked at Sully, lifting a questioning brow. "A Mr. Gunderson from Park City, Utah," Sully said. "Wandered off from his home a few days ago. On foot."

"He must've gotten a ride or something," Cal said.

"His driver's license, which was supposed to be renewed ten years ago, says his address is in Illinois."

"Stan says he'll probably have more information by the time he gets here, but this must be him. Dementia, he says."

"You can say that again," Maggie observed. "I can't imagine what the last few days have been like for him. He must have been terrified."

"He look terrified to you?" Frank asked. "He might as well be on a cruise ship."

"Tell Stan we'll take care of him till he gets here."

Maggie went about the business of caring for Mr. Gunderson, getting water and a little soup into him while the camper, Cal, chatted with Sully and Frank, apparently well-known to them. When this situation was resolved she meant to find out more about him, like how long he'd been here.

She took off Roy's shoes and socks and looked at his feet—no injuries or frostbite but some serious swelling and bruised toenails. She wondered where he had been and how he'd gotten the backpack. He certainly hadn't brought it from home or packed it himself. That would be too complicated for a man in his condition. It was a miracle he could carry it!

Two hours later, the sun lowering in the sky, an ambulance had arrived for Roy Gunderson. He didn't appear to be seriously injured or ill but he was definitely unstable and Stan wasn't inclined to transport him alone. He could bolt, try to get out of a moving car or interfere with the driver, although Stan had a divider cage in his police car.

What Maggie and Sully had learned, no thanks to Roy himself, was that he'd been cared for at home by his wife, wandered off without his GPS bracelet, walked around a while before coming upon a rather old Chevy sedan with the keys in the ignition, so he must have helped himself. The car was reported stolen from near his house, but had no tracking device installed. And since Mr. Gunderson hadn't driven in years, no one put him with the borrowed motor vehicle for a couple of days. The car was found abandoned near Salt Lake City with Roy's jacket in it. From there the old man had probably hitched a ride. His condition was too good to have walked for days. Roy was likely left near a rest stop or campgrounds where he helped himself to a backpack. Where he'd been, what he'd done, how he'd survived was unknown.

The EMTs were just about to load Mr. Gunderson into the back of the ambulance when Sully sat down on the porch steps with a loud huff.

"Dad?" Maggie asked.

Sully was grabbing the front of his chest. Over his heart. He was pale as snow, sweaty, his eyes glassy, his breathing shallow and ragged.

"Dad!" Maggie shouted.

If you tell the truth you don't have to remember anything.

—MARK TWAIN

CHAPTER 2

It's different when it's your father, when your father is Sully, the most beloved general-store owner in a hundred square miles. Maggie felt a rising panic that she hoped didn't show. First, she gave him an aspirin. Then she rattled off medication orders to the EMT, though she wasn't the physician in charge and it would have to be approved via radio. Poor Mr. Gunderson ended up in the back of Stan's squad car and Sully was put on the gurney. The emergency tech immediately started an EKG, slapping electrodes onto his chest, getting an oxygen mask over his nose and mouth.

Maggie was in the ambulance immediately, reading the EKG as it was feeding out. Beau was barking and jumping outside the ambulance door, trying to get inside.

"Beau!" Maggie yelled. "No, Beau! Stay!"

She heard a whistle, then a disappointed whine, then the door to the ambulance closed and they pulled away.

"Maggie," Sully said, pulling the mask away. "See he didn't follow. I don't leave him very much."

Maggie peeked out the back window. "It's okay, Dad.

He's in front of the porch with that guy. That camper. Enid will see he's taken care of."

The driver was on the radio saying they were en route with a possible coronary.

"The lost guy with dementia?" the dispatcher asked.

"Negative, we got Sully from the store. Chest pains, diaphoretic, BP 190 over 120, pulse rapid and thready. His daughter is with us. Dr. Maggie Sullivan. She wants us to draw an epi and administer nitro. She stuck an aspirin in his mouth."

"Is he conscious?"

"I'm conscious," Sully whispered. "Maggie. I ain't quite ready."

"Easy, Dad, easy. I'm right here for you," Maggie said. "Let's start some Ringer's, TKO."

"Not you," Sully said. "You're shaking!"

"You want me to do it, Sully?" the young EMT asked.

"Better you than her. Look at her." Then he moaned.

"We need morphine," Maggie said. "Get an order for the morphine and ask for airlift to Denver. We have to transport to Denver stat. Gimme that IV setup."

She got the IV started immediately, so fast the EMT said, "Wow!"

A few years ago Walter, her stepfather, had suffered a small stroke. *Stroke.* That was her territory and she handled him with calm and ease. He was treated immediately, the recovery was swift, his disability minor and addressed in physical therapy in a matter of weeks. A textbook case.

This felt entirely different.

"Gimme your cell phone," she said to the EMT. She didn't have hers, of course, because it was back at

Sully's in her purse. The young man handed it over without question and she called Municipal Hospital. "This is Dr. Maggie Sullivan. I'm in an ambulance with my father, en route to you. I don't have my cell. Can you connect me with Dr. Rob Hollis? It's an emergency. Thank you."

It took only a moment. "What have you got, Maggie?" her friend Rob asked.

"My dad—seventy-year-old male," she said, running through his symptoms. "The EMT is running an EKG and we can send it." She looked at the EMT. "We can send it, right?"

"Right."

"If we get medical airlift from Timberlake, we'll be there in no time. Will you meet me?"

"Absolutely," he said. "Try to stay calm."

"I'm good," she said.

"She's a wreck," Sully muttered. "Airlift. Gonna cost a goddamn fortune."

"I gave him nitro, oxygen and morphine. He seems to be comfortable. EKG coming to the ER for you."

It was not like this with Walter. With Walter, whom she'd become close to once she'd passed through adolescence, she was able to be a physician—objective, cool, confident. With Sully, she was a daughter clinging to her medical training with an internal fear that if anything terrible happened to him she would be forever lost.

Sully was not experiencing terrible pain once the morphine kicked in; his breathing was slightly labored and his blood pressure remained high. Maggie watched over him through the transfer into a medical transport helicopter and stayed with him while he was taken into the emergency room where Dr. Hollis waited.

"Jesus, Maggie," Rob said, his stethoscope going immediately to Sully's chest. "Nothing like making an entrance."

"Who are you?" Sully asked.

"Rob Hollis, cardiac surgeon. And you must be Sully." He picked up a section of the EKG tape, glancing at it almost casually. "We're going to run a few tests, draw some blood, bring down that blood pressure if possible and then, very probably, depending on the test results, go to the OR and perform a bypass surgery. Do you know what that is?"

"Sure I do," Sully said, his voice tired and soft. "I'm the last one on my block to get one."

"Maggie, this is going to take a while even though we'll push it through with stat orders. Maybe you should go to the doctor's lounge and rest."

"She should go grab a beer and find a poker game but she don't need no rest," Sully said. "She's plenty rested."

"I'll stay with my dad," she said. "I'll keep out of your way."

"You're going to be bored," Rob said.

Not as long as he's breathing, she thought. "I'll manage."

Maggie knew almost everyone in the hospital, in the ER and the OR. Because of her stature as a surgeon, she was given many updates on the tests, the results, the surgery. She even thought to ask one of her friends, an operating room charge nurse, for the loan of her car once Sully was out of recovery, out of danger, and resting comfortably in the coronary care unit.

Here she was in Denver with no vehicle, no purse, credit cards, phone, nothing, but there was a spare key to her house under the flowerpot on the back patio and she could write a counter check at her bank for cash. There might even be a duplicate or extra credit or debit card she didn't keep in her purse. In her closet there would be something to wear. In fact, there were drawers full of scrubs, if it came to that.

She wasn't bored and she'd had plenty of sleep before Sully's medical emergency, but by the time she stood at his bedside in the CCU at five in the morning she was so exhausted she could hardly stand up. She had the wiggles from too much caffeine, looked like bloody hell and hadn't had a shower since leaving Denver for Sullivan's Crossing. It reminded her of some of those days in residency when she stayed at the hospital for over forty-eight hours with only a catnap here and there. This time it was all stress.

She went home in her borrowed car to freshen up. She located an old wallet and purse, found a credit card she didn't often use in her file cabinet and was back at the hospital by eight. By nine they were rousing Sully.

"Maggie, you gotta get me out of here," he rasped. "They won't leave me alone."

"There's nothing you can do but be your charming self," she said.

"They got some breathing thing they force on me every hour," he complained. "And I'm starving to death. And it feels like they opened my chest with a Black & Decker saw."

"I'll ask for more pain meds," she offered. She lifted a hand toward the nurse and got a nod in return.

"Maggie, you gotta go run the store…"

"The store is fine. I called Enid an hour ago, gave her a progress report and checked on them. Frank stayed with her yesterday till closing, they took Beau home with them and they should be opening up about now. She's going to call Tom Canaday and see if he has any extra time to help out. It's all taken care of."

He just groaned and closed his eyes. "'Bout time Frank worked off some of that coffee he's been freeloading. What about you?" he asked.

"What about me? I'm here with you."

He opened his eyes. They were not his usual warm or mischievous brown eyes. They were angry. "I'm not good with hospitals. I've never been in one before."

She thought for a moment because surely he was wrong. "Huh," she finally said. "Never? That's something, Sully. Seventy years old and never spent a night in a hospital."

"Turns out I knew what I was doing. Look what happens. They have a tube shoved up my—"

"Catheter," she said.

"Get it out! *Now!*"

The nurse arrived with a syringe, putting it in the IV. "You should feel a lot better in just a few minutes, Mr. Sullivan."

"How long do I have to stay here?"

"In the care unit? Just a day or two."

"Then I can go home?"

"That's a good question for the doctor, but it's usually anywhere from three to eight days."

"I'll do two," he said without missing a beat. "That's all I got."

"There's recovery time involved after heart surgery, Dad," Maggie said.

"And what are you going to do?"

"I'm going to stay with you. Take care of you."

He was quiet for a moment. "God help me," he whispered.

We're going to need a lot more drugs, Maggie thought.

A great deal of maneuvering was required for Maggie to get her affairs in order, so to speak.

According to Enid, Tom Canaday, their handyman and helper, was going to adjust his schedule to spend more time at Sully's. Tom had a lot of jobs—he drove a tow truck, worked on car repairs in a service station, drove a plow in winter and did road work in summer, which kept him on the county payroll. He did a variety of handyman and maintenance jobs around the area. He'd do just about anything if the money was right because he was a single father with four kids aged twelve to nineteen. Sometimes he'd bring one or two along to help him or just to hang out with him. And now, when Tom couldn't work, he could send his oldest son, Jackson, the nineteen-year-old.

Maggie asked Enid if she could come to Denver to pick her up, drive her back to Sully's where she would get her own car and some incidentals like her cell phone, purse, extra clothes, makeup and the like. Also, she would get some clothing and a shaving kit for Sully, who was not going back home soon, a subject she was not looking forward to discussing with him.

Enid said she'd be at the hospital in the morning. "Can I see him when I get there?" she asked.

"You don't want to see him, Enid. He's a huge pain in the ass. He's been complaining and trying to get out of here from the minute he arrived and the fact that he can hardly get out of bed hasn't deterred him one bit."

"Well, I could've told you it would be like that."

Maggie was waiting outside the hospital's front entrance for Enid when who should pull up in a banged-up old red pickup truck but Frank. Maggie sighed. *Just what I need—two hours held captive by Frank.*

All the way back to Sullivan's Crossing, Frank droned on and on about the evils of government in every conspiracy theory ever imagined, including his belief that commercial jetliners were spraying the atmosphere with enhanced jet stream in an effort to lower the temperature of the earth to combat global warming. "Of which there ain't no damn such thing anyhow."

By the time they got back to the crossing, she was exhausted all over again. "I can't believe you did that to me," she said to Enid.

"You find him a little talkative, Maggie?" she asked with a teasing smile. "He got there, didn't he? We're a little short-handed around here, you know."

Maggie hurried to gather up what she needed and asked Enid to make her a sandwich.

"Already done, cupcake. Turkey and swiss on whole grain. And I packed up a box of cookies and muffins for Sully."

"I'm afraid his cookie and muffin days are over for now. Listen, Enid, we can put a sign on the door. Close up for a while. You and Frank just can't handle the whole place on your own."

"We're getting by all right, honey. People understand about stuff like this. Tom's been here with his boy. That camper with the pop-up trailer has even been pitching in. Nice fella, Cal."

"Oh, Enid, he'll probably steal the silver! If we had any."

"Nah, he's a good enough fella. He's got that spot and asked for a weekly rate. I offered him the house for his shower but he said he's doing just fine."

"He's probably homeless," Maggie said. "You know we don't really know these people."

"Tom offered to try to spend some nights around here, but we don't hardly have anybody in the park anyhow. And besides, we got Cal here if there's trouble, which there ain't likely to be. Cal's got a cell phone."

"He'll probably break into the store and clean us out the first night and—"

"Maggie, the first night's come and gone and he's still here, helping out. You've been in the city too long. That isn't gonna happen, honey. And for sure not in March! No one's passing through in this muck and mess."

But there had been times when the police or sheriff or ranger had to be called, when a few campers had a little too much fun, too much to drink, got aggressive. Sully had a baseball bat he took with him if he went out to see what was going on late at night. There was a domestic once when Maggie was young—some man knocking around his woman and Sully just couldn't resist. He decked him, knocked him out. Maggie had been stunned, not just that her dad would do that but that he was that strong. Plus, even though she'd always been told, *we never hit, no matter what*, she had adored him for it.

It was true the crossing was mostly peaceful. But

they were isolated, especially from November to March, and from time to time had a little trouble. They didn't have any paid security like some of the bigger or state-operated campgrounds. Just Sully. Maggie could count on one hand the number of nights Sully had spent away from the campground. Her graduations, her wedding.

"Was it awful?" Enid asked of Sully's heart attack.

"I was terrified," Maggie whispered back.

Maggie went back to Denver, to a hospital she knew well, and commenced what would become three of the longest weeks of her life. Sully was healing nicely and making great progress…and he was incorrigible. He sulked, he didn't follow explicit instructions, he got very constipated and it riled him beyond measure. He began speaking abusively to the nursing staff. He went from stonily silent to loud and abrasive; he wouldn't eat his food and he was moved to a private room because Maggie couldn't bear the effect he had on his roommate.

"What is the *matter* with you?" she ground out.

"Besides the fact that my chest was ripped open and I haven't had a good shit in ten days? Not a goddamn thing!"

"You haven't been here ten days, but I'm going to get you fixed right away. And you're going to be sorry you complained to me." She put two residents on the job; she told them to use any means available and legal, just make it happen. She said she didn't want to know how they did it but they were to see to it he had a bowel movement by morning.

When she came in to see Sully the next day, he was smiling. And he was passably pleasant most of the day.

After seven days in the hospital she took him home

to her house where she was cloistered with him, fed him low-sodium and low-fat foods, took him to rehab every other day and listened to him bitch for another thirteen days.

Finally, she took him back to Sullivan's Crossing.

And Sully was reborn. His temperament immediately smoothed over. His facial features relaxed. He greeted Enid, Frank and Tom, and spent about fifteen straight minutes greeting Beau. Then Sully ate a salad with turkey slices and complimented Maggie's thoughtfulness for the lunch.

"I think you dropped twenty pounds," Enid said.

"Twelve. And I could spare it. Now, Enid, it looks like I'm going to be keeping Frank company for a while. Maggie says I have to go slow. We should get Tom's boy to help out with things like stocking shelves; get Tom to finish cleaning the gutters and clearing that trench around the house to the stream so we don't get flooded, if we aren't already."

"You aren't," a voice said. "I finished clearing that trench and I checked the basement at your house."

Everyone turned to see the man standing in the doorway of the store. Cal. Maggie looked at him closely for the first time. He was somewhere just under forty, with dark brown hair and light brown eyes that twinkled.

"Cal," Sully said. "You're still here? Good to see you! You been helping out?"

Cal stuck out a hand. "Sorry about the heart trouble, Sully. Glad to see you're doing so well. To tell the truth, you look better than ever."

"What the devil you doing here so long?" Sully asked, shaking his hand.

"Well, I could say I was here to help out, but that

wouldn't be true. I'm waiting for better weather to check out the CDT. Since I was here, I tried to lend Enid a hand."

"He did a great job, Sully," Enid said. "He's been bringing in the heavy boxes from the storeroom, helped stock shelves, swept up, hauled trash, the kind of stuff that's on your schedule."

"That's awful neighborly," Sully said. "We'll cut you a check."

The man chuckled and ducked his head with a hint of shyness that Maggie was immediately taken with.

"No need, Sully. I didn't mind helping out. It gave me something to do."

"If you're camping, you must have had other things on your mind to take up time."

"To tell the truth, I messed up my planning. I thought I'd pick up the CDT out of Leadville but where it's not icy, it's flooding. A few chores weren't anything. Enid took care of me. I appreciate the hospitality."

"Are you planning to leave your vehicle in Leadville?" Sully asked.

"That was the plan."

"Well, you can leave it here if it suits you and pick up the trail just over that hill," Sully said, pointing. "Whenever you're ready and no charge. No charge on the campsite, either."

"You don't have to do that, but it's appreciated. In fact, this being your first day home, I'll stick around a few days in case you need a hand. I don't have urgent plans."

"Are you homeless?" Maggie asked.

Everyone stared at her.

"I mean, you don't need money and you're in no

hurry and you're happy to help and… It's unusual. Not that people aren't friendly, but…"

He flashed her a beautiful smile. His front teeth were just slightly imperfect and it gave him a sexy, impish look. "No problem. In fact, I am homeless. I'm on the road, probably till fall. But I have the truck, the camper, I'm always on the lookout for places to charge up the laptop and phone and I think Enid gave me special treatment—some of the meals I got here were way better than what's for sale in the cooler. I have what I need for now. And yes, I can pay my way."

"Independently wealthy?" Maggie asked. And for someone who didn't mean to be rude, she realized she certainly sounded it. "Trust-fund baby?"

"Maggie!" Sully reprimanded. "She might be a little cranky, Cal, on account of I turned out not to be the best patient on record."

"No problem at all. I'm the suspicious type myself. No, not a trust-fund baby, Dr. Sullivan. Just a little savings and a lot of patience." He shifted his gaze to Sully. "Right now I have time for a game of checkers. Any takers?"

"Don't do it, Sully," Frank said. "He's brutal."

"That makes it irresistible, now, don't it?"

That's when Maggie wandered off to the house.

Sully's house was over a hundred years old. It had been built when Maggie's great-grandfather was a young man, before he and his wife had their first child. The improvements and changes since it was originally built were haphazard at best. When old refrigerators died, new ones appeared and they never matched the original kitchen color or design. The washer and dryer started in the basement but eventually made it up to the back porch; the porch was finally closed in so a person wouldn't freeze doing laundry in winter. Furniture was replaced as it wore out but never was a whole room remodeled. It was long overdue.

But the design was surprisingly modern for a house built in 1906 and Sully himself had reroofed it. There was a living room, dining room and a kitchen with nook on the main floor. There had been three bedrooms and a bath but Sully had installed a master bath attached to the largest bedroom. He had burrowed into the third bedroom for the space, which left a smaller than usual room, so it became his office. Over time he'd finished off the attic into a cozy loft bedroom but Maggie had no idea why. He didn't marry again. It wasn't like there were offspring wrestling for space. He'd recently remodeled the basement into what he called a rumpus room. "For the grandchildren I guess I'll never get," he said. "No pressure."

"It's not really too late," Maggie said. "If I ever find the time." *And the right man...*

"There wasn't that much to do in winter so I worked on the house a little bit," was all he said.

She loved the house, though it was in serious need of a face-lift.

She spent the afternoon settling their belongings into their rooms. Sully didn't make an appearance. It crossed her mind to check on him, to make sure he wasn't doing too much, but she trusted Enid to keep an eye on him.

She came back across the yard to the store a little after four and found Sully sitting by the stove with only Beau for company.

"Tired?" she asked him.

"I never been the nap kind of man but I'm starting to see the merits," he said.

"Did you send Enid and Frank home?"

"Nothing going on around here, no need for them to stay. We can close up early. After we have a little nip." He lifted his bushy salt-and-pepper brows in her direction. "Your friend the doctor, he said that's all right."

"Did he, now? You wouldn't lie about that, would you?"

"I would if need be but he did indeed say that." Sully got up, a bit slower than he used to, and walked through the store to the little bar. He went behind while she grabbed a stool. "What's your pleasure?" he asked.

"Is there a cold white wine back there with the cork out?" she asked.

"No, but it would be my pleasure to uncork this really nice La Crema and let you steal it. You can take it back to the house with you."

"That sounds like a plan."

"Now, I'd like you to do something for me, Maggie."

"What's that, Dad?"

"I'd like you to go out to the porch where that nice Cal Jones just sat down, and invite him to join us. Right after you apologize for being such an ass."

"Dad…"

"You think I'm kidding around? Really, I didn't raise you like that and maybe Phoebe did but I doubt it. She's snooty but not nasty. I've never seen the like."

She took a breath. "After your behavior in the hospital…"

"After you get your chest sawed open, we'll compare notes. For now, the man was decent enough to help Enid and we're grateful. Aren't we, Maggie?"

She sighed. "You know what this is like? This is like getting in trouble at school and being marched back to the classroom to humbly take your medicine. How do you know he's not a serial killer?"

"I'm not," said an amused voice.

"Don't you just have the worst habit of sneaking up on people!" she said. "This old man is a heart patient!"

"That's no way to worm back into my good graces, calling me old," Sully said. "Besides, I saw him coming. Say what I told you, Maggie."

"I might've been a little impatient today," she said. "And perhaps I didn't show my gratitude very well..."

"She was an ass," Sully said. "Not like her, neither. You want a little pop, son?"

"You're on," he said, sitting on one of the stools. "How about a Chivas, neat, water back."

While Sully pulled the cork out of the wine, he talked. "So, Maggie here is very tough but tender-hearted and usually very good with her manners. Much better than I am. But I think putting up with me for three weeks since this operation just plain ruined her." He pushed a glass of wine toward Maggie. "She isn't going to do that again. Unless you give her trouble. Don't give her trouble, son. She's very strong."

Maggie the bold and strong, she thought.

"I don't have any trouble in me, Sully," Cal said with a chuckle. "I'm just checking out Colorado."

"And what are you doing here?" she asked. When both men looked at her, she held up a hand. "Hey, no offense, but people usually have a reason for finding themselves at Sullivan's Crossing."

"No offense taken," he said. "I've been doing some hiking here and there. Hiking and camping. There's a lot of stuff online about hiking the Divide, but you don't want to hit the Rockies before May, and that might even be too soon…"

"Not this year," Sully said. "It's an early thaw. We damn near washed into the lake one year with an early thaw. The snowpack flows to the west but we're not without our wash. I gotta figure out how to get that garden in without lifting a finger."

Maggie laughed. "Once again, he talks about me like I'm not even here. Of course I'll help with the garden. So, you think you might hike the whole CDT?"

Cal shook his head. "I don't think so, just a little piece of it, but I'd like to get up there and see what I see. I'll hike and camp for a few weeks, then I'll decide what's next. Montana, maybe. Or Idaho. Canada. But not in winter."

Over the years, Maggie had learned that you don't ask a hiker why they take on something like the Appalachian Trail or the CDT. They're driven. They want to be stronger than the trail, to break it or maybe just survive it. "The CDT is the longest one," Maggie pointed out. "It can get lonely out there."

"I know. I like the solitude. I also like the people I run into. People who want to do that are… I don't know how to explain it. It's like they have things to understand about themselves and every single one of them has different things to figure out."

"And what do you have to figure out, Mr. Jones?" she asked.

"I don't know. Nothing too deep. How about what to do next? Where to settle?"

That sounded like true freedom to Maggie—choosing something new. She'd eventually have to go back to work in Denver. Right now she was using Sully's rehabilitation as an excuse. She was needed here.

"If you like solitude, then that must be why you chose this campground in March," Sully said, sipping from his glass and letting go a giant *ahhhh* as he appreciated it. Maggie and Cal laughed. "Doc says this is all right but you can bet your sweet ass that bitch of a nurse didn't bring me no nightcap!"

"Dad!"

"You expect me to apologize for saying that? That was a simple, true statement!" He shook his head. "That one nurse, the one at night with the black, black hair and silver roots, she was mean as a snake. If I die and go to hell, I'll meet her there."

Cal looked at Maggie and with a wry smile said, "Long convalescence?"

"Three weeks of my life I'll never get back," Maggie said.

No man can, for any considerable time,

wear one face to himself, and another to the multitude,

without finally getting bewildered as to which

is the true one.

—NATHANIEL HAWTHORNE

CHAPTER 3

Once Sully had gone to bed, Maggie got on her computer. She might not be a trained investigator but she was damn sure an experienced researcher. She started by collecting the possible variants on the name Cal. Calvin, Calhoun, Caleb, Callahan, Calloway, even Pascal. Then she tried just plain Cal Jones. She found several obituaries but not a single reference that could be their camper, so if he was a serial killer he was still an unknown one. She wasted two hours on that.

She heard her phone chime with a text. She was surprised to see it was from Andrew.

I heard about Sully. Is he doing well? Are you?

We're fine, she texted back.

There was no response and she went back to tinkering on her laptop. About ten minutes later her phone rang and she saw the call was from Andrew. She sent it to voice mail. There was a ping—message received.

There were so many times over the past three weeks she had wished to hear Andrew's confident and reassuring voice. To feel his arms closing around her. She had a few close women friends. There was Jaycee, her closest friend. Jaycee had called or texted every day to see how they were getting along. There were a few of the women she worked with, but Andrew had been the only man in her life for a long time. Since Sergei. And Sergei had been a total mistake. An artist of Ukrainian descent who, she eventually realized, wanted to marry an American doctor or someone of equal income potential. He'd had the mistaken impression she came from money because of the show Phoebe and Walter could put on. Walter could affect an image of aristocracy.

"I am so lousy at men," she muttered to herself.

But Andrew shouldn't have been a mistake. Her eyes had been wide-open—they were both professionals with young practices and bruised hearts. She'd been thirty-four, he almost forty. His marriage had been longer but far more expensive than hers, and his ex had been so mean. Sergei hadn't been mean, not at all. In fact he'd been charming. Sweet. And after nine months of marriage expected a house, a car and 50 percent of her income for the next twenty years.

It turned out she'd had good instincts about lawyers. Thank God.

She didn't listen to Andrew's message, but she saved it. There would probably be a time soon when she'd crave that soothing voice. She wondered if he even realized that after all the storms she'd weathered lately one of her darkest hours had been the sight of Sully gripping his chest, panting, washing pale. She knew true terror in that moment.

It was amusing to Maggie that her mother thought Sully was such a loser, a simple, laid-back general-store owner, a country boy, an underachiever. Maggie didn't see him that way at all. Sully was her rock. In fact, he was a rock for a lot of people. He had a strong moral compass, for one thing. He worked hard but he wasn't a slave to his work, he saw the merits to a balanced life. He was possessed of a country wisdom attained through many years of watching people and learning about human nature. And he was true. He was the most loyal individual on earth. Sully thought Maggie was smart to strive to be as successful as Walter. But Maggie wished she could be more like Sully.

She settled back on the couch and decided to listen to Andrew's message.

"Maggie, listen, babe, I'm sorry about your crisis with Sully. Is he there with you in Denver? When I get a day I can come up and check on you both…"

"I don't want to be checked on," she said to the phone.

"It's been pretty crazy here or I might've heard sooner. I just heard about the bypass a couple of days ago but I was told he was doing great and you were with him so I didn't jump on the phone."

"Yeah, why would you do that?"

"And what's this I hear that you took a vacation? Of indefinite duration? I hope that doesn't have anything to do with our disagreement. I know you're probably upset with me, I know that. Honey, I just want what's best for you and I could tell I wasn't helping anything. Maybe I made the wrong call but I thought it was probably best if you looked further than me to get support right now. I don't know anyone who could cope with all you've been through any better than you have, but I just felt so helpless, and that wasn't good for you…"

"I sucked the life out of you, remember?"

"Call me, please. Or email me or something. Let me know what I can do, when we can talk. You know how much I care about you and Sully."

"Actually, I'm a little murky on that…"

"Maggie?" Sully said from the hall. "Who the devil are you talking to?"

She jumped in surprise. He was wearing his pajamas, his white hair mussed and spiking. "Um…the television?"

"The TV isn't on," he said.

"Okay, I was talking back to a message from Andrew. You don't dump someone and then leave a kind and caring message. Too little, too late."

"Hmm," he said, thinking on that for a moment.

"I guess I need a fresh start," she informed him. "I'd like to go back to eighth grade and redo everything."

"I think this heart attack business has taken a toll on you," he said. "I'm sorry about that."

"It wasn't exactly your fault," she said. "Aside from your genetics, you've been in good health. Your father and grandfather probably had health issues they didn't even know about. At least yours is resolved."

"I understand all that, but there's one thing you're going to have to make peace with one way or another. I'm seventy. I'm going to die before you do."

"*That* takes a toll," she informed him. "Remember you said you weren't quite ready? You remember saying that? In the ambulance?"

"If God takes me home in March it's only because he means to punish everyone I hold dear, from the folks who help run this little place to all the folks who pass through. I wasn't done with the cleanup. That's all I meant by that. Now, will you take one of them anxiety pills that are so popular and get some sleep? Unless you want to bitch at Andrew's message some more, of course."

"I thought coming back here would help me get perspective," she said.

"We been in Denver, Maggie. We haven't been back two full days. Even God needed seven to get it together. Jesus." He ran a hand over his head and wandered back to his bedroom.

"I've always had kind of high expectations of myself," she yelled at his back.

"No shit," he returned.

Maggie woke up at first light and walked into the kitchen. There were no signs of life and Sully's bedroom door stood open. He'd made his bed and was gone. This was typical of life here—he rarely put on a pot of coffee at the house, only in the worst of winter when venturing to the store was a useless chore. In spring, summer and fall he dressed and trudged over to the store where he'd start the big pot for Enid.

Before she even got up the steps to the back porch, she spied Sully. He was down at Cal Jones's campsite sitting on a small camp stool, holding a mug of coffee on his knee, petting Beau with the other hand. Cal, on the other hand, was crouched before a small grill, sitting on the heel of his boot, stirring something in a frying pan. She caught the unmistakable aroma of bacon.

When Beau saw her he got up, started wagging his tail and ran to her as though he hadn't seen her in weeks. "Good morning, gentlemen. Something smells good."

Cal cracked two eggs on top of his bacon and covered the pan. "I'd be happy to make you breakfast," he said.

"That's very nice of you. I'll get some in the store in a minute. Dad, I was hoping you'd sleep in."

"And here I was hoping you would," Sully said. "I can't stay in bed, Maggie. I get all creaky and it takes too long to work out the kinks. Besides, this is the best time of day."

"It is a beautiful morning," she agreed. She wanted to discuss the coffee—just one cup, please. And activity today—nothing strenuous. Diet, they could talk about diet, and it wouldn't include bacon... But Cal distracted her by popping open a camp stool for her to join them. "Thanks," she said.

She watched as Cal put two pieces of bread he'd toasted on the grill onto a plate. Then he lifted his bacon and eggs out of the pan. He sat across the grill from Sully, plate on his knees, and worked away at his breakfast.

"That bacon smells every bit as good as I recall," Sully said.

"If you stay away from the wrong foods you'll live longer," Maggie reminded him.

"I probably won't. But it'll damn sure seem longer." Cal laughed.

"What's Cal short for?" Maggie asked.

He swallowed and looked at her. "You've been Googling me."

"I have not!" she said.

"Is that what you were doing on the computer half the night?" Sully asked.

She scowled at him. "I'm just curious. Calvin? Caleb?"

"Why? Does one of those guys have a record?" Cal asked.

"How would I know?" she returned, but she colored a little. She'd always been a terrible liar.

He laughed at her. "I just go by Cal," he said.

"You won't tell me?"

"I think this is more fun."

A car pulled into the grounds followed by Frank's beat-up red truck. "There's Enid and Frank. I take it you started the coffee?" Maggie asked.

"I did. And ate a bowl of that instant mush," Sully said.

"What've you got to do today, Sully?" Cal asked. "What can you use help with?"

"Just the regular stuff. I can probably handle it with Maggie's help. You know—shelf stocking, cleaning up, inventory. Hardly any campers yet so we're not too far behind, but they're coming. We have spring break coming up. I'm gonna have Tom and two of his kids to help this weekend and we'll get that garden in. Once it's in, I can handle it, plus the doctor said I should be back in the swing of things in a couple of weeks."

"No. He didn't," Maggie pointed out. "He said you'd probably be moving slow for six weeks and in a few months you'd be in good shape. But no lifting anything over ten pounds for at least six weeks, preferably ten."

"Thank God you were listening, Maggie," he said sarcastically. "Otherwise I might've just killed myself planting a carrot."

Maggie got up, turned and started walking to the store. "I don't appreciate the attitude," she said.

"I'm about ready to get out a big cigar and see how strong *your* heart is!"

"Do that and you'll see how strong my right arm is!"

"This is going to be one giant pain in the ass, that's what."

"Sully, can't you appreciate that I'm just being responsible? If you live right you have many good years ahead," she said, a pleading quality to her voice.

"Let's try to relax, Maggie. The doctor said I'd be fine and to keep an eye on too much bruising from the blood thinner. He didn't tell me to stay in bed until I die of boredom." Sully stood from his camp chair to follow Maggie. "He did tell me not to have sex or take my Viagra for a while," Sully said to Cal.

Maggie whirled and gave him a dirty look as Cal smirked.

"Bummer," Sully said.

Cal puttered around his campsite, cleaning up and stowing things. Then he ambled over to the store to check things out before Sully got himself in any more trouble with Maggie. Sully was full of mischief and reminded Cal a lot of his grandfather. His grandfather had died at the age of seventy-five and it had seemed so premature at the time. He, like Sully, had been so physically strong, mentally sharp.

Maggie was a very interesting character. He didn't know all the details but he'd peg her for either a first-born or only child. She was strong like her father, that was undeniable. Or maybe she was strong-willed like a doctor? Cal had had plenty of experience with doctors and he knew they could be arrogant, stubborn and nurse a great need to be right about everything. They were also often brilliant, compassionate, sensitive and yet not sentimental. Maggie seemed to embody those qualities.

And she wasn't hard to look at, either. She had good teeth, he thought, then laughed at himself. Like he was judging a horse? He was just one of those people who noticed eyes and mouths first. It was somehow natural to him and also something he consciously thought about—you can tell a lot about a person from their mouth and eyes.

Maggie's eyes were brown like his but darker. Chocolate. She had thick lashes, fine, thin, arching brows and a sparkle in her eyes. They reflected humor, anger, curiosity and embarrassment. He'd caught her; it was written all over her face—she'd been trying to research him. Probably because he was hanging around the campground so long, even during inclement weather. And not just hanging around the grounds but also the store—she was naturally protective of her father and his property.

He said good-morning to Frank, who sat by Sully near the stove. Sully had another cup of coffee and Cal guessed he must have gotten rid of Maggie somehow to score another cup. Who knew how many he'd had before walking with his steaming mug over to Cal's campsite. Cal wasn't sure whether Sully was hard to manage or he just enjoyed watching Maggie's attempts. He was extremely curious about their family history. Where was Maggie's mother?

"What would you like me to get out of that storeroom for you, Sully?"

"Aw, I don't want to work you, Cal…"

"I don't feel put upon at all. I don't have anything on the calendar. Another week and your campground will get busy, the weather will get warmer and I'm going to take you up on your offer to park and see what these trails have to offer. So—want to tell me?"

"I'll go with you and show you," Sully said.

"As long as you don't get in trouble with the warden."

Cal went about the business of bringing out boxes of supplies and restocking the shelves. He rotated the goods so the newest went in the back and the oldest would sell first. He checked the dates on the food products if necessary and he used a dampened rag to wipe the shelving clean.

It brought back memories of his student days. Stocking supermarket shelves didn't pay particularly well but it was something he could do at night. He went to classes and study groups during the day and early evening, worked at night. And sleep? When he could. He learned to work quickly, study every second he could spare, power nap, eat on the run. He recorded facts, stats, case studies and lectures into his pocket recorder, listened and repeated as he showered, drove, shelved. The days were long, the nights short, the labor intense.

Yet it was a happy time. He was achieving all his goals, was deeply bonded with his friends and fellow students, his life felt challenging but very stable. And he met Lynne.

Lynne Aimee Baxter was the smartest, kindest, strongest, funniest person he'd ever known. They weren't headed in the same direction, not really. They both wanted to work in the legal system. He wanted to make a good living, put down roots, build a house that could hold him till he died and with space to accommodate a growing family. Lynne wanted to help people. He might end up in criminal law...maybe tax law...same thing, they would joke. She might end up a public defender or, better still, a storefront operation for the underprivileged in need of legal counsel. What was so comical—he came from nothing while she was a trust-fund baby.

Maybe that explained it. He longed for security; she wanted to shed the excesses of her life.

"You're better at this than I am," Sully said behind him.

He turned around with a grin. "I've done this before."

"I'll say it again—I just don't pay you enough. Listen, Maggie's gone over to town to pick up my seeds and starters and maybe to get away from me. Want to join me for a hot dog?"

Cal smiled. "You eat a hot dog, you're going to pay. That's for sure."

"You thinking I'll get caught?" Sully asked.

"Someone is bound to talk," Cal said. "But I was thinking more along the lines of indigestion. You've been on a pretty bland diet, haven't you? I'd work up to a hot dog if I were you. And then there's the high sodium, fat, et cetera."

"That mean you don't want one?"

"Oh, *I* want one," Cal said. "You should have something a little more easy on the stomach. If you ever want to have sex again in your life."

"Hell, I gave up on that a long time ago. Don't tell Maggie. I'd like to think of her having nightmares about it."

When he was done with the shelf stocking and his hot dog, Cal went to the area Sully had mentioned was his garden. It was easily identifiable. It was behind the house, kind of hidden from the campgrounds. Cal wondered if that was sometimes an issue—a thriving garden being tempting to campers. Did they occasionally help themselves to the tomatoes?

It wasn't too big, maybe sixteen by sixteen feet. He could see the rows from last year. He went to the shed that stood back from the property, tucked in the trees. There was a lot of equipment, from snowblower to plow attachment, lawn-grooming equipment, riding mower, wheelbarrow and gardening supplies.

Snowblower. He kept reminding himself to head south. Maybe southwest. It was just all that smog and sand and those hot rocks they called mountains...

He'd gone to school in Michigan, the state that invented winter. He was from everywhere, usually moderate climates, while Lynne was from New York. Westchester, to be exact.

He chose the wheelbarrow, spade, shovel and rake, and started clearing away the winter debris. He hadn't asked what Sully meant to do with the stuff so he made two piles—one of fallen leaves that could constitute fertilizer and the other rocks, winter trash and weeds. You wouldn't want to use weeds in mulch; that would just invite them back.

He'd been at it a couple of hours when he heard her approach. He knew she'd get around to it. He leaned on his spade and waited.

"You let my father eat a hot dog? Does that sound heart healthy to you?"

He just shook his head. "You know he's a liar and he's having fun with your close medical scrutiny. What do you think?"

"He got me, didn't he?"

"He ate a sandwich—lean turkey, tomato, lettuce on wheat bread. He asked for doughy white bread and lost out to Enid, who obviously knows him better than you do. He wanted chips—he got slaw—made with vinegar, not mayo. Really, Maggie?" He laughed and shook his head.

"He's antagonizing me, is that what you're saying?"

"Over and over. But you can stop pressing the panic button. He's doing great."

"Have you seen his incision?" she asked.

"Oh, about ten times. I offered to sell tickets for him. He's running out of people to show. But no worries. He tells me the camp is going to attract people like crazy any second now. Spring break, then weekends, then summer. I just hope he doesn't scare the children."

She thought about that for a moment. "It's impolite to act like you know more about my closest relative than I do."

"And yet, that's usually the case. You're too bound up by baggage, expectation and things you need for yourself. Like a father who lives much longer." He pulled a rag out of his back pocket to wipe off his brow. "Stop letting him bait you. He's very conscious of the doctor's orders. He's taking it one step at a time."

"Did he pay you to say this? Or are you Dr. Phil on vacation?"

Cal laughed. "You two have quite a dynamic going. You could be a married couple. Married about forty years, I'd say."

"Remind you of your parents?" she asked, raising one brow. She crossed her arms over her chest.

"My parents are unnaturally tight," he said. "They're kind of amazing, I guess. Deeply supportive of each other, almost to the exclusion of everything around them and everyone else. Protective. They're in their sixties, as in love as the day they met, and total whack jobs. But sweet. They're very sweet."

Her arms dropped to her sides. "What makes them whack jobs?"

"Well, they always described themselves as hippies. New-age disciples. Free thinkers. Intelligent and experimental and artistic. They're from that dropout generation. And Deadheads."

"As in, the Grateful Dead?"

"Exactly. Just a little more complex."

She dropped down to the ground like a child fascinated by a bedtime story filled with adventure and excitement. She circled her knees with her arms. He'd seen this before. It was kind of fun, as a matter of fact.

"Where are they now?" she asked.

"Living on my grandfather's farm in Iowa. My grandfather passed away quite a while ago and my grandmother, just a few years ago."

"Are they still whack jobs?" she asked.

"Oh yeah," he said, working his spade again. "Or maybe it's more kind to say they're eccentric. My mother doesn't hear voices or anything." Then he smiled. "But my dad is another story. My father fancies himself a new age thinker. He's incredibly smart. And he regularly gets…um…*messages*."

"Oh, this is fascinating," she said. "What kind of messages?"

"Come on, nosy. How about you? Are you the oldest in the family?"

"The only. My parents divorced when I was six. My mother lives in Golden with my stepfather. What kind of messages?"

"Well, let's see…there have been so many. One of the most memorable was when my father believed space aliens were living among us and systematically killing us off by putting chemicals in our food. That was a very bad couple of years for meals."

"Wow."

"It definitely hits the wow factor. They—*we*—were gypsies with no Romany heritage and my parents glommed on to a lot of bizarre beliefs that came and went."

"And this has to do with Jerry Garcia how?"

"He appealed to their freedom factor—no rules, no being bound by traditional ideas or values, crusaders of antisocial thinking, protesting the status quo. They were also very fond of Timothy Leary and Aldous Huxley. My father favors dystopian literature like *Brave New World*. My mother, on the other hand, is a very sweet lady who adores him, agrees with everything he says, likes to paint and weave and is really a brilliant but misguided soul. She usually homeschooled us since we were wanderers." He took a breath and dug around a little bit. "My father is undiagnosed schizophrenic. Mild. Functional. And my mother is his enabler and codependent."

"It sounds so interesting," she said, kind of agog. "And you're an only child, too?"

He shook his head. "The oldest of four. Two boys, two girls."

"Where's the rest of the family?" she asked.

"Here and there," he told her. "My youngest sister was on the farm with my parents last I checked. There's a sister back East living a very conventional life with a nice, normal husband and two very proper children. My brother is in the military. Army. He's an infantry major. That's taken years off my mother's life, I'm sure."

She laughed and it was a bright, musical sound. "You are no ordinary camper! What are you doing here?"

He leaned on the spade. "What are *you* doing here?" he asked.

"Looking after Sully," she said.

"Oh, but that's not all," he said. "Neurosurgeons don't just take weeks off when duty calls."

"True. Not weeks off, anyway. I was already here for a vacation. My practice in Denver shut down because two of my former partners are not only being sued but being investigated by the attorney general for fraud and malpractice. I am not being indicted. I had no knowledge of their situation. But I can't float a practice alone."

"And that's not all, either."

"My father had a heart attack," she said indignantly.

"I know, but there's something else. Something that made you run home, run to your father, who is a remarkable man, by the way. There's at least one more thing…"

"What are you talking about?" she demanded.

"That little shadow behind your eyes. Something personal hurt you."

"I don't know what you mean."

"A man," he said. "I bet there was a man. You had a falling out or fight or something. Or he cheated. Or you did."

"There was no cheating! We just parted company!"

"Now we're getting somewhere," he said, grinning at her.

"That's just plain rude, prying like that. I didn't do that to you. I was only curious and I asked, but if you'd said it was none of my business, I wouldn't have pushed. And I wouldn't have given you some bullshit about something behind your eyes."

"I think I'm getting a name," he said, rolling his eyes

upward as if seeking the answer in the heavens. "Arthur? Adam? Andrew, that's it."

She got to her feet, a disgusted smirk marring her pretty face. "Oh, that was good, Calhoun," she said.

"Frank told me," he said. "You weren't thinking of keeping a secret around here, were you?" He laughed, very amused with himself. "And it's not Calhoun."

She brushed off the butt of her jeans. "You're going to pay for that. I don't know how yet, but trust me…"

"Someone has to teach you how to have a little fun, Maggie," he said.

"Well, it's not going to be you, Carlisle."

He just shook his head and laughed. Then he worked on tilling the garden plot.

To find yourself, think for yourself.

—SOCRATES

CHAPTER 4

The days were getting just a little longer, a little warmer. Flowers were starting to sprout along road-sides and trails. It was turning beautiful in and around Sullivan's Crossing. Sully wasn't able to plant his bulbs around the house but Maggie did it for him, with his relentless supervision.

Maggie and Sully had been back for five days and she'd driven to Timberlake as many times. First for some fresh vegetables and salmon, then for seedlings for Sully's garden along with fertilizer, then for some fish and chicken breasts. She went ahead and stocked up on frozen shrimp and ground turkey and she spent a lot of time on her laptop looking up heart-healthy meals.

This was not how Maggie envisioned her escape from reality. She'd been hoping to relax and empty her brain of all those disappointments and worries. *But this?* She was working her tail off. She was not used to cooking, for one thing. When she was working she typically ate hospital food which, paradoxically, was not the healthiest. It was so starchy, cafeteria quality. It wasn't the food they served patients, either. If not eating at the hospital, she'd grab something on the way home, something light—there was a conveniently located grocer and deli that sold prepared meals for one. And then there were the times she went out with friends or some of the staff for a meal and they were partial to either sushi or Italian.

But now she was working hard at feeding Sully delicious things to at least intrigue him rather than bore him to death. Before, when Maggie was at the campground, they'd decide what they were having for dinner and meet at about seven, throw a steak, burgers or maybe some chicken breasts on the grill. And they'd eat their meat with fries or potato chips.

She was already tired of this new routine.

She also watched while Cal got the garden ready. This was not his first garden. He created neat, straight rows of slightly raised dirt, ready for planting.

There were two fishermen in the campground and one older couple in an RV. The couple was interested in getting pictures of the wildflowers that were springing up all over, some even popping through the snow at the higher elevations. Because there was still so little traffic there was a sign on the front door of the store—Winter Hours, 8-5.

After dinner one evening, she walked over to the store to pilfer a beer and she saw there was a campfire on the beach, one lone man enjoying the mild evening. She grabbed two beers and walked down to the lake. He was sitting on top of a picnic table, feet on the bench, his elbows on his knees. His short brown hair was wet, as was the collar of his sweatshirt. He'd had a shower and shave.

"Evening, Caldwell," she said.

He turned toward her in surprise and she handed

him a beer. *"Caldwell?"* he asked. "You're getting desperate."

"That's true, but not about your name. I'm getting a little restless."

"Maybe it's time to go back to work," he said. He toasted her, clinking the neck of her beer with his.

"I do a lot of chores around this place. Sully has always been a tough taskmaster. I've always had to haul stock, sweep, clean, chop wood, dig out trenches, clean gutters, clean that damn bathroom and shower, work in the store, but never what I've been doing this time— cleaning house, cooking dinner. I'm already bored with my little housewifely duties and I'm getting cabin fever. I'm sick of heart-healthy food. If I see one more hunk of fish I'm going to gag. Sully said he's growing fins."

Cal laughed.

"You think it's funny? I can smell your bacon before I smell coffee in the morning. I sneaked over to Timberlake for a hamburger today and Sully claimed he could smell it on my breath."

He leaned closer to her, sniffing. "Yep."

"I asked him if he had any ideas for dinner and he said he'd like a New York strip, smothered in onions on a hoagie bun." She took a pull on her beer. "God, that sounds good."

"I knew it," he said. "You're a carnivore."

"You're kind of interesting, Caliber. You shower and shave while you're camping."

"I wash my clothes and change the lining in the sleeping bag, too. I'm a very clean fellow. Are you ever going to go back to work and leave Sully alone?"

"Gimme a break, I haven't relaxed a day yet," she said. "Are you?"

"Sure. I just left a job about six weeks ago. I work. I'm just not working now, except for you."

"Well, not *me*, exactly," she said. "You work for Sully. Have I said how much we appreciate all the free labor? It's very nice of you to pitch in."

"I have time on my hands," he said.

"What was your last job?"

"I was an assistant to an assistant in human resources in a theme park. It basically meant driving a golf cart around, checking on people, helping them fill out forms or taking complaints. Or, sometimes it meant catching them screwing around on the job and reporting them to my supervisor. As little of that as possible."

"Really? A theme park?" she said, fascinated again. "Which one?"

"The big one."

"Really? Was it fun?"

"It really was. I applied to the ground crew but there wasn't anything and they offered me the job in HR. I met all the actors. It was cool."

"And you quit?" she asked.

"No, I got fired. I was checking someone's human resources very closely. Not in public of course. Not on the job. It was consensual and private, but word got out. Apparently even adults have to refrain from that. There are rules if you want to work there. Strict rules. More for some than others."

"They can't do that," she said. "That's discrimination."

"Not for everyone. Princesses are not allowed to do some things, even on their own time."

"You were doing a *princess*? Which one?"

"Get outta here, I'm not telling you."

"You're too old for those princesses!"

"Oh, she was a lot older than she looked! Plus, she was an animal!"

"So not only was it a bad decision, you didn't like it?"

"I never said that," he said. He grinned lasciviously.

"You're lying!" she said. "I don't believe one word of that!"

"Okay," he said. He took a drink of his beer. "It's true, though. A very embarrassing situation. We both got fired. I lost a pretty fun job and I think she lost her lifetime dream. I was planning to take a few months off to camp, but I wasn't planning to start until April or May. I hate being cold. However…"

"Callahan, I think you're a liar, con man and maybe a predator."

He just laughed at her. "Seriously, you ever going back to work?"

"I told you, the practice shut down," she said.

"We both know there are things you could do."

"I was picking up work here and there from colleagues. I just came to Sully's for a badly needed break. I packed up a bunch of stuff, left the disposition of the office in the hands of a broker who can be sure the equipment, furniture and supplies are sold or stored, emailed all my colleagues that I was taking a leave of absence. I was burned out, bloody well sick of all the controversy my partners had stirred up and I was exhausted. I was only home for twenty-four hours when Sully crashed. That's almost four weeks ago. I haven't thought about anything but Sully since."

"You can let go of that pretty soon. Aside from being a little ornery and sick of salmon and chicken, he's doing great."

"I know. But I don't know if I want to go back to that grind. Check with me after I've actually had some time to think. But one thing I'm not crazy about is being a caretaker the rest of my life."

"Maybe another residency? A different specialty?" he asked.

She shook her head. "I don't think so. Right now I just want to escape. Have you ever felt like that?"

He chuckled. "I've been in your campground for five weeks. Through rain and mud and heart attacks. What do you think?"

"You're traumatized by the aftershock of screwing a princess?"

"It takes a lot more than that to traumatize me," he said. He put an arm around her shoulders. "It's okay to take a break, Maggie. I'm not sure it's good for you to obsess about Sully, though. It might be misplaced anxiety. Really, he's going to be fine."

"You didn't see what I saw," she said.

"No one saw what you saw, honey," he said very sweetly. "I was right there when they loaded him into the ambulance. You saw your father slipping away. Everyone else saw a cardiac episode. I think you're a little terrified."

"Yeah," she said. "Guilty. I'm not very close to my mother and I have no siblings. And it was Sully. Maybe it's because I always felt deprived of him when I was growing up—my mother and stepfather lived in Chicago and it wasn't easy to see Sully. Or it could be that he's as special as I think he is. You don't know him that well yet. He's one of the most remarkable men I've ever known. If you were going to be around here longer, like through summer, you'd see…"

"Tell me," he said.

"Oh hell, where to start. I've seen him break up fights, rescue drowning kids and *dogs*! You didn't think a dog could drown, did you? He was tangled in fishing line. He's given refuge to the lost, tracked and killed a bad cat, a mountain lion who attacked a hiker. That almost never happens and Sully got in so much trouble! Took him forever to work through that. But maybe the most important thing he does—he creates relationships with people. Unforgettable relationships. They write him, send him pictures, mention him in their writing, their blogs, long after they've gone. They hang out at the store and he listens to their tales from the trails. He gives them tips, does little favors, lets them charge up their phones and stuff so they can make contact with friends and family. He tells jokes, encourages people, praises them, and most of that without anyone knowing that's what he's doing. He lets kids' organizations come out and camp for free—he's partial to the autistic kids. Sully relates to a lot of them and I have no idea why. He doesn't know why, either. He plows in winter— he clears our road and then he goes out to the neighbors who are snowed in and clears theirs. He's the third generation—his grandfather built the store and Sully didn't get a son to run it. All he's got is me. What's going to happen to this place when Sully can't run it anymore? Will the next owner carry on that legacy? You have no idea how much Sully is loved. Needed."

It was still and quiet for a moment. The sound of night birds and crickets and the occasional splash of a fish was all she heard.

He tightened his arm slightly, pulling her a bit closer. "What a lucky man," he said softly.

"I never looked at it that way, as Sully being the lucky one. I always thought it was the rest of us who were lucky."

"It's the rest of you, too. One of the things I think about a lot when I'm alone is what makes a life well spent? It sounds like you described one."

"Yeah, Sully is very happy. I'd say he's good at making relationships with everyone. Well, except maybe me. He never tried very hard to make a relationship with me."

"You? I thought you two were very close."

"We are, I guess. Except my mother took me away from him. And of course he never came after me. He said I was better off." She shrugged. "I guess I should get over it by now. Huh?"

He gave her shoulders another squeeze. "Some things stay with us a long time," he said. "No one knows that better than me, the boy raised on the road by Jed 'Looney Tunes' Jones."

Maggie had a new friend. The days around the store and grounds were busy but in the evenings, when things were quiet, she wandered down to the lakefront or over to Cal's campsite. One night she invited him to meet her on her front porch at the house. They talked about their lives, even though she wasn't sure how much of his was true.

"Did I mention I'm being sued?" she said.

"No. No wonder you don't want to go back to work!"

"Oh, I've been sued before. It might settle or just go away but if it doesn't it could drag on. There was no malpractice. We did everything humanly possible. It really took its toll on me—it was a hard one. A terrible accident involving teenagers. We all did what we could, but were so helpless. I've lost patients before—in my business it happens too often. It was awful."

"I'm so sorry. Are you worried about the lawsuit?" he asked.

"I worry about everything," she admitted. "But when I'm in the moment, in surgery, I'm not worrying, I'm performing and thinking hard. Before and after, I worry too much."

On the weekend, the park began to fill up with campers. The weather was outstanding—sunny and warm spring weather. Tom and his oldest son, Jackson, came to the property to help Maggie finish putting in the garden. She had several flats of flowers and vegetable starters. Cal dug in and helped while Beau did his job chasing the rabbits into the woods, and Sully watched over everyone, giving plenty of advice.

"Like I've never put in a garden before," Tom said.

"What haven't you done, Tom?" Maggie asked.

"Never did surgery," he said. "Yet."

Tom Canaday was a big, happy guy whose wife divorced him years ago. At first she wanted to take the girls, Nikki and Brenda, to her new home in Aurora, but that didn't last long. The girls were miserable away from the home and school they knew and Tom convinced his ex-wife to give them back to him, that he was in a better position to take care of them and see they were doing well in school. Nikki was now seventeen and Brenda, fourteen. His ex visited from time to time and, as far as Maggie knew from the gossip, they were amicable and got along better divorced than they had as a married couple.

Tom had indeed had a million jobs and on top of that was a volunteer on the search-and-rescue team.

The campground welcomed a lot of what Maggie referred to as weekend warriors. They began to pull in on Thursday and Friday afternoons. A few planned to stay a few days but most would pack up on Sunday night. During school breaks, whole families or large groups of young people would stay through two weekends. And school breaks came at various times all over the country.

"We're going to do some hiring for the spring and summer. Interested, Jackson?" Maggie asked.

"Doing what?" he asked.

"Everything," she said. "From spring till August this place will be busy. I'm still trying to hold Sully down. Do you have any time?"

"I can take on a little work," Jackson said, smiling handsomely. "This is not a bad place to be in summer. Girls everywhere."

"Thanks, Maggie. As if college isn't hard enough on my nerves," Tom said, staking the tomato plants.

"I have an idea. Why don't you ask Nikki if she wants a summer job, too. Maybe they can spy on each other and tattle?"

"Oh, much better, Maggie," Tom said, one knee in the dirt. He looked up at her and shook his head. "You're just looking for ways to make my life easier, aren't you? Now I have to worry about two of them. Schoolwork is a priority."

"Well." Maggie rubbed her hands together. "Until school is out for summer, if you can come after school, I'll give you dinner and when things are slow you can study. You can try to study, anyway."

"I've been working for my dad the last two years and I have good grades. He just doesn't want to part with his cheap labor," Jackson said.

"He doesn't want you looking at too many bikinis," Sully said.

"Oh? Is there such a thing?" Jackson asked, grinning.

The camp came alive in the sunshine. The lake was still too cold to enjoy swimming but women rolled up their shorts and sat in lawn chairs in the sun by the water. Maggie strung up a couple of macramé hammocks and they were filled before she could walk away. There was a steady stream of people through the store all weekend, getting ice for their coolers, grabbing items they missed like butter, Tabasco, salt and pepper. Enid left early—she wasn't usually in on weekends but was coming around to make sure they were covered since Sully's surgery. Her cookies and breakfast muffins sold like crazy.

There was activity beginning on other spots around the lake—a dozen rental cabins across the lake, a Girl Scout camp, a church camp, a US Forest Service campground with bathrooms but no laundry, showers or store. Most of them were just starting to get ready for summer vacationers. A couple of them, on the other side of the lake, had little mini-marts but no general store. A family camp across the lake sold gas for the boats. People who needed to do a little shopping had to choose between a trip to Leadville, Timberlake or Sully's.

Maggie kept the store open a little later than usual, enjoying the sound of laughter, the smell of cooking fires. Sully operated the cash drawer and Maggie knew there was no way she could leave him yet. Dusk came, the air cooled and campers settled their lawn chairs around their campfires. Cal came into the store carrying two covered plates.

"I thought you might not have time to cook," he said.

"What have you got there?" she asked.

"Look and see. Where's Sully?"

"He's checking inventory," she said. She pulled the foil off one plate. "Oh my," she said. It was a skinless chicken breast cut in strips, smothered in a light sauce surrounded by broccoli, peppers, mushrooms, cherry tomatoes, onions and a couple of baby corns tossed in for color. "Sauce?"

"Yogurt, flavored with spices. Try it."

She took the offered fork and dipped into it. "Wow. You did this on that little grill of yours?"

"The Coleman stove. I'm a pretty experienced camper."

"Gee," she said, chewing and swallowing. "Imagine what you could do with a real stove. Did you go to town today? Shop for dinner?"

"Yesterday."

"I have to stay open a little later tonight," she said. "I hope it's not past your bedtime."

"I'll manage," he said. "Go get Sully."

After eating at the checkout counter, Sully went back to the house. Maggie washed up the plates and gave them back to Cal. Then she dimmed the lights in the store and they sat on the front porch for a while. They sat side by side, their feet up on the porch rail. The store was officially closed but if someone came down the path and needed something, she'd unlock the door.

Since no one did, they talked. Softly. He put his arm around her again and told her that he admired her ability to shift gears, be flexible during this important time.

"That you put his needs above your own for now, that's generous. A lot of people couldn't."

"You thought I was overdoing it a bit," she reminded him.

"You are," he said, giving her shoulders a squeeze. "But I think it will give you both peace of mind. You're important to each other. I think you watch over each other. That's all that matters."

Maggie was working up a crush. She thought about Cal while she was falling asleep. She was probably a sucker for a soft, calm, confident voice and a steadying arm, she thought. In medical school one learns to worship calm confidence. Especially in surgery and particularly in specialties like hers where no doubt, no tremor, no hesitation could be tolerated. There were occasions she'd had to make a life-altering decision in under a minute. Maggie remembered times her knees had knocked but no one knew. She was decisive.

This was probably not what Jaycee had in mind when she suggested a break, and becoming a caretaker and full-time grocer was certainly not what Maggie had in mind. But Cal was a welcome distraction. Vacations, camping trips and campgrounds like this were ripe for romance and it was no different if you were the proprietor. There was something about the temporary quality, the way one was removed from real life for a time. Having spent many a weekend and vacation here with Sully during high school and college, Maggie had been vulnerable to that vacation dalliance a time or two. And it had been fun. When she was younger, the reality that the young man didn't follow through, didn't write or phone or email, stung. But that didn't last. Now, she knew it for what it was.

The sexy Cal Jones, probably not even his real name, would be no different. Her common sense told her it shouldn't be. He was lovely and wonderful the way he helped her dad, but he was just marking time and would be on to his next adventure soon. But her attraction to him was real. One of these evenings their twilight beer by the lake or on the porch would go a little further. She hoped.

She couldn't help that. She hadn't been in the arms of a loving man in a while, after all.

Sunday at the camp was active. People were trying to squeeze in the last of their weekend fun, then pack up their tents and campers. The store was busy—campers ran out of things to get through their last day: beer, soft drinks, snacks, sandwich fixings. Maggie was ringing up, bagging things, laughing with the customers, telling them she hoped they had a good time, looking forward to dusk when the activity would slow down. A lovely fourteen-year-old girl and her ten-year-old brother came in for eggs—they were staying one more night and then backpacking farther up the trail with their parents. They were beautiful blond-haired, blue-eyed angels and the sweetest kids. Apparently their spring break had started and the family—mom and dad both teachers—loved hiking and camping and it was their dream to one day hike the whole CDT as a family.

"We're getting up early tomorrow, eating breakfast and heading out," Chelsea Smyth told Maggie. "We'll probably get in a hundred miles during break."

"I hope you're planning to get into really good shape for the CDT," Maggie said. "It's a six-month commitment."

"I think I could do it now," Chelsea told her.

"So could I!" her brother, Remy, insisted.

"I hope when you do I'm here to cheer you on," Maggie said, giving the girl her change. "Good luck tomorrow!"

"Maggie?"

She looked up into the beautiful blue eyes of the man next in line, eyes she knew so well. "Andrew. What are you doing here?"

"I took Mindy home a little early and hoped I could catch you. Rob Hollis told me you were here with your dad. You might've let me know."

"Why? We're fine. Better than fine," she said, bagging up the eggs for the Smyth kids. "I hope you had a good time here, and have a safe hike," she said. She waited for the kids to clear the door and then turned on Andrew. "Little busy here. You should have called."

"Maggie, what the hell are you doing?" he asked, frowning.

"Bagging groceries, mostly."

"No, what are you doing here? The rumor is you quit!"

"That's not quite accurate. I decided to take some time off since the practice is closed and I've just been picking up hospital shifts here and there. Then Sully needed me, so it's a good thing I have the time. I don't have any patients counting on me."

"When are you going back?" he asked.

"That's really not your concern, now is it?" she said.

"You've lost your mind, is that it? You're a *surgeon*. A gifted surgeon. You can't stay here!"

"I don't want to talk about it with you. You really should have called. I could've saved you a trip."

"You're ignoring my calls."

"Well, there's a reason for that. We're not seeing each other anymore."

"We're not enemies, I hope. Come on, Maggie. Can we talk? Please? We have things to talk about."

"This is a bad time," she said.

Sully came from behind her, from the kitchen or storeroom. For seventy and in recovery from heart surgery, apparently his hearing was perfect. "Hello, Andrew," he said. "How've you been?"

"Sully! Damn, it's good to see you," Andrew said, grabbing Sully's hand and pumping it. "You look great! Are you feeling all right?"

"I'm doing fine. Not crazy about the new diet, but I'll live."

Andrew laughed. "You have really good color."

"I was told I'd come out of it looking better than when I went in. I have freshly widened arteries to float my oxygen through. As a beauty treatment, I don't recommend it."

"Can't say I blame you," Andrew said with a laugh. "What a relief to see you. Did Maggie say I called? Just to see how you were?"

"She might've mentioned it, thanks. But we're doing fine."

"Maggie, are you going back to Denver anytime soon?" Andrew asked.

"I haven't made any plans."

"Can you break away for a few minutes? I won't keep you long."

"Sure. Meet you out front in a few."

She watched him walk away, leave the store as a couple of guys walked in. "I'll get this, Sully," she said.

"Nah, go deal with him. I'll live through a check-out or two."

"You're sure?" she asked.

"Stop pampering me. I'm doing a damn sight better after heart surgery than he did after his knee surgery. You'd think he'd delivered a baby elephant or something. And don't you dare use me as an excuse for not going back to work. Go on now. Get rid of him."

That made Maggie laugh a little, though she was in no mood to laugh over Andrew. It was true, though—what a lot of complaining he'd done after a knee scope. It was his first experience on that side of the knife, poor baby. "I won't be long," she said.

"Be as long as you want," he said. "Just make sure you don't invite him to dinner."

Oh, Sully wasn't happy with Andrew, and he didn't even know the half of what Andrew had put her through. It was so rare for Sully to get out of sorts with someone and Maggie hadn't even explained all that went on between them. But then, Sully usually guessed right.

Andrew was leaning up against his car, texting or reading his email. He straightened when she walked out of the store and down the porch steps. He really was so good-looking. She remembered the first time he suggested dinner. She'd been so surprised—he wanted to date *her*? He was one of those classically handsome men—chiseled cheekbones and chin, tall with dark blond hair, striking blue eyes, enviable physique. And he was so nice. But he was an ER doc—they had to have certain gifts, had to know how to deal with frightened, hurting people, had to be swift and skilled. Andrew could put patients and their families at ease and get the job done quickly.

"Maggie," he said. "You're looking good."

"Thank you. Listen, we don't have anything to do here. You said you were done. Let's go with that."

"Come on, Maggie, that wasn't exactly it," he argued, reaching for her hand.

"No, that was *exactly* it. Before I came back here, before Sully's heart attack, you said I was too depressed for you, that you couldn't deal with it anymore. Of course my practice was shutting down, I was thinking about filing for bankruptcy, I was being sued by the family of a sixteen-year-old I lost on the table, and I was trying to stay ahead of the bills by picking up call for other doctors, mostly nights and weekends so I could give interviews and depositions all week. Oh—and did I mention, I'd just lost my baby? The baby I wanted but you didn't. I'm so sorry I wasn't more cheerful, but there you have it." She shrugged. "Sorry, babe, that's all I've got," she said, mimicking him. "It turned out Sully needed me. That's all I have to say, Andrew."

"Look, I want us to be friends," he said. "I want to lend support if I can…"

She laughed a little. "You want us to be *friends*?" she asked, aghast. "I've never been treated more cruelly by anyone in my life, Andrew. You asked me to abort a baby because it wasn't convenient for you, then you bitched because I grieved. Andrew, hear this, please. I don't want to be friends. I spent a couple of years as your friend. That meant taking vacation to look after you when you got a meniscus tear repaired, listening to your rants over your crazy ex-wife and hearing a million complaints about the working conditions in your ER. Being your friend appears to mean that I should be there for you, be perpetually happy no matter what's going on. But, when I need you, you're unavailable. That's not good enough for me. Please just go."

"Maggie," he said in that calm, deep, lovely voice. "You're crying."

"Shit," she said, wiping at her cheeks. "We're done. It's non-negotiable. I wouldn't take you back if you begged me. I can't be with a man as selfish as you."

"That's not fair," he said. "Would you have wanted me to lie? When you told me you were pregnant, I told you the truth. I have a daughter and a crazy ex-wife and no, I was not planning to have more children. It was one of the first issues we talked about when we started seeing each other. You said you understood completely."

"I wasn't pregnant then!"

"Be reasonable—it wasn't planned," he said.

"Just go!"

She turned and walked around to the back of the store and in the back door. She ducked into the bathroom beside the storeroom and looked in the mirror. Sure enough, she was crying. Again.

In medicine, everyone worships stoicism, thus her hiding in stairwells. She once sneaked into a bathroom and sobbed her brains out when she lost a young woman and her unborn child, even though saving them had been a long shot. GSW. Gunshot wound—so tragic. Then there was a mass shooting at a high school, several victims and they pulled them through, all of them, and it had almost the same effect on her—she cried until she was sick to her stomach. That was back when she was in Chicago doing her fellowship with Walter. The sheer violence and cruelty of a school shooting had nearly gutted her. By the time she was practicing, she'd figured out how to hide it, the overpowering emotion. But she hadn't cried over a man since she was sixteen.

Not the man, she reminded herself. The relationship and the baby.

Andrew, the sensitive ER doctor, left her because she was having trouble coping with her loss. She really and truly had not known he was that inflexible, that cold. There must be a lesson in there somewhere. And she was damn sure going to find it.

She splashed cold water on her face, dried it, went back into the store. And of course who was standing beside Sully wearing a look of concern but Cal.

"Well, Calistoga, you're just everywhere, aren't you?"

"You okay, Maggie?" he asked.

"I got a little pissed, that's all. Ex-boyfriend."

"Gotcha," Cal said. He looked at his watch. "Why don't you go home and see what you can find for dinner for you and Sully. I'll hang out here till closing."

She sniffed. "Would you like to join us?" she asked.

"Thanks, but I've already eaten."

"It's early," she said.

"It's okay, Maggie," he said. "Take a break. Get some alone time."

"Sunday night can get a little… Ah, hell. I'm going," she said.

No legacy is so rich as honesty.

—WILLIAM SHAKESPEARE

CHAPTER 5

When Maggie had gone, Cal looked at Sully. "I bet she doesn't get like that very often," he said.

"Like what?" Sully said. But he was frowning.

"Teary. Splotchy. Shook up. What did he do to her?"

"I have no idea, but I bet I wouldn't like it."

"How long was he the boyfriend?"

"Couple a years. I didn't think he was that much of a boyfriend."

"Did you ever mention that to Maggie?"

Sully laughed, but not with humor. "Maggie look like the kind of person anyone tells what to do? She's contrary sometimes. I try to stay out of her business. She doesn't return the favor, either."

There was a lot of cleaning up, putting away, sweeping and organizing to do after the last of the weekend campers pulled out. Those who were leaving had settled up and were on the road by six at the latest. There were five campsites and one cabin still engaged and according to Sully all of them were planning to stay longer.

"Should we restock?" Cal asked.

"Let's not do it tonight," Sully said.

"I bet you don't ordinarily leave the store until it's ready for morning," Cal said.

"I don't ordinarily get tired. In summer and warm weather me and Tom give the place a nice face-lift on Wednesdays, slowest day. When Enid's in the store I spend more time on the garden and grounds but weekends find me right here, ready for anyone. Nights I patrol a little before I go to bed but hardly get any trouble. A year ago I got laid up with the pneumonia—things got pretty sloppy around here but we were running real low on weirdos or drunks so it was at least quiet. Don't know why I'd get the pneumonia when the weather finally gets warm, but I never ran high on good luck, except for Maggie. Maggie's about the luckiest thing a man could get and I wasn't even trying. Imagine what I could do if I was trying?"

Cal smiled. *The pneumonia* made him grin. If you didn't pay close attention to someone like Sully you would think he wasn't terribly smart. But Cal did pay attention. Sully was sharp as a tack and had that enviable insight into people so few possessed. "Where's your wife, Sully?" he asked boldly.

"Phoebe? She's in Golden, married to someone who deserves her."

"Are you still…you know… Do you miss her sometimes?"

"Miss Phoebe? Oh, Jesus, boy. Hell no, I don't miss Phoebe! She's the biggest pain in the ass I ever met. She's everyone's pain in the ass. Poor Maggie, that's all I have to say. She tries to take care of her mother. Phoebe." He laughed and shook his head. "I don't know what I was thinking. I must've been drunk."

Call laughed with him. "Well, what do you suppose

it was?" Cal asked. "No man gets that drunk. She must have been beautiful. Or sweet. Something."

"Oh, I could put a dent in the keg back then, but that Phoebe, she was mighty pretty. And funny and sweet but God as my witness, it sure didn't last long. I shouldn't'a brought her here—it was a bad match. She found fault with every breath I took. She was difficult. Miserable, unhappy."

"What do you think was wrong?" he asked.

Sully thought for a moment. "Well, son, it's mostly my fault, I'm sure of that. I'd been to Vietnam and it didn't leave me right, if you know what I mean. I had settling to do, in my head and other places and I just hadn't taken the time. I hadn't stopped making noise enough to listen to that inside voice. I was listening to the voice in the bottle sometimes. Phoebe would bitch that I was drinking and I'd just drink more. And Phoebe? She's one of those people who's always hungry, if you know what I mean."

Cal frowned. "Hungry?"

He shook his head. "She couldn't be satisfied. I believe she tried, but she couldn't. I didn't understand until she left and took Maggie with her. Then I understood what that felt like. It's a miserable feeling, wanting something you can't have." He put a hand on Cal's shoulder. "You go on, Cal. It's a nice evening. Cool but clear. There could be rain ahead so enjoy it now while you can."

"If you need any help, you know where to find me."

Cal watched Sully put the closed sign on the door and went to his camper. He had the impression that Sully had just confided more in him than he had in his daughter, whose absence a long time ago had filled him with an aching hunger. He believed Sully might never have told Maggie she was the greatest thing he'd ever done. It wasn't a facial expression or inflection in his voice. *It's the way we don't tell the most important people in our lives the most important things.* It was how men tended to be.

He made his fire by the lake in a brick fire pit that had been there a long time. He couldn't be more obvious if he'd made his fire in front of the porch, yet she didn't come.

I should've kissed her, he thought. For the past several nights she'd found him after dark and they'd talked by the fire. Sometimes they had a beer together, sometimes just the dark and conversation. She had no idea what she was revealing. Her admiration for Sully, her concern, her annoyance with all things as though she felt completely out of place. But he hadn't suspected a broken heart.

I should've kissed her before he came back and made her realize she'd felt so lonely.

He loved the anger that made her skin mottle. He was guessing, but he bet anger made her cry as often as sadness. He wished Lynne had had more fight in her. Maybe she had at first but it was soon reduced to helplessness. He loved Maggie's sturdiness. He laughed as he thought that—what woman wanted to be admired for something like that?

It crossed his mind that a smart man would move on before things got complicated but it was already too late for that. The minute she had confided she was being sued, he'd submitted an application to the Colorado bar for license to practice here. Colorado had reciprocity with Michigan; he wouldn't have to take the bar in this state to be licensed, but he did have to apply. Which he had done without saying anything to anyone. He gave one reference in Colorado. Sully. They might not even ask him.

A part of him thought it might bring Maggie peace of mind to learn he wasn't just a homeless bum but a professional legal mind. Yet he hadn't shared. Not yet. He wasn't quite ready to tell everything. Some of it was still too private.

He sat by his fire, thinking. He gave her some time to find him. He didn't feed the fire; he let it burn out. Then he went prowling, looking for her. If he had to, he'd knock on the door and call her out. Their routine had made him happy. He didn't know if he was finally working through his issues or if it was something about the crossing—the spot where the Continental Divide separated the east from the west, where everything felt balanced. It was probably just that he'd been looking for a deeper understanding, for self-discovery, for a couple of years now and he was finally stumbling upon it. Pure accident.

She was sitting on her back porch steps in the dark. No fire. Her view? The garden, which was all dirt so far.

"There you are," he said. "Hiding."

"It's not a good night, Calvin," she said.

"All right, I get that. I was waiting down by the lake. You shouldn't do that, you know—bring me a beer at night, cozy up and talk in the dark and then shut down. I won't know how to act tomorrow."

"Don't act," she advised. "Just try to be normal. Just be a guy. You didn't see anything, you didn't hear anything. Just be a regular blissfully ignorant man."

"I'm not that guy."

"Famous last words," she said.

"He hurt you," Cal said. "I thought you might want to talk about it."

"Are you some kind of counselor? What's with all this understanding and sensitivity? Because the men I know are not like you. They don't care about how a woman feels. They're *scared* of women's feelings. And they won't admit to having feelings of their own, but boy, do they work at protecting them. Defending them."

"Well, damn, I'm honored. You think I'm not like the men you know?" He sat on the step beside her. "Were you in love with him?"

She shrugged. "Probably not."

"You're pouting a lot for nothing, then."

"He just hurt my feelings, that's all. Maybe he was right."

"I doubt it. If he was right, Sully would like him. He doesn't like him."

"He never told me that," Maggie said.

"Because he's just a guy," Cal said with a laugh. He put an arm around her shoulders. "I should've kissed you last night or the night before. I should've done that before some useless old ex showed up and made you feel like you were missing something."

She laughed in spite of herself. "You arrogant fool. What makes you think you kiss that good?"

He turned her toward him. He grabbed her so suddenly her arms were flapping like a bird's wings. He covered her gasp with his lips, tightened his arms around her waist, held her close and moved over her lips with urgency, giving it his very best effort. The fit was perfect and he thought this might be one of his most outstanding kisses. He kept his eyes closed but he knew if he peeked hers would be wide-open. He tilted his mouth over hers to kiss her more deeply, edging his lips apart just enough to run his tongue along the seam of her lips, urging her to open up to him a little bit.

Her arms finally wrapped around him. That was what he was hoping for. Then her lips opened a little bit. She took a small, experimental taste and then with a sigh, he felt her sink into his kiss. He concentrated on just that, making it a wonderful kiss for as long as he could. She was molded to him and it felt just right. When he thought he'd given her a minute of brain-numbing kissing, he slowly pulled his lips away. But he didn't let go.

Her eyes were closed now, that's for sure. Her head tilted back, her chin lifted slightly and she let out her breath. Without opening her eyes she said, "Meh. It wasn't that great."

"It was fantastic and you know it," he said. Then he nibbled at her bottom lip a little bit. "If it wasn't perfect, I'm willing to keep trying."

"Okay," she said in a breath, leaning toward him.

Cal was happy to comply, especially if it helped her mood, as it was definitely helping his. It wasn't typical of him to do much thinking while he was kissing or making love, but in this case he did a little of that. He was reminding himself that this was perfectly normal. Reasonable. He'd been around the crossing for weeks now. He'd gotten a little attached to it. He liked helping with the store, liked the locals who stopped by, the lake was lovely. Then Sully and Maggie came home and the place took on a new dimension. He was busy and starting to feel needed. He'd always liked feeling useful. The surrounding towns were friendly and quirky, there was no more beautiful landscape in the country, and Cal had seen a lot of the country.

And then there was Maggie. Yes, he had gotten to know quite a few doctors but he'd never kissed one before. Never one in khaki shorts and lace-up hiking boots.

He gently pulled away from her lips. "Am I getting any better?" he asked.

"Pretty average, so far," she said.

"Let's rest a minute, then I'll go at it again. Let's have something to drink. I have some brandy in my camper."

"Brandy?" she said. "*Bllkk.* That's for eggnog."

"We can break into the store," he suggested.

She patted her pocket to feel for a key and smiled. "Let's."

He wouldn't let her get too far away from him. He put his arm around her waist and strolled with her from her back porch to the store's back porch. She unlocked the back door. "Don't turn on any lights or people will see and come wanting something."

"Where's Sully?"

"He's on his way to bed. He just doesn't have that much stamina. Truth is, he wasn't up past nine very often when he was a hundred percent because he gets up so early. Don't trip over anything," she said as they entered the store. The only light was from the front porch. They didn't mind if people gathered there and used the tables after the store was closed but it being a cold early April night in the mountains, folks preferred their campfires and the porch was empty.

She got behind the bar and he sat on a stool in front. "What's your pleasure?"

"Chivas. Neat."

She tipped the bottle over two glasses and put it on the bar.

"Now, come around here," he said. "I don't want that bar between us. I want us together. Here."

There was no argument from her. She sat on a bar stool, facing him. She was ready to be kissed some more. He pulled her knees inside his spread legs, bringing her a little closer.

"Has Sully ever talked to you about your mother? About when they separated and divorced?"

"Some. We don't dwell on that too much. It was a hard time all around. Why?"

"He mentioned one or two things. It's come to my attention the last few years, sometimes men don't say things they should to the people that matter to them. In trying to be strong and protective, they neglect to mention important things to the people they love. He said you were by far the luckiest thing he's ever done with his life."

She smiled. "I guess I knew he felt that way, but he never said it. I didn't see my dad for about five years and I was hateful during that time. Once we were seeing each other again I constantly asked him why he let that happen. Why didn't he fight? He just said he thought of himself as a lousy father, that I'd be better off with Walter."

"Did he ever mention war issues, like maybe some PTSD?"

"Huh?"

"He said Vietnam had him pretty messed up. Of course you knew he went to Vietnam, right?"

She nodded and sipped her drink. "I didn't know

there were any issues. Why do you think he told you these things?"

"It seemed spontaneous. It was as if you were on his mind, having just had your little reunion with… What's the boyfriend's name?"

"Ex. It's Andrew."

"I think that's why he talked about some personal things. He also said your mother is a pain in the ass."

She laughed at that. "You won't be surprised to learn I've heard that from him before. At least ten thousand times. And it's pretty accurate. Phoebe is very high-maintenance. But the universe will catch up with her. Walter is older than Phoebe. He was a wealthy neurosurgeon, and he took very good care of my mother and me. He's in excellent shape, energetic and healthy and on the golf course whenever he can, but he's seventy, like Sully. Phoebe is only fifty-nine, not a bad age for a woman in good health. She's always had to be indulged and taken care of and Walter certainly stepped up to the plate. But she could end up the caretaker."

"Or she could put him in a nursing home and walk away from it all," Cal said.

"Walter turned out to be a good guy. If you haven't guessed, Phoebe has been twice a trophy wife, though I'm sure Sully didn't realize it. To Sully I think she was just a pretty little thing. I'm sure he never thought she'd be a lot of work. I think she loves Walter. And I know Walter loves her."

"You know, sometimes age has hardly anything to do with it. Phoebe's health could fail before his. You just never know," Cal said, taking a drink. "So, now that Sully is so much better, what are you going to do?" he asked her. "It's been weeks, can you even remember why you came home in the first place?"

"Oh, Cal, not you, too. Lecturing me to go back to the grind?"

"Did I say that? I asked what you're doing here."

"There was a pileup," she said. "Not only was it getting bigger than I was, I ran out of ways to practice. I ran out of ways to cope. And then Andrew..." She looked away.

"What?" he said.

"He said he couldn't take it anymore—my plethora of problems. He said I was sucking the life out of him. He broke it off, not me. And the funny thing about that is, we didn't even live in the same town. We texted, talked, emailed, saw each when we could—every couple of days or weeks. I was having too many problems for anyone, but I looked back through the texts and emails—they weren't all my problems. There were friendly, chatty little things, affectionate comments, questions about him and his ER and his daughter. In fact, there's more bitching about his alimony and custody issues than what I'd been dealing with. I realized I wasn't supposed to have *any* problems. I was supposed to be his mommy and lover and cheerleader. I'd fallen down on the job by getting needy. He wanted me to get professional help so I could get back to work. Not work as a surgeon, work as his support system." She took a deep breath. "It was my best friend, who is also my doctor, who said, 'Get out of town for a week or two! Get some rest.' There was no reason not to. I was grateful for the push."

"How the hell did he think he was going to get that kind of attention and nurturing from a neurosurgeon?

Aren't you a little too overwhelmed on an average day to take on a little boy and all his little needs?"

She was silent for a moment. "Oh, I do like you, Callum. Where are you from?"

"I'm from everywhere. If he wasn't doing anything for you..."

"Why was I with him? After he dumped me, I asked myself that question. It was comfortable in many ways. I had someone to talk to, play with, sit next to during a bad movie. Someone to go to a restaurant with, someone to make love to. But then he left me and basically said it was my fault."

Cal grinned. "You won't have any trouble filling the position. Maybe around here it'll be iffy. But when you go back to Denver..."

"Since I've been here, since Sully has been doing better, I'm starting to feel almost normal. I'm going to milk this for a little while. Since I don't have a job."

"Were you bored with surgery?"

"You don't get bored with the kind of surgery I do. There's no margin for boredom. The pressure is too intense and the odds against success, despite our progress, are still too high. Never bored. I think I might've been addicted to the rush—it's damned exciting. I might be making a change, however. I'll think about that for a while. I like it here. It's pretty uncomplicated," she said, leaning toward him for a kiss.

She tasted of Chivas and playfulness and he lapped it up. He was starting to have thoughts of going further.

"And what about you, Calico? You have no job, you've been here for weeks, you don't have a woman, you don't seem to be doing anything..."

"Shame on you, I dug your whole damn garden. I

stock your shelves every day, fish off the dock, hike around the crossing and build a fire for you at night. Then I let you talk. I've been very busy."

"What brought you here?"

"I was looking at the CDT trail map and from New Mexico to Salida across the Rockies it's frozen. I hate being cold. I'm just waiting for some of that snowpack to melt and then I want to do some serious hiking. I decided when I left Walt's World to take six months to wander, then I'll settle somewhere and get back to work. I'm just doing what you're doing. I'm just taking a break. Thinking."

"Did you graduate from high school?"

"Yes," he said, laughing.

"Did you go to college at all?"

"Yes," he said, trying to look serious. "I studied literature. I'm a romantic."

"And then went on to get a counseling degree…" she offered.

"I'm afraid not. You shouldn't ever take my advice or tell me your dreams unless they're harmless."

"Did you want to teach?" she asked.

"I did teach for a while. A short, memorable time— six months in what was called a men's academy, the oldest 'man' being seventeen. I think I'm probably better with girls. I really liked that HR job…" He put his hands on her hips and leaned toward her.

"Because it got you laid."

"I saw that as a perk, not part of the job."

"I'd really love to see that princess someday…"

He decided it was time to talk less and kiss more. She was every bit as excellent as he was. She was getting closer and closer, her hands caressing his shoulders, neck and head. He loved female fingers in his hair. She was breathing hard and so was he.

"I have a roomy tent," he said against her lips.

"That probably wouldn't be smart of me," she said.

"You worried about Sully?"

"I'm worried about *me*," she said emphatically. "You're probably riddled with theme-park diseases."

He laughed. "Making serious love to you will be hard if you keep making jokes. I'm not riddled with anything. Except, you know, things like lust."

"How long has this been on your mind?" she asked.

"Specifically?" he asked.

"Just when did it first come to you?"

"I think it was…when you asked me if I was homeless," he said. "There was a dominatrix quality about it." Then he smiled against her lips.

"I'm not spanking you, no matter how you beg."

"Awww…"

"Why do you want to? Besides the fact that you're a man?"

"You're so pretty, Maggie," he said tenderly. He tucked her hair behind her ear. "You have such a hot body, too. And you take such good care of your dad. Okay, that last has nothing to do with sex, it just makes you so much more desirable, that you're a caring person. Mostly? You're pretty and clever. I'm such a sucker for looks and brains. Gives me such a hard-on."

She sighed. "All right, Calypso. But if you leave me in the morning, I might hunt you down. And punish you."

He put his hands on either side of her face, on her cheeks. "Listen to me, Maggie. I'm going to explore this summer. But I won't leave you without saying goodbye.

Because that would be awful and if you did that to me I would be disappointed. We'll make love, we'll laugh, we'll play and when the weather is warm enough so I'm not caught in some damn avalanche, I'm going up the trail to the divide. I've been dying for two things. You and that trail. You most."

"You promise?"

"Yes. Even though I have a bad track record with promises."

"You break them?" she asked.

"They usually break me," he said. "Let's sneak out the back door."

Maggie held his hand and they walked to his little pop-up trailer. It was a tent, really, but it opened up out of a small, flat trailer that he pulled behind his truck. The base was metal, the top was canvas. It was spacious for a tent; she could almost stand up inside. It was not furnished with a king-size bed, however. There were two single but large cots, one on each side with space in the center. "Hopefully we won't take up too much room," she said.

"We'll have all the room we need," he said. He pulled her down beside him and after their shoes were off, they disrobed each other while they kissed. She was in a hurry and he was slowing her down. "Don't rush this, Maggie," he whispered, kissing her neck and chest. "Let's enjoy it."

"People can't see our silhouettes through this tent, can they?" she asked. "They can't hear us, can they?"

"You grew up in a campground and you don't know? If you're really loud, someone might get Sully out of bed and tell him someone's killing a cat…"

She moaned and lay back on his cot. He pulled off the last of her clothes, her shorts and panties. Life was good, she thought. She'd shaved her legs without the faintest idea there might be sex in her life again. It was a miracle.

She'd been attracted to him since first meeting him, but that didn't translate into making love for her. She just thought he was very good-looking for a bum. But it was really talking to him that did it to her. He was the clever one. She should have known he was learned in literature; he was so well-spoken.

Her Achilles' heel was being told she was pretty. Not just pretty, *so* pretty. Maggie wasn't used to that. People didn't say that to her. They said things like, *Of course you're pretty, Maggie*, and *You're a very attractive woman*. She was ordinary. Not homely, certainly not ugly. But there was nothing special about her looks—brown hair, brown eyes, five-nine, straight teeth. She was always picked first in sports for teams but if there was a school play, she got the part of the aunt or sister while those achingly beautiful girls played Blanche or Cinderella. Those girls who would grow up to work as princesses.

His hands on her were so delicious; his mouth was heaven. He was determined to take his time, stroking and caressing slowly. She moaned and squirmed beneath him, the craving building, but he just hummed as he kissed, sucked, licked, nibbled, caressed. Somehow, he knew exactly how to touch her, how to titillate with his lips and tongue. He brought her nipples to life with those excellent lips. Then he kissed his way down over her belly and between her legs, his miraculous tongue torturing her for a little while as she gritted her teeth to stay quiet, gripping his shoulders. Then he kissed his way back up to her mouth.

"I think I could do this for a living," he said. "You really turn me on."

"I'm ready for you to get going here," she said.

He laughed. "Are you now? You sure you want it bad enough?"

"I'm sure," she said, running her hands down his smooth back, over his muscled butt. "I think you have a better butt than I do," she said.

"Not possible. Your butt knocks me out." He reached down and fumbled around under the cot. She heard him rummaging and he came up with a condom.

"That was convenient," she whispered.

"My shaving kit," he said. He knelt between her legs and looked down at her. "Maggie," he said in a breath. "Look at you. So lovely. Ready for love." He ran one finger from the hollow at the base of her throat down her body, over her breastbone, over her navel, over her pubis. He gave her clitoris a brief tease, then lowered himself into her. "Whoa," he said in appreciation. "God, that's good."

"Good," she agreed softly.

With his mouth on hers, his hands on her hips, he slowly rocked with her, gradually setting a pace that grew deeper and deeper, harder and faster. She pushed back against him, embracing him and kissing him wildly, little whimpers of hunger escaping her until before long she froze, lifting off the cot, lifting him in her sudden strength, and she clenched as she came with heat and power. While her insides gripped and quivered he emitted a deep groan and she felt him throbbing inside her. As she was coming down from the experience, he began to move, ramping her up again, making her come again. He was limited to the one, however—so sad for the man, she abstractly thought as she indulged a second orgasm, almost as good as the first.

Then she collapsed beneath him, weak and satisfied. "Oh, Calder," she finally said. "That was amazing."

He chuckled and ran a knuckle over her cheek, giving her bruised lips little pecks.

"Did we rock the tent?" she asked.

"Who cares? I don't care. I'd be happy to rock this camper all night, entertain the neighbors."

"Unfortunately, I can't stay all night. The bed is too small, for one thing."

"You can stay a little while, till I get a second wind. I'm not like some people, on a hair trigger and able to throw out an orgasm a minute. That's a very neat trick, by the way. I bet I enjoyed that as much as you did."

"Highly doubtful," she said. She rubbed her hands over his shoulders. "You're very good at that, like a man with tons of practice. Lucky for you I have to stay right here until my bones grow back."

"We came together like old pros," he pointed out. "Like lovers with a routine. I love that. It's kind of kismet, don't you think?"

"I don't know what to think," she muttered. She ran her hands over his chest. "You're so smooth. I never saw this coming..."

"You didn't?" he asked. "The second I saw you I knew we'd end up like this. Waiting for you was hard." He moved a little inside her. "It's hard again..."

"You don't have to wait now, Caleb," she said.

Every man has a property in his own person.

This nobody has a right to but himself.

—JOHN LOCKE

CHAPTER 6

Maggie had no idea how long Sully had been up when she finally rolled out of bed at seven thirty....on about four hours of sleep. She stumbled to the bathroom and purposely didn't look in the mirror, a little afraid she'd see Cal's brand on her. She started the shower and got in while it was still cold.

Holy mother of pearl, what a night that was. He was an amazing lover. But also, he was such a sweet, smart, funny man. Of course he had to be some strange duck who was taking six months off to do odd jobs and camp. He couldn't be some ordinary, stable, reliable person, like a truck driver or forest ranger. But then, what type of man did she think she could have a comfortable fit with? Sergei, the Ukrainian artist, had been a disaster. Andrew, the doctor, should've worked—they had so many things in common—and it had been a worse disaster.

Even running her own hands over her body as she sudsed up in the shower brought delicious tinglings from the night before, little shudders of aftershocks.

When she was out of the shower she braved it, looked in the mirror. Her cheeks were either flushed or chafed from Cal's beard. Her lips were rosy from hours of kissing, sometimes so wildly she could hardly catch her breath. She lost control more times than she could count and she was pretty sure she bit him once. His fault, really. He could drive her so far into ecstasy she lost her bearings and became nothing more than a writhing body responding to a powerful force and lost all sense. She wondered if she just rocked and wailed in that little pop-up all the damn night. For all she knew the other campers brought their folding chairs over to Cal's site and created an audience. At least it had been Sunday night, the weekend warriors gone, the population down.

She put lotion on her face and some lip gloss, blew out her hair and got dressed. She was going to have to think of what to say to Sully. She'd never faced that before—worry over explaining to her father. She'd had a fling or six at the crossing, and there was Andrew—she'd never explained him. She had just said they were seeing each other and they'd be staying in one of the cabins. Something about this was different. It was probably because he'd had a heart attack, she thought. Or it could be because she hardly knew Calvert, the handsome, good-natured bum and princess molester. Better go easy on Sully.

Funny, this had never been an issue. Until she was out of pre-med, aged twenty-two, she'd been very careful with her behavior around Sully. He was so proud of her, she hadn't wanted to disappoint him. Then that summer before med school, self-designated as an independent adult, she had a little summer romance at the crossing. He was a biology teacher on summer break, living in his RV for several weeks, studying the flora in the Rockies, and she flirted with him. He flirted with her. They were drawn by common interests and lust and she stayed out all night a few times, cozy in his RV.

Sully had said nothing. Nothing at all. It was as if they'd come to the mutual understanding that it was time for her to lead her own adult life, take responsibility for her actions without his guidance or interference. Silent acceptance.

She found him on the porch with Frank, having coffee and a not very heart-healthy pastry. But she'd been out most of the night and had therefore relinquished the right to comment on his diet choice.

She got a cup of coffee and sat down. "How'd you sleep, Sully?"

"Slept like a rock. Didn't even hear you come in at three thirty."

"That was subtle," she said. Like she really needed Frank in on this.

"Mail run yesterday brought in four packages," Sully said. "They're for thru-hikers, so it's starting. Cal's in the storeroom moving things around and getting ready for some restocking, making room for the packages that are going to start coming in now—hikers on the trail are moving this way now that the snowpack is melting."

"Oh." She sipped her coffee.

"I'd be in there working, but I'm taking it one step at a time. Some of those boxes weigh forty pounds."

"I'm glad you're not doing that."

"You know more about the post office end of things than Cal. Can you go check and see if he's making sense of the storeroom? Looked like he was doing okay, but..."

"When did he get here?"

"Around six thirty, I think."

Show-off, she thought. "You give him a raise or something?" she asked.

"Funny. Jackson is starting this afternoon. I'm going to use him Saturday, Monday, Tuesday and then his sister Nikki Friday, Sunday and Thursday. No extra help on Wednesdays. Sounds decent, doesn't it?"

"Doesn't Tom usually show up on Wednesdays?"

"For cleanup around the grounds," Sully said. "That's going to get more important as spring ripens. Few more weeks and I'll be doing it mostly on my own."

She wasn't so sure he'd ever be as active as he once was. It wasn't just the surgery, it was the surgery plus being seventy. "I'll go check on Cal," she said, taking her coffee with her to the storeroom.

When hikers planned to take on one of the long trails like the Colorado or Continental Divide Trail, meticulous planning was required. They couldn't carry a lot of water with them—water is heavy. They had to know precisely where they could get fresh water along the trail. And they had to try to plan strategic stopping points. They could camp along the trail for four to as many as ten nights if there was plentiful water along the way, but they couldn't carry enough nourishment or changes of clothing for longer than that. They would plot their trek by towns and campgrounds like the crossing. At the crossing they could get showers, wash clothes, pick up parcels they'd mailed ahead as well as packages sent to them by friends or family. They'd meet with other hikers, share news, drink a few beers, grill some burgers and load up on protein. They'd charge their phones, check their email. They exchanged more than news—sometimes they'd trade off equipment or supplies to both lighten their load and pick up items they needed. They often exchanged books—Sully had a shelf set aside for that. Long-distance hikers didn't carry more than one book at a time. They'd also do some shopping for anything they'd used up, lost or forgotten—batteries, first-aid items, lighters for campfires, protein snacks, water-purification kits.

She walked into the storeroom where Cal was stacking boxes containing food and supply items on one side of the room and leaving some shelves empty to give their postal items more space.

"Sully said you were here at six thirty this morning," she said.

He turned toward her with a very large smile. His eyes were a little sleepy. Sexy and satisfied. He took her coffee cup out of her hand, placed it on the shelf and pulled her closer. "And I think your complexion has cleared up," she added.

He kissed her. Long and lovingly. Yes, this guy was a little gift. She would try not to fantasize spending every night of her life getting trimmed up like she had last night.

"I have to rent a cabin," he said when he released her.

"Oh? And why is that? I thought you liked the tent."

"I think we weakened the struts that hold up the sides last night. And I want to stretch out a little bit."

"How soon will you be checking in, sir?"

"By this afternoon," he said. "They have a bathroom, shower, etc., right?"

"They do. But we're coming into our busy season, so I don't think a free cabin is in your future, even though I have a feeling I'd somehow benefit."

His lips quirked in a superior smile. "I'm capable of paying my way. Didn't I explain that?"

"I wasn't sure whether to believe you," she explained.

He cocked his head. "I don't think you got enough sleep. You could thank me for melting your bones last night but never mind, let me play the gentleman. I'll thank you. I see your talent extends far beyond the operating room. You are a riot in bed. Thank you. I've never felt better." He laughed. "God, you're blushing."

"I think it's whisker burn," she said.

"Even better," he said, laughing. "Now, can you get me a cabin or do I have to go through the boss?"

"Oh, please don't," she begged. "Bad enough that he heard me stumble to my room at three thirty."

"I need some time off after I finish in the storeroom and stocking shelves. I have a few errands. But since I'm going to town, want me to cook for you and Sully tonight? I'd like to."

"That would be very neighborly. Would you like to borrow a kitchen?"

"Nah, I'll make do. But tell me about these hikers?"

"On their way, it seems. When the parcels start coming we know they're marching up the divide. They don't like to hit the Colorado border before the first of May but they start sending stuff before they begin."

"Are there big groups of them?"

She shook her head. "Very rarely. There might be a couple or few together, but mostly individuals. Sometimes they meet along the way and begin to watch for each other."

"How many?" he asked.

"How many hikers? Hundreds, but they're not all long-distance hikers. The number that will spend six months on the CDT are relatively few, but they all plot their own course. They might hike for a few days or a few weeks or maybe just through Colorado. Some get on the CDT on the Mexican border and head north, some hit the trail as far away as Banff to head south and there's every possibility in between. All through summer you'll see them. They get off the trail at different points—we have about five foot-and cattle paths and a north-south road all converging here. They usually get off the trail just five miles north or south and march up the road. Every once in a while some crazy fool comes down that footpath behind the house from the Hallelujah Trail straight down from the Rockies."

"Hallelujah?" he asked.

"It's a demanding trip around and down the peaks. It used to be called Dead Man's Trail but that was bad for business." Then she smiled. "Rock climbers love that area."

"I bet people get in trouble out there," he said.

"For the most part it's inexperienced people, people who haven't prepared, who run into trouble. But there's always the random accident or illness. It's very isolated. Sometimes they sit for a long time until another hiker can get word to first responders—rangers or fire and rescue. Occasionally, someone gets lost and search and rescue goes out. There's a lot of federal land out here, fire stations, forest service, public land that's remote. Then there's wildfires, avalanches, floods. And the odd wildlife issues."

"I'm going to have to get out there pretty soon," he said. "As soon as I'm sure I'll be warm."

"You've said that all along," she said. "I'm going to hate that day. For obvious reasons."

He grinned his wicked grin. "That's very flattering,

Maggie. That day is not coming too soon. Also for obvious reasons," he added.

"It would be kind of you to at least let me get tired of you."

"But, Maggie. What if you never do?"

She just sighed. The one thing you always secretly hope for can become your biggest fear.

"Any special requests for dinner?" he asked.

She shook her head. "Something very lean, please. Sully's eating a pastry."

Maggie's cell phone, left at the house, was beeping with a message. Her primary attorney, Steve Rubin, asked that she call him.

Her heart beat a little faster as she prayed. *Please let it be news that the lawsuit is dropped!*

"How are you doing, Maggie? How's your dad?"

"He's good, Steve. What's up?"

"Well, it looks like we're going to trial. It should be in about a month. Maybe two."

"Crap," she said. "Crap, crap, crap!"

"I don't see this as terrible news. In fact, it will look better for you if you win this one rather than settling. I know it's a little traumatic but our case is looking strong. Are you still at your dad's?"

"I am. I think he could manage without me now if you think it would appear better if I went back to work…"

"Maggie, it makes no difference. The closing of your practice has no bearing on this case. And if your father is recovering from a heart attack and you're the only relative, you have a perfectly good reason to be on leave. Unless you're bored out of your wits or he's driving you nuts… If you're comfortable there, relax and try to enjoy the time off. However, you have to feel good about yourself and if working helps that, by all means, go back to work. I don't consider it risky and neither do the many colleagues who have asked you to fill in for them."

"They haven't been emailing or calling, begging me to come back…"

"I know the kind of blow this is to your confidence, but I'm sure your colleagues are leaving you alone to rest and tend to family matters. With any luck we'll have this behind us at about the same time you feel comfortable leaving your dad. Just do what keeps you sane for right now."

"I'm not entirely sure I know what that is," she said. But she was thinking she could stand a couple more weeks near Cal.

"One day at a time, Maggie," he said. "I'm going to need some of your time as we get ready for a trial. I'll need pretrial conferences, I'm sure the plaintiffs will want to depose you, and I'll want to prep you before the trial begins. Call me in a few days and let me know if there are any changes in your work status."

"Sure," she said. "Listen, it's not like this brought me to my knees, Steve. It's a combination of things, really. Mostly my dad, but—"

"Maggie, go a little easier on yourself. This kind of thing brings everyone to their knees, even those big badass surgeons who didn't have a single additional stressor in their lives. Believe me, I know. I've worked with a great many of them."

She sighed. "My dad says I have high expectations

of myself," she said, when in fact it was she who carried those expectations.

"Yes, I know. Uncomfortable, I know. And that's exactly what it takes to make a good surgeon. We'll talk soon."

She sat at her dad's kitchen table for a half hour. When she went back to the store, she didn't mention the call to anyone.

Cal settled into his cabin, the farthest one from the house, and Maggie was with him after their usual fire, then sneaked into her own bed in the middle of the night. The next night she got to bed a little earlier, but one of these days soon she was going to steal a whole night with Cal and not even blush about it.

Cal's truck and compact pop-up trailer sat behind the cabin he "rented" for which Sully would not take money. Since the days were a bit longer, the store was staying open a little later. Come summer, their hours would be sunup to sundown.

On Wednesday, Tom Canaday came to the grounds early to help with cleanup, grounds keeping, grass and shrub trimming and trash hauling. Cal spent most of the day helping with that while Maggie put in her time at the store, restocking and cleaning. Sully was back and forth between the store and the grounds, giving advice, trying his damnedest not to tote and lift, getting grumpier by the hour. With warmer weather, the crossing was expecting a surge starting the next day, Thursday afternoon, and extending for ten days. They were getting ready. Even Frank was smart enough to be scarce on Wednesdays, knowing he could be put to work.

Yard work done, Enid gone home to her husband and

Tom to his kids, Cal grilled fish fillets and an aluminum foil packet full of green veggies and the three of them ate at a table on the porch so they could mind the store if any of the few campers who were still around needed something. When dinner was finished Cal went off to his cabin to shower while Sully headed for the house with Beau to catch a little of the news on TV.

Maggie stayed at the store until closing, which she'd do as soon as cleanup was complete. The sun was beginning to set, casting long shadows across the lake, when Maggie was on the front porch wiping off the tables. An old, mud-splattered, rusty black pickup was parked down the road near the lake. It looked like three people sat in the cab. She leaned on her rag on the table and peered in its direction—two men flanking a small blonde woman. Not campers. Not locals—she hadn't seen the truck before. Two big men and a small woman made shivers go up her spine.

The truck began to slowly inch toward the store and when it neared she saw the two men were scruffy-looking strangers to her but between them, wearing a frightened expression, sat Chelsea Smyth. *Where was her family?* Had they sent her to get help for some reason? The driver parked at the side of the store and Maggie tried to concentrate on her wiping up. She wouldn't give away her concern in case something was wrong. *Wrong. Wrong. Wrong.*

The men talked for a moment and then the passenger got out of the truck. All she knew for sure was that the men looked creepy and Chelsea looked scared.

The man who approached the front porch was dirty and unkempt, not a strange look around a campground. Locally there were fishermen, hunters, ranchers—also frequently messy and disheveled. His pants were baggy and dirty, his boots had seen better days and his beard was scraggly, but it was the look in his dark eyes and the rather large hunting knife holstered in leather at his belt that cautioned her. So she smiled.

"How you doin'?" she asked with a friendly smile. *How long is Cal's damn shower going to take?*

"Yeah, you got beer?"

She nodded. "Draft or six-pack?" She glanced at the truck out of the corner of her eye and the fact that Chelsea hadn't moved over near the passenger door once the first man got out told Maggie all she needed to know.

"Six'll do."

"Right in the cooler," she said, standing back so he could enter the store.

He was waiting right inside the door. He looked at her over his shoulder.

"Over there," she said, pointing.

He smelled, but not of ranching or fishing. He smelled of body odor, greasy food, gasoline and smoke, not wood smoke but probably tobacco smoke. And the way he looked at her, it was the most threatened she'd felt in a long time. They'd had a patient go postal in the ER once and that had scared her enough to pee her pants but security got him under control quickly.

There was no security team here.

She went behind the counter by the cash register, wondering if he was going to rob her and cut her up into little pieces. The broom was within her reach if he got too close or pulled out that knife. But he put the six-pack on the counter and took out a wallet he kept on a chain. Then he looked over at the bar. "Get me one a them bottles," he commanded. "Whiskey."

"We don't sell…" She stopped herself. What was she thinking? "We don't usually sell by the bottle, but you're probably my last customer for the day. I'm closing up in ten." She went across the aisle to grab a bottle of Jack Daniel's from under the bar and took it back to the cash register. She had a thought. It might be a stupid thought but Maggie usually assessed and made decisions quickly and it was the only thought she had. She knew he was wrong and she didn't want him wandering back into the vast wilderness and doing harm to Chelsea. She began ringing up the purchase. "You passing through?"

"More or less," he said.

"I got two empty cabins if you want it to be less," she said. "Fact is, middle of the week hardly anyone's around so we lower the price if it's one night. Twelve dollars. I can't do that for more than one night. Can't do that on weekends, you know—we stay full on weekends. In good weather."

Stop chattering, she told herself. Her knees felt liquid. If Cal would just walk through the back door, maybe she'd come up with a better idea.

"You can park around the back of the cabin, if you want it."

He looked at her suspiciously. It looked like he was onto her. He turned from the counter as if to leave but instead he brought back an armload of snack food—chips, pretzels, jerky, nuts. He piled it all on the counter. "Add it up. Gimme the key on that cabin."

She rang everything up, gave him the total and he handed her a credit card. The credit card belonged to Gilbert Anthony Smyth. *Wrong, wrong, wrong!* She ran it and it showed *approved* on the machine. She turned and grabbed the key, slapped it on the counter and said, "You don't need a receipt, do you?"

"Why?"

"Most people don't," she said with a shrug. "You can't deduct supplies unless you're on business."

He sneered at her. *Like he was on business?*

She bagged up his things and he left the store.

Maggie sank behind the counter, her knees useless. She heard the truck start and motor slowly around the store along the drive that led to the cabins.

No one had reported Mr. Smyth's card stolen or the machine wouldn't have approved it. That was a good sign, wasn't it? Or maybe the card was taken off his body? Or were they tracking it? Oh God, how long had that child been with those two?

Shaking, she reached for the phone to call 911. She identified herself to the dispatcher and tried to calmly explain. "Two creeps in their thirties just checked into one of my cabins with a fourteen-year-old girl I know was here with her family last week—they were camping here. Her name is Chelsea Smyth and I believe she may have been abducted."

"Was the girl in distress, ma'am?" the dispatcher asked.

"She looked terrified! Never mind, I'll call Stan!" She disconnected and dialed Stan's cell phone.

"Yel-low," he said thickly, like his mouth was full of dinner.

"Stan! Stan! There's a kidnapped juvenile and two creeps have her and I gave them a cabin! Need help fast!"

He coughed and spit. "Jesus, Maggie! The Smyth girl?"

"Yes! Yes! I just called 911 and the dispatcher asked

me if the girl was in distress! You know about this? Where is her family?"

"The family reported her missing. The bulletin went out a few hours ago—earlier today. They're searching for her. She walked away from the group to answer nature and didn't come back."

"She's here. I recognized her. She's with two creepy guys in a dirty, old, muddy truck. Where'd she go missing?"

"Northwest of Leadville, in the mountains. They aren't looking this far south. They thought she was lost but started exploring abduction just lately," he said.

"One of the men used her father's credit card—Gilbert Smyth. Please, hurry before they hurt that girl, if they haven't already."

She heard the sound of Stan's movement, running, car door opening, huffing and puffing, like he was either at home for dinner or at a diner in town. "Where are you?" he shouted to Maggie.

"I'm in the store. I'm alone. Dad's in the house, hardly any campers. I've got this shotgun..."

"Maggie, no!" he shouted. "Don't you do *anything*! You lock yourself in the store and wait for me!" Then she heard the car door slam, engine start and Stan flipped on his siren to be en route fast. She listened while he radioed a variety of case numbers and emergency calls to everyone and their brother. She heard him call out *in progress* and *Sullivan's Crossing*. "Maggie," he said, a little breathlessly. "They armed?"

"Gun in the rack and big hunting knife strapped on a belt. And Stan—they're big! She's just a little girl."

"Stay in the store. We're on the way."

Then he tossed his phone, probably onto the seat

next to him. She could hear him on the radio in the background so he hadn't disconnected. She overheard key words like *SWAT, abduction, negotiation team, air support, dogs, armed and dangerous.* She went to the storeroom for the shotgun. She loaded it. It held four rounds of small pellets and she knew how to use it. It was loud, scary and depending on where it was aimed, potentially deadly. But more to the point, it was probably *not* deadly. *Probably* being the operative word...

Where was Cal? Should she go find him?

Maggie, Maggie, her mind asked. *When was the last time you had to have a man to help you make a decision?*

Well, hell, Cal didn't seem to be in possession of a gun and who knew if he'd ever fired one. He was a theme park employee!

She grabbed a roll of duct tape out of the store. Maggie loved duct tape—it cured almost everything shy of an aneurysm. She'd even seen a maintenance guy slapping it along the leading edge of the wing of a 757 once! But, if she had the chance, she was going to tape up the hands and feet of two bad guys. She stuffed it in her pocket and went out the back door.

She had several concerns, all of which had her marching with a shotgun toward the closest cabin. *Sully.* She couldn't let him try to handle this—it could kill him. A few months ago she would have turned it over to him but not now. She could wait for Cal but something told her he might try to reason with her—make her wait. And she knew what was coming—law enforcement complete with a negotiator. They would surround the cabin and... She was reminded of an emergency case years ago, her last year of residency, the victim... Oh God, what they could do to that girl in the time it took...

"What if they already have," she said to herself.

Then they won't again, her mind whispered back.

Oh, this was crazy. She stopped walking ten feet from the cabin to ask herself essential questions—could a frontal attack make this worse instead of better? They could shield themselves with the girl...but not both of them. She could shoot the other one if that happened. It could piss them off. Oh hell, they were already dangerous. My God, he bought snacks and liquor to enjoy while they did who knew what to that innocent girl! Maybe if the police, better equipped and experts in this sort of thing, had their chance, maybe no one would... But they weren't expecting *her*. If the police and SWAT team surrounded that cabin, they'd have all the time in the world to plan how to defend themselves or hurt the girl.

Then she heard Chelsea's scream fade into a sobbing cry and Maggie couldn't stop herself. She marched to the front of the cabin and gave the door a mighty kick right at the latch. When it didn't open she gave it another right away and the door flew open. She fired a shot into the ceiling and it made an earthshaking blast, a thundering explosion. She barely had time to make out what was going on inside. One of the men was standing on the left side of the bed, crouched in a fighting position with that big hunting knife in his hand while the other was moving off the bed toward something— the gun was leaning against the wall in the corner. His pants were open and even though she didn't see Chelsea, she shot the man with the open pants, shot him below the chest, dropping him screaming to the ground. Then she swung her shotgun wide to aim at the second man, racking up the next round, a scary sound.

That's when she saw Chelsea, crouched in the corner, her hands over her face. "Run to the store," she said to the girl. Then to the man. "Put the knife on the floor or I'll shoot you. Now."

He backed away, palms toward her. She glanced at the first man, crying out in pain, crawling toward the rifle. So she fired at the wall behind him and he scrambled away, back against the wall.

"You shot me in the dick!" he screamed. "You shot me!"

Well, that was fortuitous, she thought. She'd been aiming for his head.

Chelsea whisked past her through the door and she heard lots of feet running. She imagined everyone within earshot was running toward her now.

"Lie on your stomach, flat, hands stretched out," she ordered the men. The one who'd been holding the knife did so immediately but the other one, crying, curled up into a ball against the wall. She racked up her last round. And then Cal was behind her; she could smell him.

"Maggie," he said. "Jesus!"

"Protect the girl," she said. "Take care of my father."

"Maggie, what did you do?" Sully asked from behind her.

"I'll explain after these two are tied up. Cal, there's a roll of tape in my pocket—Stan and all the police in Colorado are on the way. Can someone please secure these men up so I don't have to shoot anyone? Again?"

For a while there was the sound of grunting, heavy breathing and whimpering in that little cabin. Outside there was a lot of murmuring as campers had gathered around to see what was going on, though Maggie was not compelled to explain other than to say the police were on their way.

Then after about five minutes of that the uninjured man began making excuses. "We weren't gonna do anything. That girl come along of her own—you can even ask her! If you'd a just said something, we'd a been on our way. We got no cause to make trouble anywhere..."

Maggie, still holding her father's shotgun, snorted. "They used her father's credit card in the store."

"She shot me! I'm dying," the wounded man cried.

"He's not bleeding enough to be dying. And he's not bleeding in the right places to be dying," Maggie said.

Cal rose from his job of binding the men. He was glistening with sweat and he was barely dressed; he must have just pulled on his jeans after his shower. Their weapons were tossed outside. One was bound facedown and the injured man was bound sitting up, leaning against the wall. He had splatters of blood on him but nothing serious. Maggie was not about to give him a checkup.

"I'll be fine if you want to grab a shirt," she told Cal.

"I'm not leaving you here. In fact, I'd rather you give me that gun now."

"I know what I'm doing," she said. "I know how to use it."

"I got that message, honey," he said, pulling it gently from her hands. "I don't want you to use it too much, that's all. Why don't you go check on the girl. Sully and I will take over now."

"Thanks," she said, relinquishing the weapon. "I'm worried about her. Will you two be all right?"

"I got it," Sully said, picking up the man's rifle and checking to see that it was loaded. "Go ahead."

When she walked in the back door Chelsea jumped off her stool at the counter and ran to her, throwing her arms around her.

"Honey, honey, it's going to be okay. The police are on their way."

"My mom and dad?" she asked through her sobs.

"I'm sure they'll be notified and either come here or meet you at the hospital or police station. Are you hurt in any way, honey?"

She shook her head against Maggie's shoulder, crying.

"Do you want me to take you over to the house? Do you want something to eat or drink?"

She leaned back and shook her head. "I just want my mom and dad," she said.

Maggie pulled her toward the kitchen. "How'd you end up with those two, honey?"

"They tricked me. One of them was crying for help right by the stream where I was filling my water bottle, and when I looked one of them dragged me down the hill with a hand over my mouth. I couldn't even scream. I lost my whole pack!" She started to tremble and sob again, clinging to Maggie.

"One of them used your dad's credit card," Maggie said.

"It was in my pocket," she said. "I've had it in my pocket since we were here. I used it to pay for stuff here. It was an extra—my mom had hers. My dad said hold on to it, keep it safe."

"When I saw that card, I knew you had been kidnapped," Maggie said. "So—it did the trick."

"Did you really shoot that man in the…you know?"

"Nah," Maggie said. "I just shot him where I thought I could stop him and do the least damage. He's fine, they're just pellets. They hurt and sting, but he'll live. He'll need a few stitches and that's all. He's going to jail."

Finally, the sound of distant sirens. A helicopter neared. A few minutes later there were cops everywhere, though Sully had called Stan to tell him Maggie had rescued the girl and that Chelsea was safe. Along with law enforcement they got fire and rescue and, as could be predicted, they made a mess of things with their big trucks and heavy equipment.

It was completely dark but with a nice, big moon lighting up the property. And boy, were the police pissed at Maggie. She had specifically defied Stan's orders.

"What the hell were you thinking?" Stan raged. "You could've killed somebody! You could've hurt that little girl!"

"I took that into consideration," she said. "If she'd gotten hurt I could still do some damage to them and get her out. But no one was gonna die from Sully's old shotgun. Noisiest piece of gun in the West, I think," she said. "Scared 'em. That's what I wanted."

"You could've been killed! Those big old bad boys could've walked right through that shot and killed you dead!"

"While I was doing my best, at least," she said.

"Leave her be now. She did what she had to do," Sully said. "You gonna sit outside and listen to a little girl scream?"

"It's okay, Dad," she said. "Let 'em get it off their

chest. You can go to the house and rest. This has been a strain on you."

"You think I'm likely to miss any of this?" he said.

"You could'a been killed, Maggie!" Stan persisted.

"Yeah, but I thought there was a better chance they'd never anticipate me coming at them with a shotgun. So...look, I shot the ceiling, hoping to scare them and hold a gun on them until police arrived, but they were going for their weapons and I was without a choice."

From there she had to sit at one of the tables on the porch with her dad and Cal and police detectives, her interview recorded, while crime scene people examined the cabin where the shooting took place. They confiscated all the weapons, including Sully's, the truck and everything else that belonged to the men.

While the police made it very clear they did not approve of the action she'd taken, they also conceded that with one holding a knife and the other reaching for his gun, it was self-defense. They weren't inclined to arrest her, but they did tell her to stay at the camp and not to leave without notifying Stan.

"Are there any charges pending?" Cal asked the detective.

"The file is not closed," he answered. "But so far I haven't seen any evidence that would warrant arrest. Still, the investigation is not quite over."

A while later a paramedic she'd known for about ten years, Conrad Boyle, Connie for short, came up on the porch. He grinned at her. "Nothing to worry about, Maggie," he said. "Except the one that got hit? He says he's gonna sue you."

"Tell him to get in line," she answered somewhat bitterly. No good deed ever goes unpunished.

"He's gonna be fine. They're twins, you know that? Burt and Bud. From the Wet Mountain Valley area, back in the hills. I'm just guessing, but I bet they're pretty well-known back in those trees."

"Thanks, Connie."

"You need anything before we haul outta here?"

"Got a Valium?" she asked.

"I'll have to check you, call ER, write it up. You don't have one?"

"Forget it, Connie," she said. "After everyone gets out of here, maybe I'll have a drink or something."

He grinned at her. "I don't care what anyone says. Good on ya, Maggie. You probably saved that girl's life."

"Thanks, Connie."

An hour and a half later, the grounds finally quiet, law enforcement and rescue gone, Maggie had a nice, hearty whiskey blend over a couple of ice cubes, out on the porch with Cal. Sully had gone to bed but she was still way too wired and spooked. She could tell that while the grounds were quiet, people were still awake. She could see the glow of fires in the dark night; she heard the gentle murmurs of talking. She wasn't the only one afraid to close her eyes on the night.

"Just one question," Cal said. "What made you storm that cabin? Without help? Without backup of any kind?"

She took a sip of her drink. "There was an emergency case I remembered. Years ago, when I was a senior resident in trauma..."

It was a victim the police couldn't get to. The apartment was surrounded by SWAT, uniforms, dogs, negotiators and medical. There was only one entry and it took hours while the suspect held the victim with a gun. After hours of trying, in an act of life-threatening heroism, one officer breached the apartment through a hole in the wall and eliminated the suspect. He was a young SWAT officer with a family who braved death to save an innocent. And he was too late.

"Not only had the victim been assaulted for hours, she was critical from a gunshot wound to the head when they finally got in. She was pregnant. It was a tragedy of huge proportions and we couldn't save her. I thought, maybe stupidly, that I had a chance in this case. I thought I might have to kill them to get Chelsea out but I also thought if I fired one round and they gave up, I wouldn't have to kill them and maybe could save her before any more damage was done."

"You weren't scared?" he asked.

"Of course, I must have been."

"Don't you even know?" he asked.

She smiled contritely. "If I let being scared stop me from doing what I think I have to do, I wouldn't get far. Would I?"

He shook his head and laughed. "You were lucky," he said. "You might be an ace in the operating room but in this, you were lucky. Let's not do that again, all right?"

"I hope to never do that again," she said. "God, I must have gone mad. I don't put the bullets in. I take them out!"

Be able to be alone. Lose not the advantage of solitude.

—SIR THOMAS BROWNE

CHAPTER 7

Maggie became a legend. Word spread around the county in about thirty minutes. Phones must've rung through the night because Enid and Frank showed up at 6:00 a.m. and Tom Canaday wasn't far behind them. There were others from near Sullivan's Crossing—a couple of members of the search-and-rescue team, one of the deputies from Timberlake, the county postal deliveryman. *For the love of God.* Maggie was amused that they made her out to be some fierce avenging angel who swooped down on two giant, armed men who were holding a little girl against her will.

As a bunch of locals gathered on the store's porch, Sully tried to help. "This story might've got a little embellished here and there," he said.

"Did she kick in the door?" Frank asked.

"Yeah, she did that," Sully relented.

"Blow a hole in the ceiling of that little cabin?" Enid wanted to know.

"It was a shotgun so not a big hole, but there's repairs to do," Sully said.

"And she shot one of them in the nuts?" someone asked.

"More or less," Sully said. "She's touched that gun

under a dozen times in her life. You reckon she's a good enough shot to do that on purpose?"

"Makes me shiver to think she is," Frank said. "I heard she had 'em in two shots. I'm gonna be way more careful what I say around her."

"I think you're all being just plain ridiculous!" Sully said. "It was a damn fool thing she did with pretty poor odds!"

"If I'm ever in trouble, I want her on my team," Enid said. "Maybe the lot of you should be careful what you say around *me*."

"Aw, you're carried away, that's all," Sully sulked. "She's just a girl! Don't encourage her!"

Cal, listening to every word, smiled.

A few days later, the Smyth family paid a visit, expressing gratitude and giving Maggie great peace of mind. As it turned out, the scruffy, felonious twins had a long list of priors, including sexual assault and battery. The county was delighted to hold them without bail and the prediction was that they had reached the end of their criminal careers.

Cal made a secret pledge to follow up on those two, make sure they were securely locked away.

The crossing was teeming with people, some on vacation and others stretching out their weekends. Maggie and Cal had to insist that Sully go easy, knock off early. He was inclined to do too much.

The garden showed the first sprouts of summer vegetables, wildflowers bloomed along roads and trails and Cal became a well-known fixture. He still maintained he was just helping out while Sully got back on his feet, yet his hours had become long and duties varied.

In addition to working in and around the store, he also took plenty of time to sit on the porch or hang around the counter inside the store because warmer weather brought out the locals as well as campers. Neighboring ranchers or their wives paid visits even though they rarely needed supplies of any kind. There was a lot of hanging around the back counter or bulletin board. Gavin, the local ranger with the US Forest Service, dropped by a couple of times for a beer after work; the volunteer search-and-rescue unit had exercises nearby and most of the crew stopped at Sully's on the way home. Tom was part of that team. And Tom managed to drop by most days, either in the morning for a cup of coffee to start his day or in the afternoon to check on Jackson or Nikki at the end of their day. Tom and Cal seemed to spend more and more time together, talking and laughing like old friends.

Cal was friendly with the campers and when they asked him if he owned the store he said, "No, it belongs to Sully. I'm just cheap help. But if there's anything you need, just let me know."

Maggie took Sully to Denver to see the doctor for his checkups. Sully wanted to drive himself there and home but Maggie wasn't having it. She wanted to hear everything the doctor said. Rob Hollis gave Sully an A+. "You're cleared to lift twenty-five to thirty-five pounds, and stretching and bending is approved, as tolerated. Walking is good, as much as desired. Meds stay the same. See you in a month."

Sully peered at Maggie. "Bet that just drives you crazy, hearing that I'm fine."

"I'm delighted," she said.

"You don't have to stay to take care of me anymore," he said.

"Can I stay if I want to?" she asked a bit sarcastically.

"Long as you want, Maggie. But, don't you miss the hustle and bustle of the operating room?"

In fact, she did. The cases, especially the most challenging—she missed them. The related complications, not so much. She was keeping up with the emails and snippets of news she got during regular calls with Jaycee, not to mention being in touch with her lawyer. He said she'd be deposed in a couple of weeks and she'd have to go back to Denver for that. "The excitement of Trauma 1 calls to me," she confessed to Jaycee, the only one of her friends she kept up to date on her legal issues. "But lawsuits, complex insurance disputes and the politics of medicine does not."

"Oh, I hear you there," Jaycee said. "OBs are almost as pursued as neurosurgeons. One of our practice has stopped delivering for that reason. What were we thinking?"

"We were thinking we could save the world, or at least a nice big chunk of it," Maggie said.

"I hope you think hard on this decision to hang around the store, Maggie," Sully said. "You went to school for a lifetime to do what you do. You saved lives. I think it would be a terrible waste to spend all that training and education handing out picnic supplies."

"I need some time off," she said.

But Maggie did take advantage of Sully's clean bill of health, the extra help around the crossing and the beautiful late-spring weather by heading into the surrounding hills for a few hours here and there. On a few quiet days Cal went with her, hiking into the hills, enjoying the beautiful views and breathtaking vistas. Instead of tents they'd carry a blanket and lunch and be back at the crossing in time for a shower and dinner.

Maggie was happy.

And, she had someone to sleep with at night. Not that much sleeping was involved. It seemed to her that Cal was settling in, getting comfortable. Now that there was help after four in the afternoon till closing up the store, Maggie was having dinner with Sully and Cal, most nights at their kitchen table. Maggie and Cal traded off cooking, cleaned up the dishes together, sat out on the porch at the store or by a fire near the lake. They sat at a table together checking their laptops for email and news. And Cal liked to read. He spent at least a couple of hours every afternoon reading—maybe in one of his lawn chairs, maybe in a hammock, maybe on the porch.

He worked vigorously but he wasn't around constantly; he certainly wasn't underfoot. He drove out a few times a week, checking out the surrounding area, bringing home groceries and incidentals. He'd been to Leadville, Timberlake, Fairplay and a few other little specks of towns. He dropped in on Stan the Man at the Timberlake Police Department and they had a hamburger together, he reported. He met Paul Castor, the deputy Stan bragged was a computer genius. "He claims to be in his thirties," Cal said. "He looks twelve."

His truck and closed pop-up camper were parked behind the cabin that had become his but even though he was helping around the store and property, he was still camping. Sometimes he got out the fishing pole, sometimes fired up the Coleman stove to make his own breakfast or fry a fish he'd caught, even though he had access to the small kitchen in the store or Sully's kitchen in the house.

"We lived off the grid a lot when I was a kid."

"As in camping?"

"We lived in a lot of odd places. There was a commune near Big Sur. That was kind of cool—there were lots of kids to play with. There were times we camped, but it wasn't recreational, it was lack of proper housing. Or it was part of traveling—my parents decided we should see the country so we spent a year on the road."

"How amazing," Maggie said.

"In retrospect, my father might've been on the run from his delusions. We were essentially homeless, living in a very old converted bus. But we did have a lot of unique and interesting experiences. And every couple of years my grandparents would snag us away from my mom and dad and keep us on the farm for a while—six months or a year."

"I guess it's just in your blood," she said.

"In a way."

"If you're interested in hiking and hate being cold, why aren't you on the Appalachian Trail?" she asked.

"I experienced a lot of that trail as a kid," he said. "We spent a little over a year in Tennessee."

"Doing what?" she asked.

"Not much," he said. "In summer we picked vegetables."

"The whole family?" she asked.

"The whole family. We picked up a lot of temporary work here and there. My favorite place to pick vegetables was California, around Fresno. The Central Valley. I learned some Spanish."

"You've had a remarkable life," she said.

"That's a nice, positive spin," he said.

Maggie took that to mean it had been a hard life.

More and more packages arrived, indicating hikers were on the trails. A few straggled in here and there, but none of them had traveled great distances—it was still too early in the spring. One couple had been hiking for six weeks, having started in Wyoming, planning to head farther south through the Rockies if the snow had melted enough. Two guys came over the Rockies from the south and reported it was passable—they had picked up the trail on the north rim of New Mexico. There were several people who'd hiked from Boulder and planned to go all the way to Durango.

On the weekends there were hiking groups who were out for the day or maybe one overnight on the trail. Cal wanted to visit with each one of them, asking about what had motivated them and how their experience had been.

Then it happened, right at the end of April.

"Maggie, your dad is doing great. He must be the poster child for bypass recovery. I saw him hauling flour sacks for Enid, patching the rain drain on the outside of the store, putting a little WeatherAll on the porch rail and throwing the ball for Beau. He's been cleaning out grills, hosing down your back porch and garden and I caught him doing a little maintenance on his truck. Nothing too serious, the truck is running fine."

"I wish he wouldn't push it," she said.

"He's not, according to him. He said the doctor gave him the go-ahead. Normal activities. And if he feels any discomfort, he's supposed to rest. But he seems to be fine. You seem to be fine. Any thoughts of going back to work? Going back to your house in Denver?"

"I'm going back next week for a day to be deposed for that lawsuit, but to practice?" She shook her head. "Not yet. I'm thinking of staying through summer. Poor Sully. I can tell he wishes I'd go. My mother has been calling a lot—she's appalled by my defection. Not just that I'm not practicing at the moment, but even worse for her—I'm spending my time here. I've been here seven weeks and by the texts and emails, people are surprised I've stretched it out this long. For now, I'm staying. Do you think I'm crazy, too? Because neuro-surgeons just don't do this?"

Cal laughed and shook his head. "Listen, life's too short to choose unhappiness. Until you figure out how to live on your own terms, you do whatever you have to do. When I figure out what that means, I'll be happy to share. For me, for now, I have a little exploring to do. Many times growing up we didn't have a house any-where and you've got two. I think you'll be okay. You won't get any judgment from me."

"Well, this is Sully's place, really. At some point I'll have to work. I can't expect my father to support me forever."

He took a deep breath. He took her hands in his. "Maggie, I'm going to go away for a little while," he said. "The time is perfect. I'm acclimated to the alti-tude, the forecast is good and I want some of that trail experience."

"Why don't you just make this your base camp and go out for a day here and there, like we've been doing?" she asked hopefully.

"I want to go north from here, camp along the way, watch summer hit Colorado, maybe go through Wyo-ming…"

"That's a long hike," she said.

"Not nearly as long as some. It's what I came here to do. I have thinking to do—like where I'm going to settle, what I'm going to do for work. I'm thirty-seven and at loose ends. I had this crazy idea the Continental Divide would level me out, give me a sense of balance, make the answers come easier. I think the solitude on the trail might be good for me."

She felt a panic in her gut. "I'm never going to see you again, am I." She did not state it as a question.

"I'll come back, Maggie. I don't know that I'll stay here, but I'll come back."

"When?"

"I have no idea. I don't know if I'll get enough of that trail in three days or three months. It will do me good. I think you need time to think, too."

"You're leaving your truck and camper?"

He shook his head. "There's a place to park it in Leadville and I'll get on the trail from there. Leadville's not too far away and I don't want it to be in your way here."

"It wouldn't be in the way. Sully offered…"

"I'm leaving it in Leadville. In the morning."

"Crap," she said, getting misty-eyed. Her nose immediately plugged up. "Can't you leave in a few days? Give a girl a little time to get used to the idea?"

"This is better, honey. I told you from the day we met—I want to do this. I need to get out on the trail alone, just me and the inside of my head."

"You're leaving your truck in Leadville so you won't have to come back here to get it in case you decide you're done with this place. With me."

"Not true. I will come back, I will see you again,

but I don't want you hanging on to a piece of me with expectations. I don't want you looking at the truck and being reminded every day. I want you to be free to get on with your life. If you go back to Denver, I can find you there."

"What in the world do you have to think about?" she demanded. "You're almost the most normal man I've ever known! You are not even slightly fucked-up! There's nothing you can't think about right here. In fact, I'll promise not to talk to you for three months so you can work through whatever it is and then we can work out anything else…" She stopped herself. "I'm close to begging," she said. "I'm not going to do that."

"You know how you said you had a pileup in Denver? Everything crashed down on you at once? Well, I went through a rough patch myself. Not something I'm ready to talk about just yet. Maybe someday. That's why I need some time alone. Alone against the challenge of the hike over the mountains and through some wild country. Alone with no one in sight, where I have to rely on myself. Sometimes that's what it takes. You know, you get a little tired, depleted, deprived, you have to push yourself, then things start to fall into place. I'm counting on that. I promise I'll get in touch when I've had all I can take of the trail. Okay?"

"Whatever," she said. She tried to hide the fact that tears were leaking out of her eyes. For just a second she thought, *I can tell him I'm coming up on a trial! That I need him! That I need the support!* But she couldn't.

"Come here," he said. "Close to me. We'll hold on to each other. It's hard for me to leave, you know. But I should do this even if it's hard. I have to look around the inside of my head and sort things out. You only *think* I'm the most normal guy in town—I have a gnarly mess in there. Now come on, kiss me. You're like buried treasure, you know that? I hobbled into this camp with no idea I'd have you for a while. Maggie, Maggie, you're so wonderful…"

Just after dawn, Cal got dressed and ready to get in his truck and on the road. Maggie pulled on her clothes and joined him outside beside the truck.

"You'll be okay, Maggie. You're strong and you have good sense. Don't get talked into anything—do what feels right."

"You shouldn't say that. What feels right is following you."

"You wouldn't like it."

"I'm a great, experienced hiker!"

"No, you wouldn't like watching me think. It's like watching paint dry."

"You're a miserable tease," she said. "I don't even know your real name!"

He grinned. "I loved you trying to guess, though. It was fun hearing what you'd come up with next. You're very creative." He sighed. "It's California. I'm California Cesar Jones."

She was struck silent for a moment. "You have got to be kidding!"

"I wouldn't kid about that. It's on my driver's license and everything. But don't make me go through all that now. Just please kiss me goodbye."

"You promise you'll get in touch when this pilgrimage is over?"

"Yes, I promise. Thank you for everything you did for me."

She kissed him deeply, held him tightly, damned fate for this. Just when she started to feel she was with a man who could carry his weight, he confessed that he was nuts and had to work on his issues by trotting over the mountains. Boy, could she pick 'em. Whatever saint was in charge of her love life was terrible at it.

He slapped her on the ass. "Take care of Sully. Take care of you."

"Be careful," she said.

"You bet I will."

He climbed in the truck and pulled away. He drove slowly down the dirt drive to the road and without even thinking she followed, walking along behind him.

Beau was barking and running to her as Cal pulled out of sight through the trees. She turned to see Sully approaching.

"Gone, is he?" Sully said.

She nodded. "Did you know he was going?"

"He said so a couple a times this week. That the weather was just about mild enough for him, that he'd planned it all along. And he thanked me several times for the hospitality and for letting him lend a hand. Damn fool thing to do—thank me. Might as well a thanked me for having a damn heart attack."

"We're never going to see him again, Dad," she said. "And that's a shame."

Heaven is under our feet as well as over our heads.

—HENRY DAVID THOREAU

CHAPTER 8

On the fourth day out on the trail, west of Boulder and north of Vail in the mountains, just north of Rocky Mountain National Park where the air was pristine and the sky a beautiful blue, where he could see for miles and great, magnificent mountains rose and fell all along the horizon, Cal set up his little tent and dug a trench around a small fire. It was the end of the day. The sun was descending behind the Rockies. "This looks like as good a place as any. What do you think?" he said, aloud.

Of course there was no answer.

It was two years and two months since Lynne Aimee Baxter Jones had taken her last breath. It was approximately the same time of day, but on the first of March it had been so cold and dark. They had talked about the end for a long time, for months.

In the beginning they'd been so happy, so oblivious to the things that could go wrong. Cal had started out by working in the public defender's office, passed the bar and got a lot of great job offers. Then Lynne passed the bar, gathered a few like-minded friends, wrote grants and within a couple of years she was operating a storefront legal clinic for the underprivileged. She won an award from the city of Detroit and was appointed to a legal oversight committee by the governor, a watchdog team running herd on lawyers with intent to mislead and gouge an unsuspecting public, particularly those of low income.

Meanwhile, California Jones was becoming famous in his own right, a white knight in the criminal law community. He was actually becoming rich, kid lawyer that he was. Cal had some gifts that he'd acquired from his off-balance, crazy family. One was an incredible memory. His father had taught the kids how to memorize and since they rarely attended school, it became imperative. Otherwise, when they did have a chance to go to school, they'd be humiliated by how little they knew. Or, given what their mother taught them, they might know all the wrong things. Cal could recite almost the entire novel *To Kill a Mockingbird*. He grew up wanting to be Atticus Finch. While Lynne took great pride in accepting very little compensation, Cal was enjoying a terrific income for the first time in his life.

They married and bought a sprawling house in Grosse Pointe. Lynne thought it was so funny, Cal and his solid house, big enough for an army. "You just don't know how much trouble a big house can be!" she lectured.

"That's right," he said. "And I want to know."

They talked about the children they would have because they both wanted at least two. Cal still wasn't sure if things would be better or worse if they'd gotten right on that and had a child or two. Like Atticus Finch, he'd be a solemn widower lawyer, bringing up his children alone, filling them with pride and accountability. But they hadn't done it and now he was completely alone.

As soon as they started trying for a baby, the nightmare of scleroderma invaded their lives. The painful disease of the connective tissue presents as a hardness and inflexibility of the skin and, in Lynne's case, internal organs. At first they were optimistic and researched the disease, hoping that she'd be one of the lucky ones and get twenty years or even a cure.

It was not to be. The disease worsened rapidly and she was admitted into a research program. Again, she was not one of the lucky ones. The disease progressed quickly and Lynne spent two years battling the pain and immobility, not to mention disfigurement of her face and arms. That's when she asked him, "I know we're on the same page here, Cal. If my kidneys shut down or my heart gives out, so be it. No resuscitation. But if it takes too long, please, don't let me suffer in pain. I wouldn't let you, I swear to God. It's not like there's any hope."

He promised.

She fought hard for as long as she could and they both prepared for what they knew would happen. Ultimately she had said, "It's time. Please. I love you so much but I can't do this anymore." And Cal slid the needle into her IV, injected the morphine slowly, then crawled onto the bed, took his beautiful wife in his arms, held her and told her how she meant everything to him, kissing the tears from her face as she passed into the next world.

He looked up into the rapidly darkening sky streaked with wispy clouds. "Do you still think it was a good idea, Lynne?" He wished he knew if, wherever she was, in whatever form or realm, she was still okay with her choice. That it hadn't been even one hour too soon. Because there were so many days when he thought about what he would trade for another hour with her. He'd gladly have given ten years of his own life for one of hers.

As per her wishes, there was no funeral. There was a celebration of life, standing room only. There were poor people, rich people, common criminals mixed up with wealthy family and friends from back East. There were politicians, illegals, lawyers and well-known thugs— between Lynne and Cal, their clients had been of every stripe. The governor delivered a few words; doctors and nurses who had fallen in love with her during her illness were present. She was beloved to so many. She had been so courageous.

He reached into his backpack and pulled out a leather satchel. The mortuary had transferred her ashes from the urn for him because you don't take an urn on a long hike. The pouch was soft and solid. He held it to his heart briefly. Then he poured the ashes in a little mound on the ground. The breeze stole a little off the top right away. He remembered her last wishes.

Here's what I want from you, California Jones. I want to be cremated. No funeral, I hate funerals. If you have to have some kind of party, you go ahead, do whatever gets you through it. Then I want you to find a beautiful place and dump my ashes on the ground. Let the wind take me away, Cal. And then I want you to let go of me. The only way you can honor my memory is with your happiness.

Cal stayed for three days in the spot where he'd let go of Lynne's ashes. Water was readily available from a nearby stream. He suspected he was sharing the water with open-range cattle and wildlife, but it was good, clear water and he had a great water filter. He drank it and washed in it and it was cold as bloody hell, shocking him into awareness. He spent his time ruminating on his life with Lynne and tried to come to terms with the hard parts, the end of her life. He spent the days and nights focused on her because he was going to have to leave it behind eventually. It wasn't as though he'd forget her, but he hoped the time had finally come for moving on. The past two years had been so lonely. And he'd held on long enough.

He made a very difficult decision. He left the leather satchel on the ground where the now dissipated ashes had been. He didn't want to carry it with her remembrance just a bit of dust inside. He might obsess on it, caress it. It was time. He thought of his promise to her. She wanted him to be happy.

He started walking north. He carried a couple of maps for the Colorado and Wyoming CDT and had highlighted water access, campsites, towns and sections of road. He walked for days and got so damn tired and dry.

But his mind felt free to wander and, unsurprisingly, he spent a lot of time thinking about his childhood and about his dad, Jed Jones. In fact, he worried about his parents a lot. Jed was so flaky and unbalanced, the range of possibilities with him was endless. He'd gotten a little steadier in the past several years, since he'd been on the farm in Iowa and wasn't roaming, but Cal wouldn't be surprised to hear his parents were suddenly off on a mission to save cheetahs in the Congo or... Or that his father had taken his own life. He'd attempted suicide a few times, though they were halfhearted attempts. He jumped off a bridge and broke a leg once, but it was a low bridge. He took a bunch of pills, but slept it off—it turned out he didn't have enough for a deadly dose. He stabbed himself in the heart—missed.

In the way that the eldest child in a family with dysfunctional parents will shift into the parent role at a very early age, Cal had become the one in charge. He couldn't say exactly when. Maybe it was when Sierra was born. He was about eight and remembered carrying her around, feeding her, changing her. His mother had usually been preoccupied with their father, making sure he was happy and as secure as possible, so Cal tended to look after the children *and* watch over his parents. His mother said Jed was a genius and needed a lot of room to think and of course, Cal believed it. He still believed it—Jed had an amazing mind and was charismatic. When he started talking, people couldn't turn away. He'd lecture on everything from the solar system to the cure for cancer. Jed had studied law before marrying Marissa, Cal's mother, and he remembered every word he'd ever read. Or so it seemed.

Cal always knew there was something wrong with his father but he had no idea what. Eccentric, they called him. When Cal was about thirteen he thought he had it figured out—he blamed it on the pot. Jed smoked daily. But it was another few years before he'd learn the truth—his father heard voices. They were back on the farm because Marissa's father had fallen ill and she was an only child. It was a lucky break—they were stable for a while. Jed, who knew a lot about everything and had experience in farming from their days as migrant workers, had something to do and they were all warm and fed. And one night Marissa asked, "Where's your father?"

Cal said, "I saw him by the barn, talking to himself again. I guess he's running ideas."

And out of the blue Marissa said, "He's not talking to himself."

Cal was seventeen and suddenly it was all so clear. Jed had secret friends. Their mother was completely devoted because she was busy trying to conceal his illness. His delusions conversed with him and gave him advice, not always good advice. He smoked a lot of dope to keep them quiet and Marissa watched over him like the keeper she was and made sure the drug use didn't get out of hand. She supported him in not seeking medical intervention because the drugs doctors used would slow down his beautiful mind and he couldn't bear it. He'd tried a couple of times, she said, and it was brutal. He became a zombie. But worse, he became depressed because he couldn't think.

Things had been quiet in those quarters the past ten years or so. Cal's grandfather had died a long time ago and then his grandmother, as old as the ages, had needed Jed and Marissa on the farm, so they stayed. Then Grandma passed. Cal and his siblings were raised and gone. Jed and Marissa had no other means of support. Sometimes Cal held his breath, ready for some harebrained idea that would have them off on an adventure, but so far so good. Cal, being the father to his father, could usually talk Jed out of things. *I think if we burn the fields instead of plow them, the ash will give essential nutrients to the soil and make next year's crop richer.*

No, Cal said, *that only works on rice fields. It has the opposite effect on corn and wheat. Besides, you lease those fields to farmers.*

But God, they were exhausting. So, unable to really help and refusing to be as codependent as Marissa was, Cal limited his contact with them. He visited about once a year and talked to them every two to four weeks. He'd like to just talk to his mother but she was attached to his father and there was no way to isolate her and pull her out of that mess, not even for a conversation. They were like conjoined twins.

Interestingly, Cal, his younger sister Sedona and younger brother, Dakota, all broke out of that craziness. With a vengeance! Sedona was a psychologist, married to a businessman, mother of two children, living a very stable, happy life. Dakota was an Army major, decorated for valor. He was so rigid and conservative it almost made Cal's teeth ache to be around him.

But Sierra, the baby, was lost. She might be schizophrenic like her father but it was impossible to tell because of her drug use. She'd seemed all right into her twenties and was an excellent student, then fell apart. Cal and Lynne had staged an intervention, explaining the situation with her father, and mother for that matter, and tried to get her help. But rather than finding the source of her pain in Jed Jones, Sierra found an ally. Apparently she understood about the wild notions and mysterious voices. Sierra was now on the farm with Mom and Dad, probably weaving, reading bizarre shit and toking it up with Dad in the afternoons. "Whatever works," Marissa was known to say.

Living with, perhaps understanding how to function in such a family, had made careers for Cal and Sedona. They were the opposite of freewheeling, new-age, whack-a-doodle hippies. Maybe Dakota, too. It was almost counterintuitive—if the parents are hippies and revolutionaries, the kids end up moderate and conventional.

Cal kept hiking. Every third or fourth night he found a campground or little bit of a town where he could wash, eat a protein-heavy meal, drink a couple of beers, talk to people, resupply.

It was when his trail also became counterintuitive, when he had to hike south to hike north, that he realized how much he missed Maggie. They were a little bit alike. They were both struggling to move on from their dynamic but abandoned careers, both getting over difficult childhoods, both floundering a little as they reached for a lifestyle that brought peace and comfort. And they could both go back to where they'd been tomorrow, pick up the threads of their previous lives, and succeed in many ways. She could go back to Denver and step into the operating room and resume her role as a talented young neurosurgeon. He could go back to Grosse Pointe and his old firm would welcome him with open arms. But he didn't think either of them would do that.

He'd been on the trail for fourteen days. He'd done what he came to do. He'd left Lynne in the wind on a beautiful mountain pass. He turned right then, in the middle of the trail, and began walking south.

Maggie's muscles ached, and for good reason. She'd thrown herself into physical labor. She'd far rather enjoy the calisthenics of sex, but her lover had taken to the trail. He'd been gone two weeks and she was trying to accept the idea that her fling was over and she wouldn't see him again.

Maggie ran the store, organizing, learning, stocking,

ordering, even balancing the books, which was mostly accomplished by computer program, thankfully.

"Know how to make a small fortune?" Sully asked Frank. "Take a *large* fortune and put it into educating a neurosurgeon who decides to quit and sell picnic supplies." Then, turning toward Maggie he said, "You're going to ruin your hands in the garden and shelving. For the love of God, go home!"

"No," she said. "Not yet. And I didn't quit—I'm taking a break."

She drove to Denver one day to meet with her lawyer and the plaintiff's counsel, spent three exhausting hours in deposition and then stopped in Golden to visit her mother. That was a mini nightmare—it was one endless argument. Phoebe was outraged that her daughter would throw away all the prestige of her career to stock shelves in a little country store.

"I also garden, hike, do a little rock climbing and I'm thinking of going out on the trail for a couple of overnights."

"Dear God, what if you run into trouble?" Phoebe asked.

"I have bear repellant and won't hesitate to use it on any animal that threatens me." And by that she meant human or animal. Phoebe didn't seem to know about the predator Maggie had shot, thank God. There had only been a small story that included the names of the felons, the general location and had not named the minor child. Maggie had been described as the "local proprietor of a family-style campground."

She drove back to Sully's the same day. When she got to Leadville, she drove all around the town looking for Cal's truck with its camping trailer. She didn't see it anywhere. Clearly he'd gone. Lied to her and left her with a promise he wasn't about to keep.

Going out on the trail overnight was just an experiment, a way to simulate what Cal was doing, how he was feeling wrapped in his solitude. He had to think, he said. About what? she wondered. When Maggie let herself think too much she saw all the carnage of the emergency room on one of the worst days of her life. A bunch of teenage boys in a terrible accident, three head injuries. One neurosurgeon. It just wasn't worth the exercise.

Instead of camping in the wild she hauled stock, weeded, cleaned the public bathrooms and showers, raked, scrubbed Sully's house from top to bottom and rearranged furniture.

"Damn near broke a leg in the night just trying to go to the john. You about got it out of your system yet?" Sully asked while they had their morning coffee on the porch at the store.

"What?"

"Cal, that's what. I guess you think I'm just stupid."

"Look, I admit I wish he hadn't gone but it's probably for the best. He's just some jobless loser, living in a tent, who couldn't tell the truth about anything even if it bit him in the ass."

Sully leveled a stare at her. "You catch him in a lie, Maggie?"

"That doesn't mean he wasn't lying!"

Sully scowled at her. "I think they need you in Denver," he finally said. "I think *I* need you in Denver."

"I have too much invested in you to leave now," she said.

"God help me."

One day a letter came for Cal from the Colorado State Supreme Court. "Dad?" she said. She held it out to him. "What the hell could this mean?"

Sully took the envelope and held it for a second. "Hmm. Reckon it means he's coming back. Unless he sends me a request to forward it."

"I don't see how it could mean that," she said. "Clearly he's on the run."

"Don't be ridiculous," Sully said. "From what?"

"Well, this isn't a jury summons! He's not a resident!"

"Maybe he is. You don't know everything."

"I don't know anything! He's probably wanted!"

"Indeed," Sully said sarcastically.

"What is it, then?"

"It's a man's private mail and as postmaster I swore an oath and part of that oath is to keep my nosy daughter from picking through the mail. You better keep this to yourself, Maggie."

"Don't you agree it's pretty suspicious?"

"I agree it's pretty personal and none of your business."

"Well, jeez," she said. "Not like he's here to question, now, is it."

"You heard me," Sully returned emphatically.

When Cal had been gone three weeks, Maggie wasn't sure how long she could continue to drive him from her mind with hard work and outdoor activities like hiking. She began to slow down. But just to reassure her the universe was not yet on her side, she saw a familiar black Lincoln move slowly up the drive toward the store.

She looked skyward. "Really?" she asked God. "Like this wasn't enough?" Then she hollered, "Dad!"

Her father came running out of the store, a hunk of his turkey sandwich still hanging out of his mouth. He stuffed it back in before he could speak. "What the hell, Maggie?"

She pointed a shaking finger at the car. "Phoebe and Walter."

Sully chewed and swallowed. "Well, that took 'em longer than I thought it would. Brace yourself, Maggie. They're here to do war."

"How do you know?" she asked.

"Phoebe hasn't been near this place since she left and took you with her thirty years ago. Hell just froze over."

Walter parked the big car beside the store and got out. He walked toward the porch, alone. "Where's Mother?" Maggie asked.

"I decided to come on my own. Don't you think she must have run out of things to say by now?"

"Highly doubtful," Maggie said.

"Hey there, Walter," Sully said. "Want lunch?"

"That sounds great, Sully."

"Ham or turkey?" he asked.

"Turkey. Thanks."

Walter came up on the porch. He wore yellow golf pants with a peach collared shirt and white sweater. He was a handsome man, she'd give her mother that. Phoebe had had two husbands and both were fine-looking men. Sully was stockier and had those strong arms and shoulders; Walter was reed-thin with silver hair and a surgeon's long, slim fingers.

"Can we sit?" Walter finally asked.

"Yes. Right. Listen," she said while she was taking

her chair. "I'm sorry about the money, Walter. All the money you invested in my education and career and—"

"Maggie, do you think I came here to talk about money? I thought maybe we could have a conversation without your mother. Doctor to doctor?"

Maggie frowned. This was rare with Walter. "Where does Mother think you are?"

"The club. Where else would I be?" Then he grinned like a naughty little boy.

Maggie could count on one hand the number of times she'd had a serious and private conversation with her stepfather, yet each one had been meaningful. It wasn't just that Phoebe rarely gave him time to speak, though that was often the case. On top of that, Walter was hardly verbose. And he was relatively soft-spoken. They loved working with him in the operating room. While other surgeons were swearing and throwing things, Walter was saying please and thank you.

Sometimes it seemed as if Walter saved himself for those important messages while Sully spit out weighty and sarcastic wisdom all day long.

"Here you go," Sully said, putting a tray on the porch table. There were two wrapped sandwiches, two prepared and wrapped green salads with a packet of dressing and fork enclosed, two bags of chips and two bottled teas. "I'll leave you alone to talk…"

"Join us, Sully," Walter said. Then he looked at their surroundings. "This is a nice place. Quiet. Comfortable."

"It's usually quiet during the day, except on weekends when there are more than the usual boats on the lake," Sully said. "Most folks are exploring or hiking or rock climbing. They'll all be back, stirring up their grills and washing off the grit of the trail. Let me get my lunch. Don't wait for me."

Walter immediately unwrapped his sandwich and opened his bottled tea, taking a drink. "Well, I'll give you this—you picked a good place to unwind. What a beautiful day."

"Walter, forgive me, but I'm overcome by the strangest feeling." He just lifted one gray brow as he bit into his sandwich. Then Sully was with them again, sitting at the table, his half-finished lunch on a tray in front of him.

"You were saying?" Walter asked.

"I said, this is strange. I can't decide whether to be touched, grateful or scared to death. Whatever prompted this little meeting... Are you going to lecture me about leaving my job?"

"I was under the impression it was a time-out," Walter said. "Are you actually quitting?"

"No. I don't know," she said. She couldn't eat her sandwich. "The truth is, I don't know what to do. What if I didn't go back to it?"

"You'd hardly be the first. A good dozen of my colleagues from medical school gave up practicing. They found it wasn't right for them for a variety of reasons. One went into business...didn't do so well, as I recall. But another quit to write romance novels and she's cleaning up." He chuckled. "Another is living on a farm, growing organic vegetables and manufacturing salad dressing. Very good stuff," he added, taking another bite. "Sully, this is a delicious sandwich."

"We get a delivery from a greengrocer in Timberlake every couple of days. Enid makes the sandwiches and bakes all the cookies, brownies and muffins. According to Maggie, they're going to kill us."

"I'll have to have one," Walter said.

"Okay, now you're scaring me," Maggie said. "Why don't you get it over with? Rip off that old bandage, Walter. Say it. Yell at me. You poured a fortune into me and now I'm threatening to walk away to bag groceries and…"

"I've never once raised my voice to Maggie," Walter told Sully.

"Course not," Sully said. "I do whenever I please, however, so she's not being neglected in that area."

"We've only had a few serious talks in my life and as I recall, they were so mild I hardly realized until afterward that you had any idea what you were doing. There was that time when I was a freshman in college that you came all the way out here from Chicago. You said you wanted to see the campus again—you'd seen it before I enrolled. But that was a ruse. You wanted me to change my major."

"No, not exactly," Walter corrected. "I thought you were too young to commit to a course of study. I wanted you to check a lot of different things while you had the chance. But I didn't insist, did I?"

"No," she relented. "But you had a good argument. And then there was that little talk we had before I married Sergei, the artist."

"That one didn't go as well, regrettably," Walter said.

"You tell her to bail out while she could?" Sully asked.

"Not exactly," Walter said. "I did suggest they had little in common and she might want to think on it a while longer. The kid was penniless. So was Maggie for that matter. But Maggie wasn't going to stay penniless and I highly recommended a prenup. Nothing at all wrong with a prenup when one of the couple has great potential and the other doesn't."

"You have a prenup, Walter?" Maggie asked.

"We did," he said. "It was Phoebe's idea. It became null and void after a decade of marriage. That seemed reasonable. All that aside, you managed your situation very well. Sad but predictable."

"I wasted a perfectly good marriage on him. And then there was the time right before residency—we had a very long talk about what it was going to be like, what kind of commitment I was making, how I had to be sure my personal goals matched my professional goals, that sort of thing. I'm still not sure what that means."

"Now's probably as good a time as any to think about what it means."

"Listen, Walter, did you ever have second thoughts about important stuff? Like neurosurgery? Or maybe marrying a woman with a six-year-old? Or sinking all that money into a med student?"

"I'm a human being, Maggie. I've had second thoughts about everything. Giving important matters serious consideration and reevaluations is vital. I even have some regrets—but not about my practice, my wife or my stepdaughter. I was lucky in those areas of my life. At least, luckier than most men. Although I have to be honest—I think I'd rather have been a pilot."

"Seriously? I never heard you say that before! But I remember your flying lessons. Didn't you have an airplane for a while?"

"I was part owner of a Piper, but I didn't keep it too

long. Your mother wouldn't go up with me. Such is life—we're all different."

Maggie took a bite of her sandwich, feeling a little more relaxed. "And, there was one other time. High school. Remember?"

"I remember," he said, finishing off his sandwich.

She'd got a speeding ticket. She'd had girlfriends in the car and got caught annihilating the speed limit. She was going a hundred in a fifty-five. And of course lost all driving privileges for a long time. It didn't matter that much as she was in boarding school where they weren't allowed to have cars. But she went home some weekends. Walter was surprisingly firm in the no-driving department and even when her friends wanted to take her out, she was grounded. Then one Saturday night he said, "Come with me, Maggie. We're going to the hospital. You'll be out late."

There was an accident and it involved teenagers. Walter was called to the emergency room and Maggie followed him wearing a lab coat so she looked like she belonged. There were terrible injuries, the police were at the hospital, alcohol was involved, frantic parents came running, the waiting room was a circus. Walter was one of several doctors who then went to the operating room from ER. "Stay with me, Maggie." She remembered thinking Walter had shown her exactly what he wanted her to see, that recklessness hurt people and it could be deadly. But imagine her shock when he told his OR tech to suit her up and scrub her in.

"What?" she had asked, horrified. "What if I faint?"

"The circulating nurse will kick you to one side so you're not in our way. But I want you to be there."

She stood through not one but two surgeries on

teenagers and watched in fascination as Walter calmly and confidently called for instruments, asked for extra hands, ordered suction while blood dripped on his shoes, drilled holes in a skull, implanted shunts, carved and stitched, even had to resuscitate one patient on the table. He never panicked; he never raised his voice. The circulating nurse mopped his sweating brow. Both patients went to recovery, Walter and Maggie following. Maggie heard a nurse say, "By the grace of God and a hair." She heard Walter say to one of the parents, "We were very lucky."

Maggie had been in a silent cloud of sheer wonder. It was nearly dawn when they were driving home. "Well, Maggie?" Walter said.

In a voice that sometimes rang in her ears to this day she heard herself say to her stepfather, "I have to do that."

He pulled the car into their garage, stopped the engine and looked across the front seat at her. "You can do anything you choose to do, Maggie. But if you want to live to do it, you will not drink and drive and you will never exceed the speed limit again. Is that clear?"

"Absolutely. So, how long does it take to become a neurosurgeon?"

He was quiet a second and then said, "Forever."

Maggie smiled and shook her head. "Walter—high school. My speeding ticket. A watershed moment."

"Seems so," he agreed. "I couldn't have planned that, of course. I admit, I wanted to scare you. But it had a much bigger impact than that."

"You didn't think I'd be impressed with emergency surgery?"

"At that time in your life I was betting on a career in cheerleading."

She gave a hollow little laugh. She thought for a moment. "Would you two mind if I just… I'd like to take a short walk down by the lake before we continue this conversation. If you have the time, Walter. If you can spare me, Sully."

"We'll just have our drinks and catch up. Go ahead," Walter said. "I'm in no hurry to get back on the road."

As she walked along the edge of the lake, hands in the pockets of her shorts, her sneakers getting wet and dirty, she remembered with such clarity the night in the emergency room, that night of vivid lucidity, watching Walter save lives. She followed him at three feet, listening raptly, but he only spoke to her twice. Both times he said, "All right, Maggie?" And she had replied, "All right."

All he'd had in mind was showing her blood and fear and trauma from a car accident, but something had happened. Though a kind and gentle man, until that night she had not appreciated how strong and wise Walter was, how thoroughly competent. That night she learned a new respect for her stepfather.

Later, while in medical school, she'd scrubbed in with Walter a few times, much closer to the sterile field, watching his perfect nimble fingers work magic. That was when she learned that Walter Lancaster was a highly respected neurosurgeon. He was the one to ask for when you wanted the best. She did her fellowship in neurosurgery with him. He had since retired from his practice after a couple of small strokes, unwilling to take any chances on his health or that of his patients. He still worked now and then, taking a few days to go back to Chicago where he was licensed, where he consulted, scrubbed in with another surgeon occasionally, that sort of thing. And he continued to go to neurosurgery conferences where he was often a presenter.

It suddenly occurred to her—maybe their move to Golden wasn't Phoebe's idea. Maybe Walter liked the idea.

She dawdled for a half hour or so, just thinking. Then she went back to find someone had wrapped up her uneaten sandwich and Sully was showing Walter the garden. She walked over to take some credit for it—stuff was sprouting up all over.

"Pretty soon we'll come out here to cut a few inches off the top of the lettuce for salad and it grows back in a couple of days. Tomatoes will be coming all summer. Melon vines are starting to crawl over the yard."

"I've always wished we had a garden," Walter said, bending to pet Beau. "But between me and Phoebe there was no one to take care of one. And hiring it done just wouldn't be the same, would it?"

"Mother isn't sinking her hands in the dirt, Walter. You know better than that," Maggie said.

"Well, she's good at other things," he said.

"Like what?" Maggie asked, sounding insolent.

But Walter laughed. "She's a genius at hiring a cleaning service and picking restaurants. And she has other gifts—she's a great decorator. An excellent travel companion. She can entertain with great fanfare. And I think you don't give her enough credit for being a wonderful mother."

Maggie reserved comment on that. It might just be there were too many complications given two marriages, the separation from Sully. She was willing to give Phoebe the benefit of the doubt. Maybe under it all she was a good mother, just not that good for Maggie.

"I'm getting back to work," Sully said. "Nice to see you, Walter."

The men shook hands and Sully wandered off toward the store, Beau at his heels.

"And I should get back to Golden," Walter said. "It was nice having lunch with you, Maggie. I think you picked a nice place to hole up awhile."

"I think you came here to give me things to think about. So let me admit it—I miss my job. The patients, the surgery, some of the staff. It's just the other forces—insurance, administrators, lawsuits, politics and Jesus, even the media. They make it so hard to help people."

"I know. It's very hard to find a way to do what you do on your own terms."

"Did you? Do it on your terms?"

"Yes," he said. "There were occasional trade-offs but I managed most of the time. But it's obvious in one hour here that I wanted an entirely different kind of life than you do. I didn't grow up in the country, in the mountains. I grew up in a nice house in Chicago. I didn't play sports. I got a chemistry set when I was seven. I was in the chess club, the debate club, the science club—the old-fashioned version of a nerd. And all I wanted in a wife was everything that would drive Sully and maybe you crazy." He smiled at her. "No one can live your life but you, Maggie. But if you find a way to use your talents to help people I think you'll be happier."

She couldn't deny it. She was deeply touched that Walter would do this—ditch her mother and drive to the crossing to speak to her alone. No pressure, just a conversation. "You're a good man, Walter. You've been a good father to me."

He kissed her forehead. "I'm very proud of you. In all your incarnations."

The store was pretty quiet so they left Jackson in charge and went to the house for dinner. Maggie grilled a couple of fish fillets and sautéed some vegetables.

Sully sat at the table. "That was good of Walter to drive down just to talk to you," he said. "You're a very lucky girl."

"Yes, Walter went out of his way, didn't he? And wouldn't it be nice if my own father had gone out of his way? When I was growing up?"

Sully put down his fork. "How dare you say that to me," he said, his voice very calm.

"Well, you let them take me, you let them keep me even though all of you knew I wanted to be here. And you—"

"Stop it!" he snapped. "You were a little girl! You needed some things I couldn't give you, like a decent education! You needed a mother and don't you dare criticize your mother again—she sacrificed so much for you. I don't like her but she was damn good to you and she wouldn't have married Walter if he hadn't been the best thing for you! And before you lay that on me one more time I want you to think about the sacrifice I made—my own child, gone to another state because it was the best thing. You think you'd be a goddamn surgeon if you'd stayed here where I wanted you to be?"

She broke down. "I thought you didn't want me. I thought you found me annoying," she whispered.

"You are annoying! But I loved you with a father's

heart! I wanted more for you! It was terrible. And I wouldn't change one goddamn thing!"

She put her hands over her face, covering the tears. She was probably ten the last time she cried in front of Sully.

"Maggie, don't snivel about it. I did the best I could and I apologize if it wasn't good enough."

"It was good enough," she said. "You never say you love me."

"I just did," he grumbled. "I'll say one thing—you never thank me for all the years I did without you for your own damn good. If you had a child, you'd understand."

I almost did, she thought, emotions overflowing.

"Because I'll tell you something, Maggie—when you have a child you'll understand how hard it is when she's taken from you. I guess I was supposed to grieve for you so you'd be convinced it wasn't fun for me, but I didn't want to do that to you. I wanted you to take everything offered you in a good home and not feel the tearing inside when—"

"I just wanted to know that," she said. "I didn't know you were protecting me. I thought you were just as happy I was gone so much."

"So now you have it—I wasn't one goddamn bit happy about it. But it worked out the way I wanted it to. You made something out of yourself. If you'd stayed around here you'd be bagging groceries and cleaning up campsites." He shook his head. "You're welcome."

"I just wanted to know," she said.

"Now you know. We gonna let go of this now?"

She nodded and wiped her cheeks.

"I'll tell you what, girl. You do make a man work hard for it."

She gave a little huff of laughter. "About Mother," she said. "She's a pain in the ass."

"I know that," he said, picking up his fork. "At least she's not my pain in the ass. Now, I want you to tell me something—how long are you planning to stay here and make me pay for all my parenting mistakes?"

She took a breath. "I came for a two-week break. I stayed because I knew that despite all your grumbling, you could use my help. Then my lawyer called and said we're going to trial. Soon. In a month or so. He said it was perfectly reasonable for me to wait it out here."

Sully lifted his bushy brows. "Trial?"

"Trial," she said. "The lawsuit. It's taking all my energy to keep from running scared."

"You have nothing to be scared about," he said. "Walter says you're one of the best and it will all come to light. Meanwhile, I can stand it a little longer if you're determined to stay on a bit."

She laughed. "You certainly know how to suck up, Sully."

"Don't I?" he said.

He who is outside the door has already a good part of his journey behind him.

—DUTCH PROVERB

CHAPTER 9

Maggie was at peace. She knew her father loved her but what she had really wanted was to know that he had missed her, that her absence had been hard for him. And now that it was laid to rest, she'd think about showing gratitude. Sully had done his best by her and it hadn't been easy.

And of course Maggie thought about Walter's visit. She had begun to ask herself if there was any compromise in her situation. Maybe there was a free clinic somewhere that needed her. Or maybe she should just take a year to travel with a medical team to performed badly needed surgeries in places that didn't have readily available resources. One of those big hospital boats maybe?

She had to admit, the very thought of returning to her field of expertise purely for the joy of operating, especially if people were trying to make it easier instead of harder at every turn, was enticing. She started looking at websites for volunteer medical teams—everything from the Red Cross to Doctors Without Borders.

The days passed more peacefully. She began to fantasize. She'd be in her best physical shape from a summer at the crossing, tighten up those belly muscles, strengthen her legs, study all those medical journals she'd been meaning to go through, even read some of those classic novels Cal seemed so fond of, not that she was thinking about him. Not at all. When the lawsuit was won or settled or—please, God—thrown out, she'd join a hospital ship for a year, traveling the world, saving lives where no one else could be bothered. She'd be operating again. She'd meet new people. They wouldn't work every second, though they would be in great demand. There would still be time to see the wonders of the world, exotic and romantic places. She'd meet a man, a fascinating and brilliant man. A sexy man, but more reliable than that California Jones, wherever he was. Yes, it would be exciting. Fulfilling.

The last week of May approached, promising summer vacation just days away when school let out. Sully announced they had lots of reservations. Many packages and letters had arrived for hikers. The busy season was upon them. All this, combined with her fantasies, took Cal, who had obviously left them, further from her mind. Soon her heart would catch up. She hadn't heard from him at all and hadn't located his truck in Leadville, no matter how many times she'd tried.

It was only late in the night, in the dark, that she remembered with longing how special their time together had been. She had loved talking to him, loved making love even more. But alas, he hadn't promised anything but that he'd say goodbye. And he said promises broke him. Well, he had said goodbye. There was another crack in her heart.

After a very long day of work, just as people around the campgrounds were starting to fire up their grills,

Maggie sat on the porch with Sully, Tom and Frank. Tom and Sully had spent the day refreshing the grounds and rounding up trash. Maggie was having a beer, feet up on the porch rail.

A hiker came into view from the north. He'd obviously been on the trail awhile. He was dirty and sporting a beard. His cheeks above the beard were apple red. He had a walking stick that looked like something fashioned out of a knotty branch.

"Lookit that," Sully said.

"Looks like he could use a cold one," Tom said.

"Wonder how many miles he logged," Frank said. "He's been gone almost a month, ain't he?"

Maggie sat up in her chair, feet off the rail. She leaned forward and squinted. *Could it be?* She stood and the hiker waved.

"Reckon I'm gonna be cooking my own dinner tonight," Sully said.

Maggie put her beer on the table and went down the porch steps. She walked toward him, at first thinking it might not be him. He was barely recognizable. She walked a little faster. He dropped his stick and shrugged off his backpack, letting it fall to the ground, and she broke into a run. So now all those guys on the porch knew everything, knew that he meant so much to her, knew she'd been missing him madly. When she reached him she threw her arms around his neck and almost knocked him over.

He kissed her as he lifted her off the ground.

"Damn, you feel good," he said. "Miss me?"

"I was so busy I hardly noticed you were gone."

He laughed. "I'm going to need a ride to Leadville to pick up my truck."

She pulled away from him just a little bit. "It's not there," she said. "I looked and I—"

He grinned. "It's there."

"Why didn't you just get it on your way?" she asked.

"I didn't want to get off the trail when this was closer. Besides, I knew you'd give me a ride. And it has to be soon—there's nothing clean in my pack."

"You're pretty ripe," she noted, wrinkling her nose. "Good hike?"

"I'll tell you all about it," he said. "But can I have a beer first?"

"Sure."

He grabbed her hand and his backpack, letting her have the walking stick. "Come on, then. I bet I can clear the porch without hardly trying."

"You gave up shaving," she said, leaning into him a little bit.

"Just for a week or ten days. Once I started south, I didn't bother."

"How far did you go?"

"Not so far. Couple of weeks north with a stop or two, ten days south, no stops. Twenty-six days since I left. I was into Wyoming."

"Did you run into wildlife?" she asked.

"Here and there. Lots of cows and deer. I heard wild-life. Coyotes, for sure. And wolves. I wanted to go far-ther north to see what was up there, but I couldn't."

"Oh? Why not?"

"You were here," he said. "It was time to get back."

"Hmm. I wondered if maybe I'd just get a postcard. If that…"

"You've been let down a lot, I think. Well, join the

club. Let's get that beer and I'll treat the boys on the porch to some high-test body odor."

"Really, you've been working on it for a while. I think I'll borrow Sully's truck to go to Leadville. I like the way the inside of my car smells."

"You looked for my truck in Leadville, did you?"

"Not really," she said. "I might've glanced around. I was working on changing my life while you were gone. I have big plans. I'm thinking of joining a hospital ship, doing surgery for those in need and without resources, having a long, magnificent affair with a brilliant, hot Australian doctor."

"Is that so? You haven't gone back to work, I take it," he said.

"That's a matter of opinion. I've been working my tail off."

"Ah, that's what I saw when I got here," he said. "That was you working."

Maggie allowed him only one beer, though he snatched a second while following her to the house. She raided Sully's closet and found sweatpants, a T-shirt and pair of socks for him, and he had a pair of rubber shower sandals in his pack, something he put on his feet when he got out of his hiking boots at the end of every day on the trail. She pushed him into the shower and said, "We'll talk about the truck tomorrow. Want me to throw your dirty clothes in the wash?"

"They might have to be burned," he said. "God, these thru-hikers must be evil smelling by the time they make the Canada border."

"Are you going to shave?" she asked.

"That depends. How sexy do you find the beard?"

"I'll get you a new razor and some shaving cream," she said. "I'll meet you back at the store. Sully said he'd throw some burgers on the grill for you."

Maggie was sitting at the bar, waiting for him. She smiled, pleased with the improvement. "Better," she said. "Hungry?"

"For real food, you bet." He sat on the stool beside her. "I spent half my childhood camping but I realized, I've never been on a long trek alone. I lost four toenails and my feet are now extra ugly."

"I hear the toenail stories from everyone who comes through," she said. "Were you lonely?"

"I was, but I was also amazed by the whole thing. I ran into people. They let you hike with them for a while, but it's every man for himself. Sometimes I camped near other people, but we didn't wait for each other. We exchanged trail news—where there was a snake, where there's water, where there's an alternative to the water source shown on the map. One guy had wolves curious around his camp. No bears. I saw elk but at a great distance. It's very beautiful. I can see why some people are driven by the need to conquer the trail, why they think of it as a religious experience."

"Do you feel the need for a lot more religion?" she asked.

"I think I've had enough for now," he said. "Part of me didn't think I'd last a whole week, another part wondered if I might not be able to stop until I'd gone all the way."

"What made you stop?" she asked.

"I was done," he said with a shrug. "I turned around

in the middle of the trail, in the middle of the day and started back."

Sully came in from the back porch and put a plate with a burger on it in front of Cal. He produced little packs of ketchup, mustard and mayo.

"Sully, this is great. I promise after I eat and get a little rest, you won't wait on me again. By the way, is there a cabin free? Maggie's holding my truck and camper hostage."

"There's room in the house," he said. "Maggie, you want a burger?"

"Thanks, Dad," she said.

"I'd be happy to share my fish and broccoli with you," Sully said.

"Normally I'd jump right on that, but since Cal just got back, I'll have a burger with him." Then she smiled sweetly.

"Maggie, I shouldn't impose. I can pitch my tent…"

"It's all right, I'll take the couch tonight," she said. She smiled at him. "You need your rest."

"Hmm," he said, biting into the burger, unable to wait. He craved solid, meaty food. He was thinking he might need her even more. Hungry and depleted as he was, he'd trade the burger and the beer just to crawl into bed next to her.

Sully gave Maggie her burger, then stomped out with a huff of displeasure. He'd always been a red-meat man, so he had told Cal. Lots of red meat. Daily. Not to mention potatoes slathered in butter. And he loved vegetables…with plenty of salt. This new heart-healthy diet was taking its toll on his mood.

Cal, forgetting he hadn't spoken aloud while he was

thinking of all he'd trade for a naked romp with Maggie, spoke. "I'm commando, you know."

"I assumed so, since I didn't provide any of Sully's tighty whities."

"God," he said, putting down the burger for a second. "I think I'm delirious. I was thinking about how I'd trade the burger and beer for a night up against you."

"Relax, Cal. Enjoy your burger. After we close up here we'll watch a little TV. Remember TV?" she asked, lifting a slimly arched brow.

"Vaguely," he said. "You're beautiful, Maggie."

"It's a mirage," she said, laughing.

"No, I'm seeing you. I told you about my hike. Tell me what you did while I was gone."

"Besides the usual? My stepfather showed up here one day, out of the blue. Alone. I wish you'd been here— he was so sweet. He sneaked down here without telling my mother because she never lets us have a conversation. When you're rested I'll tell you stories about Walter. He's an interesting guy. The opposite of Sully yet he had a major influence on my life, my education."

Cal stuffed himself. Sully came in with his own plate, which he ate at the bar. A couple of campers stopped in for milk and eggs and Maggie jumped up to take their money. The ice maker on the back porch rattled and clunked. The front door was propped open and laughter could be heard as the sun slowly became lost behind the mountains.

This must be such a happy place in summer when families come here to play, to be together, to get away from their stress and worry, Cal thought.

He was in a daze and he knew it. He was vaguely aware that Maggie and Sully were talking to customers, putting things away. Maggie was sweeping behind the counter. He got up and took his plate to the kitchen. Maggie leaned her broom up against the counter and took his plate.

"Just go over to the house," she said. "Turn on the TV and put your feet up. You're a basket case. I'll be over in a while."

"I'm sorry, Maggie. I pushed it kind of hard the past couple of days. You should just give me a blanket and I'll sleep in the—"

"I think Sully would be disappointed if you didn't accept. He's missed you." She pushed him out the back door. "Try not to get lost."

Beau was lying on the back porch. "I'm going to lie down," Cal said to the dog. Beau jumped to his feet and began wagging his tail. "Okay, then," he said. "You and me, on the couch."

Maggie and Sully essentially closed down the store, but they sat out on the porch in front. They watched over the grounds while the moon cast a glow over the lake. This was the perfect end to a perfect day, in Maggie's mind. Even though Cal was in the house, even though she'd told him she'd be along soon, she felt no urgency, but a sense of comfort, of all being right in her world.

When she visited Sully's while she was in med school or residency she might study all day but come evening, they'd eat a burger or barbecued chicken and sit on the porch after sunset. From here they could hear the conversations, children running and playing, clattering of dishes from the various campsites; they could see the small fires that dotted the landscape by tents and campers or at the edge of the beach. On some nights

Sully would wander through the grounds to make sure everyone had safe fires, contained at all times of the year. A wildfire was a nightmare come to life in the Colorado mountains.

"Are you glad he came home?" Sully asked.

Maggie laughed softy. "This isn't home for him, Dad. But yes, I'm glad he came back."

"You were missing him," Sully said.

"I was just about over him. I was building a new life in my head and it had nothing to do with him!" That brilliant Australian doctor, however, bore an uncanny resemblance to Cal. "I was a little worried sometimes," she went on. "People can get lost, sick, hurt, have conflicts with unfriendly wildlife, have problems with un-friendly *people*! He was gone a long time. I assumed he had moved on. He admitted he's been a wanderer."

"Nah, I don't think so. I think he's looking for some-thing, that's all. He's respectful. He won't just take off without an explanation."

"He did once," she said.

"So far," Sully said. "He said from the start he was planning a long hike once the weather warmed. You like him a lot, don't you?"

"I think you know," she said. "I might've been a little obvious when I saw him come down the road."

"That's okay, you know. You can like him. I admit, I got a little attached to him," Sully said. "But we gotta talk. I don't want him working like he did, for free and all."

"Maybe he's just visiting, Dad. Maybe he's here for a few days and then will be on his way again."

"You get that impression?" Sully asked.

Maggie was afraid to answer. No, she hadn't thought,

by anything he said or did, that he was dropping in to get laid and then would be moving on. "He wasn't very specific about his plans, Dad." However, he had said he was coming back to *her*.

"Well, I get the impression he could be hanging around," Sully said. "That be okay by you?" he asked.

"Well, I guess. I'm hanging around. But my way isn't as clear as when I got here. I was taking a break, yet I'm still here. I've been trying to figure out what I'm going to do next. More specifically, I'd better figure out who I am and where I belong."

"Walter gave you some things to think about," Sully said. "Good."

"What did you and Walter talk about while I was walking down by the lake?"

"Oh, you know, the usual. Weather. Broncos. How you're a work in progress."

"Is that so?" she asked somewhat indignantly.

"And pretty much on schedule. We used to call it a midlife crisis," he said. "What do we call it now?"

"What are you talking about, Sully?"

"You know—the day you wake up and see that even though you been busy every second there's a whole lot missing outta your life. I was about your age when I decided it was time to get married." He shook his head. "I don't regret it but I should'a thought that one through a little better."

"Well, then there was me…"

"That's why I have no regrets. Isn't that just about what happened, Maggie? You wake up one morning and say to yourself, something's gotta change here?"

"I don't think it was quite that abrupt…"

"Everybody's got a different bottom," he said. "But a

midlife crisis used to have a lot to do with seeing forty staring you in the eye and asking yourself some important questions about whether it's time to get that old."

Oh yeah. And for a woman it has a lot to do with her eggs.

It had seemed to Maggie that it had been more like a boulder rolling down a steep hill, picking up speed as it went, rather than a sudden explosion. But it must have seemed abrupt to everyone around her—the rush of emails, the call to her neighbor to keep an eye on her house, she never did call Sully, and calling Phoebe when she was on her way out of town, headed south, her car full of luggage. She heard her mother saying, "Have you lost your mind? What do you mean you're taking an indefinite leave? You don't study for twenty-five straight years and then just walk away!"

Her bottom? She'd been building to it. She loved her work, but she wanted more. She wanted a family. She wanted a permanent partner, not some convenient boyfriend. She remembered that night with Walter in the hospital, suddenly thinking she wanted to be that doctor, that single person everyone depended on. And she'd been right—it was as if she was made for it. And then, when the pressure and frustration became overwhelming and she needed relief, she was alone. Even the short-lived joy and excitement of having a baby grow inside her was suddenly gone.

"It was both," she told her father. "It was a slow, steady build and then it was all of a sudden. I was having irrational thoughts, feeling so lonely, wondering if I'd be alone my entire life. You ever feel like that, Sully?"

He laughed softly. "Well, I got married all of a sudden, to a woman I'd known for three weeks and couldn't hardly get along with. I don't know much about all those deep feelings—I never bothered to check what I was feeling. But I know I did some things that I can't explain and they were way out of character for me. I married Phoebe and brought her to a country store to live in an old house with my elderly father. What do you think?"

"God, I hope panic attacks don't run in the family," she said. "If it's any comfort, I haven't felt that lonely since I got here."

"Well, we each have one short, crappy marriage to our credit. I'd like to think I'd have somehow got you, anyway, even if I'd accidentally married the right woman, but, Maggie, everything has a higher purpose. Walter's right—you just slow down a spell and try to remember why you decided to spend a hundred years getting ready to do brain surgery."

"I'll think about that," she said. "Let's walk over to the house."

When they got to the house, Cal was stretched out on the couch, dead to the world, the TV still on. Beau, lying on the floor beside him, perked up in greeting.

Maggie sighed and went to wake him. She jostled him, then pulled on his arm. "Come on," she said. "I'm putting you to bed." She led him to her room and he flopped on the bed, facedown.

She went back to the living room. "It's okay," she told her father. "I can take the couch. And he owes me."

"There's that bed in the loft," Sully said.

"That is the worst bed ever built. I think you pulled it off a trash heap. There's a spring sticking out of the mattress. Just go to bed. I'll turn the volume down on the TV," she said. "Sweet dreams."

* * *

Cal was having a lovely dream and in a half-conscious state he decided it was brought on by sleeping in Maggie's fragrant sheets. He felt her naked flesh under his hand, sliding down her flat belly, headed for the promised land. Then he felt her lips on his neck and came awake to the delicious sensation of her soft skin against his. He moved just enough so that her lips found his and he pulled her against him. He'd awakened sometime in the night and shed his T-shirt and he was glad. Her breasts were pressed against his bare chest, her nipples branding him. He moaned in appreciation.

"When did you decide you had to have me?" he whispered.

"I don't know. An hour ago, maybe."

"You're completely naked. Thank you."

"It didn't seem to disturb your sleep much," she said.

"I'm not sure what woke me up, your flagrant groping or this raging hard-on." He ran a hand through her hair. "I don't have a single condom. Not much need for them on a hike..."

"I have a couple," she said. "I stole them from the store while you were showering."

That had the effect of making him harder, if possible. He covered her mouth in a searing kiss and brought her over him, grabbing her butt with his hands and pressing her against him. "I must have balls of cast iron," he whispered. "I'm going to do a girl in her daddy's house..."

"If you're shy..."

"Don't even think about it," he said. "There's no stopping this now. Do you know how long I've waited for this?"

"Almost to the minute. Assuming you've been faithful…"

"You spoiled me, Maggie. I couldn't think about anything but you all the way back. I can't wait for you to wrap those long legs around me…"

"We should get you out of these sweats, then…"

She lifted just a bit and he slid them over his hips and off.

"Oh boy," Maggie said, giving him a stroke. "We better take care of this." She rolled away to get a condom and while she was fussing with the package, his hands were exploring. His fingers were stroking her, sliding into her.

"Beautiful," he said, feeling her deeply. "I'm not the only one in a bad way. You need me to take care of you, too. Gimme that thing," he said taking the condom from her and rolling it on. "God, I hope Sully is a sound sleeper."

"Shhhh," she said, and then she laughed.

"I had to get a giggler…" He rolled her onto her back, spread her knees and found the way home. "God, that's sweet."

"And it's going to be fast," she said. "Think you can keep up?"

He gave a couple of deep thrusts and felt her instantly tighten around him. He buried his face in her neck, ground his teeth and held on, letting her come. When he felt her begin to relax beneath him he found her nipple with his mouth and teased it with his tongue. Then he drew it into his mouth to suck. His fingers inched down to work her a little bit and he knew exactly what to do. He stroked, sucked, pumped and she froze, clenching again. He let it go, pulsing until his brain was empty. The orgasm washed over him in a warm haze and he glazed over. A moment later he lifted his head and looked into her glassy eyes, saw her slight smile.

"That was easy," he said with a smile. "Feel better?"

"For now," she said.

"Have I mentioned how much I enjoy that little trick you have there?" he asked. "Two for the price of one. Do you have any idea how good that feels?"

She smiled. "I believe I do. Could the princess do that?"

"Don't talk about my previous exploits while we're naked and satisfied. Let me just say, she gets an A for effort, but that was predictable. We didn't really mean anything to each other. The difference is always obvious."

"That sounds suspiciously like you're saying you care about me," she ventured.

"Maggie, it is not a secret. Not in the least. And you care about me."

"Oh yes, and damn, it's scary. I want to ask you a question right now, while you're compromised, while I have you captive, because I know you can't lie to me. Are you going to be leaving me a lot? Coming back sometimes to get laid?"

He ran his fingers through her hair. He shook his head. "I don't think that'll be enough for me. I kind of like your idea of keeping me captive."

Hard times arouse an instinctive desire for authenticity.

—Coco Chanel

CHAPTER 10

It was interesting to Cal that after all he'd been through in life he should face Sully with a case of nerves and a boyish blush. He should be well beyond such self-consciousness. Life was a little short for that.

"Relax," Sully said after taking one look at him. "This might come as a shock but you're not her first boyfriend."

His blush deepened.

"I have to get you on the payroll," Sully said. "How long are you staying?"

"How cold does it get here in winter?"

"Son, the average elevation in this county is over 5,000 feet. Leadville sits at over nine thousand with the highest airport in the world. Or at least the US. That mountain behind us there is 14,500. The best skiing in the country surrounds us. It's cold. And in case you haven't ever been here in winter, it's beautiful. The lake freezes and folks go ice sailing—it's so fast, your head'll spin. And things aren't too busy—no tents at all, just full cabins, campers, maybe a couple of RV's. Cross-country skiing, mainly."

"I hate being cold," Cal said. He cleared his throat. "I care about Maggie."

"And, if I heard correctly, you'd like to help out around here. Stay busy?"

"Sully, how about a cabin? So I can have some… privacy?" And again, his neck felt warm. He ducked his head and muttered, "Jesus…" He was a man who had defended hardened criminals at trial and he never broke a sweat. He felt ridiculous.

"I guess you think I was never your age? My cabins are pretty much booked with just a day here and there we have an empty one. No chance for you to settle in one this summer. But, I got a little behind around here, stuff I usually get done in March before it all starts still needs doing. There's things that Tom and his kids don't have the time for or can't handle and I'm just getting back in my swing. Stuff I'm talking about takes a little muscle."

"We'll get it all done, Sully. But, if there's no cabin…"

"Don't worry about it. I never even heard you last night, starting around three…" He grinned. "You're a nice guy. Maggie's a grown woman. I make no judgment. Besides, after what I saw her do with that shotgun, she doesn't need me to run interference for her."

"All right, look…" Cal rubbed a hand across the back of his neck. "I'm not taking your money. I'll earn my keep."

"And then some," Sully said. He smiled slyly.

Cal supposed he'd adjust. The problem wasn't having sex with Maggie in her father's house while her father slept in the room across the hall; it was doing that in her father's house without being married to her, with no plans to marry her. It was a great dichotomy, considering the way Cal grew up. The weird things his parents were into, not the least of which was his father's dope, and everything from nudism to Wicca, did not foster this conservative thinking. Of course none of their *interests* were as challenging as those long stretches of time Jed thought the government was monitoring his thoughts or, more fun yet, thinking he had been personally chosen by Jesus to be the next savior of the world. But conservative worries about whether or not a person was married? It never came up.

How I ever got out of that nuthouse with a working brain is a miracle, he thought.

"There's one thing," Sully said. "Sit tight." He went into the back room and came back with an envelope. "This came for you."

Cal looked at the return address of the Colorado Supreme Court. He smiled. "Thanks, Sully. I've had an eye out for this. It was nice to know if it came while I was on the trail you'd hold it for me."

"You in some kind of trouble?"

"Trouble?" He laughed. "Oh no, Sully. Just a little legal business. Never mind the Supreme Court envelope, this came from a clerk. Sully, when you're in trouble they send the police and handcuffs, not a letter. This is a license."

"For the truck?" he asked.

"No," Cal said. "No, I've worked in the court system. Been a while now, but if I need a job in Colorado it can't happen without registering and getting permission. The courts don't readily trust out-of-towners."

"You mean like a court reporter or paralegal or something like that?"

"Something like that. I told you, I've had a lot of jobs, from stocking shelves and picking vegetables to putting on a tie and shuffling paperwork."

"But you're hanging around here?"

"That okay by you?" Cal asked. "I like the pace. And I like Maggie."

"You gonna give a better explanation about that license to her?"

"Absolutely. But it's not urgent. I'm planning to work for you now."

"Listen, she doesn't need anyone to protect her, but I'm her father. I'd hate to have to ask Tom to beat you up." He rubbed his chest with his knuckles. "If I have to do it, I'll just shoot you."

Cal laughed, folded the unopened letter and stuffed it in his back pocket. "Sully, I don't want her feelings hurt any more than you do. You know she's going to go back to work, right?"

"She talking about that?"

"Not yet," he said. "But it's early. She just needs a little time to get her perspective. Her business was kicking her ass. She needs a breather. This seems like a great place for that. Maybe you should worry about my feelings getting hurt."

"Who's going to hurt your feelings?" Maggie said as she came through the back door.

"Hopefully no one. Want to take me to get my truck? Sully's got a long honey-do list for me."

"Sure. You ready to go?"

"How about a couple of coffees for the road?" Cal asked Sully. "Oh, and thanks for the pants and shirt."

Cal thought about explaining more of his history to Maggie on the ride to Leadville. It was complicated. Being a lawyer was certainly nothing to be ashamed of. At least in most circles. The fact was, he hadn't had any intention of petitioning for a Colorado license, at least not until Maggie said she had legal troubles. A lawyer in his position, licensed in Michigan, couldn't even give advice or answer questions in Colorado without being liable for practicing law without a license. Sully could tell his daughter she ought to get a better lawyer and it was perfectly all right. Cal could tell her the same thing and be fined, or worse. In fact, he couldn't even say, "I might be able to help you with this problem." His only reason for extending his license to Colorado was so she could discuss her case with him if she chose to.

And of course there was other stuff that went hand in hand with being a lawyer. His marriage, his wife's illness and death, his *role* in her death... He was an officer of the court. He would not be caught in a lie. No one had ever asked him for the details of Lynne's death and he didn't volunteer any information. Before he confided to anyone, there would have to be a vital reason and a lot more trust. He wouldn't, for example, marry again without full disclosure. And although he was crazy about Maggie, he wasn't seeing a second marriage.

He'd get around to telling her more about his recent past. But not just yet. Not until there was a compelling reason.

"What were you and Sully talking about? It sounded like two men talking about feelings," Maggie asked.

"He warned me, very nicely, not to hurt you. I said I was as serious about your feelings as he was. He threatened to shoot me. But I assume Sully is mostly talk."

"Mostly," she said, flashing him a grin.

Cal retrieved his truck and pop-up camper, put the camper behind the storage shed and parked the truck next to Maggie's car. He started working through Sully's list. He hadn't been kidding about getting a little behind. Cal scraped out old grout in the public showers, bathroom and laundry room, regrouted, painted the building inside and out, scoured the whole thing until it was like new. He painted and covered the porches and stairs on both the store and house with rain repellant. He graded the driveway and parking areas, cleaned out grills, collected trash, raked campsites, cleaned cabins, changed and washed the linens, tended the garden and helped in the store.

It crossed his mind Sully was trying to wear him out so he'd be too damned tired to have sex with Maggie. *Ha! No such luck, Sully!*

Maggie was irresistible and he felt like a teenager again, always ready. Maggie was also always ready.

"You're killing me," he whispered to her deep in the night.

"You'll be fine," she whispered back.

"Sully gives me shit about my nights in his house," Cal said. "Subtle innuendo. He thinks he's very clever. But the miracle is that I can still get it up after a day of doing chores for him and letting him needle me."

"And you do so very adequately. I know about these things. I'm a doctor."

When Cal had been back at Sullivan's Crossing for about a week, Maggie took off for the day to meet with her lawyers in Denver. It was a long day so she planned to stay overnight. She met Jaycee for sushi, something they used to do regularly. Then she had a nostalgic visit with her house.

It was a great single woman's house, large enough to give her plenty of room, small enough to hug her when she was there. Even though her schedule hadn't allowed her a great deal of time at home, she had gone to great trouble and considerable expense in decorating. Her furniture was contemporary and comfortable, dark walnut tables and accents, her sectional cozy and deep velour.

She had a wonderful mattress that she had missed, but she missed Cal more. Sometime in the middle of the night she went to the guest room bed and found it slept just as well.

When Maggie returned to Sullivan's Crossing she was driving a rental truck that she could return in Leadville and she was towing her car. In the truck was a thick area rug and the furniture from her guest bedroom. She brought a bookcase and reading lamp. Sully already had an old leather chair and ottoman that had been his father's—it was a beautiful, comfortable relic.

"What's this?" Cal asked.

"We're moving downstairs. Into Sully's rumpus room."

"Will he know everything we're doing if we're down there?" Cal asked.

"Only if he has a nanny-cam."

Cal's eyes lit up with pleasure. "Oh boy. We're going to rumpus our brains out!"

Cal was quickly absorbed into summer at the crossing. Guests and campers greeted him by name. He asked kids if they were having fun, checked to see if there was anything he could do for their parents. He worked with Tom on the care of the grounds and did any heavy lifting that had to be done if he caught it before Sully did. He also got better acquainted with the neighbors and friends who stopped by. People who worked at other campgrounds on the lake liked to grab a beer or drink at Sully's store; first responders dropped by now and then to see how things were going, get the latest gossip, grab a beer if they were off duty.

"Tom's got a lot on his plate. I can take on his Wednesday jobs," he suggested to Sully. "I can keep up with the grounds."

"I couldn't do that to Tom," Sully said. "He supports four kids on his own. He does every job he can manage and he's a search-and-rescue volunteer besides. He depends on his paychecks. And now he's helping Jackson with college."

Cal was impressed—this responsibility to each other people around the crossing shared. His own family was barely capable of that. They checked on each other and one would think, given the unbalanced lifestyle in which they'd grown up, they would cling to each other for survival, but it seemed to go the other way. Once they broke free, their contact was steady but minimal. It was every man for himself. He liked his brother-in-law, Sedona's husband, and his niece and nephew were great, but they didn't see each other often. Dakota, being a military man, wasn't easy to keep up with; he had deployed three times in the past ten years. If they didn't all have cell phones, they would hardly be in touch at all. They didn't exactly have family reunions.

"Family reunion?" Sedona had once said. "Doesn't that sound like a day in hell?"

"Nah," Cal had replied. "Just a day at the loony bin."

Summer brought Sullivan's Crossing to life—vacationers abounded. The camps across the lake were full; there were fishing boats and Jet Skis all over the water. The occasional Boy Scout or teen camp counselor escaped to Sully's to get away from their kids.

Hikers passed through in a steady stream—some

who had made the trek south from Boulder, some who had been out for a short time, some who had come all the way from the Mexican border and had already logged close to a thousand miles. They usually straggled in at the end of the day. They had a variety of reasons for taking to the trail—a cancer survivor who had a lot of living to do, a professor who was documenting his hike, a divorcée getting her confidence back, a couple of ministers who wanted to experience the CDT for the spiritual messages, married teachers doing as much of the hike as they could over summer and hoping to get across three states. They sometimes recognized each other from the trail or from names in trail logs they'd read along the way. They gathered around picnic tables, on the porch or the dock. Remembering all too well coming off the trail, Cal began grilling burgers for hikers. He kept ground beef and buns on hand just for that purpose—burgers and chips. No charge.

"You're gonna go broke that way," Sully groused.

"I can spend my money any way I like," Cal said.

Later that night Maggie told him that Sully had been doing the same thing for years. Most hikers weren't destitute at all and traveled with their credit cards. They'd leave a nice tip behind, more than covering the cost. Cal and Maggie both loved talking to them, watching them open the packages they sent themselves, hearing them describe the almost religious experience they had from taking a hot shower.

Cal particularly enjoyed watching families together, couples with two or three kids who camped in big family-sized tents and stayed for anywhere from a few days to more than a week. Sometimes they were on the move, seeing as many of Colorado's national parks as possible. They usually staked out a picnic table and grill for their meals and played cards or games at night and went hiking, rock climbing, boating or fishing by day. Cal had always expected to have a family like one of these, a boy and girl, a family having fun together in the healthy outdoors.

Cal was at peace with the place. Since he'd grown up with no security or schedule, always some new agenda or scheme, he fell in love with the routine. Mornings he used Sully's kitchen for breakfast, though Sully rose at dawn and headed for the store. Then he'd have coffee on the porch with Frank, Sully, and often Tom who would come by on his way to some job—usually a handyman project for a local home owner. Sully would let Cal know what he wanted done that day, Frank would head to his ranch to give his sons advice, everyone got to work. The end of the day found him back on the same porch, talking with hikers, having a cold drink.

He hated to go inside at the end of the day unless it was raining, which was seldom this time of year. He would sit outside with Sully and Maggie until the sun was well set. When he retired with Maggie to the rumpus room, he took at least an hour in that old leather chair, feet up, nose in a book. There was a bookstore in Leadville he'd visited a couple of times and he had a nice library forming on that bookcase of Maggie's.

"What are you reading?" she asked.

"I'm doing a lot more rereading than reading these days. Isn't that what you do on vacation?"

"As hard as you work all day, this is hardly a vacation. What are you rereading?"

"Great Expectations."

"You're the only theme park employee I've ever known who reads classics."

"Literature major," he reminded her.

"Why reread now?"

He closed his book. "Sometimes it takes me back in time, remembering who I was the first time I experienced a great book. It reminds me where I thought I was headed and how life changed and changed me. When I first read this I was a kid—it was one of my mother's favorites. I thought I might be a famous playwright. Or at least a rich novelist. I changed my mind and direction a few times. At least."

Cal didn't explain how much he liked the language of exceptional storytelling because in a way *he* was a storyteller, but he'd done it in court. He never made things up or lied, but he offered *possibilities*. Enough to cloud a jury's decision. Enough to confuse human nature. Sometimes he'd complicate an already complex process—that was plotting. That was what the greats of literature did—they got their characters up a tree and threw rocks at them.

He thought again about explaining things to her, who he was, what baggage he was bringing to the relationship. After all, they were playing house in Sully's basement. Every time he thought about it, it felt a little bit heavier. Eventually he'd unload it. But tonight was not the best night. Maggie was getting ready for bed and other things came to his mind.

He didn't explain himself but he did ask her if she wanted to talk about the lawsuit, the case against her. "Eventually," she said. "Not yet. Frankly, I get tired of thinking about it and talking about it is even worse. Thanks for offering."

Wednesday brought Tom for grounds keeping. Cal stocked shelves before getting out the rake and edger to help. Maggie, he noticed, was in the garden, which was beginning to flourish. They were already getting their salads from the backyard and the first tomatoes were coming in. At lunchtime he was headed with Tom back to the store. Maggie was on the porch with a bottled water and a lot of mud on her shoes and knees. She wore a ball cap with a short ponytail pulled through the back and just a look at her, all a mess from gardening, created carnal thoughts he looked forward to acting out later.

"You've been farming," he said.

"How could you tell? Hey, Tom," she added.

"We're going to get some lunch," Cal said. "You want anything?"

"Yes, exactly. Anything. And a green tea?"

"Coming up."

Tom and Cal returned immediately cradling wrapped sandwiches, a bag of chips, pickles, hard-boiled eggs, drinks. They put everything on the table and Cal pulled napkins and a packet of salt from his pocket. A couple of campers with a small ice chest passed by the porch and yelled out, "Hi, Cal. Hi, Tom. Hi, Maggie."

Maggie unwrapped her sandwich and froze. She was staring at the drive. "Oh God," she said.

Pulling up to the store was a shiny BMW convertible, the top down. Inside the car was a woman with dark glasses and an elaborate scarf covering her head.

"What?" Cal asked, his mouth full.

"Phoebe," she said dismally. "My mother."

"Really," Cal said slowly, smiling.

"Oops, I just remembered something," Tom said,

gathering up all his food in his big arms and fleeing the porch, into the store.

"Would you like me to leave you two alone?" Cal asked.

"It really doesn't matter. But if you stay, I'll introduce you as my boyfriend."

"This could surpass interesting. After all you've told me about—"

Maggie stood. "Mother, what are you doing here?"

Cal also stood and although he'd just given his hands a good washing in the kitchen, he wiped them on his khaki shorts.

Phoebe proceeded up the steps to the porch. "Is it enough that I've hardly seen you in three months?"

"I saw you a couple of weeks ago and called you almost every day. I'm not in Denver. It's quite a drive."

"I managed quite nicely, except that last bit. Messy, rotten road. Slow." Then she looked pointedly at Cal, waiting. She was probably five foot two and slight. She was attractive; her scarf, pushed back, revealed red hair and a beautiful, youthful face. Fifty-nine, Maggie had said. Dressed pretty well for a road trip, designer slacks and jacket, pumps... *Pumps?* To a campground? She was spit-shined, polished, her jewelry tasteful and expensive. Just her watch was worth a month's salary. A month of his *old* salary.

He lost his nerve. She scared him to death. He couldn't help with this.

"How do you do, Mrs....?"

"Lancaster," she supplied. "And you are?"

"I'm Cal Jones. I work here. I work for Sully. I'd, ah... I'll leave you and Maggie. Can I get you anything? How about lunch?"

"Thank you, that would be fine. Is there something like a salad? Undressed, of course. If it's dressed, skip it and get me fruit. And a San Pellegrino? Glass glass, if you please."

"I'll check," he said, gathering up his food.

"Oh, and, boy? A rag to wipe the table?"

Cal kept his eyes downcast. He couldn't meet her gaze. His lips twitched. She called a thirty-seven-year-old criminal defense attorney of some moderate fame and sterling reputation *boy*.

He disappeared as quickly as possible.

Maggie sat and left Phoebe to choose a chair. "Very nice, Mother. His name is Cal, not boy. Where were you raised? And the table is perfectly clean, I wiped it myself before I sat down. Now, what is it that brings you here, given you haven't been here in, how long? Thirty years?"

"I kept hoping you'd visit soon because I have something to ask you that I didn't want to ask over the phone, but you don't seem to have the time to— Oh my dear God, your *hands*!"

Maggie splayed her fingers and examined her hands. Kind of a mess. Chipped nails, calluses, damaged cuticles. "Garden hands," she explained.

"And what have you done with your hair?"

"Actually, nothing at all."

"In *three months*?" Phoebe asked, clearly astonished.

"A little more when you get down to it." She picked up her sandwich and took a bite. "I'm so amazed you're here."

"Well, Walter said it was quite a nice place and that you were doing very well."

"So, he told you he was here?"

"Of course. Really, Maggie, not exactly the lap of luxury, now, is it? How can you relax in a place like this?"

Maggie laughed and wiped her mouth with her napkin. "This may be difficult for you to understand, Mother, but this is slightly more relaxing than standing in surgery for seven hours, up to my elbows in brains. Now, ask what you came to ask."

Phoebe sighed. "It's that time again, Maggie. Missy Stanhope is having her summer luncheon gala. This year she's raising money for cancer research. I had hoped you'd be back in Denver by now but never mind that. You'll go with me, of course. After you've had a decent color and cut and a manicure."

"I don't know, Mother. I might have to bow out this year. Too many complications."

"There are always complications, Maggie! Many more complications when you were working and on call all the time! I don't ask much."

"Yes, but what you do ask is always hefty." She took another bite and swallowed. "Have you ever asked yourself why a seventy-year-old woman goes by the name Missy? Come on."

"She's a lovely person and I didn't pick her silly name!"

Missy was a wonderful person, but Maggie knew that wasn't why Phoebe had chosen her for a friend. Her friends all had tons of money, all belonged to the same club, all played bridge and golf and had luncheons and participated in fund-raisers—an exact replica of Phoebe's life back in Chicago. Only now Walter had more time to participate. And most of the women in Phoebe's circle skied, which Phoebe did not. Phoebe also did not do volunteer work. She found it depressed her.

"You're looking good, Mother. Is that a new color?" Maggie asked, touching her own head to indicate Phoebe's hair.

"A little darker on the red. What do you think?"

"I think it's very attractive. Listen, I'm going to have to think about this luncheon. I like some of your friends, but right now it's awkward—I don't want to talk about my ex-partners, the lawsuit, my leave from work."

"I think it's better to be seen," Phoebe advised. "Be seen looking perfectly fine and then say you're not allowed to discuss any of that on advice of counsel, but you're confident it's going to work out just fine."

"I'm not confident of that, as a matter of fact," Maggie said.

"Say so, anyway, and if you're worried, you should talk to Walter."

"Mother, I have talked to Walter. He's given me all the advice he can and helped me choose an excellent lawyer, but it's very messy. I'd rather not."

"Please, Maggie! My friends are starting to miss you, too! I look forward to these events you attend with me. You're my best friend."

Phoebe should raise her standards for best friends, Maggie thought. She'd attended about a half dozen of these mucky-muck affairs with her mother because it was so important to Phoebe, but she didn't enjoy them much. There were some nice women involved in these events and fund-raisers, but none Maggie would choose as friends. Phoebe was only involved because she thought these women were elite and important and she wanted to be a part of a group like that. She had a hard time being around the baseborn, though she came from nothing. Maggie sighed.

Sully came onto the porch with a small tray bearing a salad in a plastic container, a packet of ranch dressing, a bottled water, glass glass and a beer. He put the tray down in front of his ex-wife. "This will have to do," he said, completely ignoring any greeting. Then he took a seat across from her. "How have you been, Phoebe?" he asked, taking the beer from the tray for himself.

"I'm well," she said. "Thank you for asking."

"Did you want to ask Sully how he's doing since heart surgery, Mother?" Maggie needled.

"I believe I'm up to date on everything, Maggie, since you and I talk regularly." She looked at Sully as she struggled to open her plastic salad. "I hope you're well, Harry."

She was the only person on earth who called him by his given name.

Phoebe managed to get the container open after a brief struggle and a few chunks of lettuce and the fork popped out onto the table. Out of habit, Maggie just scooped it away and arranged the meal for Phoebe, putting the fork beside the container and shaking out the densely folded napkin and snaking it onto her lap.

"Well," Phoebe said, moving the clumps of lettuce around a bit. "Walter said he enjoyed his visit to your camp."

"He told you?" Sully asked, surprised.

"Of course he told me! Why would you think otherwise? Do you think we have secrets from each other?"

"I meant no offense," Sully said, taking a long pull on his beer. "He said you thought he was playing golf," he added. "I thought that meant…"

"He's always playing golf!" Phoebe said.

"New hair color?" Sully asked her.

"My hair has always been red," she said.

"Was it red?" he asked. "I can't remember."

"Well, at your age, that's to be expected, isn't it?" Phoebe said. "Maybe if you weren't always headlong into the bottle—"

"Oh, Jesus," Maggie muttered, rubbing her temples.

"I haven't had a beer before five in the afternoon in at least twenty years," he said. "Hadn't felt the need until now."

"At least I don't have to point out where your sore spots are," Maggie said. "Be nice to each other or you'll be sent to your rooms."

"When will you be done with this hiatus?" Phoebe asked. "When will you be back in Denver?"

"I don't know. Not much longer."

"Leave her be, Phoebe. She hasn't had a proper vacation in years and she's burnt out. She can stay here as long as she likes. Don't bully her."

"I've been more relaxed since I've been here than I have been in years and that should make you happy, Mother."

"Of course your health and happiness are paramount. And I *don't* bully."

"Course not," Maggie said. She took a big bite of her pickle.

There was a loud burst of laughter somewhere in the campground and Maggie looked around. A man wearing a backpack but no clothes was coming down the trail. He had excellent hiking boots on his feet, a straw hat on his head and that was all. His thing was swaying in the breeze.

Maggie hadn't seen something like this in a long time. She covered her mouth to keep from bursting into laughter.

"Oh my hell," Sully swore, slamming down the beer and jumping to his feet. "I should shoot his pecker off! Doesn't that idiot know this is a family place?" And he charged down the steps toward the naked man.

Maggie started to laugh and slid down in her chair.

"Dear God," Phoebe said. "Maggie, you can't stay here! This is why I took you away. This is the bowels of hell!"

Just be what you are and speak from your guts and heart—it's all a man has.

—HUBERT HUMPHREY

CHAPTER 11

"You're a coward, that's what you are," Maggie told Cal.

"Don't be so hard on me. Tom ran for his life and he said he'd never even met the woman, just heard about her. I'm sure she's very nice but she just intimidated the hell out of me. So, what happened with the naked man?"

"Oh, he gave Sully some song and dance about being over-heated, taking off his shirt first, then his sweaty shorts, being dehydrated and confused and forgot to get dressed again before hitting camp. All bullshit, I'm sure."

They sat on low beach chairs by a little fire near the lake. Lots of small fires dotted the grounds, being enjoyed by campers. This was the first chance they'd had to talk since Phoebe's visit.

"Sully was occupied with him, dragging him out of sight of the other campers—not so many around at lunchtime—and out of sight of the porch. Just another loony-tune. They pop up regularly, though that's the first nudist I've seen. But I've heard naked hikers are seen out on the trails from time to time. If one of the forestry guys, a park ranger, sees one they throw the book at them. That was pretty brazen, walking into camp that way. Why anyone wants to hike naked is beyond me. Imagine the interesting places you could get a mosquito bite. And here's a little-known fact—they're never women."

"Exhibitionists," Cal said. "I bet it made your mother's day."

"She'll be talking about it for years, trust me. So then we had a little chat. Not too long. She wants me to go to a charity luncheon with her. She has these social obligations from time to time and in the past I've gone to some with her. They're not horrible and she likes to show me off, I think. My daughter the doctor, you know? When I'm in Denver I try to spend a little time with her. Sometimes I take her to lunch and endure a little shopping. It makes her happy and quiet. What intimidated you about her?"

"The very look on her face," he said. "Looked like she was here for a takedown."

"And you abandoned me? Some knight in shining armor you are!"

"You didn't ask me to stay. You said it made no difference!"

"Well, I think she was here for more than her need to corner me and convince me to go to her friend's charity luncheon. I think she wanted to see it again because Walter had been here and told her he enjoyed himself and that it was a nice place. It wasn't up to her standards, of course, which I think came as a relief to her. She'd die a thousand deaths if this had been an exclusive spa or something. She wants to see Sully as a country bumpkin, an idiot with no taste. She hates that I love his campground. It's been a thorn in her butt all my life."

"I'd love to meet this Walter," Cal said.

"I'm sure it'll be another thirty years before either of them will be back. They live in an entirely different world. But Walter isn't uppity. He's rich, of course—he not only comes from old money but is a highly respected neurosurgeon, but his gift is his passion. His patients have always been his priority. He's compassionate and brilliant, very soft-spoken and quietly powerful. Since I've known him, he makes the money and Phoebe spends it. And that works fine for him." She smiled at Cal. "Phoebe means well, I suppose, but she's shallow. She can't help it."

"Everyone can help it, Maggie," Cal said.

"She was poor growing up, she said. I don't know the details because to my memory we never had anything to do with her family, but clearly she plotted her escape from her roots. She fully intended to marry up, as they say. She started off with a tech school that would teach her what she needed to know to get a great job in a high-level corporate setting where she would meet men with money. She concentrated on beauty, intending to snag a rich husband. Sully was an accident."

"Oh?"

"I think he was working as a welder at the time they met. They met in a classy uptown bar in Chicago. He was a handsome, sexy guy, midthirties, had been a Green Beret, had been to war a couple of times, had medals, liked to have fun. She fell for him. He told her he was coming into a big property near Aspen and so she married him. She was twenty-two. He brought her here and knocked her up. It was all downhill from there."

Cal whistled. "Best laid plans..."

"She obviously played a better hand with Walter. Ohhh, I so hated him. They wouldn't let me see Sully for years. Of course that was Phoebe, but Walter went along with it. Later, much later, I came to like him. Then respect him. Now I'm more fond of Walter than of Phoebe. He's always been on my team. He tried to talk me out of marrying my husband. I should've listened to him."

Cal came to attention. "You were married?"

"Didn't I tell you that?" She laughed a little, slightly embarrassed. "I apologize. It was so insignificant. Sergei was...*is* an artist. Painter, sculptor. He was a dirt-poor immigrant but hung out with important people who endorsed his talent. Someone introduced us—I was still finishing residency, which might account for my brain atrophy. I didn't realize Sergei would do absolutely anything for money and I was the trifecta—I came from Walter's money, sort of. I had great earning potential. And I had the prestige of being a neurosurgeon who was the stepdaughter of a very well-known and highly respected neurosurgeon. But Sergei had a very short attention span and once the wedding was done, he began to flirt and rove and we didn't last long. We were divorced before our first anniversary. Honestly, it's the dumbest thing I've ever done. I should've listened to... Hey! What's that look? Have you lost all respect for me because I married badly?"

He raised his gaze to hers. "I didn't know you were married."

"I could've sworn I told you that..."

"Maggie, I was married."

"Well, that's okay. A lot of people our age—"

"Mine wasn't short," he said. "It wasn't a mistake.

I was married for eight years. My wife died two years ago."

She was stunned silent for a moment. "Wow. I'm sorry."

"Thanks. Listen, I'm not trying to be secretive, but is it okay if I don't talk about it right now? She died of scleroderma, a difficult disease. Let's save that discussion for another time. Okay? It's still hard to talk about."

"Sure," she said quietly. "Wow. I mean, I had no idea."

"How could you? I'll fill in the blanks one of these days. When the time feels right. Okay?"

"Are there a lot of blanks?" she asked.

"Details, that's all." He reached for her hand and squeezed it. "I'm moving on the best I can, but I still find it very personal. And emotional. Right now, I want to hear about Phoebe and Walter and anything else. I want to laugh with you, then I want to hold you and take you to bed. Let's cover my background another time. A better time."

"Okay."

"Tell me about your childhood with Phoebe," he suggested.

"Ohhh, you're not going to believe any of it," she said.

"After the family I came from?" he asked, lifting a brow. "Really?"

"You mean that's all true?"

"Maggie, I may be guilty of withholding, not being ready to talk about some things, but I've never lied to you."

"How can you manage that?" she asked.

"Force of habit, I guess. Tell me stuff."

"Well, Phoebe had it hard," Maggie said. "She rescued me from this *shit hole*, as she called it, and took me to Chicago where she somehow managed to get a very nice apartment. I have no idea how she did it. Sully swears she never asked him for any money. She got herself a very good job in a posh restaurant and although I seemed to spend most of my time with the next-door neighbor lady, Phoebe only worked or looked after me. When she got home in the middle of the night, her feet were swollen and her head ached. After about a year she brought Walter home—she met him in the restaurant. She must have picked him on sight. And I hated him because I knew what he meant—Walter getting together with Phoebe meant I'd never see Sully again. I was horrible to him. And to Phoebe, for that matter. They even had me sitting with a psychologist for a while. I ran away several times but I only made it a couple of blocks. I got bad grades, had temper tantrums, wouldn't eat, or so they thought... I was a growing girl—I sneaked food. And then when I was eight Walter said to me, 'I think you should visit your father, but if you'd like to do that, this is no way to go about it.' When I tried to explain that Phoebe would never let me he just said, 'Let me work on that. Try to be patient. And for God's sake, try to behave. You and I both know what you're doing.' It wasn't just the fact that he had me nailed that made a difference, but that he spoke to me as if I were an adult."

"And he won you over," Cal said.

"Not yet, but he was getting closer. You have to remember, Walter was a busy surgeon. We didn't spend a great deal of time together."

"He must have loved Phoebe very much to put up with you," Cal said.

"I don't know that Walter cares that much about love, though clearly he cares about Phoebe. I asked him once why the devil he married her and you know what he said? He said she was uncomplicated. How's that for an assessment?"

He pulled her chair closer to him, put his arm around her and drew her in. Lips hovering over hers, he asked, "And what are you looking for, Miss Maggie?"

"Well, obviously I like 'em real complicated, California."

Maggie made Cal laugh with stories of being a grave disappointment to Phoebe her entire youth. She wouldn't take tap and ballet but played soccer and volleyball, forcing Phoebe to sit in the hot sun or smelly gymnasium. And when it came to the debutante ball? Of course Maggie wanted no part of that and her mother cried for a month. She wore a uniform at school but the rest of the time could hardly be pried out of her tight, torn jeans, boots and gauzy blouses that showed her bra. And just to see her mother freak out she'd leave out pictures of tattoos she was thinking of getting.

"I was a serpent's tooth," she said, sending him into peals of laughter. "And oh God, if she ever found out I lost my virginity here at the camp when I was fifteen, she would die. But first she'd kill Sully."

"But of course you were safe and protected and—"

"I was fifteen! I worried about being pregnant for a year and the guy broke my heart by being a summer dude who never called or wrote or came back. But all things considered, I'd rather go through that than put on a white formal gown and dance a waltz."

Cal sprinkled sand on the embers and they left their chairs sitting out. He had his arm around her shoulders as they walked toward the house. As they grew closer, his hand slid down and he began to caress her butt. "Are you worried that I'm just a summer dude?" he asked.

"If there's one thing I've learned, no one stays here. This is a bump in the road."

"Sully stayed," he reminded her.

"Well, that's different. It's his legacy."

"You haven't made any noises about leaving," he said.

"I was born to this. I might be different like Sully. But mostly this is a place people escape to. Most of our guests are getting out of the city or away from work. Some think better in the solitude and serenity of the trail—they work things out. But no one stays."

"You think I'll go? That I'll love you all summer, right in your father's house, and leave you?"

"Probably," she said.

He stopped walking. He turned her toward him and took her into his arms, kissing her deeply, passionately. He backed her up a couple of steps so that she was against the thick trunk of a big tree and he pressed the length of his body against hers. He was already aroused and if he knew Maggie, so was she. "You don't think this time it might be different?" he whispered against her lips.

"I can want it to, but there's been nothing to convince me. I don't really know you. I'm trying to know you but there's new information every day."

"Maggie, you know the best parts of me. When I make love to you, I give you everything I have."

"Will you deny there have been quite a few women

along the way who have benefited from your rather amazing erotic skills?"

"Not really quite a few. Not as many as you might think, but at least one princess…"

"At least?" she said, already a little breathless.

"Come with me, Maggie. You're way overdressed."

"So, after all that you're just going to play with my feelings again?" she teased.

"I won't be playing…" He kissed her again and grabbed her ass, giving her a hard squeeze. "Come on, angel. Let's get comfortable."

Comfort was the least of his intentions. He stripped her and played her body as if it were a Stradivarius and he knew every note perfectly. He wanted to give her everything within him. It all came so naturally with her. He'd been aware of every nuance since that very first night they were together, and making love to Maggie allowed him to pull all his deepest feelings together. Sex with Maggie was more than just sex; it was intensely personal. All he had to do was think about getting into her body and his chest expanded a little; his wounded heart seemed to grow stronger.

What she gave back to him fulfilled him. Her natural abandon, her complete trust reminded him that this was like a smooth pathway to his most private emotions. Lovemaking wasn't always like that. Sometimes it was all physical—just a need satisfied. Not complicated at all. Sometimes sex was emotional—a blending of spirits to strengthen each other. And then there were times like this when the give-and-take of bodies in the act of loving made one's very soul feel sturdier. More sure. More stable. Sometimes making love relieved a deep tension. It could be exciting, stimulating and electrifying. And then there were times it felt like the one person you were destined to find came into your life and all the jagged edges you struggled with had smoothed out, calmed down, quieted.

He knew what it was. It was at once a great comfort and dangerous. When a man gives all of himself to a woman who gives everything she has, the bond is so powerful it can be the ultimate fulfillment. And if lost, the ultimate destruction.

Their love play left them panting, wrapped around each other, holding on for dear life. They whispered to each other. Praise, mostly. Compliments and simple adoration. Then he loved her again. He was falling in love with her. It was a terrifying concept.

Cal rose early, leaving Maggie to sleep. She was naked, twisted in the sheets, looking like she'd never had a deeper, more comforting rest. He'd worn her out, his objective.

After his shower he walked over to the store and of course Sully was there, getting started on his day. There was no denying the man looked a little better each day—his cheeks slightly pink, his hands steady, eyes alert and sparkling.

"Morning," Cal said. "Good night?"

"Mine was. And I heard yours was, too."

"You're full of it, Sully," he said, gambling on a lie. "There wasn't anything to hear."

"Well, I'm old. I gotta have my fun where I can."

"Aren't you afraid you'll go to hell for lying?" Cal asked.

"For *lying*?" Sully roared with laughter. "Son, I'm going to hell for way worse than that. Trust me."

"I'm taking a morning off, Sully. If there's anything important you need me to do either tell me right now or save it for this afternoon."

"Nothing I can't manage. Errands?"

"Yep. I'll be done by noon."

"Jeez, son, take the day if need be. I'm not exactly an invalid, you know."

"Not even slightly. I'll check in a little later."

Cal walked around the end of the lake, five miles, and it took over an hour. There was a perfectly service-able road and he could've driven but the morning was clear and cool and he thought the walk might be a good idea. The cabins on the other side had a bay of small watercraft—five or six Sun Dolphin boats with small motors. These could be rented for fishing or just tour-ing the lake, getting some sun, having a date.

Cal rented one and motored over to Sully's dock, tied up his boat and went looking for Maggie. He caught her just coming out of the house, on her way to the store. "Well, sleepyhead. I wondered when you'd roll out," he said.

"You are the best sleeping pill…"

"We all have our gifts." He reached for her hand. "Grab a hat and come out on the lake with me for a couple of hours. I rented us a boat."

"This should be interesting. Let me go tell Sully where I'll be."

Ten minutes later they were under way in the little boat, putt-putting across the narrow part of the lake to the turn where it opened up into a big, round body of water. Sully's and some of the other camps were built around the north end because the boats had more play on the wider expanse of the lake, making the camp-grounds' swimming areas safer.

"Where are you taking me?" she asked.

"I don't know," he said. "Just somewhere quiet where we can talk. Maybe right over there," he said, pointing to an area of the lake that seemed out of the way. He let the small engine idle and then stop, leaving them floating quietly. He faced her. "I think I should explain a few things."

"Are we out on the lake so I won't panic and run?"

He chuckled. "Nah. I'm not wanted or anything. Yet, anyway. I'm an attorney," he said. "My wife was an attorney. We had very different practices—she was part owner of a nonprofit legal clinic that operated mostly on grants and donations. I was part of a large firm. We met in law school—University of Michigan. We married as soon as I graduated. I was only twenty-seven, in a brand-new job, studying for the bar. Her name was Lynne Aimee Baxter and she was an amazing woman. She got sick before she was thirty but for a while we considered it a nuisance. We researched it, got a lot of medical opinions, but we got on with our lives. We had a few years before things got worse. You know about the disease…"

"I know about it."

"She suffered tremendously. After she died, I tried to be half as brave as she was and just carry on. I stayed in our house, I went to work every day, I called my in-laws every Sunday. I did that for a year. And then suddenly I just couldn't do it anymore. I finished up or handed off what was on my desk. I tried to resign but my boss wouldn't let me. He insisted it could only be an indefinite leave of absence and that my position would be waiting for me when I was ready."

"Doesn't it figure that we'd have that in common? Why didn't you just admit you were a lawyer named California Jones right away?"

"The stages," he said. "First, it's because to tell one part invites questions that insist on answers. Why aren't you a lawyer now? Why walk out on a great job at your age? Et cetera. I don't talk to everyone about my wife, about her illness and the way she suffered. Then the next stage is this—I can't give legal advice anywhere I'm not licensed. And I wasn't licensed in California or here."

"Really? Because I don't have to have a medical license in the state of Michigan to advise a friend with blinding headaches to get a head CT."

"There's an argument that if I don't get paid for the advice I'm not breaking the law, but it's an argument that's been challenged. Doctors and attorneys volunteering their services are still culpable for practicing without a license. Screwing it up could not only get me in trouble, it could compromise your defense. It wasn't worth the risk."

"Well, I can't count the number of cocktail parties where I've been backed into a corner and asked if an eye twitch could be a brain tumor."

"The problem for me was that I'd have to be so careful not to be involved—and you told me you were being sued. So instead of saying anything, I petitioned the state of Colorado for a license to practice. There's reciprocity between our states. It was just a formality, but a requirement. Now, if you need me, I'm available. And…" He shrugged. "I wanted to tell you I was married before. That seemed like something you should know. It wasn't important for me to share with anyone before, Maggie. It wasn't important until it was you."

"I'm sorry for all that, Cal. It must have been so terrible. So after a year, you just got in your truck and…"

"First, I packed up everything with Sedona's help. I put a lot of stuff I thought I'd want again someday in storage and sold the house and most of the furnishings. And then I relived the odyssey of growing up, living in a different place every few months. I can't explain why, Maggie. It makes no sense. The best time of my life was when I was settled, when I had a job, a house, a family even if it was only me and my wife. It was instinctive, I think. Reaching back in time to see if I could retrace my footprints."

"That's what I said to Sully," she said. "That I wanted to go back to the eighth grade and rethink everything."

"You should definitely try that debutante ball thing," he said. "I bet you'd look like a regular princess." Then he grinned at her.

"So…is telling me now significant in some way? Meaning you trust me?"

"It's more than that. Whatever is happening between us is growing. For me, anyway, and I think for you." He laughed but not out of humor. "I hope you're a patient woman because… I'm probably fucked-up. I'm wound too tight. I'm working on that."

"What's the prognosis?"

"That I'm determined to keep working on it until it's fixed. At least fixed enough to have a life again."

"Then you might not need me anymore," she said.

"I don't need you now, honey. It's all *want*. It's powerful want. It's driving me forward."

"Hmm," she said. "So, you're a widowed lawyer and I know your resources. You have access to court documents and you know how to research. You've studied my case."

He shook his head. "I'm not going to do that. I'm not even tempted to do that, although I do want to know. But I only want to know if you want to tell me."

She sat up a little straighter and took a deep breath. "Have you got any idea how bad the mortality rate is in neurosurgery? There was a time, when Walter started practicing, that he could face losing half his patients to brain surgery but he put his personal feelings aside and took the emotional risk for the ones he could save. It's better now but it's still high. The suit against me alleges that I made a bad choice in a triage situation, that I left a patient to die by not taking him to the OR immediately."

"So the lawsuit is for malpractice?" he asked.

She shook her head. "Malpractice charges have not been filed, though there was an investigation and it's still possible. Not likely, the investigation returned no malpractice. It's a wrongful death suit filed by the parents of a teenager who died in the emergency room. We were in triage hell after an accident that brought five teenagers to the trauma unit. The call I made was practiced, logical and routine protocol. I took the patient who was the most critical—unconscious with an obvious epidural hematoma—to surgery and sent the conscious patient with a head injury for a CT."

He frowned as he listened. "How do you make the call?"

"Besides experience and sound medical judgment? The ABCs—open airway, breathing, circulatory function, conscious. My patient was unconscious and he had a blown pupil, classic epidural hematoma—bleeding between the skull and brain. We had to drill holes in the skull immediately to get pressure off the brain. Another patient we pronounced; his heart was still beating but there was gray matter all over the gurney. We put him on life support for possible organ donation. The patient we sent for a CT was crying, bleeding, conscious, coherent." She stopped talking and looked away. "He had a fatal hemorrhage before we could get him to the OR."

"If he'd gotten to the operating room first, would he have lived?"

She shrugged. "Who knows? I can't control everything that happens during surgery. Sometimes we get a brain bleed, a reaction to anesthesia, any number of things can go wrong. It's always a risk. Always."

"So a stroke was the cause of death?"

"The cause of death was five teenagers in a car traveling at a high rate of speed, lubricated by alcohol, hitting a guardrail and then a semi," she said, almost defensively. She took a breath. "Yes. Stroke. With circumstances."

"At least you got one to surgery."

She sighed. "We lost him, too. He was the more critical. He was touch and go. Three teenage boys died that night. Two more were critical. It was devastating."

"Aw, baby," he said.

"You know, I don't mind that they think I made the wrong call. I don't mind that they're angry and hate me. I don't even mind if they sue me. But what I do mind is they think I don't *care*. How could you do this job if you *didn't* care? Sometimes I care so much it almost brings me to my knees. For the toughest of us there's still an emotional cost."

"I understand. As a defense attorney, I've faced people that think I want crime to pay or that it's my intention to get bad people off. Neither being true."

"I can imagine, though it's unjust of them to judge you for your clients. But you must admit, with the unsavory element seeking your support, it's at least understandable. You represent criminals. I save lives! I do everything humanly possible to save lives. That they're not all savable isn't my fault."

Cal smiled patiently. "I don't represent criminals. I represent individuals charged with crimes. Whether guilty or innocent is not up to me but decided by a judge and jury. The element I represent is the accused. The element I represent is *you*."

Rather than love, than money, than fame, give me truth.

—HENRY DAVID THOREAU

CHAPTER 12

Cal listened while Maggie explained, this wasn't the first time she'd been sued. She'd been sued before and even though she'd never lost a suit, never even gone to trial, once the insurance carrier settled, that alone had caused her malpractice insurance rates to skyrocket. There were endless, time-consuming interviews and depositions before a judge just threw out the lawsuit. Even with a lawyer provided by the insurance carrier, on the advice of Walter, Maggie hired her own counsel and the hours invested cost her money, cost the hospital money. The absence of a surgeon was expensive.

This was her third suit in four years and while anyone can sue anyone for anything, it was still more than the average neurosurgeon faced in such a short period of time. The first went nowhere. The second settled early, in the pretrial motions because the plaintiffs took the first offer from the insurance company. This one had legs. Because so many of her colleagues would be deposed or subpoenaed, they were cool toward her. Maybe angry, maybe frightened, maybe just sick of the inconvenience. All of it left her in a toxic work environment.

She was weary, discouraged, lonely and broke.

Maggie had shifted positions so she was leaning up against Cal and they floated aimlessly, talking.

"And yet, I feel robbed," she said. "I love what I do and I don't feel I can do it. Every day it's swimming against the current."

"You might feel a lot better about that once you're through this lawsuit."

"I feel so guilty, walking away like I did. I meant to take a couple of weeks off, then I had Sully on my mind and it stretched out. I don't mean to paint myself as some kind of savior, but what if people died because I couldn't step up? After all the years and all the educational funds, I should be more committed, but I ran out of gas."

"It's okay to get tired, Maggie. Life's too short to live with unnecessary pain and frustration. I ran away, too."

"I plan to testify, to defend myself," she said.

"If I were your lawyer I would strongly advise against it."

"Why? I'd tell the absolute truth! I have nothing to hide."

"The plaintiff's attorney will hand you your ass. In trial, we never ask a question we don't know the answer to and we never make a statement that can be convoluted into an exaggeration or change the direction of the case. If I were suing you and you told your side of things, I'd draw attention to your many lawsuits—"

"Not that many! And they were frivolous! Even though the insurance company settled one I never admitted to any guilt! No guilt was ever proven."

"I would never let you get to that explanation. I'd have the jury believing you're sued every other week— that you're incompetent and lack good judgment."

"But why? What sense would that make? I want to save everyone."

"As the plaintiff's attorney, I would convince the jury you shouldn't practice and that you should be punished by a big settlement. But, if you don't speak, if you don't open the door, I wouldn't be able to lead you down that destructive path. Let your lawyer defend you."

"It's outrageous," she said. "I can't defend myself, I can't say anything, I'm paying a fortune for representation and when I win, I can't sue the plaintiffs for putting me through it. They're barely existing as it is. They have nothing. The only thing that allows them to bring a suit is a contingency attorney who will either draw a large percentage of their settlement or take nothing as payment. I'm probably going to have to declare bankruptcy and they're going to walk out of the courtroom with the same assets they brought in. They can afford to sue and I can't. It is not a level playing field!"

"It is if you don't hand them anything that can be used against you. You are a highly trained, impressively educated surgeon of sterling reputation with many next-to-impossible saves to your credit. Stand on that. Stand on it silently."

"Oh, you're as frustrating as anyone else I've spoken to. Do you have any idea how hard this is?"

"Well, just lie back and relax awhile," he said. He pulled off her straw hat and began to massage her scalp. He just talked to her, said things that required no response. "They're not really suing you. They're suing the injustice of it all. Sixteen-year-old boys shouldn't die, even stupid sixteen-year-old boys who take foolish risks. The brokenhearted parents only want to strike out and feel some sense of relief. It won't bring relief, of course, but it will keep them busy until relief eventually begins to come. I always try to walk in their shoes, see the world from their perspective, understand what they hope for. There are two kinds of plaintiffs I've never understood—the kind that can forgive immediately, forgive without any struggle or hint of hate or rage. And the kind motivated purely by profit. And the lawyer, even the contingency lawyer doesn't know if you're exceptionally gifted or if you're a silly klutz who shouldn't be allowed to hold a scalpel. He is an expert on your credentials by now but those can be manufactured just as realistically as a highly credentialed surgeon can be accident-prone. Both lawyers will seek the truth in the court. The court seeks the truth in the lawyers, charging them with the responsibility to produce honest and powerful cases for their clients so that there's evidence to show a decision that serves the truth. The plaintiffs, however, will be disappointed no matter what. Oh, they might cheer with a win. They might even give a press conference and say that justice was served and their son's death was vindicated, but they'll go home to find his room empty and the photographs of him will bring gut-wrenching tears. They can't win, Maggie. No matter how hard they try.

"The attorney for the accused will show them that the boy had the best possible care, though the outcome was destined to be tragic. Hopefully the attorney, the smart attorney, knows how to do that with compassion—it always wins more points. Cruelty toward the bereaved just never works. Sensitivity toward the parents is particularly essential since their beloved son made such a disastrous mistake. My gut tells me the plaintiff's son was the driver—possible, since they're not suing the parents of the driver, all victims being minors. They're not suing whoever provided them with alcohol. But of course, as you know, you might be the most logical defendant, the one with the deep pockets.

"The most important thing to remember is this—no matter the outcome, the plaintiffs will always have the greater suffering. You can't help them. It's impossible. So you must save yourself. A good defense attorney can help with that or, at the very least, lessen the damage."

They floated for a while, not talking, but Cal continued to play with her hair. He noticed an early strand or two of silver that he was smart enough not to mention, but it made him happy. Every woman should have the luxury of growing older, growing into her skin, settling her emotional debts.

"Did you learn that in law school?" she finally asked him.

"Sort of, yeah. I mean, that's what we do, right—we're seeking justice. But that stuff about understanding the other guy—that came from Atticus Finch. I grew up wanting to be him. Partly because he was the most fair-minded man on the planet and partly because he was so sane, so stable. I had to contend with a crazy father, remember. If I couldn't have a father like Atticus, then I'd like to be a father like Atticus."

"Atticus?"

To Kill a Mockingbird.

"Oh. Right. Sure. So…you wanted to be a father?"

"I did. I wondered if I was being ridiculous, given the dysfunctional family I came from. But my sister forged ahead, fearless, and had a family. A perfectly normal family. They have all the usual issues—she fights with her husband sometimes, the kids drive her bat-shit crazy, she's overworked, underpaid, running around trying to be a professional woman and a full-time mother, and she's happy. I think for us, for kids raised in so much uncertainty and occasional deprivation, being grounded in relationships and having relatively stable homes is reassuring."

"Do you still want a family?" she asked bravely.

"I don't know," he said. "I think so. If it's not too late."

"Men can have families forever," she said. "They can have 'em so old it's like having their own grandchildren. I worked with a guy who's on his third wife and just had a baby at the age of sixty. He's happy as a pig in mud."

Cal laughed. "God bless him. Men are all a little obsessed about when it goes away—the erection. Is it at sixty? Sixty-five? Didn't Groucho Marx or someone reproduce at ninety?"

"Really? Men never let on, do they..."

"Never. But hardly anything trumps erections. I guess brain tumors and heart attacks, but..."

"So do you think about whether you'd actually be alive to raise them? These children you'll have if it's not too late?"

"If I'm pushing that envelope, I won't have them. On purpose, anyway. But, Maggie, I think there's still time to consider this. I fully intend to be at least ninety. And I'm not just being ridiculous. That's completely reasonable for a healthy male my age."

"Huh," she said. "I never think about that. How long I want to live. I wonder why I never think about that. Especially since I had this crazy, irrational fear of dying alone."

"You did? When was that?"

"Oh, right before I came here. I'd been under a lot of pressure. I certainly wasn't the only one—the whole hospital was under a lot of pressure. We had a new administrator, a change in chief of staff, a scandal, a tragedy followed by a lawsuit... I was hardly the only one affected. I think I was the only one who's looking at bankruptcy. But while I was trying to figure out how to proceed I suddenly felt completely isolated. Well, Andrew broke up with me. Dumped me when I was inconsolably depressed. That probably contributed."

"Dying?" he asked.

"I thought about dying. No particular way, no particular age, just random lights-out. And I thought about being so alone. It was the last straw. It might've been the fact that all those combined stresses made me feel pretty unloved. Know what I mean? So I ran home to Sully and he surprised me with a heart attack."

Cal found it interesting that the fear of death threw her into a panic. For him it was the fear of living.

"Are you over that now?"

"Oh yes, completely. I shot at Dumb and Dumber, didn't I? Even though it crossed my mind I could be in real trouble. I just have steps to take before I move on in my life. Step one—get beyond this suit. Then I have to figure out if I can ever make those life-or-death decisions again. Simple, no?"

"Lawsuits can take years," he said.

"We're having a preliminary hearing in a week. The judge is going to hear the lawyers, has all the pretrial motions, will get a list of evidence and witnesses from both, they'll decide on judge or jury resolution, mediation might be suggested, but doubtful... It is my dream that the judge looks at the lawsuit and says, *Get outta here.*"

"My dream, too," he agreed. "I can go with you," he said. "I can find a suit to wear."

"Thanks, but I want to go alone. I'm going to stay over, go visit Phoebe and Walter on my way home."

"If you change your mind at the last minute, I have a white shirt and a pair of dress pants…"

She was still leaning against him, not looking at him. "I'd like to ask you a personal question. If you can't talk about it just say so and I'll ask again later. How did you meet your wife?"

He chuckled softly. "I saw her sitting in a coffee shop, studying. She was so pretty. She looked so intense. She'd get a line between her eyebrows when she concentrated. I approached her and said, *Excuse me, can I buy you a cup of coffee?* And she said, *As you can see, I have coffee. And I'm too busy to be picked up.*"

"She was onto you…"

"Oh, from the start. So I waited outside for her to come out. I waited forever. She finally came out and I asked her if she had time to be picked up now. She laughed at me and said that as a matter of fact she hadn't been picked up in a while, so what the hell. We went back into the coffee shop, had more coffee and I asked her a million questions. She said she felt like she was being grilled and asked me if I'd been stalking her. I could tell she didn't believe that I'd just seen her for the first time. Against her better judgment she agreed to meet me again, same place. I was an hour late for work, that's how gone I was. I didn't think she'd keep our date so I went to the coffee shop two hours early— I figured I'd catch her escaping. But she was already there, eating a muffin, drinking coffee, book open. So I went right to her and said hi. And she said, *You're two hours early and I'm busy. Go walk around or accost some other girl until it's time*. And I did."

"Oh, I like her," Maggie said.

"Yeah, she was fierce. And soft—she was so soft. She was a law student and she could be so powerful. I loved watching her."

"You fell in love with her instantly."

"I think so, yes," he said. "But in the end, she asked me to marry her. I mark that as one of the great victories of my life."

"Was it good, then? Being married?" she asked.

"I liked marriage. At first we were so busy trying to settle into our lives it was insane. We both had to pass the bar, get on our career track, find the work-life balance so we could actually be a couple. It wasn't simple but it was still fun. We took different paths—I wanted the big, powerful firm, she wanted the small legal clinic. We both chose right. We were happy."

"I'm sorry, Cal. Sorry you didn't have a fifty-year marriage."

"I have no regrets, that's the only important thing now. Right?"

"You'll never get over her," she said.

"I'm not supposed to get over her, Maggie. I'm supposed to treasure what was good and move on. That's a tall enough order." He took a breath, doubting his own wisdom, yet knowing what he had to do. "There's one more thing. It'll be obvious to you why I've never talked about it before, why it's a closely guarded piece of information. It's hard to tell you, of all people. You might find it unforgivable, dedicated as you are to saving lives. See, I made the ultimate commitment to my wife. She was dying of a painful disease. She asked me to give my word I wouldn't let her suffer, to promise that I would help her let go. She asked me to help her die. And I did."

Time stood still. Not even the water moved. It was actual minutes before Maggie moved, turning around in the little boat and kneeling to face him. She had tears on her cheeks. She put the palms of her hands against his cheeks. "Of course you did," she whispered. "Of course."

One way to move on, Cal discovered, was to have a heart-to-heart talk about both personal and professional things, leaving nothing unsaid. He unburdened all of it. And then they made out like long-lost lovers reunited for an hour or so, rocking the little boat until they were wet and laughing. When they got to the point where they either had to try to find a way to make love or at least get satisfied somehow, they gave it up. Cal took her back to the dock at the crossing and motored across the lake to return the boat. Although he told her he'd be happy with a long walk home, she drove over to the camp and picked him up.

They didn't have any more of those serious, deep conversations again, at least through the following week. In fact, Maggie grew very quiet. Cal suspected she was worried about the hearing.

There were questions he could taste on her tongue that she didn't ask and it could only be because she was afraid of the answers. Questions like, *Can you ever love like that again?* And *How long will you stay here?* And *How do I fit into your life, your plans?*

He hoped that was what was causing her silence and not anything else. He did have some answers stowed away in the privacy of his heart. *Yes, I can love again but like that? Maybe it will be a different kind of love but equal.* And he wanted to stay there as long as staying there worked for everyone, including Maggie. And how did Maggie fit? He wasn't sure, except that he couldn't imagine letting her go. The caveat was—could she truly accept him as he was? Because he already knew he wouldn't be going back to that other life, a partner in a big firm in a big city.

He had no regrets about leaving all that, either.

It was almost the middle of July when Maggie's court date came around. Cal was sitting out on the porch of the store in the morning having coffee with Tom Canaday and listening to his tales of the weekend with his family—he had a complicated list of activities from work to chores to commitments the kids had that required juggling schedules and transportation.

"At least with Jackson and Nikki driving now, I get a little help with chauffeuring," he said. "Problem is, not enough cars."

"How you manage all your jobs and still get those kids to everything they signed on for must take some interesting logistics."

"I start with one workable solution—if I'm available to them from four to seven, we can manage almost anything else. They're old enough to get themselves up in the morning and get their own breakfast—I start my jobs early most days. The bus comes for the younger three, Jackson can drive himself to school and jobs. But from after school through dinner if I'm not around homework doesn't get done and games, plays, dances, all that goes missed. And that stuff is just about as important if they're going to be balanced. Right?"

"I guess," Cal said.

Campers were just beginning to come awake. The aroma of coffee and bacon around the campsites filled the air, as did the sounds of people getting ready for a day of fun. A couple of dogs barked.

"Whoa," Tom said, looking over at the house.

Maggie stepped out onto the porch. She wore a slim-fitting sleeveless black dress, black hose, black pumps. She carried a jacket over one arm and had a briefcase in hand. She'd fussed with her hair, that was obvious. It was smoothly turned under at her collar but still had that life in it, moving with her. She was decked out somberly but classy.

"Wow," Tom said again.

Cal got up and walked over to the house. He'd already kissed her good-morning, once in bed and once when she was in the shower. He'd already told her she'd be great today. He wasn't about to let her leave for court without another boost to her confidence. He took the steps up to the porch and stood before her.

"You look beautiful," he said.

"This is my funeral suit," she said. Then she winced. "How do you feel?"

"Terrified, but as ready as I'll ever be."

"If you've changed your mind I can still go with you. I can be ready in five minutes."

She shook her head. "I'm just going to do it."

"My phone is charged and I'll keep it on for you."

"You've been wonderful," she said. "In case I didn't say it or in case I forget to say it, you've been so wonderful. Helpful, encouraging, supportive."

"How about a dynamic lover who's taken you to heights never before experienced, taking your mind off your more cerebral legal affairs?" he asked.

"Satisfactory," she said. Then she smiled her teasing smile. "Okay, above average."

"The way you make me beg, it turns me on," he said, returning the smile.

"I'll call with updates, if there are any. I don't know the process so if you don't hear from me as soon as you…"

"It's okay, honey. I know the process. And the rule is—unpredictable and leveraged on the mood of the judge and the paperwork involved."

"Well, we're ready. At least that's what the lawyers say."

"It's going to be okay. Just remember, you did the right thing."

"I did my best," she said. "It's been good enough so many times…"

"Maggie, you did the right thing. You'll do the right thing today. All you have to do is listen and confer with your attorneys. You're going to be fine. This will soon be behind you."

"Only to happen again and again?"

He grabbed her around the waist and pulled her to him, kissing her passionately. She couldn't embrace him, coat in one hand and briefcase in the other. But she certainly gave full attention to his kiss.

"Did you smear my lipstick?" she asked.

"No. Now listen to me. *Everything* is going to happen again and again, Maggie. There will be accidents, there will be lawyers, there will be grieving family members.

There will also be magnificent victories and lives saved. And there will be joyous occasions."

"I'm remembering that book, *When Bad Things Happen to Good People*."

"Good things also happen to good people. This isn't the only outcome you're going to have to live through, you know. Now, are you ready to go? Do you want to tell Sully you're leaving?"

"I saw him for a moment before I got in the shower and he wished me luck. Will you tell him I'm on my way, please?"

"I'll be glad to."

He led her down the porch steps and helped her into her car. When she was getting in he gave her fanny a pat. "Break a leg," he said. "Call when you can."

"Thanks, California. I'll return the favor if I can."

Cal watched her leave and then walked back to the porch where Tom sat, waiting. When Cal sat down with his coffee cup again, he looked at Tom to see wide eyes and lots of teeth.

"Whoa," Tom said. "You know what you should do? You should lock that down right away," he said, giving a nod toward the house, toward Maggie. "Seriously. Right away."

Cal laughed. "And what makes you think Maggie's ready to get locked down?"

"Are you kidding me? You need my advice? You a novice?"

"Pretty much. What's your best advice?"

"Well, at least you're an adult. I fell for my girl when I was a kid…"

Tom launched into the story of his marriage, family and divorce. It was both complicated and predictable.

He fell in love at sixteen, knocked up his girlfriend at seventeen, married her, went to work before finishing high school, had four kids. Then the girl grew up and wanted more of a life, but she felt suffocated by a husband and four kids, so…

Cal was only half listening. He was thinking about how beautiful Maggie looked and how brave she was. Not for facing a lawsuit in court, although that took guts. Every time she clocked in to her role as a neurosurgeon she was facing the unknown and laying her reputation and indeed, her future, on the line. Making those life-and-death decisions in seconds took great skill and incredible confidence. She amazed him.

Amazing women, it seemed, were his lot in life. For this he pushed aside his trepidation and said a little prayer of thanks. Complaining of finding not only one but two of these remarkable females should not be condoned. Time to give thanks.

As Maggie drove, something Cal had said came slinking into her mind. *Good things happen to good people, too.*

Had she been properly mindful of the good things? Every time she held that cranial bone flap in her hand she was performing a small miracle. There were surgeries she'd come to think of as routine and yet she was conscious of the fact that whenever she was near the brain or spinal cord, it was a matter of life and death.

There were some procedures and surgeries that were more memorable than others. There'd been that inoperable brain tumor in a seven-year-old that Maggie dared to remove. No one would touch that little girl, it was just too complicated and dangerous. And no surgeon liked performing an operation that was 99 percent likely to fail. Yet the child was headed to certain death with a very minimal chance of prolonging her life—and suffering—through radiation and chemotherapy. But Maggie was willing to risk it for the child's sake. She'd once scrubbed in with a neurosurgeon who had excised a similar lesion. She had a very impressive team backing her up.

They had several pre-surgical conferences to discuss it before taking it on. There was doubt all around her but it had worked. That little girl not only survived, she was now perfectly healthy. It was a total success. The surgeon who had scrubbed in to assist was an older man and he said, "You have the most beautiful hands I've ever encountered."

There was a cyclist thrown over the hood of a fast-moving truck, paralyzed from the neck down. Maggie took him into surgery and performed a partial cervical laminectomy and repair and when he woke up he could wiggle his toes. A month later he walked out of the hospital.

She was not by any means a religious person; she could count on one hand the number of times she'd been inside a church in the past four years. She did have a deep spiritual core and every time she went into the operating room she had a mantra: *God, still my hand and clear my head.* And when she came out she said, *Thank You, God.*

She had always scheduled her surgical cases for Tuesday and Thursday. She saw patients on Monday and Wednesday. She tried to take a couple of three or four-day weekends a month just to fill the well, catch up on her reading, organize her office and her head, but she was on call a couple nights a week. Blessedly she wasn't always called in to the hospital and the occasions of being called to a major catastrophe like the MVA that had taken the lives of three youths were rare.

They had tried to prepare her in residency for the toll her specialty would take, yet it was more devastating than she had imagined. She had to fight the disappointment when things went poorly. Sometimes the emotion had driven her to the stairwell. And yet she met each new case with renewed vigor and enthusiasm—how?

She hoped the lawyer was going to talk about her good results, for she had them. Fantastic results, really. She was one of the best spinal surgeons in the area; many of her patients who were experiencing chronic pain realized complete relief and full mobility after surgery.

It was not in her nature to be negative. Why had she failed to remember all the victories?

Honesty and transparency make you vulnerable.

Be honest and transparent anyway.

—MOTHER TERESA

CHAPTER 13

Maggie had an early lunch with her primary lawyer, Steve Rubin. For once it was just the two of them, not the whole legal team plus a rep from the insurance carrier. They'd be before the judge at one o'clock and he warned her it might be a long afternoon. Both attorneys had already submitted all their paperwork, motions, witness lists, anything pertinent to this hearing. The judge would use all this information to determine the approximate length of the trial.

"Could the judge just throw it out today?" she asked hopefully.

"Very unlikely," he said. "We've been in this process for a year and a half and if he were so inclined, that might've happened already."

"Will you at least be able to bring up my exemplary record as a neurosurgeon?"

"Not until or if we get to closing arguments. Then, certainly. But I want to stay away from statistics if possible. I have expert testimony ready if necessary, but once we start talking about your saves we open the door to discuss your failures."

She grimaced.

"I'm sorry to put it that way, Maggie. That's not a very accurate conclusion, it's just that the numbers in this specialty are bleak. Especially when it comes to emergency neurosurgery.

"Try very hard not to take this personally," he said, and then launched into a short speech about motives and strategies and presentation, saying almost the same things Cal had said, that we mustn't blame the plaintiffs for doing what they have to do. "We might suggest there is no blame here while there is access to considerable financial gain. But we'll treat that with care—judges and juries don't like the implication that we intend to hammer the grieving plaintiffs.

"On the other hand," he said, "your malpractice carrier has not offered or agreed to a settlement, so without saying a word we imply we're in for a fight. And I want you to be prepared, the judge we drew is not known to be sympathetic toward doctors. His record shows he decides most of these suits in favor of the plaintiffs."

"Swell," she muttered.

He didn't speak quite as eloquently as Cal had. Oh, how she wished he were here! Just the soothing sound of his voice brought her such a serene feeling even when talking about this debacle. But she'd been afraid. She hadn't wanted him to see her fail.

She listened to Steve Rubin talk, picking at her food. She was not on his witness list, he thought that ill-advised. They went from the restaurant to a small meeting room next to the courtroom. The courthouse seemed to be so busy, people everywhere. When they went into the courtroom via a side door, she saw that it was full.

"Who are all these people?" she asked Steve.

"There are always spectators. Or perhaps witnesses are—"

"Oh my God," she said, momentarily frozen in place. "I know some of them! I know a lot of them!"

A woman separated herself from the crowd and came to the rail that divided the gallery from the attorney's tables. "Jaycee!" Maggie exclaimed, reaching over the rail to hug her. "What are you doing here?"

"I can't really do anything except show support. I just want you to know I'm here. I might not be able to get here more often—babies, you know. They're relentlessly being born. But I wanted to make sure I was here for this evidentiary hearing. I've been in your shoes and it's so difficult. Think positive, the outcome has to be good!"

"Steve, this is my best friend, Dr. Jaycee Kent, ob-gyn."

"Pleasure," he said, sticking out his hand.

"Thank you," Maggie murmured to Jaycee. Next to neurosurgeons, OBs were very vulnerable to civil suits. "You told me to take a week or two off and I haven't been back yet."

"Then you needed the time to regroup. Maggie, you're not unique. A lot of doctors who are under enormous pressure have to schedule downtime just to recover. Now think positive. We're here for you."

Over Jaycee's shoulder Maggie saw Terry Jordan, an RN from the operating room, a round and stern fifty-five-year-old woman who ran that OR with an iron fist and had saved Maggie's ass more than once by knowing almost as much as Maggie did. And next to her Rob Hollis touched two fingers to his brow in a salute. She spied her old office manager, Susan, a smile on her usually tight and grim face. And there was Kevin from radiology, Kevin who could read those emergency CTs better and faster and more accurately than anyone she knew. There were three OR techs, a couple of nurses, a couple of paramedics she ran into in emergency quite a lot. An audience. They were here for her. She prayed she wouldn't just draw their pity.

She hadn't even told her mother and Walter about this preliminary hearing! Now she remembered, she had told Jaycee and Terry in emails when they asked for updates on the lawsuit. Word must have spread like wildfire.

Maggie turned around. She was faced with the plaintiffs for the first time in over a year and it was shattering to see them. They were young, not that much older than Maggie at right around forty, yet they looked so devastatingly old. Mr. and Mrs. Markiff; she remembered telling them their son had expired. She'd held Mrs. Markiff in her arms for several minutes as she sobbed. Mrs. Markiff appeared to be losing her hair and was painfully thin, sallow, her face so deeply lined. She looked so weak. Mr. Markiff, on the other hand, looked so much bigger than she remembered. He had a fierce look on his face and a huge belly that strained the buttons on his white dress shirt. Both of them looked at her with loathing.

She had tried. She had tried so hard. Losing those kids was horrible. And yet it was her work and she didn't have time to second-guess split-second decisions or pause to reconsider.

"All rise! The Honorable John Bestover White presiding."

The judge entered, the entire courtroom rose and Maggie studied him. He looked very big in his robes but she thought, given the perspective of him passing the bailiff, he was actually a small, chunky man with a large, intimidating mustache and a ring of white hair around his otherwise bald head. And he was scowling.

He was efficient. They began going through the paperwork, first the complaint of wrongful death, then the motions—each one was read and had Maggie's attorney not explained them all, she would be lost. There was the complaint, which was the plaintiff's case. There was the counterclaim, which was essentially her side of the story and as close as she'd ever get to testifying, which she probably would never get to do. With the help of her lawyer and depositions, they had reconstructed the emergency in a timeline with supporting facts. There was the reply to the counterclaim in which the plaintiff alleged it should be obvious to any certified and experienced neurosurgeon that the patient to take to surgery was their son and not the unconscious boy—they alleged she had mismanaged triage. Then there was the statute of limitations, forcing the trial in a timely manner. She found that laughable a year and a half after the event. There were several more motions as well as evidence in discovery. All of these motions, each one read and explained and denied, took almost two hours. Denied to the defense team was the district attorney's report in which he declined to prosecute any malpractice. A blow to the defense.

Then, finally, the plaintiff's attorney offered a motion of summary judgment. Steve whispered to her that meant they'd go with the judge's decision rather than a jury. They had no doubt heard Judge White wasn't crazy about doctors.

"Your Honor, we make a motion to dismiss," Steve said.

"Sit down, Mr. Rubin."

The courtroom sank into dark quiet. The judge took a deep breath before he spoke.

"My heart is very heavy today," he said. "I've read the claim, the counterclaim, all the motions and pleas. Inclusive in those materials was the accident report. In the plaintiff's claim the focus is on two sixteen-year-old boys but in fact there were five—it was a catastrophic event, all arriving in the emergency room critical, one of them beyond help upon arrival. I preside over many civil malpractice and wrongful death suits. Many of them emerge from emergency rooms and emergency operating rooms. There is not only a reconstructed time-line provided by the defendant but notes from paramedics, RNs, attending physicians and ER physicians, not to mention the OR staff. From the time the first of the injured arrived in the emergency room until the fifth patient arrived, only six minutes had elapsed. From the time triage was complete until the first patient was anesthetized and the surgeon at the ready, four more minutes. From the time patient Markiff was assessed and sent to radiology for his head CT—two and a half minutes. There were also other decisions and designations made within this time frame—one boy sent to surgery for splenectomy while yet another was put into the care of an orthopedic surgeon and on to surgery to deal with two life-threatening broken femurs and yet another put on life support for possible organ harvest.

"If anyone had trouble following that—the time from the very first of five injured arriving in the emergency room until Dr. Sullivan entered the OR suite—ten minutes. If you could break it down, she probably had less than thirty seconds to make a decision. Her notes are written by the attending physician and verbally recorded.

I not only looked at the accident reports—police, paramedic, fire and rescue—but the postmortem reports. And I must tell you, the entire scene must have been horrific, and yet the record is not only flawless, it is flawlessly consistent. The only report lacking in this vast collection of documentation is a blood test done on the emergency room and operating room staff to measure drug or alcohol use. It was not done because there was no indication. Fifteen emergency room and operating room employees were deposed and under oath stated that the physicians in question appeared rested, sober and efficient.

"I pored over all of this detailed information and yet the most telling and crucial fact came down to a single number—the time of death. Rory Busch in the operating room and Carl Markiff in radiology for a CT both expired ten minutes after arriving in the emergency room at the exact same time. Well, resuscitation began on both patients at exactly the same time and continued for several minutes. Their injuries and cause of death were nearly identical as well—both died of head injuries that led to massive brain hemorrhage. This fact alone made it physically impossible for Dr. Sullivan to make either choice work, although the testimony of the staff establishes that her decision to take the unconscious lad to surgery first is indeed protocol.

"But let me say this—I believe it needs to be said. For any doctor to enter a melee such as that emergency room, filled with critical teenagers, make a sound decision, move to intervention in the midst of chaos and try to save a patient under such dismal circumstances and against such overpowering odds is nothing short of heroic.

"Because we have access to the many reports and depositions, I don't feel anything further can be gained by reading or reciting them aloud in this courtroom. I'm dismissing this case with prejudice. I find no case here. Mr. and Mrs. Markiff, my deepest sympathy for your tragic loss. We are adjourned." His gavel struck and the courtroom began to stir, first with voices, then cries of happiness, cries of devastation from the Markiffs.

"With prejudice?" Maggie asked, though she thought she knew what it meant.

Steve Rubin was looking at her, smiling somewhat sadly as he wiped the tears off her cheeks with his thumb. Maggie didn't even realize that when the judge started going through the events of that night it took her back and the tears were automatic, rolling down her cheeks. "That means the case is closed forever," he said. "Of course, in the event of new and previously undisclosed evidence, the plaintiffs can petition the court, but it would have to be stunning and they'd have to find a lawyer willing to do that when the odds of winning are so remote. This is it, Maggie. You're through here. You did nothing wrong. There was no mistake."

"Oh God," she whispered weakly.

"I think some people are waiting for you," he said.

She looked up to see Rob Hollis leaning over the rail, grinning like a fool. "We're going to O'Malley's down the street, Maggie. Terry sent a posse ahead to hold tables. We're taking you out to celebrate."

"Jaycee?" she asked, looking around.

"She'll be there. She just had to call her service first. You coming? Of course you're coming!"

"Of course, yes," she said. "Go ahead. I'll meet you. I'm going to get out of the courthouse parking garage and drive down. And thanks," she said.

She turned to Steve. "Will you join us?" she asked.

"I'm going to pass," he said, laughing. "I wish I could, but there's always work to finish. Not for you, though. Your work here is done."

She hugged him. "We were lucky, weren't we?"

"You were in the right all along, but there's no such thing as a slam dunk in this business. Now go enjoy your friends. And get a good night's sleep."

"Thank you, Steve." She smiled. "Pleasure doing business with you."

"Hardly anyone is actually pleased when they have to do business with me..."

"Then we have that in common," she said. She grabbed her purse and briefcase and headed out the door.

She wanted to be alone. She wanted to be away from people. She saw a ladies' room sign at the end of a long deserted hallway far away from the courtroom, in the opposite direction from where the crowd seemed to be heading. She walked that way and ducked in. There was only one occupied stall so she washed her hands and checked her appearance. A little blotchy, but not bad. The toilet flushed and a uniformed female security officer came out, smiled hello, busied herself at the sink for a moment and departed.

Maggie pulled out her phone. She dialed Cal's cell phone number and mentally prepared a message. Since he'd been at the crossing he hadn't carried his phone during the day. He sometimes took it with him when he ran errands and checked it once or at most twice a day. He was free of encumbrances and seemed happy about that.

"Maggie?" he said.

"Cal? You're there?"

"Right here, baby," he said.

"Where are you right now?"

"I'm at space number eleven, cleaning out the grill, raking up the site."

"And you have your phone with you?" she asked, though she immediately thought it was such a foolish question. He answered, after all.

"I told you I would. I knew you were in court, Maggie. I wanted to be able to answer if you called."

She started to sob. She backed against the cold tiles of the bathroom wall and slowly slid down until she was sitting on her heels. Sitting on the heels of those dressy business pumps.

"Honey? You okay? Need me to come?"

"I'm okay," she whimpered. "It's over, Cal. It's over."

"Tell me," he said.

"Dismissed with prejudice. The judge made a fantastic speech... I wonder if it's possible to get a copy. He said the doctors were heroic."

"We'll get a copy," he said. "I know how to get a copy."

"There were friends there," she said, still crying and gasping a little. "I thought they mostly hated me. They were all listed as witnesses, deposed, subpoenaed. I didn't tell them but they came."

"Honey, where are you?"

"Oh. I'm in the bathroom. Why?"

He laughed. "There's an echo."

"I'm falling apart. They're having a celebration at a pub down the street and I'm in the bathroom, falling apart."

"You're just unloading the tension of a long ordeal. You're not going to fall apart. You need me to drive up there and sleep with you tonight?"

"No, I'm okay. I'm going to visit my mother and Walter on the way home tomorrow. But then..." She stopped and sniffed. "Then I'm coming home and I have nothing to do but you. Do you get that, California? I have no more court case, no job, no stress, no nothing. Nothing but you. I have to get something started or finished or figured out with you."

"Do you, now?" he asked, laughter in his voice.

"No pressure," she said. "We just have to figure out where we're going because I just don't want anything else. I want you in my life. While you're missing me tonight, figure out what I have to do to get that, will you?"

"Sure, Maggie," he said. And his voice was, if possible, smoldering.

"I think I'm falling in love with you, damn it. You're probably a worse risk than the artist or the ER doctor. I didn't do this on purpose. I had no intention. Please don't make me wait, Calhoun. You're a smart lawyer, come up with a statement of intent and a plan because I don't want to be strung along or crushed."

"Go have a glass of wine, Maggie," he said. "Everything is going to be fine. Don't drink and drive!"

"All right, then. But you better think about it!" She cried a little more. "I'll be back tomorrow."

"You'll be okay after a little cry and a few deep breaths," he said.

"Oh my God, I told you I love you on the phone in a courthouse bathroom! Crying! You probably don't believe me but I don't cry that much, just over huge ordeals, which in my life…"

"Are you going to try to take it back now?" he asked.

"This is why no one ever casts someone like me in a chick flick, because I don't even know how to stage words of love! Do you think I'm socially handicapped?"

"Maybe a little bit," he said.

"Oh, stop it! Well, it's probably true. You miss a lot of social training when you want premed…"

"And when you refuse debutante balls. I hear there's tons of social training for debutantes."

She laughed and slowly rose. "This must be so hard for you," she said. "Here you have experience with princesses and find yourself with a debutante reject."

"Only one princess," he reminded her. "And fooling around with me cost her the crown, so maybe you should be careful. Have you called Sully?"

"I'm going to do that right now, as soon as we hang up. I'll see you tomorrow, Calvin. Be prepared. I'm coming back with emotions blazing."

"I can't wait. Now go have fun! You've earned it."

"Maybe I'll call you tonight and interrupt your reading time."

"That'd be okay. Just call Sully. I'm not good at keeping secrets and he's been a little anxious today."

They said goodbye and Maggie tucked away her phone, deciding she could call Sully before going into O'Malley's. She occupied a stall briefly and when she came out she was facing Mrs. Markiff. The woman was waiting right outside the stall, a fierce look on her face.

"Mrs. Markiff!" she said, startled.

"I hope you're proud of yourself," she said bitterly. "You let my boy die and you got away with it."

"I did everything I could," Maggie said pleadingly. "I'm so sorry for your loss, but I did the best I could. There just wasn't anything more I could do."

"A person could try! You didn't try!" Then she whirled around and stormed out.

So there, Maggie thought. Just in case I needed to

be reminded that I'm not allowed even the briefest periods of happiness without a dark cloud passing over.

She left the ladies' room to call Sully, forcing any melancholy from her voice for his sake.

When Maggie walked into the pub, there were cheers. There were more people there from the hospital, those who hadn't made it to the courthouse but had been called with the news the case was dismissed. She was pulled into a party of at least twenty that grew as the hour got a little later and the day shift at the hospital ended. Doctors, nurses and techs showed up in jeans or scrubs to congratulate her, to show their support.

At first, overwhelmed by all the tension of the day and the presence of so many people who appreciated her, all she could do was nod and smile. After a glass of wine, she began to laugh as jokes and gossip were traded. People came and went as though it was an open house. At five o'clock, food appeared.

"It's going to be fine now," Terry, the RN from the operating room said. "Have another glass of wine. I'm driving you home in your car."

"But how will you get home?"

"I came over with Rob Hollis from the hospital and my husband, Jake, is coming." She shrugged and smiled. "Free food."

"Who put this together?" Maggie asked.

"I don't know. Everyone, more or less. Once the word got out that the first day of your suit started with the hearing, we all wanted to be here. The ones who had to work are just getting here a little later, that's all. Maggie, it's over."

"Mrs. Markiff met me in the bathroom to let me know how bitterly she hates me."

"You were the only chance her boy had. We go through this, Maggie. We go through it because who will they have if we don't?"

"I think I'm used up," she said.

"I hope to God not," Terry said. "We need you. What are you finding at Sully's we can't give you here?"

She gave a short huff of laughter. "I shot a guy who had abducted a fourteen-year-old girl."

"That was you? At Sully's?" she asked, surprised. "The news was pretty good at keeping the identity of the girl, the woman and the exact location of the incident quiet, but they did say it was a campground on a lake near Timberlake. I should've known." She laughed and clapped a hand on Maggie's shoulder. "You're a tough broad, Maggie."

"I always wanted to be something else," she said. "One of those frail, pretty girls who men felt they had to protect. Maybe I should have let my mother dress me up and send me to dance lessons."

"Yuck," Terry said.

"I played touch football, with some tackling. My mother almost died of heartbreak."

"Thank God you've never had an ounce of compromise in you," Terry said. "Listen, it's understandable if you need a break, but will you come up one of these days and have dinner at my house with Jake and maybe my daughter and her family? I miss you. I boss around those residents and I swear they pee their pants. When you're not around there's hardly any muscle in the operating room. It's sad. It's pathetic."

Maggie was so touched she sighed. "I miss you. I miss the OR."

"I like to hear that."

"I have a boyfriend," she said.

"Oh? Dr. Mathews, right?"

She shook her head. "We've been off a few months now. A new boyfriend. I met him at the crossing and he just won't go away. He's a lawyer."

Terry laughed. "Well, that'll probably come in handy."

At eight o'clock Maggie said goodbye to Jaycee, Rob and her other friends. Terry drove Maggie to her house, her husband following. She pulled into the drive behind a truck.

"Who's that?" Terry asked.

Maggie smiled. "The boyfriend. Want to meet him?"

"Bring him when you come to dinner. We'll get to know each other then."

Maggie got out of the car, Cal got out of the truck and they met in the drive. "Why are you here?" she asked.

"Just in case. If you need to be quiet and alone, I brought a good book. But I wanted to see you. I wanted to get my arms around a free woman."

"They had a celebration for me. That's my OR nurse…" she said, turning.

But Terry was moving toward the waiting car. She waved and yelled, "Bring him to dinner so we can look him over!" Then she jumped in her husband's car and off they went.

"Very outgoing, isn't she?" Cal said.

"Did you bring an overnight bag?" she asked.

"Always the optimist," he said with a nod. "Have you eaten?"

"Ate, drank, laughed," she said. "I wish I hadn't told you I wanted to do it alone, Cal. I wish you'd been with me tonight. I have some very good friends, it turns out."

Earth and sky, woods and fields,

lakes and rivers, the mountain and the sea,

are excellent schoolmasters, and teach some

of us more than we can ever learn from books.

—Sir John Lubbock

CHAPTER 14

Cal suggested he drive back to the crossing rather than join Maggie for her visit with Phoebe and Walter. "When the time is right, I'll visit them with you," he said.

"I can't wait to see what makes the time right," she said. But she let him off the hook.

This was a new experience for Cal, this kind of courtship. When he'd met Lynne he knew the second he saw her that she was the one. Crazy as it was, he'd felt it reaching way down inside him. There was something about her that signaled stability, sense of purpose, commitment—the things he had desperately needed at the time. It didn't hurt that she was beautiful, sexy and fun.

Maggie wasn't really so different, it had just taken him longer to see it. She was equally stable with an uncanny sense of purpose, even though she was on hiatus from her purpose at the moment. He was attracted right away, but how hard was that? Maggie was hot—tall, lean, muscular with high cheekbones and a quirky, slightly crooked smile. And she didn't know that about herself—that she was stunning, which only added to her sexiness. He loved the way she stood, one knee bent, her foot balanced on a toe like some kind of dancer. And there were a dozen other qualities that kept turning up, making his attraction stronger and stronger. Her strength was empowering. It was ironic—she thought her strength was running out and that she had to step back, but it was only growing stronger. She was a little afraid, given all the complications in her life, that's all. She wasn't weakening. She was so demanding of herself. She was demanding of others, too, but fair. He thought watching her with Sully was a premonition of what was to come when her future husband became old and infirm. She might not know it yet, but she was going to be just like Sully toward her children when she was old and creaky. She loved hard, but with compassion. She was fearless. Because she hurt over things that had happened to her professionally, she thought she was running out of courage, but it was the opposite. She was afraid her fast action and fearlessness was going to keep giving her trouble over and over. She was partly right—at some point you have to decide if you can take the heat. More specifically, you have to decide if what you do is worth the trouble. She was asking herself that question right now. He bet on her finding the answer soon.

Cal had certainly been down that road. His profession was no easier. Stress management was almost a hobby for him. The rush he got from winning kept him going back for more.

Then things changed.

It wasn't just losing Lynne, though that was huge. It was the fact that those things he had done to protect himself and his wife hadn't worked. He'd gotten himself a great education and then a big reputation for success. They said he had stars in his pockets, that he was destined for greatness. He bought a large, sturdy house, exactly the kind of house he thought people who knew what they were doing and where they were going would live in, large enough to hold a family and a future. They put down roots, got enmeshed in the community, poured themselves into each other and work. They even dealt very admirably and intelligently with Lynne's condition.

Then one day she was sick and in pain. The next couple of days were okay, then bad days followed, then a few good... It wasn't long before Lynne suffered disfigurement and chronic pain. She couldn't work. Their lives became more of coping and praying than living and working. Her last six months had been hideous. Cal went to work because Lynne wanted him to, because she believed his work fed a need in him and that he'd have a life after her.

He had tried to make that true for her sake but it took every fiber of his being to keep from crumbling in front of her while she was going through the last months. Weeks. Days. The only thing that kept him upright was an overpowering need to match her courage; the only reason he tried to get on with his life was for her. The truth was, there were so many hours he just wanted to go with her. He felt like his insides had been pulled out, stomped on, stuffed back into him. Life without her seemed unendurable.

He kept trying after she was gone, and he did it not for himself but to honor her. All she wanted was for him to live, to find joy in life.

Well, that had taken a while. But here he was, remarkably, having a life. One he hadn't planned but found intensely satisfying.

Between insurance, Lynne's legacy, a couple of bonuses and the sale of the house, he had some money. He tried to turn the trust back to her parents but they wouldn't have it—he had been a devoted husband and they appreciated his love and loyalty, especially during the darkest days. Lynne's will left a few special items to her parents for remembrance's sake but the rest to Cal. Now his quest was simple—he just wanted to belong to someone and something. Life was precious and not to be taken for granted, and he would not disgrace his wife's memory with self-pity or misery. Part of that was being of service. It didn't have to be winning the most high-profile case. Sometimes it was stocking shelves.

One of the many things Cal had learned was that the role he'd assumed as a kid, becoming the parent in a dysfunctional family, wasn't temporary. He still had that need—to take care of people, watch over those he loved.

He was watching over Maggie. He was pretty sure she had no idea.

Maggie had packed a pair of jeans to wear on the drive home but instead she showered, blew out her hair and put on her dress, the one she had worn to court. She knew it would please Phoebe. She called her mother and asked if they could meet at her club for brunch because she wanted to talk.

While Cal made breakfast, she checked her email. She thought there might be a couple—word travels fast in hospitals. "Holy shit," she said. There were over fifty!

"What do they say?" he asked.

"Mostly congratulations, I think. It's going to take

me forever to read through them. I had no idea people were paying this much attention. People didn't say much. Just things like *good luck* and *it'll be okay* and *tough break, Maggie*—that sort of thing."

"All doctors probably relate," he said. "If you didn't express a need to talk about it, they probably didn't want to pry too much."

"Would I have heard from them if I'd been beaten to a pulp instead?"

"How will you ever know?" he countered.

Maggie couldn't help her doubts. *Do they really like me? Respect me? Or only like and respect me if I win?*

They ate a quick breakfast, Cal washed up the dishes while she read through email after email, then he quickly got out of her hair so she could read and answer as many as possible before it was time to drive to Golden.

There was one from Andrew.

Maggie, love. You've been on my mind since the day I last saw you. Before that, to tell the truth. I don't blame you if you're still angry with me—that was a stupid ass thing for me to do, telling you I couldn't take it anymore, rejecting the idea of our baby. So now I hear the suit is over and your life can get back to some resemblance to normal, as much as lives like ours can. I just want you to know—I'm not over you. I'm sorry. I'm filled with regrets. I miss you and I'd do just about anything to have another chance. We can even revisit the idea of a child, the little matter that had us at each other's throats. If it's that important to you, let's talk about it. At least think about it, will you? We were happy; we had a good time together despite the complications of our lives. I love you, Maggie. And I think you loved me. Tell me what to do and I'll do it. Andrew.

She stopped herself before emailing back, *Kiss my ass, Andrew.* She'd think of something profound to say to him on her drive home.

There were emails from colleagues who wanted her to talk about possibly leasing office space, joining their practices, offers of part-time work on call, even suggestions of teaching assignments. *Teaching?* She thought she was a basket case, yet some surgeons thought she was stable enough to teach.

It was the first time in too long that she felt there were many wonderful possibilities ahead. She felt strong and above all, with Cal's encouragement embracing her, she thought her future was bright. Their future had great potential. She vowed to consider all the offers and see if she could do that thing Walter had long ago advised—find out how to make her personal and professional goals match.

She drove to Golden with that on her mind.

Phoebe's eyes lit up when she saw Maggie all dressed up. She told her she looked beautiful and got a little misty-eyed.

"There was a hearing yesterday," Maggie told Phoebe and Walter. "The judge threw out the lawsuit with prejudice, which means they can't retry it or appeal it. He said he didn't see a case. In fact, the judge said some very encouraging things, complimentary things. I'm going to try to get a copy of the hearing. If I do, I'll share it with you."

"Oh, thank God!" Phoebe said. "Then you're coming back to Denver!"

"Mother, I have no practice," she said.

"That's a mere formality. You can work, I know you can. You can take a position with the hospital. Or the university medical school! Walter can ask around. You can figure out what to do about a practice and start seeing patients again. I know you wouldn't waste that marvelous education and spectacular gift."

Phoebe proceeded to stop people in the dining room of the club and announce, with great excitement, that Maggie's lawsuit was over and she won! The maître d' brought champagne to the table.

"Now stop, Mother," Maggie said firmly. "I didn't actually win. I failed to lose."

"So now you'll go back to work, correct?" Phoebe said.

"I don't have everything all sorted out just yet," she said.

"What on earth is there to sort out?" she asked.

Maggie lifted her glass and took a sip of champagne. She put down the glass and looked at her mother. "Remember, way back when you were a young woman with a child living at the crossing? Remember, you hated it and one day you decided that wasn't enough of a life for you?"

"One day? Maggie, I starting planning to leave the second I got there! I put aside money for at least a year! And I'd really rather not talk about that right now, if you please. It's a very unpleasant memory."

"A year," she said. "Huh. Well that explains a few things, like how you had enough money to get us to

Chicago and rent a very nice downtown apartment. You were skimming money, weren't you?"

"Be civil," Phoebe hissed.

"I took a brief leave of absence from my practice when I was forty," Walter said. "I think it was three months. Maybe four. I traveled some. I went to Tibet. I was in search of something. Those monks…" He smiled.

"Not a lot of serenity in neurosurgery, Walter?" Maggie said.

"Problem was, I was already too serene. Even neurosurgery couldn't beat it out of me. I wasn't bothered by the risk or the critics or my envious colleagues. My problem wasn't burnout. Not so much. I had no balance in my life. My family, God bless every one, would bore the paint off an old Chevy."

Phoebe gasped. "Your mother was a lovely, genteel lady!"

"My mother was a hopeless snob, but the two of you got on admirably. My colleagues were about as interesting plus twice as pompous. My house, which was large and impressive, echoed. I loved surgery, even the most challenging cases. But my life was empty. You'd think saving lives would be more fulfilling, wouldn't you?"

"Walter," Maggie said. "Why didn't you ever tell me this?"

"Well, that was all before I met your mother. And there didn't seem to be any need to. Didn't you have what you wanted?"

She wasn't quite ready to face that. "Back to you. So you went to Tibet. To find balance?"

"Tibet was another extreme. I was looking for the median. The radical center." He grabbed Phoebe's hand.

"I found your mother in the restaurant. She was the hostess. I started to eat there every night."

"Oh, Walter..." Phoebe said, touched.

"But wait, Phoebe had a daughter. What was I then? Seven? Eight?"

"Yes, a daughter." He chuckled a little. "You did nothing to enhance my serenity, by the way."

"Now, Walter," Maggie said with a smile.

"Maggie, you were abominable," he said. "Most days I couldn't tell if I was anxious to see what bad thing you'd done or excited to hear you'd been a good child for a change. It was a bundle, see. It was nothing like the family I grew up in—it was *interesting*. It took me a little while but I suspected you had a very high IQ, not that you needed one to be a surgeon. But there was such intelligence in you, especially when you were bad. I had you tested."

"I thought that was Mother!" Maggie exclaimed.

He was shaking his head. "I gave strict instructions that you never be told the results. That Phoebe, especially, never be told!"

"Walter?" Phoebe asked, as if deeply hurt.

"You have so many wonderful qualities, darling, but humility is not one of them. You would have had the number put on T-shirts. Besides, the most brilliant scientists in the world don't have the recipe for happiness."

Maggie took a sip of champagne. "Well. I'm thirty-six and have been around the block. What's the number? How brilliant am I?"

"You must think I just fell off the turnip truck," Walter said with a laugh. "All evidence is gone. It's right here," he said, tapping his temple. "And right here is getting less reliable by the day."

"I can't believe you think I'm a snob," Phoebe said in a little pout.

"Don't complain, Phoebe. You taught me to have fun. And to value the frustrations of a real home life. I even half enjoyed all those parties you carted me off to." He rolled his eyes.

"How'd you two manage to be happy with all you were up against?" Maggie asked Walter.

"It was probably all the great sex," Walter said.

"Ah! God!" Maggie said. "I can't believe you said that!"

He laughed and sipped his champagne. "I'm not a very exciting guy, Maggie, I know that. Hardly anyone would take me for a complicated man with many layers. They saw one thing—a nice but boring man with a skill for neurosurgery. I was told many times that I wasn't personable. One patient said he was so grateful for me, I changed his life forever. He also said he wouldn't want to go to a ball game with me, but he sure was grateful. Most of my colleagues had way too many layers—booming personalities, many needs and desires, more emotions than one genie could stuff in a lamp. They were exciting men and women. I don't even have much of a sense of humor.

"But I did need things. I wasn't much fun but that didn't mean I couldn't want a fun-loving woman. I wasn't much of a romantic but I certainly appreciated how important love was. I wasn't full of great wisdom but I thought I could be a good father. I thought I knew enough and felt enough to raise a child successfully, though you did cast doubt on that idea a million times. There were twenty or thirty empty places inside me that could not be filled by neurosurgery, although that part

of me did seem vital. One thing I found objectionable…
When you make a steel worker walk again after he can't
even wiggle his toes, he shouldn't say, 'You might not
have much of a personality, Doc, but you sure know
how to untangle a spinal cord.'"

Maggie gave a snort of laughter and realized she was
tearing up. *Sweet Walter, brilliant Walter, just as complicated as everyone else.*

"How in the world did you think you could fill up
the empty places inside you with an incorrigible child?"
she asked.

"I didn't," Walter said. "But up until you and your
mother came into my world, I was living only for myself. I needed more. I needed someone to live for." He
chuckled softly. "You certainly filled the bill, Maggie."

"Weren't you afraid of being taken completely for
granted?"

Walter shook his head. "I didn't say I was looking to
be used. I said I needed a purpose greater than myself."

"Enough," Phoebe said. "Enough melancholy! We
should be celebrating! Maggie won her case and is coming back to this part of the world. I'll get my decorator
to go over to your house and make sure everything is
like new. I'll send Carmen and her cleaning crew over.
We'll get back to our lives. Our *real* lives!"

Walter and Maggie just looked at each other and
smiled.

Before Maggie left the club to drive home, she em-
braced Walter. "Thank you, Walter. You were a wonderful father. And I love you."

Since Cal was driving through Leadville on his way
back to the crossing, he stopped at that little hole-in-

the-wall bookstore he liked. The bookstore was one of the places he was reminded of things he wouldn't willingly change—he liked the old classics, he liked maps, he liked paper. He had an electronic reader and he used it sometimes, but he liked holding the book, smelling it. Books equaled freedom to Cal—the freedom to keep a few books of his choice, for one thing. You don't store much of a library in a converted bus, the family's favorite home on wheels. It was a little like hiking, like stocking the backpack—if you wanted several books, you had to sacrifice a few other items, like jeans and shoes. For Cal, those choices weren't hard—he loved his books. Then it was the freedom of thought. Finally the freedom learning presented; the ability to achieve, to move forward.

Once he was in the bookstore, he was in no great hurry. He'd choose with care. He took a few books off the shelf and sat in a leather chair, carefully looking at the cover, copy, binding, first pages.

Someone on the other side of the shelf was fanning pages, sighing and grunting a lot. It sounded like a man who couldn't get comfortable. But there was something a little familiar about the sounds. Cal left his short stack of books on the table beside his chair and walked around the double-wide shelf. Sitting in the corner, a couple of thick, oversize softcover reference books on his lap, Tom Canaday groaned again and rubbed his head.

Cal chuckled. "One of the kids forget to do a report or something?"

Tom looked up. "They're all out of school, man. Well, Zach's got some summer school because he won't pay attention and he gets behind." He looked down at the books in his lap. One was about lawsuits and the other—Colorado laws. "I got issues."

"Need a hand?"

Tom had a pained expression on his face. "I can't talk about it," he said. "The kids don't know anything about this and I can't tell 'em."

"Okay."

"My folks don't know anything about this. No one knows anything. No one can know."

Cal sat on the thick table in front of Tom and lifted a book. "Legal issues, Tom?"

He sighed heavily. He looked like maybe he was going to cry.

"Maybe I can help?"

"I don't think so, Cal."

"Two heads are better than one," he said. "I know how to keep a confidence."

"I don't know."

"Whatever it is, you think there's a book on it?"

Tom nodded. "I got a workbook on divorce in here. But what I need... I don't know..."

"I'm a whiz at the library," Cal said. "If there's a book to help you solve your problem, I can find it for you."

"You won't say anything to anyone?"

"It's in the vault. Let's go get a cup of coffee."

They walked down the street and around the block off the main drag to a diner the locals favored. While they walked, Tom talked.

"My ex-wife, Becky, she's in trouble. Bad trouble. I don't know where to start. I think I should start by telling you about us. Me. Maybe I should tell you about me.

"One of the problems with growing up in a small

town, some of us just don't think big enough. My dad had a small ranch. I played football in high school and helped my dad and the idea of growing into that ranch worked for me. I had a serious crush on Becky, who was a year younger, but I was planning to go to college and we were going to get married after. But being the genius I am, I got her pregnant. My dad's real old-fashioned, he told me to quit school, get a job or two, marry her and sleep in the bed I made.

"Getting married, even though we were way too young and it was way too hard, that wasn't so bad. We lived in my folks' basement for a year or so, then we rented part of a house from a widow and it was pretty awful so I fixed it up until it was pretty darn nice. By the time Jackson was a year old the folks had come around and my dad and brother helped me fix up the house. In fact, I bet they paid for as many materials as I did. So, life was okay—I worked a lot, but I had good jobs. I drove a trash truck for a few years—dirty job but damn, the county pays good and the benefits are great. Then I started driving the plow and that pays great.

"We had Nikki and were a real content little family just barely old enough to vote. Then, after that there were a couple of accidents—Brenda and Zach. I don't know if it was me or four kids or just the natural order of things, but when Zach was about four, Becky had had enough. She wanted a life. Can't say I blame her. Four kids and a husband who works all the time—not much of a life."

"What about you?" Cal asked. "You had just as many kids. And you worked all the time."

"Yeah, but I had the life I wanted," he said with a shrug. "Still do. Pretty much."

"So you've been divorced how long?" Cal asked.

"She left about eight years ago, we've been divorced about six years now. We did it ourselves. Becky's never been far away. She moved to Aurora, worked and went to school, came back to Timberlake and stayed with us all the time. At one point she thought it'd be a good idea if the girls lived with her and the boys with me." He snorted and shook his head. "We tried it, but it didn't last long. But she shows up regularly. In fact, sometimes it's just like we're married, only nicer."

Cal thought it might be impolite to ask, but it sounded like those were conjugal visits.

They sat in a booth in the back of the diner, ordered pie and coffee and Cal waited for Tom to get to the point. Instead he talked about his on-again-off-again relationship with his wife.

"And now Becky's in jail," he finally said. He hung his head.

"Ho, boy," Cal said. "For?"

"Solicitation." He shook his head. "I said it had to be a mistake, she wouldn't do that. She said it was all a mistake. And it had been a mistake the first two times, too. It's the third time. She said they're going to make her go to jail. She needs help. She called me for help. What the hell am I gonna do? And if she's in jail, the kids are gonna know something is terrible wrong."

Cal's mouth didn't even hang open in awe, though he was a little surprised. Tom and his kids seemed so homespun, such simple rural folks without the kind of problems they have in the city. But given Cal's experience as a defense attorney, he'd seen and heard just about everything.

"I never suspected anything like this, not in a million years. I thought she lived pretty good for an office worker. But she's so beautiful, I thought she had boyfriends. Generous boyfriends. She didn't talk about her love life, but I figured she had one even though I didn't have one. But she could afford things. Nice things."

"Did you pay support?" Cal asked.

"I didn't really pay alimony," he said. "We didn't have an arrangement for that since I had the kids. But sometimes she ran short and I gave her money. I paid some child support for that little while when she had the girls. I wanted to be sure they were getting what they needed, you know?"

"Your original agreement is for joint custody?" Cal asked.

"We wrote it that way, yeah. The idea was to help each other out with the kids."

"What about property?" Cal asked.

"What property?" he asked with a laugh.

"Furniture? Cars?"

He shrugged. "I told her to take anything she wanted, I didn't want to fight. What I wanted was for her to stay."

"Have you gotten over that now?"

"I guess it's about time, isn't it? I don't know that I'll ever be able to let the kids visit her now. And her coming to us?" He shook his head. "I can't think about that right now. Zach and Brenda, twelve and fourteen, at the absolute worst time for teenagers, they don't need this. But she loves her kids and they love her. I want to believe it's a mistake, but three mistakes? Man, I'm so screwed."

"Does she have a lawyer?" Cal asked.

"Not yet, but she said she'll have to find one. She has nice stuff but she doesn't exactly have money. And she's heard bad things about court appointed lawyers, like they get a little lazy on these free clients."

"I don't think that's necessarily true. But I think you're going to need a little help here, Tom. Legal help."

He shook his head. "I'll go online and study up. There's gotta be lots of help online. I bet if I break down and tell Jackson, he'll help me look things up. After he recovers from his nervous breakdown. That kid is smarter than anything. But I—"

"Tom, you need a lawyer."

"Cal, I can't hire a lawyer. I can't even bail her out— she's gonna have to sit there till her court date in a week or so. We get by job to job. We're doing all right but there's not two nickels left over, trust me."

"You have options. There's got to be a legal clinic around here somewhere. Might be Denver or Colorado Springs, but there's help out there. An attorney with experience in criminal defense would be best. Or maybe I can help you. I'm an attorney. But I have no experience in Colorado statutes. I can learn, though. It's not complicated, just a matter of looking things up."

Tom's mouth was hanging open. "You're a what?"

"Lawyer," Cal said. "A defense attorney, as a matter of fact. I practiced in Michigan and the state of Colorado has graciously extended licensing to me here."

"You're a *lawyer*? And you're raking campsites and taking out trash?"

Cal smiled. "I am a man of many talents. I also have a checkbook in the truck. Let's go by the bank so you can get Becky out of jail."

Maggie enjoyed the drive back to Sully's. She used the time to think about her conversation with Walter.

The first thing she was going to do—she was going to find a way to show Walter how much he mattered in her life. She had two pretty awesome fathers, nothing alike, and each in his own way, sensitive and astute. She wasn't sure what would have become of her if she hadn't had both of them in her life.

So here we are. Four and a half months ago she'd felt she had lost everything. She'd thought she had nothing. No one. No one but Sully. And even Sully, she'd thought, hadn't really wanted her. And no one needed her. Oh, there had been patients but she was hardly the only neurosurgeon.

Almost five months later her biggest discovery was that she wanted it *all.* She wanted her fathers, her dippy mother, a husband or at least a full-time partner. And a child. She wanted that child she felt had been taken from her. She wanted a full home life—and she wanted to practice again. She wanted to pull her salad out of the garden but also to go to excellent restaurants now and then. She wanted everything. There would have to be compromises, but she'd figure that out.

Who was that husband going to be? It was not going to be Andrew; that relationship was far behind her. But was there any way to convince California Jones he'd be happy with her? She had the slightly paranoid fear she was a placeholder and that he hadn't yet decided what his life would look like in the future.

As she drove into the campground, she came upon the strangest sight. There were people on the porch of the store, the porch of the house, and several were sitting in cars. And Stan's big SUV police cruiser was parked between a huge bull and the store. There were a couple of turned-over picnic tables, a collapsed tent and a healthy dent in the police cruiser.

"Maggie, stay in the car!" Stan's voice boomed over his loudspeaker.

There, in the grassy area between the store and the campsites, the bull was grazing lazily. But it was very clear that before he settled down to lunch, he'd scared everyone half to death.

She looked at the ceiling of her car. "When I said *all*, I wasn't counting on this!"

Come forth into the light of things,

let nature be your teacher.

—WILLIAM WORDSWORTH

CHAPTER 15

Colorado was an open-range state. That meant the cattle roamed where they would, though ranchers took some measures to keep their herds segregated. The lake and the campgrounds and homes around the lake were surrounded by cattle ranches and grazing land. The entire valley was cattle land with a little silage farming for feed. If you didn't want cows in your yard you had to fence yourself in, and that included public roads, lands and parks. Though it wasn't a daily issue, there were times a piece of fence was down and cattle wandered onto the roads and highways, into parks and yards.

Ranchers usually kept closer tabs on their bulls, especially if they were a little testy, as this one was.

Maggie spied Cal on the porch and gave him a sheepish wave. He waved back.

She put her car in gear and oh-so-gently inched her way around the store to the rear entrance. Cal stepped out of the store onto the back porch and signaled to her that it was safe to get out of her car and come inside.

"Better stay indoors. You're not dressed to try to outrun that bull," he said, taking her hand and tugging her into the store.

"Where's Sully?"

"Trying to keep everyone back. And don't surprise him—he's got the shotgun out."

A little laugh escaped her. "What's he going to do with a shotgun besides piss him off?"

"We've had that discussion. He said not to worry, that Stan has the big gun, but he's not convinced Stan's a better shot."

"Lovely. Maybe they'll have a shoot-out," she said. She walked toward the front of the store, which was full of women and children. But the men and a couple of young women, it seemed, just couldn't resist the porch. "Hi, Sully. That the Mitchells' bull?"

"Yeah, and they're taking their sweet goddamn time coming after him. I'm going to send them a bill. That goddamn bull had himself a party."

"I thought that might be Cornelius. Anybody hurt?" she asked.

"Scraped knee or two. I think we're all okay. Bet some folks'll never trust this campground again."

"Others will think it's the best entertainment they've had," Maggie said. And right then and there she decided. *I'm going to stay here, raise my family here.*

"Here she comes, about time," Sully said. "I ought to load that bull with buckshot just for good measure. Can't she keep an eye on her bull?"

"Watch this, Cal," Maggie said. "You're going to love it. When the truck and trailer pull in and park, get some of the kids up front to watch them wrangle Cornelius."

A well-used truck, a big dually pulling a roomy trailer, pulled up alongside the bull. The driver, a young guy in a cowboy hat, gave them a wave. The passenger door on the other side opened and a young girl in tight jeans, boots and hat with long blond hair running in a braid down her back, came around the truck with a lead and a big harness. She stood for a minute in front of the bull, a hand on one hip, staring him down. The bull pawed at the ground twice and snorted meanly.

"Don't start with me," the girl said. She approached the big animal. He backed away. "Corny! That's enough!"

The young man jumped out of the truck and opened up the trailer, putting down the ramp.

The bull stood still. He put his head down and the girl shook hers.

She attached the lead to a huge harness. "Come on, Corny. You're in trouble."

She led the enormous bull to the trailer. The bull went slowly. Calmly. When he was inside the girl jumped out and helped the young man close up the trailer. He ran to the driver's side of the truck. He waved at Sully. "Sorry for the inconvenience," he yelled. Then they pulled slowly away from the campground.

"What the—" Cal stuttered.

"She raised him from a calf," Sully said. "Some nights she slept in the barn with him. His mother didn't make it and Casey fed him from a bottle. She and a couple of the Mitchells can seem to manage him, but no one else. Don't get the idea he's safe—he's a big, ornery bull. But he's fathered half the herd and he takes orders from Casey Mitchell. She got a blue ribbon for him."

"Isn't it the cutest thing you've ever seen?" Maggie said.

"He turned over two picnic tables. Stan was going to shoot him. People were running and screaming," Cal said.

"Yeah, I didn't say he wasn't a troublemaker, but I

don't think he's ever hurt anyone. I mean, if you get between Cornelius and a heifer when they're courting, there could be trouble, but usually he just likes people out of his way and sometimes he likes to show off a little bit. He's mostly a big spoiled baby with only one mommy and she's a hundred-and-five-pound teenager," Sully said.

Maggie grinned. "I told you you'd like it. Better than a magic trick, isn't it? The truth, California—isn't this the most awesome place?"

"Oh, awesome! Escaped Alzheimer patients, kidnappers, naked hikers and a crazy bull so far."

"We're just getting warmed up. Summer's not over yet."

It made Cal uncomfortable keeping things from Maggie, but it was the nature of his profession that all cases, no matter how small or large, were confidential. So, when she asked him why he was on his laptop so much the very next afternoon, he made up a small, partial lie. "Someone I met at the bookstore in Leadville was asking questions about Colorado law and I offered to help research. A good excuse to get a little more familiar with Colorado statutes."

"Does she have a name?" Maggie wanted to know.

"*He* does, but I think I should keep that confidential. Just as you would keep a patient's medical information confidential."

"Hmm. It occurs to me that if we were both working we wouldn't have much to talk about."

He presented her with his finest lascivious grin. "I believe we will never run out of interesting and stimulating subject matter."

Cal had told Tom to ask his ex-wife if she'd like to consult with an experienced defense attorney and if so, he would have to see her at once. The next day he called and said Becky was very anxious to talk to a good lawyer. Since Cal didn't have an office, he made arrangements to go to Becky's house.

Cal parked across the street from a nice-looking town house in a pleasant little neighborhood that backed up to a golf course. This was his first time in Aurora and clearly it was upscale, with lots of building going on, wide clean streets, impeccable landscaping and more than the average quotient of late-model SUVs and sports cars. Becky, Tom had told him, worked for a plastic surgeon in Aurora.

Aurora was not a cheap place to live.

He knocked on the door and she answered. "Hi, Becky. I'm Cal Jones."

"Thanks for coming," she said, opening the door for him.

His first impression was—*attractive*. The first thing he noticed was boobs. Yes, they were larger than average yet not obnoxiously so. Her crisp white blouse was open just enough to showcase her cleavage and those *ta-tas* were standing proud. Through the fabric of the blouse he could discern bra straps about the width of string. The bra was not capable of holding her up meaning, after four children, those thirty-six-year-old breasts had been enhanced.

Becky was casually dressed in denim capris and wedge-heeled sandals. Her red hair was pulled back in a demure clip and she wasn't wearing a lot of makeup. She walked ahead of him to a sunny dining room.

"I made coffee and lemonade," she said.

"A cup of coffee would be nice," he said. "Black."

She preferred lemonade and he waited for her to get settled. He had his laptop with him but he pulled out a simple tablet from his canvas bag. He told her a little about himself, that he'd been practicing law for ten years but the last year he'd been on leave, traveling, just kicking around. Then, mainly to see how she'd respond, he said, "I lost my wife to a long illness and needed time to adjust."

She ran her thumb and forefinger up and down the icy glass of lemonade. Her nails were perfect. Her eyes were large and luminous. "I'm so, so sorry. She must've been very young."

"My age. So, I don't have an office and I haven't had a firm in a year, but I'm licensed in Colorado."

"Bless your heart," she said, her eyes so soft and warm. "I can't imagine how difficult that must be. You must miss her so much."

"So, once you decide you want me to represent you, you can notify the DA's office and I can pick up a copy of the police report. But first, maybe you should tell me what your expectations are."

"I don't know what you mean," she said, tucking a leg under herself, leaning an elbow on the table.

"What do you think I can do for you, Becky?"

"Hopefully you'll keep me from going to jail," she said. "It's such a terrible, unfortunate misunderstanding."

"Shouldn't you be expecting a fine? Maybe a fine and community service? It's not typical for a jail sentence for soliciting."

"I don't dare take any chances and go without a lawyer," she said. "The last time the judge said if it happened again, he'd give me ninety days. *That* was a misunderstanding! But I never had a chance to explain. I'll lose my job and everything."

"Everything?"

"Well, my income, my benefits. And people will know. The people at work, the family, probably the whole neighborhood. The kids…"

"Your arrest is a matter of public record," he informed her.

"But why would anyone look?" she asked. She teared up, her blue eyes getting a little glassy.

A blue-eyed redhead? Well, they weren't really blue, it was probably contacts, and was the red hair real? None of the four kids had red hair. She smoothed her hair over one ear and looked at him with those big blue eyes. And she slowly lowered her lids. A hand went gently to her throat.

"I was so careful."

"Careful?"

"I'm not a prostitute. I'm more of an escort. There are a few men who come to town regularly and we go out, that's all. Sometimes they're a little lonely and need someone to talk to. It's like performing a service. You know?"

"Becky, you don't have to convince me of anything. Just tell me the facts because I'm going to find out the reason you were arrested. And it wasn't for going out on a date or performing a service. How long have you been in this business?"

"The escort business?" she asked.

"Precisely," he said, encouraging her.

Her graceful hands moved around as she talked, stroking the glass, touching a button, smoothing her napkin. Her tongue touched her lips and she blinked sometimes. But her mascara didn't run.

"Business, yes. A friend I once worked with invited me to dinner with a couple of gentlemen from out of town. She was an escort. She said we'd be paid by the hour just to have dinner with these men and it was a lot of money. I can't remember how much, but I think fifty dollars an hour or something. And when dinner was over, I just went home. I did that a few times. Then a couple of the gentlemen I'd been out with called me and asked me for a date and I said yes and they paid me—as if it was a paid date, just like before. I was thinking it was just an ordinary date—meet at the restaurant, have dinner, go home. I didn't do any more than that for a long, long time. After a year or so, with a gentleman I happened to be quite fond of, it went further. But the money was the same so you see, I wasn't selling my body. I was selling my time. I was a paid escort who made an adult decision to be more intimate with a client. Consenting adults."

"I understand completely," Cal said. "And you should know, the judge isn't going to buy that."

"Very narrow-minded of him, don't you think?" she asked.

She's throwing off pheromones like crazy, Cal thought. And while she started out as pretty, she was growing beautiful. Sexy. She was very good at this—the way she talked, moved her hands, adjusted herself in the chair, her soft voice.

"What was different about this last time?" he asked.

"I'll tell you what—I was tricked, that's what. Something I hardly ever do because I just don't have the time, I was going to meet a girlfriend for a drink. There were no gentlemen involved. I wasn't meeting a man. While I was waiting in the bar a man took the stool two down and after he got his drink, he started to talk to me. He was very nice, very friendly, and he asked me if I wanted to go on a date and I said, *What kind of date?* Because I was waiting for a friend. And he said, *How about a short date to my room?* And I laughed at him and said that didn't sound like a date. Dinner in a nice restaurant sounded more like a date, but unfortunately I was busy. And he said, *Well, if you changed your mind, what would something like that cost?* He was harassing me, annoying me. Like I'd ever go anywhere with someone that pushy. And I told him I didn't have the first idea because I wasn't about to go on a *date* to his hotel room. And he pushed and said, *But if you did? What would it cost?* And I said, *A lot! Hundreds and hundreds of dollars!* And he arrested me!"

"Did he give you money?"

"No. He just talked about it."

"And did you go to his room?"

She shook her head. "No! He was leading me out of the hotel bar when my friend was walking in. He put me in handcuffs! And my friend said, *What the hell is this?* And the man pulled out his badge to show her. And she asked him if he was crazy."

"And this friend? Also an *escort*?"

"As it happens, she's a yoga instructor! I called her as soon as I got home to tell her it was a terrible misunderstanding. But I think she wonders about me now. This is awful."

"Did he *show* you money?" Cal asked.

"No," she said.

"Listen to me carefully, Becky. If that police officer

was wired, will the recording be exactly as you say? Or will it sound more like you were setting a price and telling him the rules for the game?"

"It will sound exactly as I told you. Ex-act-ly."

Cal scribbled a few things on his tablet. "Well, the next thing to do is get a copy of the police report, the arrest report, and plan a defense in time for your court date."

"It's in a week," she said.

"What happened the last two times you were arrested?"

"Does that matter?"

"Just to me. The fact that you were arrested could come up but the details won't affect the outcome of this situation."

"Well, a gentleman I was having dinner with told a maître d' that I was a hooker and he called a cop. Apparently he was irked at the escort price when he wasn't getting sex and didn't want to pay it. So see? I was in trouble for not being a hooker! That was the first time. The second time it was a female police officer undercover and she was asking me how I managed to get into my escort business because she wanted to get into the business, so just for fun I demonstrated how easy it was to attract a man in a bar and interest him in an escort. It was very confusing because I wasn't going to do anything then, either. But the man was her partner and they *both* took me to jail. I paid a fine because it was less than it would cost to hire a lawyer. But I'm telling you, I'm not doing anything to break the law!"

"What you're *not* doing happens to be against the law. Working as an escort who occasionally supplies sex is illegal, whether the price is affected or not and something tells me you already know that. But we might get lucky this time. I'll have to see the arrest documents before I'll know for sure."

"I want this to go away," she said.

"What's your job position? With the doctor you work for?"

"I'm mainly a receptionist, but I also do some computer work. I check patients in, check them out. It's a cash business—most plastic surgeons don't run insurance paperwork. I really love my job."

"And you've done this for how long?"

"I've been with him for five years now."

"Okay, that's all I need for today," Cal said, sliding his tablet into his bag and getting to his feet.

She stood as well and looked at him sadly. "But you hardly touched your coffee," she said sweetly.

"Another time, Becky," he said. At the door he turned toward her. "I suggest that you don't go on any dates with anyone before your court date."

"Sure," she said. "Unless you want to get together. To talk?"

"If I need to talk to you, it'll be business. Have a good day."

"Cal?" she asked. "Will you be talking to Tom about this? I know you're friends."

He shook his head. "I won't be talking to anyone about this. What you tell me is confidential."

"Thank you," she said softly.

He threw his canvas bag in the passenger seat of his truck and started the ignition. He chuckled as he thought about the case. *She's a hooker. A pricey hooker who probably rarely gets dinner but commands a decent hotel room and an excellent price. Very likely she meets*

*clients in the doctor's office. She probably doesn't have
more than one, at most two appointments in a single
night. She's discriminating and her gentlemen probably
appreciate her very much. And she's going to be one of
my repeat customers for legal representation.*

Cal spent the next day at the courthouse rounding up
documents and lining up a witness he hoped he wouldn't
be using. He met with an assistant DA and suggested
he not press charges based on the arrest report alone,
but the young man wanted to go to court. So they were
on for the following Wednesday.

The weekend found the campground full and busy.
People were floating out on the lake, sunning, fishing,
swimming. There was a tent or small trailer on every
campsite, grills in constant use, lawn chairs out, beach
towels spread and picnic tables moved around—first
come first serve. The smell of hot dogs cooking and
the sound of softballs *thwacking* into mitts filled the
air. People were coming and going to the nearby trails
and cliffs all day. The store was teeming with business
and probably one of the most gratifying scenes was
Sully, enjoying the pinnacle of good health, greeting
old friends from years past, customers returning to the
crossing for their vacations or long weekend.

During summer, every hand was employed, though
Enid kept shorter days since Sully had extra help.
Once she got her baking done, she went home—
summer meant Frank's grandkids hanging around the
ranch more and she liked spending time with them.
Cal and Maggie worked all weekend. A few college
girls from across the lake came over to Sully's to sit on
his side of the lake. They had a cooler, a few beers and

staked out a picnic table by the lake under the shade of a big tree. One of the girls, probably the only one who was twenty-one, came in and bought a six-pack.

Cal sat on the porch, taking a break in the early-afternoon shade with his laptop open. Maggie came out and sat at his table.

Jackson drove up to the store in his dad's truck. He got out, still wearing his climbing harness, and began to put the accoutrements of his favorite hobby, rock climbing, into the back of the truck—harness, ropes, ascenders, pulley, lightweight backpack. He pulled off his sweaty shirt and grabbed a fresh shirt out of the front seat. He changed from his climbing shoes into dry socks and hiking boots. He tossed the clean shirt over his shoulder and headed for the store, obviously planning to do a little wash up in the bathroom before putting on his clean shirt. His canvas cargo shorts rode low on his hips. He was about six feet, his arms and shoulders powerful and strong from months of working out with the rescue team, his grin infectious. He had a tattoo on one bicep.

"Hey, Cal. Hey, Maggie." He walked past them into the store to get to work.

Cal was looking toward the lake, a secret smile on his face. Maggie followed his gaze and started to laugh. All four of those girls were gazing after Jackson. They started to swoon, giggle and one of them pretended to faint.

"He's gotten so manly," Maggie said. "He even smells manly."

"That he does," Cal agreed with a laugh.

It wasn't long after that that the girls were back in the store. Jackson was working the counter, Cal was stocking, Beau was hanging out in the storeroom with Sully. There was a lot of excited talking and laughing and it was a long time before the girls were leaving and Jackson was getting back to work.

Cal peered around the end of a grocery aisle at Jackson. Jackson chuckled a little in embarrassment and blushed. But Cal had a feeling there would be more than fireworks over the lake that evening.

It was an exhausting weekend but just what everyone needed. On Saturday night Tom came to the camp with his kids and as soon as the sun was down, he and Jackson shot off some fireworks.

The rest of the weekend was more of the same. It was busy and there was plenty of work to do but Cal enjoyed the friendly, happy energy of the crossing. There was a lot of cleaning up on Tuesday after the bulk of the campers had headed home. In the afternoon, Cal sat on the front porch of Sully's house, out of reach and earshot, and called Becky.

"We have court at nine o'clock tomorrow morning. I thought I'd touch base, make sure you're ready and know what to wear."

"You don't have to tell me what to wear, Cal. I know I should be conservative."

"Not Amish, just conservative. That trick of trying to look like a Sunday school teacher usually has the opposite effect. Be prepared for the judge to ask you a few questions about what happened. Answer just as you explained to me."

"Is it going to be okay, Cal?"

"There are no guarantees but it's my educated guess that you're not going to spend any time in jail."

"I hope you're right," she said.

He pulled his suit, the only one he'd brought with him, out of the back of his truck. The day he met Becky, he took it to the cleaners. It was covered in blue dry-cleaning plastic. He dressed early in the morning. His shirt was starched, his tie was probably still in style. He'd shined his dress shoes.

"Can I borrow your briefcase so I look like a real lawyer?" he asked Maggie.

"You didn't bring a briefcase?"

"I packed everything. I only brought a suit and a couple of shirts and ties in case I had to dress for some reason, but I honestly didn't think it would be for a court appearance."

"That is a fine suit, California," she said. Maggie sat cross-legged on the bed. Her long, brown legs stuck out of her khaki shorts and a white shirt covered a blue tank. "Did you go to work looking like that every day?" she asked.

"I had a few good suits," he admitted.

"I bet you were a clotheshorse," she accused.

"I thought if I could have all those things I missed out on growing up it would make me a better person. It was a great lesson."

"Because it didn't?"

"You know the answer. You have to work on who you are from the inside out."

"Are you going to tell me about this court case when it's over?"

He grinned at her. "Probably not."

"Well, you're very hot and I want to jump you. That suit turns me on."

"I'll be wearing the suit when I come back. Be ready," he said with a naughty grin.

Cal met Becky just inside the courtroom doors and went through security with her. She was wearing a nice dark suit with a colorful scarf around her neck—no cleavage, no extra jewelry. She wore nude hose and black pumps and looked like a lawyer. Or one of the rich women from Aurora.

Waiting outside their courtroom was Steve, the bartender from the hotel bar where Becky had been arrested. Cal shook his hand and thanked him for his appearance, but Becky looked confused. "Do you remember Steve?" Cal asked her.

She shook her head. "But you look familiar."

Cal laughed. "He's the bartender, Becky."

"Oh," she said. "Well, I only had that one glass of wine."

"Am I going to have to testify or something?" Steve asked.

"I don't know. That's not really up to me. If you do, it'll just be that one question I already asked. We'll have to wait to be called so let's find a place out of the way to sit down. I'll let them know we're here."

Just as Cal was turning to go, a uniformed police officer appeared.

"Now *him* I remember!" Becky whispered.

"Best if we don't talk to him now," Cal said. "Just go sit over there."

It was over an hour before it was their turn to appear. Cal guided Becky to the defense table and indicated for Steve to take an empty chair in the gallery behind them. Then it was only minutes.

The charges were announced. "The county versus Rebecca Canaday on the charge of soliciting."

"Everybody here?" the judge asked.

"Yes, Your Honor," Cal and the young ADA said in unison.

"What've we got," he said, turning pages.

"We move for dismissal, Your Honor. The motion should be there. According to the arrest report, Ms. Canaday didn't solicit anyone for any reason. There's no probable cause or evidence."

"Approach," he said.

Cal and the ADA both went to the bench. The judge looked at the young ADA over the rims of his glasses. "You read this police report, Mr. Lockhart?"

"Yes, sir. The police officer signed the report and will testify that they had an agreement on sex for money."

The judge raised an eyebrow. "The same police officer who wrote the report and failed to mention taking the defendant to a hotel room or giving her money? That police officer?"

"They made a deal," the ADA argued.

"And was there a wire?" The ADA shook his head. "Witnesses?" Again the head shaking. "Corresponding evidence?"

"We can supply the witness and corresponding evidence, Your Honor," Cal said. "The bartender was a witness to the fact that no money changed hands. No money was even visible. He heard the whole thing and was about to ask the gentleman to leave the lady alone. The police officer cuffed her while she was sitting at the bar."

The judge gave the ADA a very tired, bored look. "I'm feeling very generous today, Mr. Lockhart. I'm going to give you a chance to drop the charges before I dismiss. Your boss doesn't like it when his young ADA's get their cases thrown out, so do be efficient. Do the right thing. And then get a remedial reading class. If it's not in the report at least round up some proof that it happened."

"Yes, sir," the young man said. "No charges will be filed."

"I'd prefer a dismissal, Your Honor," Cal said. "I don't want this charge visited on Ms. Canaday again. She doesn't need the aggravation."

"Consider it dead, Mr. Jones," the ADA said. "We're done with this."

"Then an apology."

"Come on," the ADA said.

"Frankly, I think you should apologize," the judge said. "Or we can go through the motions, swear the bartender and listen to his testimony. But—"

"All right, all right. Sorry for the inconvenience!"

"In writing," Cal said.

The ADA sighed. "Yes. Of course."

The judge gave his gavel a rap. "We're done here. Next case."

What lies behind us and what lies before us

are tiny matters compared to what lies within us.

—RALPH WALDO EMERSON

CHAPTER 16

Becky threw her arms around Cal's neck, thanking him. The ADA promised there would be nothing on her record and when Cal left her, the bartender was chatting her up. Cal suspected he hoped for either an assignation or perhaps a business deal, though he was probably twenty-five to her thirty-six.

He called Tom from the parking lot. "I'd like to talk to you when you have a little time. A private conversation. I'll meet you wherever you like."

"I'm headed home for a little lunch between jobs. Is Becky all right?"

"She's fine, Tom. There are no charges."

He heard him sigh in relief. "Thank you. Thank you so much."

"It wasn't too difficult. So—will we be able to talk privately at your house?"

"Yeah, the kids are all gone today. Noon?" Then he gave him the address in Timberlake.

Cal pulled up to a good-looking, restored three-story Victorian. He remembered Tom's story about the half a house and expected to see side-by-side doors, but there was just one set of double doors. There was a great wide porch, the floor painted blue and the porch rail white. The double doors were oak and leaded glass.

When Tom let him in, Cal was speechless. He stepped into a roomy foyer, living room on one side and open staircase with a rich-looking banister on the other side. Straight ahead a hallway led past the living room and dining room. "Come on back," Tom said. And Cal followed him into a large kitchen with what appeared to be fairly new stainless steel appliances. He turned around in a full circle.

"Tom," Cal said. "This is amazing!"

"Thanks," he said. He had bread, cold cuts, mayo and other stuff on the table and was building a couple of sandwiches. He shuffled everything together and finished quickly. He put each on a plate, sliding one to Cal. Then he grabbed a bag of chips and put it on the table.

"You do that like a guy who's been making school lunches for years."

"Tell me about Becky," Tom said.

"I can tell you the results of the proceedings. No charges were filed."

"So it *was* a misunderstanding!" he said, relieved.

"I guess you could call it that. The assistant district attorney was a young, inexperienced guy who didn't really vet that arrest report thoroughly—the police officer had not provided sufficient probable cause for the arrest. It was a sting, Tom. The officer shouldn't have arrested her unless money changed hands, which it did not."

"What are you saying?" Tom asked, putting down his sandwich.

"All arrests and court proceedings are a matter of public record. If you're ever so inclined, you can look these things up and draw your own conclusions. The important thing is, Becky doesn't have this on her record, doesn't go to jail, doesn't pay a fine."

"So it's all good," Tom said. "Want a Coke?"

"Thanks, that'd be great. Can you tell me about this house? I thought you had part of a house?"

"Eighteen years ago. Not quite half. We had our own entrance to the second floor from a staircase out back. Mrs. Berkshire had a small galley kitchen installed and we didn't need much more than that. We had two rooms on the second floor, two on the third or attic floor. It was perfect for us. Especially when the kids were little. We fixed it up. And I helped Mrs. Berkshire with everything she needed. My dad and brother even pitched in a lot because Mrs. Berkshire was older than dirt and her son didn't pay her any attention at all. We were all she had. We even put on a new roof. Then she died about ten years ago and left me the house." He shook his head and laughed. "Her son didn't like that much. He tried fighting it. But her will stuck. So we started tearing down walls and making it one house."

"Tom, it's beautiful."

"Well, I work construction when I can. And I do a lot of built-ins for rich folks up on the ridge. Those are my best jobs."

"But this is incredible. How'd you do it?"

"Well, hell, Cal—I had eighteen years to work on it! And my dad and brother helped. I had four kids and just got by the best I could—they were awful generous with their time. I try to help my folks and brother, too. You know, when we all work on the same team, stuff gets done."

Cal finished his sandwich and asked for a tour of the house and was astonished by the finishing detail work, not to mention the fact that a man and four kids lived in the house and it was spotless. "I run a tight ship," Tom said. "I have to."

"I think you're amazing."

"Cal, what's going on with my wife?" Tom asked.

Cal put his hands in his pockets and looked squarely at Tom. "I'm not at liberty to share our professional conversation, Tom. That's the law—I could lose my license over it. But I can tell you a couple of things you already know, the most important being—she's not your wife anymore, Tom. And you told me yourself—this isn't the first time. That's just fact."

"She said it was always a misunderstanding..."

Cal just looked at Tom, great sympathy in his heart for the man.

"I've been kidding myself, haven't I?"

Cal didn't respond because he couldn't.

"Becky is one of the sweetest, most considerate women I've ever known," Tom said. "She's so loving and kind. She really cares about her kids and the kids love her."

"She's their mother," Cal said. "While not all mothers are so wonderful, I'm glad to know she's a loving mother."

"But...?"

"Tom, you're going to have to figure this out for yourself. I wish I could somehow make this easier for you but the truth is, there's nothing more I can tell you. I'm just glad we managed to work out this court case so neatly. You're going to have to take it from here."

"I'll pay you somehow." He laughed uncomfortably. "I don't even know what a lawyer gets for a case like this."

Cal put a hand on Tom's shoulder. "Don't worry about that, buddy. We're friends. We help each other when we can. Right?"

"Right. Well," he said, rubbing a hand around the back of his neck. "Thanks for everything. I really appreciate it."

July ended toasty and warm, the lake was refreshing and the landscape was lush. The garden was plentiful and since his schedule wasn't demanding most days, Cal was out on the trails several times a week for a few hours. He came across the search-and-rescue team running exercises along the mountain face, climbing a steep rock and rappelling down. He watched Jackson training with them for a while, wearing his rock climbing rigging proudly.

Cal thought he might have to try that one day soon. Then he looked straight up to the top of that mountain and almost swooned. He decided he could probably find better things to do with his time. Some of the trails that wound around the steep side of the mountain were challenging enough.

Maggie, however, was like a goat. She went along with him sometimes; she was sure-footed and lithe. They usually didn't talk until they reached a summit and relaxed, enjoying the view. They'd sit, guzzle a pint or so of water, let the breeze cool them and unwind before they talked.

"I think you're starting to like Colorado," Maggie said.

"Colorado has a lot to offer," he said, putting his arm around her.

"What are the chances you'll stick around?"

"I haven't made any plans to leave yet, Maggie. You getting tired of me?"

She laughed. "Do I act like I'm getting tired of you? You're almost like one of the family. If you leave now it might upset Sully more than me."

"I hope that's not true. I haven't spent much time with Phoebe and don't know Walter yet."

"I don't want to scare you off," she said. "I've been wondering—how did it feel, doing a little lawyer work?"

"Very familiar," he said with a laugh. "It wouldn't be a big deal to rent space, take a few clients here and there. I don't want to make any fast moves," he added.

"I know you're in flux, that you left Michigan in a state of grief and by the time you got here you weren't sure what kind of life you wanted. Are you getting any closer to knowing? Like where you want to be? How you want to live? Work? Any of that?"

"I kind of like the life I have right now. It's satisfying."

"What about lawyering?"

"Turns out there's a use for me in that regard, as well," he said. "I worked a little bit."

"But were you paid?"

"I'll be paid one way or another," Cal said. "But then it turns out I don't need much money, living off my girl like I am."

"I'm your girl, am I?"

"I'd say we're pretty attached. Wouldn't you say?"

"What I want to know, Cal, is will you ever be able to talk about the future? Because I might want to. Talk about the future."

"And I'd love to hear what you have to say about it.

From what I've heard so far, you and I are in the same bucket here—trying to figure out what to do next."

"Well, for starters, I want to stay here. I'm planning to raise a family here."

"Ah," he said. "Are congratulations in order?"

"I'd like to tell you something very personal. Sully doesn't know. No one around here does and only a couple of people in my other world. Can you keep a confidence?"

"You know I can."

"I *do* know you can. A little too well for my tastes. I'd love to know about your court case, and yes I know you weren't teasing me—it was really court. You were dressed way too pretty for just giving legal advice or helping someone understand statutes."

"Could have been a meeting with an IRS auditor," he suggested. "It's smart to dress up for those guys, too."

"Never mind," she scoffed. She took a breath. "Here goes. I think I loved Andrew. I was seeing him for a couple of years. I was prepared to marry him. We lived in different towns but the distance was commutable if our situation changed, like if we wanted to live together. Then it did change. I got pregnant. And," she said, taking a breath, "he was very clear, he didn't want to have a child. He's forty and is the single father of an eight-year-old daughter. He had a pretty unhappy marriage and ugly divorce and he was not inclined to be the happy daddy. The fact that I was excited about it didn't seem to change things. But I guess all that's kind of irrelevant— I miscarried."

He pulled her a little closer. "I'm sorry, Maggie."

"Thank you."

"Was that the cause of the breakup? The pregnancy?"

"Not completely. Even through our disagreement, and it was pretty fierce, I stuck. He wanted me to abort, I refused, we fought. Then I lost the baby and he was very sensitive and supportive. Kind. But I couldn't get beyond it—my heart was so broken. I was so grief-stricken it surprised even me. I cried all the time. I was a total basket case, but there was so much going on—my ex-partners being indicted, my lawsuit, the threat of bankruptcy... No one noticed there was one more disappointment in my life. Except Andrew, he noticed. He said he couldn't take it anymore. He told me to get myself together. To get professional help if necessary."

Cal grimaced. "That was decent of him."

"He did me a favor, I can see that now. I can't be with a man like that. With or without a child."

"I bet he's kicking himself now..."

"He's too late."

"He's back?" Cal asked.

"Begging for another chance. Seriously, he's much too late."

"How about me?" he asked. "Are you sure I'm the right kind of man? Dead wife, crazy family, living in the rumpus room, practicing law for free?"

"Is that what your life is always going to look like?" she asked.

"What if it does? What do you want *your* life to look like?"

"I don't have all the details worked out yet," she said. "But I'm getting closer. I want a man who adores me— check. I want to live around here—check. Baby? Am I too old for that?"

"You have plenty of time," he said. "You do very

well with Beau. You'll make a fine mother. Are you going to work?"

"Maybe. Are you?"

"I will always work," he said. "I'm not sure I'll work as a defense attorney, but there's always a lot to do. Are you going to raise this alleged child in the rumpus room?"

"I said I haven't worked out all the details yet! Probably not, but I haven't come up with a good alternative. Do you want to grow old with me in the rumpus room?"

"I'd say yes to the first part of the question and reserve judgment on the second. Maggie, are we in a hurry? Do you sense your eggs hatching?"

"Do not make fun of me," she said.

He tightened his arm around her shoulders, pulling her tight. "I'm not making fun of you. I think you know I love you…"

"Even though you haven't bothered to say so?" she asked, a little sarcastically.

"Even though I haven't exactly said so. But you did ask me to get together a… What did you call it? A statement of intent and a plan? Very sexy, Maggie. I've been working on that. Working like mad, really."

"You have?"

"I have. I'm not quite there yet, but I'm trying. You can't be cranky about that since you don't even know where you're going to raise your child. I should get the summer to devise a really excellent mission statement, don't you think? You can't accuse me of stringing you along until the end of August. Right?"

"Are you planning to take your sweet time and let me down easy?" she asked.

"Actually, I was planning my statement of intent. But

then someone needed my help and I spent a lot of time reviewing the law. But more important, Maggie." He stroked her upper arm. "I'm not taking any chances falling for you, but you're risking plenty getting involved with me. Just the gene pool alone should give you second thoughts. Don't you want to meet my family before you make a final decision?"

"Humph, what does it matter? You never know what's going to hatch."

"It's schizophrenia, Maggie. I'm pretty sure my youngest sister has it but it's hard to tell because of her drug use. In fact, we'll never know unless she stops using and since she doesn't want help with that…"

"That would be a grandparent and an aunt, not a parent or sibling. Less than ten percent likelihood of a genetic component. The odds are worse she could turn out like Phoebe."

"You looked it up," he said.

"Well, yes. I look up everything. You're also not wanted for murder anywhere, congratulations."

"I don't want you to have regrets."

"I don't want *you* to," she said.

"You have to do your part. You have to know how you want to spend your life. People can change their plans, that's all right. I don't want you giving up things to be with me. Things like neurosurgery."

"I'm not sure giving it up would be the worst idea. It's fraught with complications and stress."

"It took a lot of that to break you and you still didn't really crack," he said. "You took a leave. You cried. Just remember when you're thinking about this—it's your identity. I don't want to strip you of it. I want to be part of it."

She was silent for a moment. "Wow. You're so amazing. Is this how it was with your wife?"

"Lynne," he said with a tender smile. "Most of the time. She wasn't as bossy as you." He nuzzled her neck. "There are still things for us to talk about before you let those eggs loose, okay? This is a good start. Let's keep at it, all right?"

"Listen, there's something," she said. "I was ready to tell you about the pregnancy and miscarriage sooner, but then you told me about Lynne and her death and it was just…it was inappropriate. My loss wasn't nearly equal to yours. It wasn't just because my loss was less; it was because I was a little afraid to tell you what it meant. Cal, I wanted that baby. I want a family. I was reminded that I'm thirty-six, that there might not be a lot of time for that. Getting hooked up with me might be more burdensome than you signed up for."

"I don't think so."

The next day Cal called Tom. "There's something I'm going to need your help with. It might be a little complicated. And it's top secret. Is there a time you'll be alone at your house and I can come over? Because my business is never my business at Sully's place."

Every summer Sully invited special groups of kids out for the day or even an overnight. No charge of course. As she watched her father with a group of special needs kids, Maggie realized as never before how fantastic he was as a leader of children. He showed them how to drop a line and catch a fish, how to pitch a tent, how to roast marshmallows. He made hot dogs for lunch and went out on some of the shorter trails with them. The only thing Sully wasn't doing this summer was getting in the lake with the kids.

Maggie supposed it was because she'd been thinking about a family for the first time. For all these years she'd been so busy working, scrambling to keep up, she hadn't had the time to think about children of her own. In fact, she hadn't had time to think about a lot of things. But she'd been at Sully's for five months and in that time some of her most immediate pressures had resolved themselves.

Her practice was permanently closed and all the equipment, office and medical, and furniture had been sold. Most of it had been picked up by colleagues who were expanding while she was downsizing her life. The office space she'd been leasing was taken back, rented and bankruptcy was no long inevitable.

Her partners had been indicted but they didn't go to trial. One gave up his license in a plea deal and the other was reprimanded and fined, and he moved to Florida. If there were civil suits lurking out there, no one seemed to know about them.

And she'd been invited by more than one of her colleagues to join their practices. John Halloran, a noted neurological surgeon from University Medical Center, advised her to keep a hand in. "Don't stay out of the operating room too long, Maggie," he said. "At least assist a few cases a month so when you do decide what you're going to do next your decision won't be forced by lack of practical application. Operate, Maggie. It's what you were trained to do."

It was good advice. She decided she'd drive into Denver a couple of times in August, scrub in with a colleague who could use a hand. While she was there she planned to see friends, so she took Cal with her once. It wasn't at all surprising that her friends fell in love with him, even if he was a little hard to understand. She introduced him as a homeless criminal defense attorney who had a big crush on her. He explained himself as someone recently escaped from the rat race, simplifying his life. Maggie's type A friends had trouble understanding that.

Maggie's friends from the hospital, having had the mother lode of medical experiences, were fascinated by criminal law and plagued him with questions about his work, his clients, his experiences. They wanted to know if he'd ever defended murderers and he was quick to point out he had defended people *accused* of capital crimes. Had his life ever been threatened? Had mafia bosses tried to control him or had he ever been afraid for his life, being involved with scary people? And the one that interested Maggie the most: "Will you die of boredom being a maintenance man at a campground?"

"I'm not bored yet," was all he said.

He only went to Denver the one time. He didn't want to leave Sully shorthanded while Maggie was away in Denver for a night or two. Besides, there were other things going on over summer in addition to fishing, roasting marshmallows, and cleaning the public bathroom and showers. There were wildfires. One had been contained recently after raging for two weeks northeast of Colorado Springs. Another took out hundreds of acres near Salida and the smoke drifted over the crossing. Even though they were in no immediate danger, Cal wanted to be nearby in case Sully had to evacuate the camp and himself.

Maggie adored him for his care for Sully and others.

The summer routine was relaxed and low-pressure but Maggie noticed that Cal had become mysteriously morose and quiet. He went off by himself several times; she spotted him standing at the edge of the lake a few times, tossing pebbles into the water. She tried asking him what was bothering him and he brushed her off, saying he was just thinking.

Frankly, Maggie was getting a little scared. Had he been thinking about his mission statement and come to the conclusion that it was time to move on? She decided the best approach was to demonstrate that she was mature and rational, but, unable to help herself, she pitched a fit.

"What the *hell* is up with you? Why are you depressed? Why aren't you talking to me? When did we become strangers? How do we go on from here if you can't talk about whatever is on your mind that makes you go silent? How am I supposed to take it? Are you ready to dump me? Is that it?"

Cal took a deep breath. "I have to go to Iowa for a few days. My sister is in the hospital and my father has gone off the rails. I'd like to ignore the situation but I can't. And, I think you should come with me. In fact, I insist, unless there's some reason you can't leave here. Maggie, you have to know where I come from so you can decide just how involved you want to be."

If any man seeks for greatness,

let him forget greatness and ask for truth,

and he will find both.

—HORACE MANN

CHAPTER 17

"Let's get this over with," Maggie said. "I know your family's troubles are hard on you and you worry about the effect on me, but I'm a doctor. I'm sure I can keep this in perspective."

"We'll see," Cal said.

"You have so little faith in me," she said.

Cal explained to Sully that he wanted Maggie to meet his parents because they were pretty wacky. He didn't want to terrify Sully so he described his father as unstable and his mother as nutty but loving. He could've said schizophrenic, but he hadn't.

When Cal was out of earshot Sully spoke to Maggie. "Be nice to his wacky parents and don't screw this up."

"Oh, very nice, Sully!" she said.

"You know what I mean. I like him and he fits in and I don't know that I've ever been around a man who treats you better, including one husband and one steady boyfriend."

"Oh my God," Maggie said. "I had more than one boyfriend! And I was engaged in med school for three weeks."

"You were engaged?" Sully asked.

"It wasn't worth mentioning," she said. "I didn't want

to be engaged, but… Never mind, it doesn't count. But I've had boyfriends."

Sully just shook his head. "Be nice to his wacky parents. And don't tell them where we live."

Cal took care of the tickets—Denver to Des Moines, one plane change. Maggie packed and as she did so, she was confident she could handle meeting Cal's parents, even if they were in crisis. She'd been around plenty of mostly functional people with mental disabilities. It was standard fare in emergency rooms. She knew neurological disorders weren't exactly easy on behavioral patterns. But, Cal was completely sane and nearly ideal. And she was of above-average intelligence and had a great deal of medical experience. She could help him and put his mind at ease.

We all have our issues, she reminded herself.

Pratt, Iowa, a tiny farming community between Des Moines and Iowa City, had a small population—just a couple hundred. The drive from Des Moines with all the crops in lush maturity was lovely. It was hot and humid and buggy and there were some dark clouds gathering in the west. Cal stopped at a motor inn in Newton and checked them in.

It was perfectly adequate and she decided not to even ask why they wouldn't stay with his parents. It was early afternoon so they had a bite to eat and headed for Pratt. They drove another thirty minutes to a completely charming little village. The Jones farm was just on the outskirts of town. It was shaded by big leafy trees and the fields were full of wheat and corn. There was a big barn and a darling little farmhouse at the end of a drive through the fields. As they got closer Maggie noticed the details. The windows were covered with tinfoil. The weather vane on top of the house had tinfoil streamers on it.

"Oh boy," she said.

"Yeah," Cal said. "We'll visit for a couple of hours and get the lay of the land, then head back to Newton."

"Just a couple of hours?" she asked.

"I'm sure that'll be enough," he said.

Finally, she was starting to see why bringing her here was important to him and she grew nervous.

"Your dad farms all this?"

"No, he leases the land to local farmers. Sometimes he thinks he's done a lot of farming, however. But, so far, there hasn't been any problem with that and the lease income is helpful."

Up close, the house seemed to be in poor repair—the steps up to the porch were slanting one way, the floorboards were rickety and creaked and it had been a long time without paint. But the inside was pleasant and clean. It was very old-fashioned—overstuffed furniture with doilies, mission-style dining chairs around the table, appliances that had seen better days. There was a TV tray in front of a chair that still bore the imprint of its frequent occupant. And on the tray, a pile of spiral notebooks.

Cal's mother, Marissa, turned from the kitchen sink, saw them, and immediately looked worried.

"Cal. I didn't know you were bringing anyone," she said, her voice very soft.

Her gray hair was very long, tied in a band and trailing down her back. Her expression was pained but her complexion was the picture of health. She seemed to be in good physical shape, not too thin, not too heavy. She wore a long, flower-print skirt, brown leather lace-up boots and a shirt over a tank top. Her breasts were small, but she was braless and they swayed. When she smiled at Cal her eyes glittered sweetly.

But Marissa twisted her hands.

"Mom, this is Maggie, my girlfriend."

"Oh, hello. I'm sorry my husband isn't here."

"Where is he, Mom?"

"He's in the barn." She looked at Maggie. "I'm sorry it's such a bad time."

Maggie murmured a greeting.

"Why is it a bad time, Mom?" Cal asked.

"I told you," she whispered. "On the phone, I told you. It's been fine till Sierra went to the hospital. I don't know what she was thinking, bringing all that attention."

"What attention?" Cal asked.

Marissa's pretty face became pinched. She spoke so softly Maggie could barely hear her. "She sent people here. County people. To look at us, at your father. He's been hiding in the barn since they were here."

"For two weeks?" Cal asked, sounding appalled.

"He's started to come to the house after dark. He's afraid of them."

Cal looked at Maggie. "It was probably social services. He's afraid of being taken to the hospital. He's afraid of their drugs and tests and electric shock." Then to his mother he said, "Make him something to eat. I'm going to go get him now."

"He won't come."

"Make him something to eat," Cal said. "Maggie? Will you be all right here?"

"Certainly," she said. "I'll help your mother in the kitchen."

* * *

The barn wouldn't keep out the cold in winter, it was that rickety. It hadn't been used to house animals in a good twenty years. Sunlight shone through the spaces between the boards. Cal's father had latched the big double doors but as Cal remembered from long-ago visits, all you had to do was lift the door on the right and the latch fell away, allowing him to walk inside.

His father had constructed himself a desk by putting an old door on top of two wooden barrels, using a third to sit on. There were papers scattered on top of the desk, held down by rocks. An empty bean can held pens and pencils, a couple of large sheets of paper were rolled up. Butcher's paper. There was a grocery store bag sitting beside the desk, filled with balls of string. On the other side an identical brown bag filled with balls of tinfoil.

Cal hated the tinfoil periods. His father hadn't suffered continuous bouts of paranoia but when upsetting things happened in his world, he started covering things in foil to keep the radio waves from penetrating.

But Cal loved the old barn. He and his brother and sisters had spent many happy hours playing here—all sorts of games—hide-and-seek, pretend, you name it. They'd swung on a rope from the loft, a pastime his grandmother said took years off her life and his grandfather said generations of farm kids had survived.

"Dad? It's me, Cal. Can you come out, please?"

No answer.

"Come on, Dad. I don't want to have to search the barn for you."

"You don't sound like Cal," his father said from a distance away.

"Well, it's me. I came to see you. Looks like the

house needs a little work—painting and stuff. I thought I might do some of that while I'm here. Mom is making you something to eat. Come on out."

There was some rustling around in the hayloft. This didn't surprise Cal. His father was as far away from the door as he could get. Jed peeked over the edge of the loft, a tinfoil cap on his head. Someday Cal was going to find out why so many schizophrenics during periods of paranoia adopted the same self-protective traits. *Tinfoil?* Hadn't their fears evolved beyond the point they believed the superpowers couldn't read their minds through household foil? It was almost as though there was collective thinking among this entire subculture.

"Come on down, Dad. I'll stay with you. Let's go see what Mom has to eat."

"I shouldn't go outside," he said. "They're probably still around."

"The people from the county? Nah, they've been gone for a couple of weeks now. Mom told me they were here and asked me to come to be sure you're safe."

"She did?"

"Didn't she tell you? I bet she told you and you just forgot."

"They took Sierra, you know. Took her away."

"I'm going to look into that," Cal said, but his mother had told him the truth—Sierra had checked herself into a hospital. "But first, let's get you something to eat and while you're eating, we can talk about fixing up the house. It needs some paint, that's for sure."

Jed Jones sighed heavily. "This could be a mistake."

"Nah, I checked around. We're good. You're safe in the house."

He slowly descended the ladder from the loft. He

was as skinny as Frank Masterson. His dad had always been so thin, losing interest in food sometimes. When he stepped down, Cal hugged him. "Feeling a little stressed, are you?"

"What do you expect, with all the pressure?" Jed replied.

"I guess it's reasonable. What've you been working on here?"

"Another lecture and a design. I have a deadline and I'm behind."

"The class could be postponed while you catch up," Cal said, though of course there was no class.

"It's not a class!" Jed snapped. "It's a *briefing*, for God's sake. It's important!"

Cal thought if he unrolled those large papers he might see some amazing drawings—machines or solar systems or even spaceships, and they would look fabulously complex and perfect. And completely useless. He grew up being told Jed held several PhD's in law, engineering, psychology, chemistry, etc. In point of fact, he wasn't entirely sure of Jed's level of education. He eventually came to find out that when Jed's schizophrenia began to take hold, when he was a young man studying prelaw in college, his family rejected him, left him to his young wife to deal with. For that reason, Marissa had never taken him back to his relatives in Pittsburgh and none of the kids had ever met that side of the family.

Marissa's parents did what they could to help, however.

"I stand corrected," Cal said. "But you know when you're under pressure you don't think as clearly. You probably need sleep. I know you need a shower and food."

"I need to be left alone! Why doesn't anyone leave us alone? We never broke the rules!"

Cal wondered, as he often had, what things must be like in Jed's world. He kept his arm around his father, leading him to the house. He was a little embarrassed that Jed had his foil cap on and wished he could bring Maggie a father more like Sully, a healthy, wiseass, happy, cognitive person. Although he wanted to yank the foil cap off his head, he stubbornly didn't. *Maggie should know how it is around here*.

They walked in the door and there was a sandwich and glass of lemonade on the table. Jed jumped when he saw Maggie.

"It's okay, Dad. This is Maggie. My girlfriend. She's visiting with me."

"I'm pleased to meet you, Mr. Jones," she said.

"It's Dr. Jones," he said, correcting her. "You shouldn't be here. It's not safe."

"It's all right now, Dad. I told you, I checked around. No one's here but Mom. And now us."

"I'll be careful, Dr. Jones," Maggie said.

Mollified, Jed sat down at the table and applied himself to the sandwich.

Maggie washed her hands at the sink. "Marissa," she said. "You're a little low on supplies. Would you like me to take you to the grocery store now that Cal is here with his dad?"

"Oh, thank you, but no. I'll go when the check comes. We get by eating out of the garden till the check comes, then Jed's fine at the farm while I go. It's just a few more days."

"Tell you what, let's go now. Cal will cover the cost—it'll make him feel useful. That would be all right, wouldn't it, Cal?" Maggie asked. "I could take your mom to the grocery store now while you spend a little time with your dad?"

"You sure you want to do that?"

"There's a grocery in Pratt, isn't there?" she asked Marissa.

"You don't want to go to that one," she said. "The prices are terrible there."

"That's okay this one time, Marissa. So, should we go while Cal visits with his dad?"

"Are you sure?" Marissa asked a little nervously.

"We're sure, Mom," Cal said. "Go get some groceries."

So their visit began. Maggie and Marissa went to the small grocery where Marissa was greeted familiarly and kindly by a few people. They asked after Dr. Jones and she replied that he was fine and staying busy. When they got home with a few bags of groceries they found Jed had washed and was sitting in his chair, writing in one of his notebooks, rocking sometimes, muttering as he wrote.

Maggie assured Cal that the trip to the store had gone well and asked him how things were at home. "As normal as they ever get. We can leave now."

Cal helped put the groceries away, hugged his mother and promised to be back the next day.

The next morning, after breakfast, they stopped at a store to buy paint and supplies, and returned to the farm. Cal talked Jed into helping him sand and paint the porch and the front of the house, while Maggie spent most of her day with Marissa, getting to know her and seeing the garden, which was only a small patch but impressive. In the second bedroom of their house Marissa had a loom and showed Maggie some of her decorative weaving, something she'd been doing for decades. The other thing she kept in that weaving room was a book-shelf stuffed with books, all of which had been read to death. It reminded Maggie of Cal's treasured books that he read and read and read again.

"Your family does love books," Maggie said.

"It always gets us through," Marissa said.

They all had lunch together but Cal and Maggie left them at dinnertime. On the third day Maggie went to a bookstore and bought Marissa and Jed some new books. She had noticed the books they kept were mostly science, law or literary classics so she bought a nice big stack, including a few large art books, hoping she wasn't duplicating what they had. Marissa was breathless with excitement and gratitude.

"I notice you don't have a computer in the house," Maggie said to Marissa.

Marissa looked at her in shock. "We can't have a computer," she said. "Jed wouldn't be able to get along with it. There are enough voices in his head without the internet. We had a computer for a short time and he didn't sleep for days."

"I thought it might keep him busy and help him communicate," Maggie said.

"He would soon be communicating with aliens from outer space. I'm very careful with what we have on TV."

"Marissa, has your whole life been like this?" Maggie asked. "Taking care of Jed?"

"My whole life has been loving my husband," she said. "Jed's a brilliant, wonderful man."

Of course every night they talked it to death. Maggie lay in Cal's arms and they went over the details of the day. Jed would be better on medication except that he refused it. "My mother claims they tried psychiatric help but I honestly don't remember anything like that ever happening. Maybe it was one of those times we kids stayed here on the farm with Grandpa and Grandma. When my dad was much younger he could conceal his hallucinations and work. And he was a gifted lecturer—when he started talking, people gathered around him. But even then my mother stayed very close to him, coaching him, managing him, making sure he wasn't acting crazy. Mom and Dad were just day laborers, farm workers, warehouse workers, that sort of thing. He got arrested a couple of times, I can't even remember what that was about because he's not one to draw attention to himself by breaking laws. Maybe that's when someone tried giving him medication. His hallucinations really intensified when I was a teenager. The bottom line appears to be that he's not aggressive, not dangerous to anyone but himself, and he's not going to see a doctor. Ever. But he's been on the farm for twenty years and as long as he stays on the farm, he seems to be safe."

"There's a nice little patch of cannabis behind the tomatoes in your mother's garden," Maggie told him.

"Oh, I know," Cal said with a laugh. "Good old Dad has been keeping his voices under control with weed for a long time now."

"It could be adding to his psychosis," she said.

"Everything could be adding to his psychosis," Cal said. "Under any other circumstances, without my mother and the farm, he'd be homeless and wandering the streets."

"Your poor mother!"

"It's her choice, Maggie. Not the choice I would have made."

"What choice would you have made?" Maggie asked.

"As a parent? I'd have drawn a line in the sand—get help for the mental illness or you're on your own. I know my mother is a loving woman but I'm not sure this devotion is helping him and I know it's not good for her. She had children to be responsible for. She could've been a better role model. Instead, we grew up knowing a woman who devoted her life to her crazy husband. He was her priority, not the whole family."

"And yet, look at the family. Look at how you turned out. You, your sister, your brother…"

"My mother was a teacher—she taught us. She read to us constantly, until she was hoarse, and the minute we could read even a little bit, she took turns with us reading. And she read from adult literature when we were small, the same books over and over and over."

"Something about that worked—you're all so brilliant."

"But, Sierra…"

"Are you going to find out what's happening with her?"

"I have the name of the hospital she admitted herself to. I'll get in touch. But she's an adult. If she doesn't want to talk to me or have me know about her condition, that's her prerogative."

"So, you don't approve of the way your parents are handling their lives and your dad's illness. How does that impact you?"

"I feel a natural obligation to them, but I won't take it to the lengths my mother has. Sedona and I visit once a year at different times, more often if there's some kind of crisis. Dakota comes less often—that whole situation is hard for him to take. I come to be sure they're fed, warm, safe. There's a family practitioner in town I've become friendly with and he's my mother's only physician. She'll go to his office if she has to, but Jed won't. The doctor is willing to go to the house if Jed's sick, like with a flu or something of that nature. But Jed, who smokes pot every day, won't get a shot or take pills of any kind. Really, he should be dead by now. But while they're alive on that farm, I'll call regularly and check on them sometimes. That's all."

"Was your childhood horrific?" she asked.

"I hated the way I grew up," he said. "I hated the instability of it, the constant worry, the embarrassment. Some of the best times were when we went back to the farm or lived in a hippy-dippy commune type community where everyone was a little wacky and we didn't stand out so much. I worked so damn hard to leave that lifestyle behind. You can't even imagine how hard I worked to appear normal, how driven I was to have stability and security. I worked and studied like a damn dog, achieved considerable success in the practice of law early in my career. I had the house, the car, the money in the bank, the reputation. It was like I was on a treadmill set at high speed and to get off was to die. Then, when it hit a snag, when I lost Lynne and couldn't stop the pain, what did I do?" He laughed. "I went back to the gypsy roots of my childhood, living loose and lean, trying to find myself all over again."

"Because you learned that true happiness isn't material," she said.

"Everyone knows that, right? But I was pretty damn happy in my material world, being one of the most sought-after young defense attorneys in the state. I didn't need the lesson, Maggie—I knew money can't buy love. Love buys love. And hard work is admirable. But loss is inescapable. It's part of life, and one thing a bank account won't help you do is get over it faster." He took a breath. "I shut off the treadmill."

"Are you happier now than you were a year ago?"

"You know I am. But there's one thing that remains from my dissatisfaction of my childhood—I feel best when I'm useful and when I'm helping people. Although they don't talk about it, the same seems to be true for Sedona and Dakota. We knew from early ages that our father is mentally ill and our mother is a flaming codependent and enabler. I think we might've overcompensated."

"Ya think?" Maggie asked with a laugh. "A lawyer, a psychologist, a decorated war hero?"

"I really think you had to see that," Cal said. "Now if you want to talk about the future, you can do that knowing I come from a family with some very obvious cracks in the porcelain."

"Cal, it will never be like that with me," she said. "I've seen a hundred men like Jed, delusional and afraid. Most of the time they have nowhere to go, won't take their meds when they have them, don't have the means to get help even if it's available. If he didn't have your mother, he'd probably be homeless or dead. In fact, I'm sorry to say I think your mother stands in the way of Jed getting help by protecting him and taking care of him as she is. I'm sure she's doing the best she can with what she has to work with."

"Well, you should know up front, I'll always look after them, but there will always be definite boundaries. My mother has no boundaries where my father is concerned—he has her full attention. Sedona has very smart boundaries—if there's some kind of crisis, she comes alone and never stays at the farmhouse. If they don't appear to be in crisis, she has brought her kids to visit them a few times, but the kids are well educated on the problems their grandparents live with. Sedona brought them as a kindness to our mother."

"Makes sense, I guess."

"I don't think my parents have ever been on a plane so there's no danger of them visiting. I think."

"You think?" she asked.

"I always brace myself for the day he goes off on a wild hare and decides it's time to pile in that old minivan and get on the road again…"

"God help us all," she said. "What do you do in a case like that? Call the highway patrol?"

"Hell if I know," he said. "You know, you were amazing with them both."

"Cal, he's ill. It's not his fault. He shouldn't be punished for it. But you have to remember—it's *his* illness. I'm sure there have been multiple times there were options other than a reefer a day. Between your mom and dad they've decided to deal with it this way. If there are consequences, they belong to them, as well. He wouldn't be the first patient I've ever had to refuse medical treatment." She shrugged. "Happens every day."

"The day will probably come when the thing he fears the most will become his reality. When my mother can no longer care for him, he'll be committed. It's all Sedona and I can do. We decided that a long time ago."

"Understandable," she said.

"Does it give you the cold willies?" he asked her.

"No," she said with a smile. "I don't know that your dad would be all that much better off in a group home, except that he'd be on regulated meds and get some therapy. Might have a better quality of life. Your mother definitely would have better quality of life. But as far as I could tell, you're right—they're safe and warm and have food to eat. Even their neighbors seem very understanding—they greeted Marissa in the grocery store and asked after Jed."

"I think they're as happy as two people with those circumstances can be," he said. "Or want to be."

"Well, I intend to be happier," Maggie said. "Do you have a mission statement yet?"

"Almost," he said. "Before we get to that, I'll find out what's up with Sierra, but if we keep moving in this direction, I think we should consider genetic counseling. Maybe donor insemination."

She just smiled at him. "First, your statement of intent. Your mission statement."

"It needs a little tweaking. Want to hear it so far?"

She sat up straighter. "Lay it on me, Calvert!"

"I want to build a healthy, balanced family life in a beautiful place with the woman I love."

"Awww, I like that very much," she said. "What are you going to tweak?"

"Well, I think I know how I can help keep that life afloat. Since we're not independently wealthy and I don't want to live out my life in a rumpus room, work would be good. It appears there's a local need for a multitalented attorney. I have to work in order to feel competent. I'm just waiting to see where you're headed."

"I'm not entirely sure yet," she said. "I might do some part-time teaching."

"Is that where you feel the most actualized?" he asked. "The most authentic?"

"Why do you have to ask me hard questions? We've almost got this nailed down. I think we'll be happy every day."

"I think we'll be happy every day for six months and then you're going to realize there's a little something missing, that something that makes you your best self. It doesn't have to be sixty hours a week as a neurosurgeon, but you do have to know what makes you happy."

"Besides you? I might be my best self just loving you."

He leaned close to her and whispered, "That's what my mother's doing."

Maggie hated to admit Cal might be right. She had the slightest problem with needing to be right. But it was true, she'd been thinking about earning some money and when she wrapped her head around teaching med students it filled her with about as much excitement as watching a tree grow. She tried thinking in terms of fertilizing their nubile young minds with the exhilaration of making good medicine, academically, and there it was again—watching the tree grow. She did like feeling the excitement of thinking about work, however.

She'd been in the operating room a few times in the past few weeks, but she'd been assisting in pretty tame cases. When she even thought about emergency work it sent shivers up her spine. She couldn't imagine another ordeal like that horrific MVA that took three young lives.

But there was one thing. Just scrubbing in got her a little jazzed. The nurses and techs were so happy to see her and kept asking when she was going to be back in the loop.

How Cal knew what he knew was a mystery. It was probably something his wife had taught him—he said she was an excellent attorney who had gone her own way, not seduced by the same things that drove him.

Maggie would like to have a daughter. She had very definite ideas about what she'd like that daughter to see while growing up—a mother with confidence and a skill, a talent she had worked at developing.

Then she had a sudden fearful thought. *What if she wants a debutante's ball?*

Maybe we should adopt, she thought.

Maggie bought a copy of *To Kill a Mockingbird*. She wasn't sure if she'd ever actually read it before; she probably either bought the CliffsNotes or watched the movie. But in reading it, she moved into another world, the world of Atticus Finch. She saw him so clearly, dressed in a meticulous but threadbare suit, walking around his town, making time for every human being he passed, working laboriously yet never hurriedly, never impatient or judgmental. In fact, he granted the most understanding to those hardest to understand. Clearly the most admired of all men, rigid in his values yet tolerant. She saw him.

She saw California Jones.

If a man doesn't know what port he is steering for,

no wind is favorable to him.

—SENECA

CHAPTER 18

Some very familiar emotions visited Maggie as the end of summer drew near—the feeling that something wonderful was coming to an end. It had nothing to do with Cal, except that her romance with him had begun in early spring. Labor Day weekend approached and that signaled the end of the heavy traffic at the crossing. They would still have some campers, mostly weekend visitors, and the coloring of the leaves in fall brought out the nature lovers. In just a couple of months snow would fall in the higher elevations; in a few months the lake would freeze and the ground would be covered with snow. Cross-country skiing and ice sailing would be in full swing.

The summer camps across the lake would close and the lake would fall silent. The lake cabins for rent would stay open a little longer, but they'd close from November through February.

In winter there would be a few RVs and the cabins would be rented on weekends, but tent campers? Hardly ever. Those hard-core campers who braved it built big, toasty fires at their campsites and spent a lot of time around the potbellied stove in the store.

Life at the crossing would slow down. There just

wasn't going to be a lot of activity, therefore not that much work to do. There would be little to fill the days.

Maggie felt she'd been levitating at the crossing for six months. Her week or two had become half a year. And the thought of going back to that insane pattern she'd lived in exhausted her. But the idea of a long, snowy winter with only Sully and Enid for company held little appeal. The days would be endless.

"You can do anything you want to do," Cal said. "Listen, life's short. Be sure whatever you decide to do fills your well."

Most of her immediate problems had resolved themselves. Her economic issues were taken care of with the closing of the practice and selling off of equipment, furniture and supplies, leaving her portfolio intact. There had been a rather impressive credit card bill; while trying to conserve her cash, she'd charged everything from utilities to car insurance. She complained about that a lot.

"I'll pay it for you, if you like," Cal offered.

"I couldn't let you do that," she said.

"Maggie, I've lived here rent-free for six months. I'm still coming out ahead. And I have money, you know."

It was more complicated than just a money issue—it was that whirlwind a woman can get sucked into, trying to deserve a man just because he's nice sometimes. She'd rather be the woman he had to live up to. Or better still, meet him on equal ground.

Two days later he asked her if she was in such a grumpy mood because he offered to pay her credit card bill. "No, I'm in a mood because it's the end of summer. Labor Day weekend is our last hurrah."

He pulled her into his arms and kissed her neck. "Don't panic. We're not seasonal."

That last holiday weekend of the summer was a full house, only two campsites left empty and the cabins in use. Just keeping up with the most mundane maintenance—from stocking toilet paper in the bathrooms to sandwiches in the cooler—had them hopping. Campers had started showing up for the long weekend on Thursday and all the camps across the lake were full to capacity, including the Christian church camp and Boy Scouts.

On Sunday in the early afternoon, Tom came driving up to the crossing from the south road, blowing his horn as he approached. By the time he stopped in front of the store, Maggie, Cal and Sully were already out on the porch.

"We got a missing ten-year-old back in the Patternix Mountain area. His parents lost track of him on the trail around there about three or four hours ago. They notified the ranger. Search and rescue has been activated—we have to get him before dark. I'm going to drive up to the ridge about five miles past the site and start down from there. Some of our crew has already started up that way. We're setting up a perimeter."

"Let me get together some stuff," Maggie said. "Three minutes, tops. I'll go with you."

"I'll go, too," Cal said. "What do we need?"

"Let me gather things here. Run over to the house and get us each clean, dry socks, our hiking boots, backpacks, light jackets in case we're out there late. And one blanket," Maggie said.

He ran to the house while Maggie grabbed bottled water and bandages—more for possible blisters than injuries. She added a cold pack, compresses, antibacterial ointment, a small bottle of rubbing alcohol, aspirin, rolled gauze, thin tape and duct tape. She added a Swiss Army knife and binoculars.

Cal came back and they quickly loaded the packs. She put the blanket in Cal's pack. "In case we find him and he's cold or hurt," she said. Then she grabbed her hiking boots and ran for Tom's truck. They changed out their shoes in his truck as Tom drove. He told them the boy's name was Justin Blaisdale, ten years old, kind of small for his age, blond, freckled, wearing a green shirt and khaki shorts.

"Green," Maggie scoffed. "Why not just camouflage, for Pete's sake."

"Be better if he had a red shirt, right?" Tom said. "Weekenders."

Tom took the access road that wended north of Sully's and up the mountain, one of the few roads with several lookout points and wide enough to park the truck in some places. He went beyond the last sighting spot and pulled off to the side of the road to check his map and coordinates. He had a radio. The team was armed with walkie-talkies. "This should do it." He radioed his team their location, gave Maggie a radio and told them to take it nice and easy, be alert and cautious. "We don't want to be rescuing or hunting members of the search group," he cautioned.

Maggie and Cal had been on this trail before and it was buried in trees and shrubs. In fact this was one of their favorite trails because of all the trees and the shade. But it was hot and steamy today, and if there was a little boy lost out there in the woods, he would have a hard time finding his way. He could stay on this particular trail for dozens of miles without seeing a campground, ranger's station or road. They used the binoculars to scan the area beneath whenever there was a break in the trail and they saw other searchers at a distance, across the deep chasm. Tom and Cal were both looking in and around bushes and tall grass. The sun was blinding when it broke through the trees and there was chatter on the walkie-talkies but nothing of substance. The sun was high overhead as they continued on the downward route.

"We're going to hate life when we're headed up again," Maggie said. "We usually start down there at the crossing, come all the way around this hill until we meet the road."

"If you're feeling like a real candy-ass, you can take the long way back to Sully's," Tom said. "It's not uphill at least."

As the trails were beginning to come together around the site where the boy was last seen, they spied more and more of the search team on trails in the distance. They all went up and down and around the hills, but the searchers had to veer off the paths to check behind trees and shrubs. The trail they were on was close to the edge in places and Cal, being a little worried about heights, hugged the hillside as the path curved around.

"He wouldn't have wandered off the trail, would he?" Maggie asked Tom.

"He might've wandered off the trail before he realized he was lost. He's ten. He could've seen a fawn or a squirrel or something. Maybe he wanted to pee. Then he could've turned around to go back to the trail and couldn't find it. Half the time they wander around in circles."

They'd been out about an hour and a half, logged

maybe three miles of trail when the radio sputtered. *We got him. Everybody come in.*

"That was easy," Maggie said.

"Up we go," Tom said, turning on the trail.

"Can we have a minute to rest?" she asked.

"Not too long," Tom said. "There's a cold beer with my name on it waiting for me at Sully's."

"Some men have a one-track mind," Maggie groused, though her mind was on the same track.

They got in the truck and started down the mountain when there appeared to be a lot of activity along the road. Members of the search party had gathered on the side of the road above a steep and intimidating ridge. A couple turned and waved for the approaching truck to stop.

Tom pulled over. "Tom, it's Jackson," a man said. "There was a small rockslide and he went down! We called rescue—they're on their way!"

Tom was out of the truck so fast it was as if smoke came off his shoes. He ran to the edge of the ridge and looked down. "Jackson!" he yelled. "Jackson!"

Maggie was right beside him. The hill was steep, too steep to walk down, but beyond that narrow shelf was a sheer drop. Jackson lay on a ledge about twenty to thirty feet below the road.

"He moved, Tom!" someone yelled. "He's alive. We saw him move!"

"What's rescue's ETA?" Maggie asked.

"We don't know exactly, but at least we have the access road. They're going to need transport."

Tom ran to his truck and began to dig around in the back for his ropes and climbing gear. Maggie followed him. "What are you doing?"

"I'm going down," he said, stepping into his harness.

"And what are you going to do when you get down there? Move him and break his neck? No, uh-uh. *I'm* going down." Then she ran back to the edge, looked down and thought, *suicide*. There were loose rocks along the ridge, part of what caused Jackson to slip and fall, and the drop to the ledge was sharp. And, beyond the ledge down the hill, deadly. She wiped her sweaty hands on her shorts.

She put her pack on the ground, dug around for her knife and asked Cal for the blanket. "Cal, cut this blanket in strips about one foot wide. Roll them up and put them in my pack." She put on her gloves. "Faster!" she said to Cal. "Tom, do you have a drill?"

"A *what*?"

"A small drill, cordless."

"Maggie, what the hell are you going to do with a drill?" Cal asked.

"Try not to think about it," she said. Someone handed her a flashlight, then Tom gave her a drill and a plastic case holding bits. She stuffed her backpack. It was heavy. She hefted it, then put it on.

"Maggie, no," Cal said.

She completely ignored him and grabbed one of Tom's nylon climbing ropes, starting to wrap it around her waist. "I don't have rappelling shoes and the pack is too heavy."

"Let me go," Tom said. "You can tell me what to do."

"That's not going to work. Get me down there. There isn't time to talk about it."

One of the other search-and-rescue members pulled the rope out of her hands and took over, making sure it was securely and safely tied around her waist. He fashioned a loop she could slip a hand through to hold on. Someone else handed her a helmet, which was just dumb luck—they didn't typically wear helmets on the trails.

"Thanks. Let's do this. I'm going down on a drop," she said. "Way over here, the shortest distance to the ledge and the farthest from that weak spot that crumbled. I don't have the right equipment to rappel and I don't want to disturb any more rock and have it fall on him. You have to lower me. Take me down very slowly."

She knew he probably had broken bones. She could tourniquet with a heavy length of double gauze or rope if necessary. She wasn't wearing a belt but she had shoelaces and she could even take off her bra and use it as a tourniquet if necessary. He probably had a head injury; she could confirm or rule out. If there was an intracranial hemorrhage, he would die if it wasn't relieved quickly. He could have a fractured skull, but if there wasn't gray matter leaking, he had a chance.

She stood at the edge and sat down. "Tom! Get airlift support."

"Done!" he said.

She turned, kneeling at the edge, facing the cliff. She edged backward and noted three men held the rope and slowly, let it out. It was the longest, most terrible twenty-five feet of her life and she didn't remove that rope from around her waist when she felt her feet touch. She yelled up to them. "Hang on to the rope. In case…"

She squeezed into the very small area between Jackson and the ledge and removed her backpack. Remarkably, his legs seemed to be intact at first glance. Possible internal injuries. He was breathing; his respirations were good, his pulse stable. She wanted to know more about his spinal column and head. Right now she'd sell her soul for a real neck brace, but she thought she could improvise. She doubled a strip of blanket, slid it slowly and cautiously under his neck, over his shoulder to his chest. Then she did it again on the other side of his chest. She took a third strip, stabilizing his neck so she could carefully turn him. Then she reinforced that makeshift brace with the duct tape. He moaned. "Jackson, Jackson, don't move, honey."

Flashlight in hand, she looked into his eyes. She swore. The left pupil was huge; blown pupil. "Jackson, oh, Jackson," she said.

His other eye opened, looking at her blankly.

She heard the sound of moving trucks, a helicopter in the distance. She dug in the backpack for gauze, alcohol, drill.

She prayed. *God, I will trade anything for this kid's life. Please, this once, make my mind clear and my hand steady.*

"Gotta do this," she said. She poured alcohol over his head on the same side as the affected pupil—that's where the pressure would be. If she worked that drill bit too hard she could drive it right into his brain.

Trucks were moving, doors were slamming, rotor blades were spinning. She shut down her ears. She could only hear one thing, the inside of her head. She carefully turned him, lifting his shoulder and upper torso and holding him there, immobile. She fit a bit into the drill. The bit was bigger than she liked but she'd had patients in surgery with bullet holes in their head and pulled them through.

Zurrr, the drill said. *Zurrr. Zurrr.* Three tidy little burr holes. Thank God the current fashion was buzz cuts. She noted the discharge and crossed her fingers. She covered the holes with clean gauze, then a few seconds later, checked it. She was never so happy to see blood. Red blood.

And then his eyes popped open; pressure relieved.

"Jackson, do not move. We're going to get you out of here but do not move."

"Maggie?" he whispered, not understanding. He probably didn't even know where he was.

"It's me. You fell. Do not move."

"Stay put, Maggie!" Tom yelled. "Help on the way!"

And exactly where was she going to go?

Jackson moaned and despite instructions, began to try to turn his head. Her duct tape brace held him in place. A swivel on the neck could be disastrous, so she put her palms against his cheeks and held him still with all her might.

"Jackson, listen to me. Jackson, you can't move. I'm here, I've got you. We're going to get you out of here. Don't move. Don't talk. Be still, honey. Still, still, still."

It was the longest five minutes of her life, waiting. She kept whispering to Jackson, checking his pulse and respirations, watching the bleeding and soaking it up with gauze.

Finally, someone was on that ledge with her, down by Jackson's feet. "Maggie, what the hell you doing?" Connie Boyle asked. He handed her a neck brace and she actually sighed in relief.

"I think you're better off hoisting him up with my duct tape brace in place. You can cut it off in the helicopter and replace it, but I think it's risky to do that here. Do you have airlift support?"

"Fifty yards up the road," Connie said. "We can't

pull him off this shelf via cable to the helicopter. We're going to have to take him up this way. First, I have to get rid of you. You go up," he said, handing her a harness.

"Connie, I can't get this on," she said. "We have about a three-foot width here. I'll never make it. Can't they pull me up on this rope?" she asked, tugging on the rope.

"I don't know what you were using for a brain, sliding down on that stupid rope tied around your waist. Stand. Back to the hill. Easy does it. Don't make me step over Jackson to dress you."

"Oh, Jesus," she said. She hugged the wall, carefully attaching the harness. It seemed to take her forever and while her hands had been steady to drill holes in Jackson's head, they shook as she tried to fasten her harness.

"Take your time," Connie said.

"Got it," she said. "I hope."

He disconnected the rope from his harness and she clipped it on hers. Then he yelled for them to haul her up. And with a jerk, she was lifted upward, her butt dragging along the hillside. The second she got to the top, a paramedic was lowered, along with an emergency basket and another cable.

With shaking hands, she began removing her harness. Cal was instantly beside her, helping her out of it. "If anyone tells you I passed out while you were being lowered to that little ledge, they're lying," he said.

"You okay now?" she asked.

"I'm better with you up here. Honey, you have blood on your hands," he said.

"Damn, I left the backpack down there with Jackson," she said. "I'll get a hydrogen peroxide from the paramedics for my hands…"

"Forget it—it's all over you," he said.

"Is he all right?" Tom asked.

"He's alive and has to be taken into surgery right away. I'll go with him in the helicopter. I'll make a couple of calls to get a room in the OR ready and call another surgeon, get a CT so we have a better idea of what we're doing. Time to hope for the best, Tom. His vitals are steady and he's semiconscious. He was lucid. He's got a chance. A good chance."

"I'll go with," Tom said.

"We need room to work, Tom. We'll be busy until you and Cal get to Denver—we'll have to take him to the hospital there. If anything changes, anything at all, we'll be in touch by phone."

Someone handed her a rag, hydrogen peroxide and a bottled water and she rinsed and washed off her hands.

"It's taking them too long," Tom complained, watching the edge of the ridge, waiting.

"It's all right, I think the immediate danger is past," she said. "I relieved the intracranial pressure. I'd like more information, but we can't get that until we get him to Denver. There isn't any place closer."

"Isn't Colorado Springs closer?"

"It's a tie," she said. "And I know the hospital and staff in Denver. I know who to call." There was a shout and the basket was lifted over the lip of the cliff. The men carrying the basket to the helicopter were moving quickly and carefully. She jogged after them. "I'll be in touch. Drive safely."

She jumped into the helicopter behind her patient.

Her hands only shook when she was being lowered down a steep hillside or trying to get into a harness on a thin shelf. When she was with her patient, she was steady.

Terry met her in the OR. "You're on call?" Maggie asked.

"Hell no, it's a holiday weekend. I was having time off. I got a call that you were coming in with a critical patient you'd rescued off a cliff. I decided I could party later."

"I didn't rescue him," she said, hurrying to the locker room. "I did drill a couple of burr holes in his cranium with a shop drill, however. Go prep him, Terry. We need a CT. And thanks for coming in. I need all the help I can get."

"Yes, ma'am," she said. "Good to have you back."

"I'm not back," she said. "I'm just helping out."

"Me, too," Terry laughed, her short round form jogging off in the direction of the OR.

She came in for me, Maggie thought. She was probably hosting a barbecue at her house for her grown kids and grandkids. No one would have scheduled surgeries for a holiday weekend, but there would always be emergencies. One of her favorite colleagues, Jake Morris, was the neurosurgeon on call and he joined her at the sink to scrub. "Your case, Maggie. I'll be in there with you if you need anything."

"I need this kid to be okay," she said.

"Rumor is you shimmied down a mountain to get to him," he said.

"Mostly true," she admitted. "That was a lot more terrifying than this. I think he's stable. Let's go see what the CT says."

"Did you notice his hands are scraped almost raw?" Jake asked.

"I did. I'm hoping that means he was able to lessen the impact of his fall because the kid got a bad head knock."

Two hours later Maggie walked into the OR waiting room. Tom and Cal both jumped to their feet.

"He's stable, Tom. He's still unconscious and we're not rousing him right away. We won't know the extent of his injuries until he wakes up and has a little recovery time but I like his chances for a full recovery. There was a second small epidural hematoma and that's all that showed up on the CT. His brain was slammed around inside his skull—there will be issues. Hopefully issues rehab can resolve. But he's stable, his reflexes are good, he's going to make it."

"Thank God," Tom said, sinking to the chair and holding his head in his hands as he wept.

"Someone's going to take you into the recovery suite so you can see him, though he isn't awake and he won't be for a while. You can sit with him, if you want to. I'll stay with him until he's out of the woods."

Tom looked up at Maggie, tears running down his cheeks. "How'm I ever gonna thank you for this?" he whispered hoarsely.

"That's not even an issue," she said. "You're my friend. You have to know I'd do whatever possible."

"Come with me, Mr. Canaday," a nurse said.

Maggie was left looking at Cal.

Cal smiled at her. "Long day, Maggie?"

"The Canaday boys tried to get the best of me but I was one step ahead of them, I think."

"I think you were."

"I'm going to be stuck in Denver for at least a couple of days."

"I'll check on Sully, get you some clean clothes and a couple of overnight supplies and come back. I'll stay with you, if you like."

"I might be mostly at the hospital, but I'd like it if you were in Denver. If I have any time at all, I want to spend it wrapped around you."

He grinned largely. "I don't have any pressing appointments."

"This," she said. "This is who I am. I have to find a way to be this person."

"As long as it doesn't involve a lot of cliff scaling, it's doable," Cal said. "It's just details. I'm really good with details."

The leaves began to change in mid-September and by the second week in October, the hillsides were resplendent with color. The crossing had just about twenty weekend guests in residence, most in RVs and cabins. They were seasoned leaf peepers, all. They toted around their cameras, binoculars and wore thick sweaters and socks.

Most people regarded spring as the fresh new start but Maggie didn't. Her favorite season had always been the fall—the color, the crisp air, the new snow on the tallest peaks. She loved it this year, more than ever before because she had started her life over, something she had wanted to do for quite a while and didn't really understand was possible. But California Jones, as it happened, was an expert. He showed her the devil is in the details.

As they were driving back to Sully's after a couple of days in Denver, Maggie described each case she'd handled. She was seeing patients on Wednesday and Thursday mornings in her friend Dr. Morris's office.

There were several neurosurgeons in the practice and they were more than happy to add her name to the marquee, even though their contracted agreement was still being studied by Maggie's lawyer, one very detail-oriented California Jones. Maggie would see patients and operate from Wednesday to Friday afternoon, two to three days a week. She would be on call for emergencies one weekend a month. It was a very manageable part-time schedule, leaving her plenty of time off. But there were a couple of doctors in the office who were spending some time in small towns that served rural areas, seeing patients who didn't have any other access to neurosurgeons. They provided services at a reduced fee scale, giving back. Maggie knew at once she'd like to be involved in that.

Filling the well.

Cal was taking a few clients besides the eminent Dr. Sullivan. A variety of simple cases—things like real estate sale and purchase, rental agreements, one prenup, a couple of wills and a couple of misdemeanor defenses. His office was Sully's front porch or kitchen table. Now that fall was here, he went to Denver with Maggie whenever he could, which was most of the time.

He did snag a weekend to fly to Minnesota to visit his youngest sister, who agreed to speak with him. As it happened, her issues were limited mostly to addiction. Their family life and dysfunction certainly didn't help, but she didn't suffer from schizophrenia. In fact, Sierra had been in touch with Sedona and together they had laid down the family roots—it seemed probable Jed Jones was among that number of schizophrenics, some 63 percent, who had no family history.

"Tom told me Jackson is getting along great," Cal

told Maggie as they drove to the crossing. "You'd never know he had some whacko woman drill holes in his head out in the wild."

"Did Tom ever get his drill back?" she asked.

"I have no idea. But Jackson is the star of PT. He's taking a semester off from school, maybe two. He wants to get caught up. He's still having some memory and cognitive issues. Not serious though. He's about as infirm as someone who had a very mild stroke and it looks like full recovery is just around the corner. You do good work."

"That's my first and last time doing something like that," she said.

"You were never sexier."

"How would you know? You fainted!"

"That's a lie!" he said. "I got a little woozy. That's all."

"Hey. You turned too soon," she said. "You're lost."

"I'm not lost, I want to show you something," he said. "Have you ever been out here?"

"Probably," she said. "We're not all that far from Sully's. Nothing much out here."

"Pretty though," he said. "Isn't it?"

"You can't find a part of Colorado that isn't pretty."

"Did you know Tom was raised in this area? His dad was a rancher. Tom said when he was a kid he expected to grow into that job, but then his life took a different turn and in the end it was probably better because he said his dad had to sell the property."

"I didn't know all that," she said.

He turned down a pretty, tree-lined lane and followed it until it opened up into a pasture with a big barn. He stopped the car. "Are we on private property?" she asked.

"I'm sure, but the only part of that I care about is the private part. Isn't this a nice scene to make out to?" he asked.

It was indeed beautiful, a big old barn sitting in a crop of trees in the middle of a pasture on a wide, deep plateau. Mountains to the west, a valley to the east, a babbling brook just south of the structure. He put an arm along the back of the seat, around her. "You know, I've been in love with you since about the first day," he said.

"When I brought Sully back to the crossing after his surgery?" she asked.

He shook his head. "Before that. When you were taking care of that old guy who was lost and confused. Then minutes later you were handling Sully's emergency. Barking orders, taking charge, confident, powerful, and yet so gentle. I knew right then I'd never known anyone like you in my life."

"I was a wreck that day," she said.

"I wanted you right then." He laughed a little. "You really gave me a hard time."

"I didn't trust you at all, California," she said.

"I learned a few things in the last couple of years, Maggie. Or maybe I should say, I remembered a few things. Since I was a little kid I wanted to feel settled and safe. I wanted the respect of the people who knew me, I wanted a family I could devote myself to, I wanted to learn the kind of everyday wisdom Sully has. Being widowed screwed me up. I was too lonely. But that changes if you'll marry me. I think we can do this, Maggie. I never thought I would know love like this—I never thought I could feel this kind of bone-deep passion, yet a sweet peace and steadiness. You changed my life. And it needed changing."

"And can you have that if I keep doing what I do?" she asked. "Because what I do tends to have its complications. The majority of my cases are routine and require training and good hands, but there are times... You can't dare to take brains and spinal columns into your hands with impunity. It's risky. It's stressful."

"It's admirable," he said. "Maggie, I think you know yourself well, yet I'm not sure you realize just how amazing you are. It's not a lack of confidence, not at all. It's more that your focus is not on yourself when you act. You do exactly what you realize is within your scope, even when it takes a toll. I wouldn't have another wife if she wasn't you. I'm sure of it."

"Can you be happy in a rumpus room?" she asked.

"For a year or so," he said. "We'll also be in Denver sometimes. But I'll be here a lot. If it works for you."

"Here?" she asked.

"See that barn? The barn and the land it sits on are for sale."

"Huh," she said, confused. "You going to get horses or something? Maybe bring in a double-wide we can live in?"

"Nope. That barn is going to make a fantastic house. With Tom's help it's going to be a big, spacious, family home with a view of the mountains and the valley. Come on," he said, getting out of the car.

He grabbed her hand and pulled her to the barn and opened the big double doors. They stood in the center of an enormous space with the remnants of previous tenants all around—stalls, troughs that had once watered animals, ropes hanging from walls, even a harness and yoke that looked as old as the barn.

He pointed to one end. "Kitchen, mudroom, laundry, dining room." He turned. "Great room, office. I'm happy taking clients at Sully's but I don't know how long he'll be happy with that." He pointed to the hayloft. "Master bedroom and bath, two rooms for kids." He pointed to the other side. "Guest room."

"Kids?" she asked.

"Whenever you're ready."

"Are *you* ready?"

"I thought that ship had sailed, but then I met you and so many things became real again. All the things I thought were past became the future. I thought my one chance at happiness was behind me, and I found out I was wrong. Maggie, you're a game changer—you'll dangle on the end of a rope over a three-hundred-foot drop to save a kid's life and you'll trust a vagrant lawyer with a piece of your heart." He pulled her into his arms. "Make a life with me, baby. I love you so much it blurs my vision."

"It wasn't just a piece of my heart," she said. "You sneaked in there and took the whole damn thing."

"Time to say yes, Maggie."

"Are you kidding me? I feel like I've wanted you forever. And Calbert—I love the barn. I love it. I can't fill it up with kids, there isn't time. But I can put a couple of good ones in here and add pets."

He laughed at her. "You're a genius."

"I love you, Cal. Like a house on fire. Will you marry me fast, before you change your mind?"

"I'm never going to change my mind, honey. You're everything to me."

This above all:

To thine own self be true,

And it must follow, as the night the day,

Thou canst not then be false to any man.

—WILLIAM SHAKESPEARE

In the long run, we only hit what we aim at.

—HENRY DAVID THOREAU

EPILOGUE

There were no wedding invitations. Maggie and Cal got on the phone and told their friends and family they were getting married before the glorious fall colors were over. In the old barn. Phoebe almost had a stroke, but Walter thought it was appropriate and suitable. Tom, Jackson, the other Canaday kids, Enid, Frank, Conrad Doyle, aka Connie, and some of the paramedics cleaned out the barn and decorated it with streamers, dried fall flowers and hay bales. Tom used Sully's riding mower to cut down the pasture so cars could safely park there without sparking a fire. Maggie called her friends and colleagues from Denver and was pleased that so many wanted to be there.

A caterer from Colorado Springs brought tables, folding chairs, food, drink, floral arrangements, decorative candles, linens. Enid insisted she could make the wedding cake and it wasn't exactly professional-looking, but it was unique—a two-tiered sheet cake with lots of fall leaves created out of frosting and food coloring. Maggie did not laugh, but she wanted to. There were no printed programs and the minister got his license on the internet. Jaycee Kent and Terry Jordan from the

OR were the bridesmaids. Cal's brother, Dakota, made the trip on short notice to be Cal's best man, the other witness was Tom Canaday. Not to be left out, Sedona and her family flew to Denver and drove down to the barn for the festivities.

Aware that Cal kept in touch with Lynne's parents, Maggie asked him if he had invited them and was rather surprised when he said he had. "They declined. They're very happy for me and don't want to distract me. But they'd love to meet you and asked if they could visit when we're settled."

"I'm sorry your father isn't well enough to be here," she said.

"We'll send them lots of pictures. You're beautiful," he said.

"And you're wearing that suit that makes me want to send everyone home early."

Maggie wore a simple, short, ivory dress with lace sleeves and nude patent leather pumps. In the car were a couple of packed bags. After a night in Denver and brunch with Dakota, Sedona and her family, they'd be taking a short vacation to a warm, private resort in the Bahamas.

At a little before four in the afternoon, when the sun was casting long shadows over the Rockies, Cal and Maggie greeted their guests, introduced some of them to each other. Before long, the minister urged them to stand at the front of the barn under a beautiful fall wreath and he began. He talked very briefly about the great joy he felt in helping to bring people together in marriage. The usual vows were recited, some of them, anyway—Cal and Maggie wanted to do things their way.

"Maggie, until I met you, I was lost. There were

so many times I asked myself what I would do next, where I would be, if there was anyone I could be right for. Then I met you and instantly loved you. Instantly. Those long talks by the fire, late at night, meant *everything* to me. The walks through the hills and valleys, not talking—*everything*. The evenings of intimacy when no words were needed, *everything*. Looking into the future with you, my heart is so full there's no room for anything but promise. And I promise you a lifetime. The best I have."

"And I promise you, California Jones, all the passion in my heart, all the joy in my being, all the laughter on a sunny day, all the thrill of day after day knowing we are one, that when my heart beats in my breast, it beats only for you. I love you. I promise you my life. The best I have."

* * * * *

ACKNOWLEDGMENTS

First and foremost I'd like to thank my readers, not only for reading my books and talking about them with friends, book club members, online, everywhere, but also for sending me thoughtful letters of encouragement and praise. It's so kind and means the world.

Thanks to Dr. Brian Carr for research help—I knew what I was doing when I raised a doctor! And thanks also for reading an early manuscript, looking for technical errors on the medical aspects of the story.

A great big thank-you to MAJ Scott Trexler, MD, Chief of Trauma/Critical Care, San Antonio Military Medical Center. I appreciate the resource, but even more than that, I thank you for your patriotic service—I am in your debt!

Thanks to Kevin Tourek, Esq., for always answering my questions to the best of your knowledge and for researching some legal issues for me. Your help and friendship are very important and special to me.

Any errors or alterations in the technical aspects of this book are not the fault of my technical advisers but mine, most often license to create a strong story, and I appreciate the readers' indulgence.

I have a couple of early readers who never fail to offer insight and commentary that very often change and invariably improve the story—thanks to my daughter, Jamie Prosser, and to Kate Bandy. Kate has been reading manuscripts for me for almost forty years and has never once complained! And a very special thanks to my dear friend the lovely Kristan Higgins who brings light into my life and work.

Special thanks and appreciation to my husband, Jim, for your unwavering support, for being a sounding board, for your patience and commitment. I love you.

Thanks to Liza Dawson, my agent, for your brilliance, loyalty, tender loving care, wicked sharp wit and, most of all, friendship.

And my thanks to Craig Swinwood, Loriana Sacilotto, Margaret Marbury and Nicole Brebner, Harlequin's A-team, for providing this magnificent opportunity. I will try every day to deserve the honor.

And thanks to everyone at Harlequin. There are a lot of fingerprints on my books. I'm having a good time, loving my work, while all of you do the heavy lifting. Thank you for the quality work, the sincere commitment, the quality product. Nobody does it better.

*Turn the page for a special preview of
the next wonderful story set at Sullivan's Crossing,
ANY DAY NOW,
a novel about finding family in unexpected places
by #1* New York Times *bestselling author Robyn Carr.
Available April 18, 2017, from MIRA Books.*

CHAPTER ONE

So, this is what a new life looks like. Sierra Jones opened her eyes on a sunny Colorado morning to that thought.

She had given this a great deal of consideration. Colorado had not been her only option but she'd decided it might be the best one. Her brother Cal, with whom she shared a deep bond, was making a life here and he wanted her to be part of it. Sierra needed a new place to start over. A place with no bad memories, where she had no history and yet had a strong emotional connection. Her big brother was a powerful pull.

When she was a child, it was Cal who'd protected her, loved her unconditionally, cared for her, worried on her behalf. He was eight years older but had been more than just her brother. He had been her best friend. And when he'd left home, or what passed for home when she was ten years old, she'd been adrift.

When she'd finally made up her mind to give this place a chance, Cal had wanted her to come directly to his house. His house in progress, that was. But that didn't sound like a good idea; there was only one bedroom finished so far. And more important—she wouldn't be a burden to anyone and absolutely did not want to be in the way of a new couple who were just feeling their way into marriage. Cal and Maggie had been married less than six months and were living in the barn they were converting into a house. Sierra had thanked them kindly and said she'd prefer to find her own lodgings and live on her own. A very important part of creating a new life was independence. She did not want to be accountable to anyone but herself.

That was what she'd told them. The truth, hidden protectively in her heart, was that she was afraid to depend on Cal again as she had when she was a little girl. He had a new family, after all. She remembered too well the pain from her childhood when he'd abandoned her. It was awful.

Independence was a little frightening. But, she reminded herself, she did have her brother near and willing to lend a hand if she needed anything, just as she was more than eager to be there for Cal and Maggie. She was thirty years old and it was high time she built a life that reflected the new woman she was becoming. This was a joyful, challenging, exciting and terrifying change. If a little lonely at times…

She had a short checklist of things she wanted to settle for herself before seeing Cal. First—she wanted to look around the area. Timberlake was the town closest to where her brother and Maggie lived and she thought it was adorable. It was a little touristy, a little on the Wild West side with its clapboard shop fronts and Victorian-style houses, surrounded by the beauty of snow-topped mountains and long, deep fields. The first day she spent in the small town, there was a herd of elk cantering down the main street. One big bull was bugling at the cows and calves, leading them away from the town and back to grazing land. They were at once majestic and klutzy, wandering in a little confusion through the cars. An old guy standing in front of a barbershop explained to her that with spring, they were moving to higher elevations, cows were giving birth, grazing was found in different areas. And in the fall, he said, watch out for rutting season. "Those bulls get real territorial."

That was all it took for Sierra to begin to hope this would be the right place for her, because her heart beat a little faster just watching that grand herd move through town. The old guy said, "You don't see that every day."

She found a comfortable, clean, cheap hostel that would let her pay by the week, and they were just starting to get an influx of students and adventurers who wanted to take advantage of the Colorado springtime. She'd have to share a bathroom, but it wouldn't be the first time; she wasn't fussy and it would make decent housing until she could find something more permanent. The owner of the hostel, a woman in her sixties called Midge, said there were rooms and apartments being let by local home owners all over town.

The best part about the hostel—there were people around, yet she would be on her own.

She found a part-time job right away—the diner needed early-morning waitstaff help a couple of days a week. They'd lost their main morning waitress and the owner's wife had been filling in. As it happened, Sierra loved the early morning. The money wasn't great but it was enough to keep her comfortable and she had a little savings.

The most important thing she'd researched before coming to Colorado was locations and times of AA meetings. She even had an app for her phone. There were regularly scheduled meetings everywhere. In Timberlake and in all the small towns surrounding it from Breckenridge to Colorado Springs. They were usually held in churches but there were some in community centers, in office buildings, hospitals and even clubhouses. She would never be without support.

Sierra was nine months sober.

Sierra had reconnected with Cal about seven months ago, right before he and Maggie married. He'd visited her twice since and called her regularly. He'd begun lobbying for her move to Colorado a few months ago. For the eight years previous, they'd been in touch but not much a part of each other's lives, and for that she had regrets. Those years had been especially difficult for Cal; the past five years had been brutal. His first wife, Lynne, had suffered from scleroderma, a painful, fatal disease, and had passed away three years ago. Cal had been a lost soul. If she'd been a better sister, she might've offered her support.

But that was in the past and the future was her opportunity. She hoped they could rebuild the close relationship they'd once had and become family again. Right before she started the long trek south to Colorado, Cal had shared a secret—he was going to be a father.

Sierra was thrilled for him. He would never know how much she looked forward to a baby. She would be an auntie. Since she would never have children of her own, this was an unexpected gift.

Cal Jones laid back against the pillows, his fingers laced behind his head, sheet drawn to his waist. He watched Maggie preen naked in front of the full-length mirror, checking her profile.

"We got a thing going on, Mrs. Jones," he said, his voice husky.

She really didn't show much yet. Just the tiniest curve where her waist had been. She kept smoothing her hand over it. "I passed the dreaded first three months with no issues," she said. She beamed at him, her eyes alive. "I'm not sick, I've logged on fourteen weeks, I feel great. I'm going to tell my dad it's okay to tell his friends now."

"Don't be too surprised if you find he already has."

"I wouldn't be at all surprised."

He watched her with pride. Thin as a reed with that little bump that he'd put there, her smile wistful and almost angelic. She wanted the baby as much as he did; she thrilled with each day it grew in her. This baby had healed something in her. And it filled him with a new hope. She was more beautiful now than she'd ever been.

"Mrs. Jones, you have to either get dressed or come over here and do me."

She laughed. "I already *did* you. Magnificently, I might add."

"I said thank you."

She reached for her underwear, then her jeans, then her sweatshirt. The show was over. Now he'd have to wait all day to have her alone again.

"It's time for you to get to work—I need a house. Tom will be here anytime. I'm going over to Sully's store," Maggie said. There was much cleanup and restoration to do at her dad's general store and campground at Sullivan's Crossing. It was the first of March, and it wouldn't be long before the campers and hikers started coming in force.

Cal and Maggie were living in the barn they were renovating into a big house with the guidance of Tom Canaday, a local with some amazing carpentry and other building skills. Tom had good subcontractors to help, speeding up the process. Maggie and Cal had married last October, and they'd lived at Sully's, in his basement, while the roof and exterior were being re-inforced and sealed, dormers were added to what was once a hayloft, the wiring was refreshed, the interior gutted and windows installed where there had been none. Tom, Cal and a few extra hands had finally fin-ished off a bedroom and functional bathroom along with a semi-functional kitchen. That bedroom, on the ground floor, would eventually be Cal's office when the house was finished. The proper master bedroom would be upstairs. They had a good seal on their tem-porary bedroom door so they could sleep there and not be overcome by sawdust or the dirt of construction. They'd been in residence two weeks, thanks to warmer weather and a good space heater.

Maggie spent most of her free time at the store help-ing her dad. Then there were those three or four days a week she was in Denver, where she practiced neuro-surgery. On her practice days, she stayed at the Den-ver house she'd owned for several years. During her days away, Cal and Tom did the things that were noisi-est, smelliest and messiest—the pounding and sawing, cutting granite and quartz, applying the noxious sealer, installing the floors, sanding and staining. Every time Maggie came home, it was like Christmas—she'd find new stairs to the second floor, a bathtub, a new kitchen sink, ceramic tile on the kitchen floor, half a fireplace. But the most precious addition of all was the Shop-Vac.

That little beauty kept dirt, sawdust, spillage and debris manageable. It was their goal to have the house finished before the baby came, due in early October.

Tom Canaday was at the house, his truck backed up to the door, before Cal had finished making Maggie breakfast—very likely by design. Cal got the eggs back out and started making more breakfast.

Tom had brought his twenty-year-old son, Jackson, something he did whenever Jackson had a day free of classes. In the cavernous great room, they sat at a long picnic table. Tom had thrown it together and it became the table they ate at, laid out plans on, used as a carpenter's bench, a desk when they held meetings. They met with subcontractors there, spread material samples or design renderings on it, looked through catalogs. It was truly multipurpose.

Once Maggie had gone to Sullivan's Crossing, the men were still seated at the picnic table, finishing a second cup of coffee, when there was a knock at the door.

"She forget something?" Tom asked.

"Maggie wouldn't knock," Cal said, going to the front door.

Standing just outside on the step was a pretty girl with light brown hair streaked with honey. She had peachy skin and a pretty mouth stretched into a smile. She wore tight jeans with fashionably torn knees, but Cal guessed hers weren't purchased that way. Her hoodie was tied around her neck. The sight of her made his eyes glitter with happiness.

"Well, you finally got around to me," he said. He lifted her off the ground with his hug. "How are you?"

"Good. Brand-new. I love this place."

"You might get a little tired of it this month—March is pretty sloppy."

"Yeah, that happens," she said.

He looked beyond her to the little orange VW parked on the road. Not new, that was for sure. He thought he saw a piece of twine holding the front bumper in place. Then he looked back at his sister. "The pumpkin," she said with a smile.

"You must've looked hard for that thing," he said.

"She came at a good price."

"Hard to believe," he said facetiously. He always forgot how beautiful she was. She was thirty now but still looked like a girl. He put a finger under her chin and tilted her face to look into her clear brown eyes. "How are you feeling?" he asked softly.

"Never better," she said. "Really."

"Are you going to stay here until you find something?" he asked.

She shook her head. "Found something already. It's temporary, but clean, safe, comfortable and convenient. The hostel in town. It'll keep me very well while I look around some more."

Sierra looked past him. Wires were hanging from the ceiling and sticking out of walls, building debris was scattered everywhere, stacks of wallboard, tarps, doors leaning against walls, piles of supplies from plumbing fixtures to hinges. "Love what you've done to the place, California."

Someone cleared his throat and Cal turned to see Tom and Jackson staring at Sierra with open mouths and wide-eyed wonder. "Oh, sorry, guys. Tom, Jackson, this is my sister Sierra. Sierra, that's Tom and his son Jackson. We're building together. Remodeling the barn. Like I told you the last time we talked—it's going to be our house by the time the baby comes."

"Amazing," she said, looking around the massive interior. "Put up some walls, California. You don't want to be living in an arena."

"Right," he said, smiling. "Listen, guys, Sierra and I have some catching up to do. I want to take her over to Sully's to see Maggie. I'll be gone for a couple of hours but I'll be back. You okay without me?"

Jackson grinned. "Sometimes we're better without you."

"Way to pump my ego," Cal said. "See you in a while." He pulled the door closed and steered Sierra toward her car. "Can I drive?"

"The pumpkin? I guess… But she's very sensitive. You'll have to be gentle. Don't grind the gears or pump the brakes." She pulled a key out of the pocket of her tight jeans. "But why?"

He grabbed it. "Indulge me. I want to see how it handles on these mountain roads."

She slid into the passenger seat. "Okay, but no matter how much you love her, you can't have her."

The first thing he did was grind the gears. "Sorry," he said. She groaned.

He was smoother then, driving around the foothills. There were a lot of sharp turns, uphill and downhill grades, narrow roads that briefly widened, and some amazing mountain vistas. At a widened lookout, Cal pulled the pumpkin right up to the edge and stopped.

"Not bad, Sierra," he said. "Kind of creaky, isn't she?"

"She likes me better," Sierra said. "I have a sweet touch and you're a clod."

"It suits you, this little orange ball. How was your drive down?"

"Pretty. A little rainy. Colorado is beautiful."

"I worried, you know. Thinking about you making that drive all alone when I could have ridden with you…"

She laughed outright. "God, I needed to be alone more than you'll ever know! Do you have any idea how rare time alone was for me the last nine months?"

"That wasn't one of the things I thought about," he admitted. He'd spent all his energy fearing her relapse. Or worse.

"I've been living with people for nine months, first in rehab and then in a group home. It taught me a lot. I'm the first to admit that. But it also drove me crazy. For a long day on the road, I could actually hear the inside of my head. My first day in Timberlake, there were elks right in the town. On the main street, weaving through the cars."

"I've never seen anything like that. I've heard it happens but never saw it." He gave her knee a pat. "Tell me if there's anything you need. If there's anything I can do to make this move, this transition, easier for you."

She shook her head. "Nothing at the moment. I planned it very carefully, down to the tiniest detail. If I need anything, I'll be sure to let you know."

"You're being very brave," he said. "You left your support system and came all the way to—"

"I have a phone, Cal. I'm in touch with my sponsor and will be going to meetings now and then, looking for a local sponsor. I'm in touch with a couple of the women in recovery I lived with the last six months. We shore each other up and…" She took a breath. "And I'm not fragile, all right? See—no sweaty palms. It's all cool. I'm excited about being here."

"You never said, what did it? What finally got you

in rehab?" Cal and his late wife, Lynne, had tried intervention, offering support if she'd consider sobriety, but it was a failure. Sierra wasn't interested. She'd said they were overreacting.

"Listen, something you should understand, I didn't know I had a problem, okay? I should have, but I didn't. I thought I drank a little too much sometimes, like everyone. I kept meaning to do better but it wouldn't last long. I mean, I hardly ever missed work, I never got a DUI, never got DTs when I didn't drink, and even though I did things I regretted because of alcohol, I thought that was my fault, not the booze. I decided to give rehab a try but I honestly thought I'd go into treatment and learn that everyone else had a problem and I was actually just an idiot who didn't always use good judgment. But it didn't work out that way. Now I know all the things I should've known a long time ago." She chuckled and looked out at the view. "Imagine my surprise."

"I thought you were doing a lot of drugs," he said.

"Hardly ever," she said. "I didn't need drugs. I was busy drinking."

He was quiet for a long moment. "I'm really proud of you," he finally said. "Nine months is good," he said.

"It's excellent, to tell the truth. And I'll be honest, in the early days I wasn't very confident of nine days. But here we are. Now you—tell me something—what does it feel like, knowing you're going to be a daddy?"

His felt his face grow into that silly smile he'd been wearing lately whenever he thought about Maggie. "Unbelievable. Overwhelming. I was getting used to the idea this wouldn't happen to me."

"But it's not a surprise, is it?" she asked. "The baby?"

"Nah, we wanted a family. Maggie's way more fertile than she bargained for—it happened right away. We're still getting used to the idea, but it feels great. You'll see someday…"

She was shaking her head. "I don't think so. Don't get me wrong, I look forward to being an auntie but I'm not all that into the mommy scene. I didn't grow up looking after little kids like you did."

"You saying you don't like kids?" he asked.

"I love kids," she said. "When they're someone else's. But… Can I ask a personal question?"

"Sure. Be gentle with me," he said, but he smiled when he said it.

"Do you ever worry about the schizophrenia thing?"

Their father, Jed, was schizophrenic and he wasn't medicated. Rather, he was self-medicated—he smoked pot every day. It kept the delusions a little quieter. Jed was, quite honestly, crackers. And schizophrenia sometimes ran in families.

"I worry about everything, including that. It appears Jed didn't inherit his disease or pass it on, unless someone's holding back information. But I have Maggie. She's much more logical and pragmatic. She began listing things we could worry about—the list was long. It covered everything from childhood cancers and illnesses to teenage pregnancy and she suggested, firmly, that we deal with each problem as it appears. You have to remember, Maggie handles catastrophic head injuries and brain tumors for a living—you can't scare her. And if mental illness is one of our problems, trust me— we'll be managing it in a different way than Jed does." He paused. "How are they?"

"I saw them briefly before I left and they're exactly the same. Mom said she was glad I was going to be around you, that you probably needed me. I have no idea where she got that idea. I told her not to tell anyone but Sedona and Dakota where I was. I don't know who would ask but I want to cut ties with that old life. I mean, I still have my Des Moines support, but we don't give out information on each other. Mom was fine. Dad was getting ready for a big security briefing of some kind. In other words, he's in Jed's world. You call them, don't you?"

"I haven't talked to them in a couple of weeks—I've been busy with the barn. I'll check in. Sierra, are there debts to clear or something?"

"No," she assured him. "I just don't need anyone from rehab or my old party days tracking me down. I'm good."

"If you have issues like that, tell me. Better to straighten it out than ignore it."

"I don't have those kind of issues, Cal."

"Okay. But if I can help… Just get settled."

"I worry about them, too, Cal," she said.

"But there's nothing we can do," he reminded her. "Let's go find Maggie. She's dying to meet you in person."

Sierra drove the pumpkin, following Cal's directions to Sullivan's Crossing. As she oohed and aahed at the scenery, she thought one of the great things about rehab had been learning she was not the only person with a totally screwed-up family. Given the fact that her sister, Sedona, and brother Dakota were living functional and what appeared to be normal, conventional lives, it seemed to boil down to her parents, and all because Jed didn't want to be treated for his schizophrenia and Marissa, her mother, didn't push him. Crazy parents weren't unusual in rehab. In fact the number of people who had been drinking or drugging their way through delusions was astonishing.

She had told a small lie. She'd told it cheerfully and with good intentions. Truthfully, she wished she could have children. But there were multiple problems with that idea. First, she had a very bad history with men— she chose the worst ones imaginable. And second, not only did she have to deal with schizophrenia in the family tree but also addiction, which also tended to run in families. How could she risk cursing a child with such afflictions? Add to that, you'd have to trust yourself a great deal to be a good parent and she wasn't even close. Self-doubt was her constant companion.

"You get to see this scenery every day," she said to her brother. "I was mainly coming here because you and Maggie are here but it's an amazingly beautiful place."

"I wonder if you ever get used to it," he said. "I still can't believe I'm lucky enough to live here."

"How'd you end up here?" she asked.

"You know," he said. "Wandering. Trying to find myself, sort of."

"Sort of?"

"I was roaming. It's in our genes. Plus…" He hesitated. "I was looking for a place for Lynne. A place for her ashes. I gave her my word—I'd leave her in a beautiful place and then I'd let her go."

"And did you?" Sierra asked.

He was quiet for a moment. "I found a beautiful place. By that time I'd met Maggie. And my life started over." He reached over and touched her knee. "Your turn to start over, kid."

"Yeah," she said, suddenly feeling tired. Scared. It came upon her at the weirdest times, that fear she'd turn out to be a failure. Again. "Right. And looks like a great place to do that."

"I think of this as home," Cal said. "We never really had a home."

"We had the farm," she said. "Sort of."

"You had more of that than I did," he said.

Their parents, who described themselves as free spirits, hippies, free thinkers and nonconformists, had raised their family on the road, living in a bus converted into an RV, but it was really just a disguise. Jed was sick and Marissa was his enabler and keeper. Marissa's parents had a farm in Iowa and they landed there quite often, all of them helping on the farm and going to school in Pratt, Iowa, a small farming community. Then they'd take off again, on the road. By the time Sierra was eight, they'd settled on the farm full-time, taking care of the land for Grandma after Grandpa passed away. Cal finished high school there.

Then he left to seek his fortune, to go to college with the help of scholarships and loans. She had been only ten. He passed responsibility for her on to Sedona, next oldest. When Sierra was twelve, Sedona left for college. She got herself a full ride and went to a hoity-toity women's university back east and though she called, she rarely visited. When Sierra was fifteen, Dakota left, enlisting in the army at the first opportunity. Then it was just Sierra. Sierra with Jed and Marissa. Counting the minutes until she could get away, too.

Not long after they all left her, she'd discovered beer and pot.

The Crossing, the place where Cal had found his woman and his second chance, did not look anything like Sierra had expected. It was a completely uninhabited campground. Little dirt pads were separated by trees, the foliage just beginning to turn leafy. The sites were dotted with little brick grills here and there. The picnic tables were all lined up by the side of a big old store with a wide porch that stretched the length of the building. There was a woman sweeping the porch—had to be Maggie. She stopped sweeping, stared at them, smiled and leaned her broom against the wall. She descended the steps just as they got out of the little car.

"Sierra!" she said, opening her arms.

"How did you know?"

She hugged her and then held her away to look at her. "You couldn't be anyone else. You belong to your brother as if you were his twin. Maybe I'll have a daughter and she'll look exactly like you."

Sierra blushed. "Would that be a good thing?"

"That would be perfect," Maggie said.

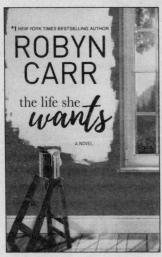

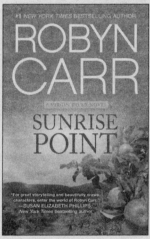

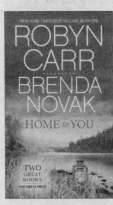

ROBYN CARR

32931	WILD MAN CREEK	___$7.99 U.S.	___$9.99 CAN.
32899	JUST OVER THE MOUNTAIN	___$7.99 U.S.	___$9.99 CAN.
31890	REDWOOD BEND	___$7.99 U.S.	___$9.99 CAN.
31854	FOUR FRIENDS	___$7.99 U.S.	___$8.99 CAN.
31787	A NEW HOPE	___$8.99 U.S.	___$9.99 CAN.
31772	ONE WISH	___$8.99 U.S.	___$9.99 CAN.
31763	BRING ME HOME FOR CHRISTMAS	___$7.99 U.S.	___$9.99 CAN.
31761	HARVEST MOON	___$7.99 U.S.	___$9.99 CAN.
31749	WILDEST DREAMS	___$8.99 U.S.	___$9.99 CAN.
31742	PROMISE CANYON	___$7.99 U.S.	___$8.99 CAN.
31733	MOONLIGHT ROAD	___$7.99 U.S.	___$8.99 CAN.
31728	A SUMMER IN SONOMA	___$7.99 U.S.	___$8.99 CAN.
31724	THE HOUSE ON OLIVE STREET	___$7.99 U.S.	___$8.99 CAN.
31702	ANGEL'S PEAK	___$7.99 U.S.	___$8.99 CAN.
31697	FORBIDDEN FALLS	___$7.99 U.S.	___$8.99 CAN.
31644	THE HOMECOMING	___$7.99 U.S.	___$8.99 CAN.
31620	THE PROMISE	___$7.99 U.S.	___$8.99 CAN.
31599	THE CHANCE	___$7.99 U.S.	___$8.99 CAN.
31590	PARADISE VALLEY	___$7.99 U.S.	___$8.99 CAN.
31513	A VIRGIN RIVER CHRISTMAS	___$7.99 U.S.	___$8.99 CAN.
31459	THE HERO	___$7.99 U.S.	___$8.99 CAN.
31452	THE NEWCOMER	___$7.99 U.S.	___$9.99 CAN.
31447	THE WANDERER	___$7.99 U.S.	___$9.99 CAN.
31419	SHELTER MOUNTAIN	___$7.99 U.S.	___$9.99 CAN.
31415	VIRGIN RIVER	___$7.99 U.S.	___$9.99 CAN.

(limited quantities available)

TOTAL AMOUNT	$ _____
POSTAGE & HANDLING	$ _____
($1.00 for 1 book, 50¢ for each additional)	
APPLICABLE TAXES*	$ _____
TOTAL PAYABLE	$ _____

(check or money order—please do not send cash)

To order, complete this form and send it, along with a check or money order for the total above, payable to MIRA Books, to: **In the U.S.:** 3010 Walden Avenue, P.O. Box 9077, Buffalo, NY 14269-9077; **In Canada:** P.O. Box 636, Fort Erie, Ontario, L2A 5X3.

Name: _____
Address: _____ City: _____
State/Prov.: _____ Zip/Postal Code: _____
Account Number (if applicable): _____
075 CSAS

*New York residents remit applicable sales taxes.
*Canadian residents remit applicable GST and provincial taxes.

MIRA®